Bloodsworn

Book 1 of the Avatars of Ruin

D1206743

Also by Tej Turner

The Janus Cycle
Dinnusos Rises

The Last Days in Existence is Elsewhen

Bloodsworn

Book 1 of the Avatars of Ruin

Tej Turner

Elsewhen Press

Bloodsworn
First published in Great Britain by Elsewhen Press, 2021
An imprint of Alnpete Limited

Elsewhen Press, PO Box 757, Dartford, Kent DA2 7TQ
www.elsewhen.press

British Library Cataloguing in Publication Data.
A catalogue record for this book is available from the British Library.

ISBN 978-1-911409-67-0 Print edition
ISBN 978-1-911409-77-9 eBook edition

Designed and formatted by Elsewhen Press

This book is dedicated to my siblings,
Natalie, James & Phillip.

And also, because not all of the sibling-relationships
you make during life are so direct,
Sean, Aidan, Nicki, Erin & Simon.

Contents

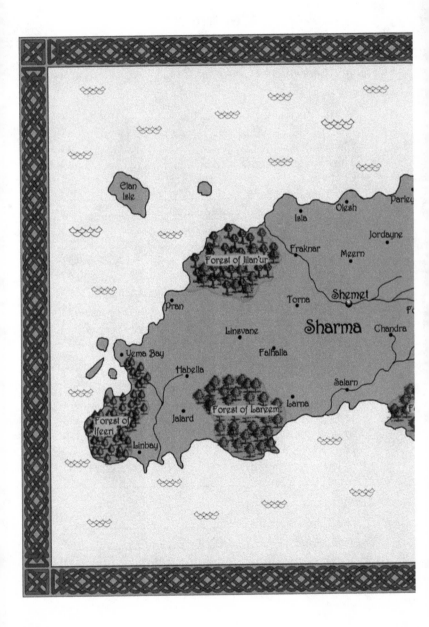

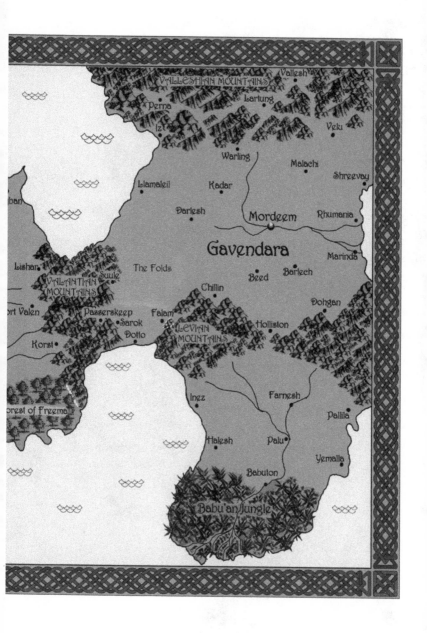

Chapter 1

Yearly Visitors

Kyra was running late.

This was not something unusual for her. Kyra would be the first one to admit that punctuality was not her forte, but this day was an important one and she was determined to be on time on this occasion.

It wasn't even her fault. Kyra *had* been on schedule until her mother sent her on a fool's errand to track down a missing goose. It had escaped from the enclosure again, and it took her half of the morning to track down the ruddy thing.

Kyra cursed as she ran. She looked up at the sky, checking the position of the sun to determine the time of day. There was still some time, but she wasn't sure it was enough.

She took a shortcut, abandoning the walkway and sprinting through the middle of a field. Kernels of wheat whipped her legs, sending grains showering in her wake. She warily looked around to make sure no one was witnessing her trespass. Not that she cared all that much. A tongue-lashing from a ruffled farmer was not a great matter of concern compared to the wrath she would face if she didn't arrive on time.

She reached the end of the field and entered the woodland, feeling some relief as she wound her way between the trees towards the central grove. She began to hear voices, meaning she was near, and quickened her pace, mustering one last burst of speed.

She found them; they were huddled in the middle of the clearing. She squeezed through one of the gaps to assert some room for herself. The two boys on either side scowled at her, but she paid them no heed; instead, she focussed her attention on Baird, her mentor, as he delivered a speech.

"The representatives from the Academy will be here soon," he bellowed, casting his steely gaze across the circle of youths gathered around him. If he noticed Kyra arriving a little later than the others, he didn't say anything. "And you all know what that means... some of you will be Chosen.

11

And to be Chosen, you need to prove yourselves worthy. I am writing your reports tonight, so this is your last chance to impress me. Make it count! Now back up and make some room!" he yelled, gesturing with his hands for them to spread out. "I will call you up to duel each other in pairs! First up are Fergus and Mavi!"

Kyra watched as the boys that Baird had just selected walked over to the rack of wooden weapons to pick a sword each. They were two of his youngest students and both novices.

Once they were both armed, they nervously assumed positions and everyone else gathered in a circle around them to watch. Baird counted down.

Kyra didn't pay much attention to their brawl. It didn't last very long.

And the next two combatants Baird called up were only a marginal improvement. Kyra realised that Baird was pairing them off in order of their skill level.

Which meant she was going to have to wait a while till her turn came.

Her eyes went to Rivan, who stood on the opposite side of the ring to her. He was, as usual, surrounded by his cronies. He was Baird's favourite, and would no doubt be sent up last. He had seen eighteen summers – only a year older than Kyra – yet with his massive frame and bushy, russet-hued beard, he had the appearance of someone much older than his peers.

Kyra was the only woman present that day, but she was used to that. A few of the other girls from the village had tried to follow in her footsteps, but none lasted for more than a few days. In one case, mere hours. Kyra knew why. The males of Jalard were possessed by a proclivity to make life difficult for any woman who showed an interest in arts they considered belonging solely to them. Kyra's existence was one they found particularly vexing because she had persevered and proved them wrong.

She could now beat most of the men of Jalard hands-down when it came to fencing.

All except for Rivan. He was the only one who still bested her.

He caught her looking at him, and their eyes met. The two of them had been rivals for so long they could now provoke each other with merely a glance. It was a challenge.

Bring. It. On, Kyra thought as she stared him out.

"Jonan, good!" Baird roared, once the third duel had ended. "Benin, you need to stop leaping around so much! This is fencing, not dancing!"

He summoned the next pair, and it became more interesting. Kyra watched the confrontation with a critical eye, noting where each of them went wrong. *He lets people in his range too easily,* she thought before their swords had even met. *No! You shouldn't crouch! It leaves you vulnerable!* she almost yelled a few moments later, but restrained herself. Baird had already, on several occasions, told her off for doing that. *Let your sword do the work for you!*

The duels generally got better as time progressed, and Kyra found herself having less to criticise internally. Baird observed them all with a stony expression on his face; one hand on his hip, the other on his chin. When each bout was over, he usually yelled some form of criticism. Most often to the one defeated. That was his way. He was a former soldier – a veteran of the War of Ashes – and he had been sent to their village ten years ago to turn its boys into warriors. His method was to make them all feel like they were treading upon eggshells. Berated outbursts were courtesy for any cracks. The ones he favoured were pushed even harder.

When there were only four students left to be called up, there was a brief silence as Baird ran his eyes across Kyra and the other three who were yet to be paired. Her body tensed as she wondered who she would end up sparring with. She knew that Rivan was the only one who was any real rival to her, but still, she doubted Baird would actually acknowledge that by picking her to fight him. For some reason, Kyra always fell short of earning her mentor's favour.

"Dareth. Sidry. You're up," Baird decided.

Kyra drew a breath. A part of her was glad, but another apprehensive. If Baird was writing their final reports that night, this was the fight which could earn her a scholarship at the Academy. Only yesterday she had proven, once again, that she was Jalard's finest archer, but she knew that it was your skill with a sword which Baird held in the highest esteem.

If she had been paired off against Sidry or Dareth, she would have almost certainly won, but Rivan was going to be a much tougher challenge.

Her hand went to the necklace about her neck. It was in the shape of a large rose thorn. The symbol of Briggan, the patron goddess of warriors and maidens. Kyra held onto it, barely watching Dareth and Sidry's bout, and only dimly aware of the loud thwacks which occurred each time their swords met. She didn't register who the victor was. Her mind was rehearsing. Praying. Mentally preparing herself for her own duel.

"Good!" Baird declared, clapping his massive hands together. "See!" he turned to the others. "That's how it's done! Dareth, you let your guard down at the end, but until that point it was great! Next! Rivan and Kyra!"

She felt eyes glaring at her as she walked over to the rack and tested some of the wooden swords to find one whose weight she liked. Some of them muttered to each other too. She didn't hear any of the words, but she could make a fairly educated guess as to the sentiment. Most of them despised her, and Baird selecting her to fight Rivan was an admission that she was more accomplished than the rest of them.

After choosing a weapon, she strolled over to one side of the ring while Rivan claimed the other. They both assumed stances.

"Are you ready?" Baird called.

She nodded. As did Rivan.

"Go!"

Rivan charged, and Kyra braced herself, holding her sword steady as he rushed her. His sword came swinging. It was not a particularly technical move, but it had the full brunt of his strength behind it.

He was, as usual, trying to win with brute force.

She parried the strike, twisting the downswing of his weapon towards the ground and then making a thrust at his mid-section. He drew back.

They circled, measuring each other up. She switched stance and, when she had her back to the sun, stepped into his range and attacked, hoping to trap him in melee while he was facing its glare. But he was no fool; he blocked and sidestepped, shirking that advantage. He went on the offensive, flashing his weapon at her in a sequence of swings and drives. She blocked and countered them all, and the space between them became a blur as they dodged and skirted around each other, searching for an opening.

They had fought each other so many times that they knew each other's moves all too well. Their bouts had recently begun to resemble a dance, and it frustrated her.

Their swords locked and Kyra almost lost her balance from the pressure of Rivan's weapon pushing down upon hers. She dug the back of her heels into the dirt to help hold her ground.

All around her, the boys were cheering for Rivan. It was distracting. She blotted it out.

Focus!

She turned her attention back to Rivan, and they stared at each other, face to face. He usually won. It was because he was bigger. And stronger. But she was faster, more agile, and it was usually when she played that to her advantage and caught him off guard that she earned her victory.

She let him bear down upon her a little, feigning weakness, and then, when he leant towards her, she ducked to the side and rolled, leaving him almost toppling over from the sudden missing weight.

The cheering – the chanting of Rivan's name coming from all around her – swiftly turned into a cacophony of boos and jeers. She ignored them and strode towards Rivan as he righted himself.

She was tired of this place. Tired of the constant battle to validate herself. Tired of working twice as hard as the men yet only receiving half of the credit. Most of all, she was tired of Rivan, and the way the other boys all idolised him.

He blocked, but she came at him again. She was tired of them always repeating the same strikes, counters and parries on each other.

Kyra remembered a new ploy she had been practising in her spare time. She hadn't had a chance to test it yet but now was as good a time as any. Rivan's motions had become all too mediocre recently; it was time to surprise him with something fresh.

She sent her sword in an arc towards his shoulder. He blocked in the usual fashion. She then circled her sword behind her to distract his eye and gain some momentum, and brought it swinging towards Rivan again – it was a common feint they had both learnt years ago – and he, of course, parried it, flicking her blade to the side and leaving one of her legs exposed. He always did that, and Kyra was all too familiar with it, so she easily countered.

Righting her weapon, she thrust at his belly, and he blocked again, twisting his sword around her own in an attempt to get within her range, but she knew that manoeuvre all too well.

He was falling right into her trap.

The next move Kyra made was a common one. Exactly the sort he would have expected, and she already knew how he was going to respond. She aimed for his neck. He raised his sword. She feigned a low swing, but instead, twisted around him, whirling her sword in a crescent motion.

And, just as she predicted, his back lay exposed. She grinned. She had a free opening! He *might* react just fast enough to face her, but he had no way of knowing which direction her sword was heading. She aimed for his legs.

But then, between all the clamour of boys cheering and heckling, a singular voice raised itself, becoming distinct.

"Rivan!" someone yelled. "Low blow!"

Kyra was struck. Pain rang down her shoulder. She toppled over, her sword falling from her hand as she landed face down on the grass.

There was a moment of pause – it seemed everyone was aware that mal-play had occurred – and they turned to their mentor for judgement.

"Rivan wins!" Baird decided.

And then his voice was drowned out by everyone cheering.

Kyra lifted herself from the ground, ignoring the pain throbbing down her arm, and looked at her mentor.

Are you scitting me!? she thought.

Rivan's friend cheated. Why was Baird letting them get away with that?

Rivan turned to the other boys and raised his sword to the air. They applauded. Kyra glared at the back of his head, seething. The sounds of their adulation only furthered her fury. She clenched her fists.

She charged at Rivan, twisting her foot between his own and thrusting her knee into the back of his thigh, toppling him over. It wasn't a conscious decision. It was an act of pure impulse. The only way she could deal with how enraged she was.

And she instantly regretted it. When Rivan's huge mass fell to the ground with a thud, everyone went silent and stared at her.

"*Kyra!*" Baird bellowed, and the ferociousness of his voice made several people flinch. "Come with me. *Now!*"

Kyra knew she was in trouble. Deep trouble. She followed Baird to a cluster of trees nearby and resigned herself to take the coming reprimand humbly or risk only stoking her mentor's ire.

"What the blazes were you thinking?" he demanded, once they were out of earshot.

"It wasn't fair!" she screamed, all her sensibilities forgotten the moment Baird raised his voice. "They–"

"Don't you dare take that tone with me!" Baird roared.

She lowered her eyes to the ground, and the rest of what he said was lost to her ears.

They cheated! she thought, biting her lip to stop herself arguing. She knew from long and bitter experience there was nothing to be gained by quarrelling with Baird.

"Do you realise how much grief I get for training you?" Baird said. She unwillingly became aware of his voice again. "I'm constantly sticking up for you, telling the villagers you shouldn't be spinning yarn with the other lasses – that you're worth all the time I put in – and then you pull stunts like that!"

"I have just as much right to be here as they do!" Kyra said, pointing to the grove.

"Well act like it then!" Baird scolded. "None of them–"

"None of them have to put up with the crap I do!" Kyra exclaimed. "They're always ganging up on me!"

"No one forces you to come here, Kyra," Baird said. She turned away and went back to not listening to him again. She hated Baird sometimes. She hated Rivan even more. He was always receiving all the adoration, but she was a better archer than him by far. And a better tracker.

"You're not listening to me, are you?!" Baird screamed, pulling her out of her thoughts.

"I am!" she lied, turning her attention back to him.

"No you're not!" Baird retorted, his face turning red again. "If you're not even going to listen to me then just *go!*"

"But–"

"*Go!*" he roared, pointing in the direction of the village. "Go home and cool your head!"

"But it's not even midday yet!" Kyra said. "I want to–"

"You've already done enough fighting today," Baird said.

"I'm sorry!" Kyra pleaded. "Look, I will apologise to Rivan if you want me to. Just let me–"

"Go home, Kyra…" Baird repeated.

"Please, Baird!" Kyra said. "I want to be Chosen for the Academy. It's not fair!"

Baird hesitated and looked at her, crossing his arms over his chest. "I tell you what… go find Jaedin for me…"

"*Jaedin?*" Kyra repeated. "What do you want with Jaedin?"

"He was supposed to be here today, but he didn't show up. *Again!*" Baird said. "Go find him and tell him that I want him here. *Now!* Drag him here if you have to. Whatever it takes. If you manage to get him to come, I *might* let you join us again this afternoon…"

"Fine!" Kyra exclaimed, turning away and marching down the hill.

She knew she needed to compose herself before she saw anyone else, so she took a longer route back to the village, passing through woodland. It was often not a bad spot for hunting wild hares, or even deer if you were lucky, but Kyra didn't have her bow that day. She did, however, notice some edible mushrooms at the base of one of the trees, so she crouched down, opened up her burlap sack and gathered them, huffing as she did so. Kyra had recently become conscious of how dependent upon her parents she was – many of the young women her age had already started working as weavers or farmers, or had even found themselves a mate – so she was making an effort to earn her keep. She spent most of her free time looking after her little sister Luisa now and brought as much food to the table as she could.

She was hoping she would be Chosen for the Academy and no longer be a burden on them, but her chances of that happening had just been thwarted.

After collecting all the mushrooms she could find, Kyra

rose and continued making her way down the hill, emerging from the trees and entering the fields. She saw the rooftops of Jalard below her.

It was summer. Everything was turning green, and the sun bathed the village with a charming incandescence. Jalard was a quaint place; Kyra could admit that. Most of the homes were single-storey huts made from cob, and they were connected by a network of dirt trackways. There was a gently rolling brook which snaked its way through the centre and the bank was lined with willow trees.

After seventeen years, Kyra had come to feel restless. She was bored of Jalard. She was one of the few women lucky enough to have ventured outside their village and seen other places – she had even visited a town once, albeit briefly – and she understood that there was much more to the world. She wanted to see the ocean. Mountains. Cities.

Most of the people born in Jalard were destined to spend their entire lives there. They worked, mated, had children and died without ever leaving. Kyra was determined to not be one of those people.

When Kyra reached the bottom of the valley, she passed the mill. Mabonna opened the shutters and tried to coax Kyra to come inside for a hot drink, but Kyra, as usual, made an excuse. She didn't find any of the older woman's gossip particularly enthralling, and Kyra had an errand to run. She needed to find Jaedin so that Baird would let her back into training this afternoon and she could prove she was worthy of the Academy.

Kyra spotted someone crouched over a flowerbed and recognised them; it was one of her friends. Bryna. She quickened her pace to reach her.

"Hello Kyra," Bryna said, without so much as turning her head. She had a gathering basket cradled beneath her arm and was foraging for leaves.

Kyra could never quite remember how she became friends with Bryna. It was an odd pairing, for Bryna was everything Kyra wasn't – serene, reserved, mysterious – but somehow it worked. The one thing they had in common was that they were both outsiders; many of the villagers feared Bryna because she was Blessed.

"Gaddythistles," Bryna said, as she rose to her feet.

"What?" Kyra blurted. Her friend was confusing her, but this was nothing new. It was as if she lived in her own little world sometimes. Probably because she spent more time in the company of flowerbeds and trees than people. She was the daughter of the medicine woman and on a path to becoming one herself. Bryna could often be found on the outskirts of the village, foraging for the fruits of their craft.

She had leaves caught in her hair that day, again. Most of the other women had begun to tie their hair up and abandon wintery garments in favour of light, airy frocks because of the warmer weather, but Bryna was still clad in a dark blue cloak and letting her long black locks run freely down her shoulders.

"Gaddythistles," Bryna repeated, holding up a green stem with blue petals to Kyra's nose. They smelled lovely – like mildly-spiced honey – but it would take more than pleasant aromas to placate Kyra. "They are calming and help with nerves. Why are you upset, Kyra?"

"Who said I was upset?" Kyra asked, stepping back and putting a hand on her hip. Bryna just looked at her with her purple eyes. No matter how long they had known each other, Kyra could never quite get used to those eyes. It always felt like they were looking through you.

"Okay, I'm pissed off," Kyra admitted. "Baird told me off, and I probably deserved it, but the boys were cheating!" she exclaimed. "And now I have to go and find Jaedin like I'm some bloody messenger! Oh, wait..." Kyra remembered. "Do you know where Jaedin is?"

Bryna nodded. "He's at Miles' place. I'll come with you."

Chapter 2

Jaedin

In the beginning, there were just four gods. The Ancients. And their names were Lania, Vaishra, Ignis, and Ta'al.

Lania ruled over the lands, and Vaishra ruled the seas – they were sisters and lived in harmony.

When the first day began, Ignis lit up the world with the sun, and his brother, Ta'al, hummed to life, stirring up the oceans with his wind.

Vaishra fell in love with Ta'al, and their first union filled the sky with clouds, birthing a son. Manveer, a tempestuous god who brought rain and thunder.

Lania and Ignis fell in love as well, as was destined, but for them the arrangement was not so idyllic. The first time Lania saw Ignis, she craved his warmth. She reached for the sky, creating mountains to reach him, but when she got too close she was seared by his fire. The flare of his passion was too strong, and she was proud. She wanted to be his equal, not his vassal. They quarrelled, molten earth roiled from the highlands, and the land burned.

Perhaps it was their turbulent relationship which caused her to act the way she did when The Others appeared.

There is no singularly consistent tale of how or why they came into existence – some accounts claim that they were always there, waiting for their time, while others say they came from the stars – but what they agree upon, is that eventually, a new group of gods were graced upon the world: The Others.

From the moment these new, alien gods came there was hostility and distrust. Over time this culminated into war, and The Ancients and The Others fought a long and bitter contest for supremacy.

Somewhere between it all, Lania had a secret love affair with their leader, Gazareth, and with him, she bore three children.

The first two, Flora and Fauna, were joined by the hands but never wished to be separated. Lania disguised them as the offspring of Ignis and they were accepted by The Ancients. Together, these two goddesses brought abundant life to the world.

The third child was called Verdana, but Lania knew from the moment she laid eyes upon her that there was no way she could disguise who her father was, so she hid her away, deep within a cave, so that the sun god would never shine upon her.

But Verdana could not be kept a secret forever and, when Ignis discovered her existence, the war between the two factions erupted into a final confrontation. A battle of immeasurable destruction; one which left all sides weakened.

At the end of it, Verdana crawled out from her hole, into the desolation. She was finally free, and became – to the horror of The Ancients – the womb of mankind.

* * *

Jaedin slammed the book shut and sighed.

Miles, his mentor who sat on the other side of the room, paused his quill above the parchment he was writing on and peered at him. "Yes, Jaedin? What is it this time?"

"It doesn't make any sense," Jaedin muttered, gesturing to the book. It was entitled, *Sharma's Pantheon Through the Ages.*

"How many times have you read that book? Five? Or six? Why don't you find something else to do?" Miles suggested.

"Such as?"

"You could go outside and enjoy the sunshine. When was the last time you held a sword, rode a horse, or even went for a *walk*?" Miles replied, turning his attention back to his writing. "It isn't healthy for a young man to be cooped up indoors all day."

Jaedin raised his eyebrow. Miles was no one to criticise him for lack of sunshine; his mentor was *always* in this study, poring over his books and writing in his scrolls. With a lazy shadow of stubble on his face, he was very much the picture of a scholar approaching middle age.

"I'm just not into that stuff," Jaedin said. "I'm not a warrior."

He did not tell Miles that he was scared of going outside –

that whenever he was tricked into learning to fence with the other boys, they picked on him – because it was too embarrassing.

Miles fixed Jaedin with his grey-blue eyes. "What is it that keeps you here, Jaedin?"

"What do you mean?" Jaedin replied.

Maybe he doesn't want me here... he thought to himself.

"You have worked through my entire collection," Miles declared, gesturing to the shelves of books which lined the walls of his study. His home was a generous size considering that he lived there alone, but he was a teacher and one of the privileges which came with that role was custody of the village library. "You're almost fluent in Ancient, and now you spend your time nit-picking."

He doesn't want me here... maybe I am just an annoyance to him, Jaedin thought, as a sad feeling twinged in his chest. *But where else is there for me to go?*

"It... interests me..." Jaedin replied weakly. "I want to learn more."

A smile warmed Miles' face. "That's a fair enough reason..." he relented. "So then, young scholar, what is it *this* time?"

Jaedin felt a huge wave of reassurance. "Well, I was just reading about the creation story again. When Lania, Ignis, Ta'al, and Vaishra encountered The Others."

Miles nodded. "Gazareth and his horde."

"It implies here that The Ancients were against the creation of mankind," Jaedin said. "How can that be so?"

"Humans have flaws, don't they?" Miles suggested.

Jaedin knew this very well. He had received enough bruises from the fists of other boys during his childhood to know that people could be cruel, and he had also read accounts of many bloody and destructive wars in Miles' history books.

"But that would mean we worship, *revere*, deities who hate us," Jaedin said.

"Who said they hated us?" Miles challenged.

"This book!" Jaedin said, holding it up. "Verdana was hidden away, and became, *'to their horror'*, the creator of mankind."

"That isn't stating they hate us *now*," Miles argued. "It is implying they had misgivings when we were created. That is only one book. Records from other regions have different theories and tales."

Jaedin knew this as well; he had read a good few of them. "I just don't think *this* one makes sense."

"Jaedin, you have never been outside Jalard. Humans are capable of uncountable evils–"

"I know," Jaedin protested. "I have read–"

"No you *don't*," Miles interrupted. "Reading about it in books is nothing like experiencing it firsthand."

"Don't you think it is ludicrous that people worship deities who are against their very existence?" Jaedin challenged.

A look of nostalgia crossed Miles' face. "You sound like a Gavendarian… They worship Gazareth above the other gods because they see him as their creator."

Jaedin paused and thought about their neighbours to the east. He sometimes forgot Miles was a refugee from there. He moved to Sharma shortly after the War of Ashes ended, and he had an accent which sounded very formal and made him stand out from the rest of the villagers. Jaedin barely noticed it anymore.

"What was it like growing up in Gavendara?" Jaedin asked.

Miles frowned. The light which was always in his eyes when he was enjoying a good theoretical discussion dimmed, and he turned away. "You know I don't like to talk about that…"

"Please Miles," Jaedin coaxed. "I want to know. It's weird… I've known you for so long, and you've taught me so many things, but I still don't know much about you, or–"

"Jaedin!"

Jaedin flinched. He had never heard Miles raise his voice before. He realised he must have struck a nerve. He looked to the window.

Luckily the awkward moment was interrupted by a knock at the door.

"Remember," Miles said as he got up to answer it. "The Ancients are the air you breathe, the land that grows the crops which feed you, the water that quenches your thirst, and the fire which warms your hearth at night. If they really hated us, they would have rid the world of us long ago."

To Jaedin's surprise, it was his sister, Bryna, with whom Miles returned a few moments later. She breezed into the room with a basket of flowers cradled beneath her arm. They smiled at each other, but there was no spoken greeting; such things were not necessary between them. Bryna was his twin.

"I should have known I would find you here," Kyra said, appearing from behind Bryna and striding into the room. "Baird sent me to find you. He wants you in the training fields. *Now*."

"I have already tried to speak to him—" Miles began to explain.

"I'm not going!" Jaedin said. The thought of spending a day being ridiculed by the other boys and shouted at by Baird terrified him. "No way!"

"Tough!" Kyra replied. "Cause he said that *I* can't go back unless *you* come with me, so get up off that ruddy chair and—"

"Since when did you become Baird's messenger?" Jaedin asked, raising an eyebrow at her and then turning back to the book he was reading to make himself appear busy.

"Baird sent me away early…" Kyra said between gritted teeth.

"Why?" Jaedin asked tiredly. "What did you do *this* time?"

Kyra's face went red, which only confirmed Jaedin's suspicions.

"That is none of your business!" she raised her voice at him. "Just get up and come with me! Baird said to drag you if I had to, so don't make me do it. You *know* I will!"

Jaedin caught Miles and Bryna grinning to each other in the corner of his eye, and he shot his sister a dirty look. She always seemed to find it amusing when he and Kyra bickered.

"If I may…" Miles said, rubbing his hands together. "I would like to point out that, while I wholeheartedly agree that a little sunshine wouldn't do Jaedin any harm, do you not see what Baird has done here? He is playing you off against each other, and you are reacting *exactly* how he intended you to."

"I don't care!" Kyra crossed her arms over her chest. "I want to get into the Academy, and Baird said he is writing his final reports tonight. I can't go back this afternoon unless *he* comes with me!" she pointed at Jaedin.

"And you suppose your chances of being Chosen are going to be based *solely* upon your actions today?" Miles shook his head and smiled to himself. "That man really knows how to goad you, doesn't he... why don't you just sit down, Kyra? Take an afternoon off. Relax. I doubt whatever misdeeds you got up to today are going to eradicate a whole year of hard work. Not to mention all the other misdeeds you've done..."

Kyra scowled at Miles and turned back to Jaedin. "If I don't get into the Academy I am blaming *you*!" she said before storming out of the room and slamming the door behind her.

"Are you okay, Jaedin?" Bryna asked, a few moments later.

"Yes..." Jaedin said, forcing a smile. He hid his hands beneath the table so Miles wouldn't see that they were shaking. He didn't like confrontation. It made him nervous. "I know she didn't mean it..."

"Yes," Miles said. "You know well enough what she's like... tomorrow she will be all light and sunshine again, and all will be forgotten... Want to join us, Bryna?" Miles said, turning to Jaedin's sister. "Jaedin and I were just talking about the goddess Verdana, and how she was demonised by The Ancients..."

Bryna sat down with them. She didn't contribute to their discussion, but Jaedin could tell she was engaged by it. Once it was over, the three of them passed the rest of the afternoon by playing card games. Jaedin relaxed a little. He almost forgot about his squabble with Kyra.

When daytime turned into evening, he realised that their mother would be expecting them so he suggested they leave. They bid Miles a warm farewell and made their way home.

It wasn't far away. He and Bryna lived in one of the few houses in Jalard which had more than one floor; a homely cottage covered in ivy and surrounded by a garden brimming with bright and aromatic plants.

When they stepped into the house, their mother was stirring a pot of stew at the hearth. "Evening darlings," she greeted.

Their mother, Meredith, was tall and elegant, with long eyelashes and an ageless face curtained by chestnut hair. She was a Devotee of Carnea – the goddess of healing – and her ability to restore people to health made her feared and respected in equal measure. To most of the villagers she held an imperious grace, but behind closed doors she was warm, and when she smiled at her children her hazel eyes lit up her face.

As well as being Jalard's only medicine woman, she was also a teacher: Baird taught outdoor skills and combat; Miles taught reading and history; and Meredith was in charge of educating the girls in basic herblore, spinning yarn, sewing, and – for those who were Blessed – how to control their magic.

Jaedin sat at the table and his mother placed a cup of tea in front of him.

"Did you find any rosebane?" Meredith asked Bryna.

Bryna nodded and reached into her basket for a handful of flowers with pink petals. "Do you want them dried?" she asked.

Meredith nodded. "Yes, please."

Bryna walked over to the cupboard where they kept most of their herbs and drew back the curtain.

Jaedin sipped his tea as his sister organised the herbs she'd gathered that day, tying them into bunches and hanging them up. Bryna was Blessed, and one of the forms her Blessing took was the ability to heal. It was something she had inherited from their mother, so Meredith was training her and passing down the legacy of her craft.

Jaedin couldn't help but feel left out sometimes. He knew that his mother loved the two of them equally, but his twin spent much more time with her than he did.

Jaedin was Blessed too. He could perform a few simple acts of sorcery, such as summon a gust of wind to help start a fire or create a ball of light to see in the dark, but performing any of these conjurings exhausted him. The only use his Blessing had ever been was as an excuse to get out of things he didn't want to do, such as learning to duel with the other young men from the village. Jaedin often claimed that he was spending his days learning to control his magic, under his mother's guidance, but it was no secret he was actually in Miles' study most of the time. It was within the pages of books that Jaedin found solace during his childhood, when he realised he was both physically weak and less Blessed than his sister, and something which began as mere escapism eventually blossomed into a genuine passion for history and scholarship.

"Miles asked for some garanwort," Bryna said when she returned to the table. "He's having problems sleeping again."

"Oh, that must be why I haven't seen him for a while…" Meredith commented.

"I'll take some over to him," Jaedin offered. "I'll be going there tomorrow anyway."

"No you won't," Meredith said. "The Academy representatives arrived earlier."

"Really?" Jaedin asked.

His mother nodded. "They'll be making the announcement in the morning, outside the Hall. I expect both of you to be there."

"Baird's going to be busy tonight," Jaedin laughed. "He still hasn't finished writing his reports!"

Meredith frowned. "The reports have already been done…"

"What?" Jaedin said. "Kyra said he was finishing them tonight! He made them all fight each other today and told them it was some final test or something. Kyra was really stressed about it."

"Sometimes that man goes way too far trying to push them…" Meredith said, shaking her head. "He was lying, Jaedin. Baird has already done all of your reports. He handed them to me aeights ago!"

"Are you sure?" Jaedin asked.

She nodded. "Parchment isn't cheap all the way out here! Only one page is used for each of you, and it is divided into three parts. Baird begins by writing an account of how you are all doing with the things he teaches you… Then he hands them over to me, and the middle section is mine – I provide an account on how much, if anything, any of you have learnt from me – and then, finally, I give them to Miles, and he compiles them."

"I never saw them in his study…" Jaedin muttered.

"Of course not," Meredith said. "It wouldn't be proper for you to see your own report – or other peoples, for that matter. Imagine if you peeked at Kyra's and told her what Baird and myself had said about her. I hid them from you."

"It does make sense…" Bryna agreed.

"I think we already know we've had somewhat less than favourable reports from Baird…" Jaedin said to his sister, and they grinned at each other. Girls were expected to spend a couple of aeights each year training with Baird too, but Bryna had never attended hers.

Their mother smiled. "Remember, Miles also writes his own account, and I bet you both had glowing ones from him which more than made up for it. And Kyra shouldn't worry so much. Does she really believe he is going to base *everything* he writes about her on a single duel?" she asked, shaking her head. "That girl has always been highly strung… anyway…" Meredith rose from her chair and walked to the hearth. "I trust you are both hungry?" she asked as she stirred the contents of the pot suspended over the fire. "I am up early tomorrow to help the Academy representatives prepare, so I have already eaten. As I said, I want you to both be there for the announcement."

She looked at them in a way which made it clear it was not a matter up for debate; both Jaedin and his sister were habitually averse to public events.

Jaedin sighed. He had his reasons, but he was too ashamed to tell his mother about them. At least on this occasion there would be plenty of adults around. The other young men bullied him less when there were witnesses. "I'll be there…"

* * *

That night, Jaedin awoke to screaming.

He leapt out of his bed, realising it was coming from Bryna's room. The sound was so hoarse it didn't even resemble his sister, but the part of him which was connected to his twin – the part which had been present since the day they were born together, that tugged upon him whenever she was in distress – *knew* it was her.

And that she was in pain.

His knees were a little slower to wake up than the rest of his body and he almost fell in his rush to the door. He opened it and caught sight of his mother racing down the corridor in her dressing gown.

He followed her.

"Bryna!" Meredith yelled.

Jaedin didn't know what to expect when he and his mother burst through the door, the idea they could be in danger was only a secondary thought to him. His sister was in distress. He needed to help her.

Bryna was alone. She was convulsing. Screeching. Her

limbs flailing wildly, and her black hair flitting through the air.

"No!" she cried. Her hands went to her face, and she clawed at her eyes. "No!"

Meredith ran to her side and grabbed her wrists, but Bryna fought back.

"Jaedin!" Meredith yelled, turning to him. "Help me!"

The sound of his name snapped Jaedin out of his stupor; all he could do at first was stare in dismay. He ran to his mother's aid and tried to grasp one of Bryna's ankles, but she thrashed and her other foot swung at his face. He ducked.

"Bryna!" Meredith said once they managed to restrain her, her voice soft yet firm. "It's okay! It's just a dream… it's just a dream. Bryna!"

"It hurts!" Bryna shrieked. She tore one of her hands free and clawed at her face again, but Meredith grabbed her wrist and pinned it to the bed. "It *hurts*! It hurts! It hurts!"

"Bryna! *Wake up!*" Meredith said.

Bryna's eyes opened, but there was no purple in them; her irises had turned black. She stared at the ceiling. "Jaedin!" she whispered. A tear ran down the side of her face. "Don't hurt him!"

"Jaedin's here," Meredith said and stroked Bryna's temple. A red line had formed where she scratched it. "He's fine…"

Bryna turned to Meredith, as if only just noticing she was there, and her eyes cleared.

"You *left* me!" she said to her mother, accusingly. "You left me to die!"

"No Bryna. It was just a dream…" Meredith said and ran her hand through her hair. "I am here. Breathe."

"Why did you leave me?" Bryna cried.

"I didn't leave you," Meredith said. "I'm right here. So is Jaedin. Look."

Jaedin crept to the side of the bed again. He was careful to not make any sudden movements because he didn't want to risk startling his sister into another frenzy. He put his arms around her. Meredith held Bryna too. Her crying softened.

"They were all dead…" she whispered.

"No one has died, Bryna," Meredith said as she stroked her head. "It's okay."

"I know," Bryna said. "But they will. I watched the village burn."

"Shhh," Meredith put a finger to her lips. "Don't wind yourself up again."

Bryna ran a finger down the centre of her forehead thoughtfully and then looked at Jaedin in a way which gave him goosebumps. "They took you away…"

"Don't go saying things like that, Bryna!" Meredith admonished. "You know it was just a dream. It doesn't mean anything."

"But I–"

"Stop it, Bryna!" Meredith raised her voice. "You don't want to worry your brother, do you?" She rose to her feet and her expression softened. "I am going to make you something to help you sleep. Jaedin, can you give me a hand?"

Jaedin thought it peculiar that his mother – a fully-fledged Devotee of Carnea – needed help brewing a potion but she gave him a look which warned him not to argue, and he knew a hint when he saw one so he got up and followed her.

Just before they left the room, Meredith reached for one of Bryna's toys – a doll in the shape of a bird, made of linen and filled with straw – and placed it in her daughter's arms.

Jaedin and his mother walked down the stairs in silence and, when they reached the kitchen, he stoked the fire as she filled the kettle with water. They sat down and stared at the flames as they waited for it to heat.

"I thought she grew out of it…" Meredith said. "But she's getting worse."

Jaedin nodded sombrely. That wasn't the first time Bryna had woken them up in the middle of the night recently, but it was by far the most ominous. "Do you think any of the neighbours heard?"

"Let's hope not. That's the last thing we need. They're superstitious here… they'll think she's possessed or…" Meredith shook her head and looked Jaedin in the eyes. "Did *you* feel anything? From her, I mean. I know you two have that link with each other."

"It's mostly Bryna who senses things about me… I'm not as Blessed as her. You know that," Jaedin shrugged. "She was in pain… I could feel that. She was more terrified than she's ever been before."

The pot balanced over the hearth began to bubble and steam. Meredith stepped over to her herb cupboard and reached for one of her jars.

"Do you think there's anything in it?" Jaedin asked, as his mother sprinkled some leaves into the water.

"What do you mean?" she responded, raising an eyebrow.

"I think you know what I mean," Jaedin said, returning his mother's challenging expression. In the past, Bryna's incoherent ramblings had proven all too premonitory. Meredith often received advanced warning and time to prepare for the injured and sick people who called at their door, thanks to Bryna.

"Don't go having thoughts like that, Jaedin," Meredith said. "Bryna is gifted. And yes, she often sees a shadow of something true, but it comes at a price..." she shook her head. "Your grandmother was much like her, so I have seen this all before... trust me, I know... the best we can do for her is try to keep her as grounded as we can. Not let her dreams and nightmares take over who she is."

Jaedin was surprised by his mother's words. It wasn't often she spoke about her family. Or even their father, who died shortly before they were born. Meredith had always been mysterious about her past, and Jaedin had learnt from a young age to not ask questions.

"So what do we do?" Jaedin asked.

"Go to bed and get some sleep," Meredith said. "Tomorrow, take Bryna to see the Academy representatives make their announcement. Then to Miles' place, if you so wish. Or something else... We need to keep her occupied on *real* things so that her mind doesn't drift into that place again. Can you do that for me?"

Jaedin nodded.

"I'm going to take this drink to her now," Meredith said as she grabbed a steaming cup and walked towards the stairs. "There's one for you, too."

*   *   *

Jaedin slept the rest of the night without any further disturbance and, when he rose the next day, Bryna seemed relatively calm and composed. They didn't speak of the incident, but the atmosphere during breakfast was somewhat marred because the memory of it lingered thickly in the air around the table.

"I guess we should leave," Bryna said.

Jaedin looked at her.

"To see the announcement," Bryna finished. "To see who is Chosen."

"It would make Mum happy if we were there," Jaedin said.

"And Kyra," Bryna reminded him. "It's important to her. Kyra's our friend. It would be good for us to be there. For her."

"Yes it would..." Jaedin agreed. "Let's go,"

He got up from the table and put on his cloak. He was glad his sister was being somewhat coherent again, and he would do whatever he could to keep her that way.

They put their shoes on and left the house, closing the door behind them.

"Do you think Kyra will get in this year?" Jaedin asked as they strolled into the village. He knew conversations about mundane things were usually the best way to keep his sister's mind from drifting.

"I don't know," Bryna shook her head. "I haven't... seen anything about that. Can girls get in?"

"Sometimes, apparently..." Jaedin said. "But never in Jalard. She would be the first."

They turned a corner, and Jaedin's eyes widened at the sight before him. Hundreds had turned up to hear the announcement, and they were all crowded around a stack of hay bales which had been erected as a temporary platform outside the Hall. The representatives from the Academy stood upon them. Their azure-blue vestments stuck out from among the villagers, who mostly wore dun clothing in various shades.

Their mother was up there too and, as usual, one of the exceptions; Meredith's dark and exotic garments always made her stand out from the rest of the villagers. Even Baird, beside her, was clad in his old military uniform for the occasion, aberrant to his typically humble attire. Miles was up there too. Jaedin tried to catch his mentor's eye but Miles seemed distracted that day.

"Where's Kyra?" Jaedin asked.

"Over there," Bryna pointed her out between swarms of people.

"I don't think we're going to be able to reach her…" Jaedin said. The crowd was too tightly packed. He waved to catch her attention though and, when she saw him, she smiled.

It seemed yesterday's quarrel was forgotten, just as Miles predicted. Jaedin mouthed 'good luck' to her, and she mouthed back 'thank you'. He hoped for Kyra's sake that she would be Chosen, as he knew that there was nothing in the world she wanted more, but he would miss his friend.

All the loud chatter going on around him quietened, and Jaedin turned his gaze back to the platform and saw that Baird was preparing to address everyone.

"Good morning," he greeted. "This is the ninth year now, so you all know the drill. Some of you have been Chosen for the Academy. This is a great privilege, so don't take it lightly. You will be expected to work hard to keep your place." He then turned to one of the men behind him dressed in blue. "This is one of their representatives, and his name is Ne'mair. He and his companions have travelled all the way from Shemet to be here today."

Ne'mair came forward and held a rolled-up scroll to the crowd, which prompted a chorus of cheering. Everyone knew, from tradition, that the scroll contained the names of the lucky individuals whose fortunes were about to change.

Eventually, Ne'mair let his hand – and the scroll with it – fall to his side, and he waited for everyone to quieten down before he spoke.

"Greetings people of Jalard," he said. "My companions and I only arrived yesterday and are still weary from our journey, but we will delay you no further. Before I announce who we have Chosen, I would like to say that it was not an easy decision and many of you were promising candidates. This is a small community but, as you have such a fine trainer," he motioned to Baird, "we have often selected a high proportion of nominees compared to your numbers. We even stopped physical try-outs after a couple of years of his service because we trust his judgement when he writes reports about each and every one of you. The same goes for Miles and Meredith here," he added, gesturing to the other two teachers. "Of course.

"I would, however, like to say that it has been very competitive this year, so please do not take it to heart if you do not find yourself selected. If we had the capacity, we would have taken many more."

He untied the string and unravelled the scroll.

"All that said; it is my pleasure to announce that, this year, we are offering two people the opportunity for a scholarship with us."

A second wave of cheering erupted from the crowd. Two being selected was a good year; sometimes they only took one.

"And our first candidate is…" Ne'mair turned his eyes down to the parchment. "Sidry!"

Some were surprised. The most surprised of all appeared to be Sidry himself; his mouth fell open, and he looked at his friend Rivan beside him.

"Come on Sidry!" Rivan said after a few moments had passed and Sidry had not moved. "Get up there!"

Rivan pushed his friend into the crowd, which separated to let him past. People clapped and cheered as the bewildered young man made his way towards the platform. When he climbed it, he was greeted by Baird who patted his back, grinning. Sidry then shook hands with Miles and Meredith, and the cheering peaked when he repeated the gesture with Ne'mair.

After the formalities were over, he turned to his fellow villagers with a flustered and embarrassed expression, but still, they cheered for him.

Beneath the ovations, a tension was rising; one Jaedin could feel in the air. Sidry wasn't a completely unexpected choice, but he wasn't Rivan or Kyra: the two whom everyone had been expecting.

Everyone went quiet and stared up at the stage expectantly. They were getting impatient; it was now a certain fact that either Rivan or Kyra would not be sent to the Academy that year, and they wanted to know who was destined to have their hopes crushed.

"Sidry has been offered a place in the Academy barracks," Ne'mair explained. "Where – if he accepts – he will be trained in the arts of combat and war strategy." His eyes then ventured further down the scroll. "I will now announce our second candidate."

"Jaedin!"

At first, a stunned silence hung upon the air, and then a couple of people chuckled as if they thought it some kind of joke.

"Is there a Jaedin here?" Ne'mair repeated.

Dozens of heads turned from side to side to search for his face, and when they found him, they stared.

"Are you Jaedin?" Ne'mair asked, peering down at him.

Jaedin nodded meekly. He could feel everyone's eyes upon him, and anxiety curled in the pit of his stomach. He wanted nothing more, during that moment, than to disappear.

"Well come up then!"

Jaedin hesitated and swallowed a lump in his throat. Between himself and the platform was a mass of people, all of them bearing hostile expressions.

"You should go to them, Jaedin…" Bryna whispered.

Jaedin took his first tentative step forward. The crowd did not split apart to give him room as they did for Sidry, so he was forced to squeeze through. He heard them mutter to each other as he passed. He couldn't make out any of the words, but he knew from the tone that none of it was favourable.

"Jaedin has been offered a space at the more scholarly institution of the Academy," Ne'mair began to explain. "He wrote a very impressive thesis on–"

But Ne'mair's voice was drowned out by the audience who became less restrained with their dissatisfaction. When Jaedin made it to the platform, he climbed up, and Ne'mair took his hand. Jaedin kept his back to the crowd, but he could still feel them glaring at him. Some of them began to shout abuse. Baird was notably dismayed and barely managed to bring himself to complete the formality when it was his turn to shake Jaedin's hand. Jaedin couldn't look him in the eye.

His mother came over and placed a protective arm around him. She whispered something into his ear, but Jaedin was too distracted to take in what she said. Miles was next, with an encouraging smile and a pat on the back.

When Jaedin finally brought himself to face the crowd again, he looked for Kyra, but she was gone.

Chapter 3

Chosen

After a couple of hours of being harassed by well-wishers and people congratulating him, Sidry finally managed to escape.

They all seemed so intent upon applauding him that none of them had remembered to ask him a simple question.

Did he actually *want* to go to the Academy?

This all felt like a dream to him, but it was not one he had been given the relief of waking up from yet. He never considered the possibility he would be Chosen. Not when he had both Rivan and Kyra to compete with.

There was also the matter of his parents.

They only let him attend Baird's lessons because they were put under pressure by the Elders. All of the boys from Jalard were required to spend some of their early years schooling survival skills and the arts of combat under Baird — it was an edict put into place shortly after the War of Ashes ended — but most of the farmers' sons only learnt the basics before they returned to tending their family's land fulltime. Sidry's parents were getting old, and they had always made it abundantly clear the future they intended for him.

Being a farmer had never been what Sidry wanted — from the day Baird put a sword in his hand, he spent every daylight hour he could get away from his parents learning to duel, hunt, and track — but he had always known that he would have to give it up one day. He accepted it as inevitable.

And he would do it because he loved them.

No. Sidry couldn't go to the Academy. He didn't even have a choice over the matter.

He then had a thought.

Maybe, if he turned the offer down, they would ask Rivan to go in his stead.

He needed to find Rivan, and he had a good idea where his friend would be. He left the village behind and made his way up one of the nearby hills to their secret place at a small clearing near the peak. It was where he and Rivan used to build dens and play games when they were younger, but more recently it was where they practised outside of Baird's lessons and drank bottles of ale Rivan pinched from his parents

When Sidry reached the top, sure enough, there Rivan was; sitting with his back against a tree.

"Rivan," Sidry said as he approached him. "It's okay–"

"I know what you're going to say," Rivan cut him off. "And no! You're going!"

"I can't!" Sidry said. "My parents–"

"Screw your parents," Rivan said. "This isn't about them."

"But it is," Sidry began to explain. "They need me on the farm. They–"

"Will you just shut it!" Rivan yelled. He got up and strode up to Sidry, so they were face to face. "You're going, even if I have to drag your ass there myself. How many people would give anything to be in your boots right now? You're not throwing it away, you ungrateful little cavecrawler!"

Sidry turned his gaze down to the valley. He could see Jalard below them.

It had been easy to resolve the matter by convincing himself he didn't have a choice, but it suddenly dawned upon him that he *did*.

But could he really leave this place – and everything he knew – behind?

The thought was both exciting and terrifying.

It scared him, but it also dawned upon him that, if he didn't take this path, he would regret it for the rest of his life.

He and Rivan went silent for a few moments, but they looked at each other, and their expressions carried more meaning between them than words could convey.

"You're going to hate me, aren't you," Sidry said.

"I will hate you even more if you stay here and I have to see that damn face of yours every day."

Sidry held back tears. It finally sank in that his life had just changed forever.

He was going to the Academy. He was moving away. He might not see his friends for years.

His parents. What was he going to say to his parents?

"Now go, you little scit!" Rivan exclaimed, pointing at the path which led back to the village. "You need to pack."

Sidry couldn't think of anything else to say, so he turned and made his way home. He took one last look at Rivan.

"And watch yourself!" Rivan yelled. "I'm training for another year, and when I get into that damn Academy I'm going to kick your ass!"

* * *

When Sidry got home, his parents were waiting for him.

"Sidry," his father said. He shifted in his seat as if he was about to stand but changed his mind. "Will you... come here, please?"

Sidry walked over to the dusty table and sat with them.

"Did you hear about the Academy?" Sidry asked. His parents just stared at him. It was obvious that they had.

"Aye," his father nodded. "We did. Have you told Baird you're not leaving yet?"

Sidry swallowed a lump in his throat as he looked at his father's weathered face, and he almost changed his mind. Almost. A hard, laborious life had taken its toll, and Sidry realised that the thought of being stuck here for the rest of his life, toiling the land and turning into his father, was a bleak one.

"No," he said.

"Well you should," his mother said, and Sidry turned to her. "People are saying that they'll be leaving tomorrow... you shouldn't waste any more of their time."

"We'll go together," his father decided. "We'll help you explain."

"No, we won't," Sidry took a deep breath. "Because I'm going with them."

His father's eyes widened.

Strangely, it was his mother who spoke up next. She had always been an amiable woman, but during that moment, her voice was surprisingly firm. "No, Sidry, you can't..." she shook her head. "We need you here. Who's going to take over the farm? We have no other children."

She turned her eyes to her lap. None of them said anything, but Sidry knew what was on his mother's thoughts: the gods only blessed her with one child. She never had any more. She visited Meredith once and, after examining her, the Devotee of Carnea told her that the delivery of her firstborn had taken its toll and she would never conceive again.

Sidry was their only child, and they had always made it clear to him that it was his destiny to take over the farm.

"What use is all that nonsense Baird's been teaching you, anyway?" his father added. "We're nowhere near the border. There's been peace for over ten years now."

"That doesn't mean there's always going to be," Sidry argued. "Baird said that it might happen again. And if it does, Sharma will need warriors."

"Sharma needs food," his mother said. "And we need you here to help make it grow."

"What's your plan?" his father cut-in before Sidry's mother had even finished. "You want to become a soldier, do you? Get yourself killed?"

Sidry paused, realising he still hadn't considered that. What exactly *was* he going to do?

"Not all of the Academy students become soldiers," Sidry said. "Some of them join the Synod. Or become teachers. Like Baird. Maybe that's what I'll do!" he said, smiling, hoping to win a smile on their faces too, but failing.

"Baird, Baird, Baird!" his father spat. "You know, that is all we've heard since you started those lessons. This village already has a teacher."

"Well he's not going to be here forever, is he?" Sidry argued. "If I become a teacher, I'll make enough coin to look after you. We won't need the farm."

"This farm," his father said, his voice tightening as he pointed to the ceiling. "Was my father's, and his father's, and his father's before that. Are you saying it's not good enough for you?"

Guilt twisted in Sidry's gut, and he hesitated, considering what angle to try next.

This was going even worse than he predicted.

And he knew now that he had a long and painful evening ahead of him.

*　　*　　*

"What did she say?" Jaedin asked, the moment the door opened and Bryna entered the house.

"Well..." Bryna began as she hung up her coat. "Obviously, she is upset..."

In her sixteen years, Bryna had never told a lie – it had just never been within her to utter words which were not truthful – but she understood that sometimes to be kind one had to be delicate with the truth, and what she just said was an enormous understatement.

She had just witnessed a tantrum which would put most children to shame.

Jaedin frowned. "I want to talk to her, but I'm afraid."

"You shouldn't be afraid, you should be proud," their mother said. She had an assortment of herbs laid out on the table and was organising them into the sections of a medicine bag she was making for Jaedin to take with him on his journey.

"It didn't feel like it," Jaedin replied. "Did you see Baird's face?"

"He was just surprised," Meredith said. "When they said two, everyone thought it was going to be Kyra and Rivan."

"There's something strange going on..." Bryna whispered.

"Stop that, Bryna," Meredith looked at her reproachfully. "Jaedin has done well. It's just the first time someone from here's been Chosen for what's up there, that's all," she tapped the side of her temple. "It's not right for Baird to assume it is always going to be *his* students."

Bryna knew this, but she couldn't shake off the feeling that something was not right. Why couldn't anyone else feel it?

"Should I go see Kyra?" Jaedin asked, turning to her.

Bryna paused as she considered the most tactful way to respond. She had a feeling that if Jaedin went to see Kyra right now, things could get messy. Bryna knew Kyra well – enough to know that, in a few days time, she would be the first to admit that Jaedin was not to blame for her misfortune – but, at this moment, it was still raw, and she was angry.

Bryna had tried to calm her down and reason with her, but she found it difficult to be supportive to a friend who was screaming curses about her twin, so she eventually gave up and found an excuse to leave.

"I think deep down she knows it's not your fault, Jaedin," Bryna went with. "But she's not ready to see you yet. She's upset."

"But I'm leaving tomorrow…" Jaedin said.

"You'll see her again. She's only seventeen," Meredith pointed out. "There's a good chance she'll be Chosen next year."

Jaedin put his face in his hands.

"Are you okay?" Bryna asked, placing one of her hands upon his. She didn't like it when her brother was upset because she felt it too. "It wasn't nice the way people responded earlier."

"I don't care," Jaedin muttered. "I'm not going to miss idiots like them…"

*   *   *

"You can't go!" she yelled.

Sidry paused from packing his clothes. His mother was standing in the doorway again. This had been going on all evening: repetitive arguments which went around in circles, followed by tears and slamming of doors. Between each heated exchange, Sidry was left in his room where he listened to the raised voices of his parents ranting to each other by the hearth, followed by the thunderous footsteps of them coming back to reignite the argument.

Over and over again.

"Do you have any idea what this means to me?" he asked her.

"And we mean nothing to you?" she asked. Her voice almost breaking.

"You mean everything to me…" Sidry whispered.

His mother was close to tears, and it was an effort to keep himself from crying.

His father appeared beside her. "Who's going to help me with the farm?" he asked.

"You can hire someone," Sidry suggested.

"We can't afford it."

"You can now you have one less mouth to feed," Sidry pointed out. "The Academy will provide for me the next few years. I'll help with the farm when I come back."

"We want you on the farm *now*!" his father yelled. "It's what we always planned."

"And when did you ever ask me what *I* wanted to do?"

Sidry blurted, feeling angry. All night he had been trying to bottle up his feelings to make this as painless for them as possible, but his father's words popped the lid. "I've always been so caught up in what *you* wanted for me, I never even considered what *I* wanted!"

"Please Sidry... stay," his mother pleaded, and her voice finally broke.

He turned away and returned to packing his clothes. He couldn't watch his mother cry. "I'm sorry, but this is something I have to do."

* * *

Bryna couldn't help but be amused at the disdainful expression on her brother's face when he stepped into the room in his new clothes. She was used to seeing Jaedin clad in billowy, loose-fitting black robes but now he was dressed plainly, in a faded brown tunic and fitted leggings. Apart from his shoulder-length hair and distinctive green eyes, he could have been any other young man from the village.

"See!" Meredith appraised. "It's not so bad, is it?"

"I'm sure my other clothes would've been fine..." he grumbled.

Bryna smiled at him teasingly. It had been entertaining watching their mother fuss over him all night and morning – but it did make Bryna wonder how well her twin was going to cope on his own when he left.

"You'll be thanking me after a couple of days. You've never been on a long journey," Meredith said, placing a hat on Jaedin's head.

"What's that for?" he asked, scowling at Bryna.

"To keep the sun out of your eyes," Meredith explained. "Maybe you should have spent more time in the fields with Baird... you're obviously not used to the outdoors."

"If I wasted time with that stuff I wouldn't have got into the Academy in the first place..." Jaedin said.

"Now... I think that is everything..." Meredith decided as she went to check his bags one last time. "I have packed some food for you, as I doubt their rations for the road will quite meet your finicky tastes..."

She was interrupted by a knock at the door, and Bryna got

up to answer it while their mother continued to fuss over Jaedin. She opened it to find Miles standing outside.

"Hello," Bryna greeted. "Are you here to say goodbye to Jaedin?"

As she spoke, she noticed Miles was wearing riding boots and carrying a large burlap sack.

"Well, not exactly…" Miles began.

"Is that Miles?" Meredith called.

"Yes, Mother," Bryna replied over her shoulder.

"Well, bring him in then!"

Bryna stepped aside, and he followed her into the kitchen.

"Hello Miles," Meredith greeted, before turning back to Jaedin. "See, Jaedin! Even Miles is dressed…" and she then paused in realisation and craned her neck to look at Miles again. "What's in that sack?"

"I'm going to Shemet as well," he announced.

"Really?" Jaedin's eyes lit up – perhaps a little too much, in Bryna's opinion, but she knew there was nothing she could do about that. "How come?"

"Well, you're my only student this time of the year anyway…" Miles said.

"You're coming to look after me?" Jaedin asked, bemused.

"Not exactly," Miles shook his head. "I also haven't collected for the villages' share of the library for a fair few years…"

"That's great!" Jaedin smiled. "I was worried I would go insane with boredom. That Sidry has the brains of a goose."

"Keep an eye on this one for me," Meredith said, patting Jaedin's head.

"I'm sure he's sage enough to look after himself…" Miles said. "Are you ready? I think we are due to meet them soon."

"Yes," Meredith answered as she lifted one of Jaedin's bags and dropped it on his shoulder. "Just about…"

They filed outside while Bryna put her boots on. After she had finished tying her laces, she made her way to the door and found her brother standing there, staring into the house.

"What are you doing?" she asked, realising that she had not managed to get a moment to speak to her twin alone since he had been Chosen. With him being so busy packing and their mother fussing over him, she had not had the chance.

"Just taking one last look…" he replied.

"You'll be back," she reassured, touching his shoulder.

"It's just…" he said, staring into their home anxiously. "I have this feeling…"

"What is it?" Bryna asked and, for a brief moment, she thought that she was not alone. That there was someone else who knew that something was amiss. Someone else who sensed there was something in the air which wasn't right.

Someone who didn't think she was just crazy.

"Come on, you two!" Meredith interrupted them. She and Miles were waiting for them on the other side of the gate.

"Let's go," Jaedin said, closing the door.

The moment was lost, and that bleak, barren feeling settled inside Bryna again. It was a lonely place, but a part of her was glad her brother had been spared from the burden she had to endure.

They caught up with Miles and Meredith, walking towards the centre of the village. Bryna gazed up at the sky. It was sunny that day, but there were a few clouds. Often, when Bryna looked up at them, images formed in her mind, but they didn't have any messages for her that day. She was glad of this. Omens had been harrowing of late.

They turned a corner, and Bryna saw the Academy representatives ahead, preparing the horses.

Sidry was there too, sitting upon a bale of hay. Bryna could tell from his posture and the forlorn expression on his face that, for some reason, he was deeply sad. She did not know him, but Bryna never liked to see anyone upset, so she waved. He smiled back at her thinly.

Things must be hard for him as well, she realised. Jaedin wasn't the only one who had been Chosen over his friend.

"Morning Jaedin. You're just in time," Ne'mair said as he walked over to greet them. He shook Jaedin's hand and then their mother's. "Don't worry about your son, we will take good care of him."

He looked at Bryna. "And who is the young lady?" he asked.

"My daughter," Meredith introduced them. "Bryna."

Ne'mair turned his attention back to Jaedin, who seemed eager and was already loading his bags onto one of the horses. "I trust you know how to ride that beast?" he asked.

"Just about," somebody appeared behind them. "It was *one*

thing I managed to drill into him…"

They all turned at the sound of Baird's voice, and the burly ex-soldier, without a word of greeting, strode past them and claimed one of the horses.

"Good morning, Baird," Ne'mair said and looked at the people gathered around them. "I believe everyone is now present…"

"What's going on?" Meredith asked, turning to Baird quizzically.

"I'm going to Shemet as well," Baird explained as he climbed onto the horse's back.

"Since when did you start accompanying the Chosen to the Academy?" Miles mumbled.

"I could ask you the same question…" Baird said.

"I need to go to the library, to–"

"My business in Shemet is none of your concern…" Baird interrupted him.

Bryna sensed tension between them.

Why is everyone acting so strangely? she wondered.

Ne'mair turned to Sidry. "Is this horse okay for you?" he asked and gestured to a black mare yet to be laden.

Sidry nodded and began loading his possessions.

"I guess everyone is a bit nervous," Ne'mair chuckled, in a rather transparent attempt to dispel the awkward atmosphere.

"Where are your parents, Sidry?" Baird asked.

"Not here," he said flatly.

Bryna walked over to her brother, who was now mounted on his horse and ready to leave. As she neared, she held her hand up to its nose.

"You like him?" Jaedin asked as he ruffled its mane.

"You mean *her*," Bryna corrected.

"I'll miss you…" he said softly.

"I will write," Bryna promised.

"But it's not the same…"

"Jaedin… I will always know of your wellbeing," Bryna reminded him. "We are connected."

"But we've never been this far apart," Jaedin said. "How do you know it'll still work?"

Everyone was almost ready to leave now. Baird, Sidry, Miles, and the men from the Academy were all saddled. Bryna turned back to Jaedin, and they both sighed, realising their last moments together were rapidly vanishing.

"Good luck, Jaedin," Bryna said.

"Bye, Bryna."

That moment, a cloud in the sky behind Jaedin caught Bryna's eye and an overwhelming sense of unease passed through her. It was in the shape of a claw, reaching towards the sun. The welkin darkened.

"Don't go!" she whispered.

"What?"

"It's not safe," she gasped, but the words were choked out of her. She was enveloped by a grey miasma. The village vanished. She spun around, coughing, searching for a way out, but all she could see was grey.

She tried to tell Jaedin that something was wrong. That something terrible was going to happen to them all, but she could no longer see him.

The mist cleared, but she was no longer in Jalard. There was a woman before her, sitting on a throne of gnarled tree roots knotted around each other. Bryna looked up, and their eyes met – the woman's were grey and sharp; they pierced into Bryna's soul and made her spine tingle.

Say no more! The course he is being pulled is far less treacherous than the puddle you will drown in, my pretty one. Remember, a fish is better risking the waterfall than drying out on the bank.

* * *

"Bryna…" Jaedin cooed, waving a hand in front of her face.

His sister continued staring at the sky. Her lips were moving, but Jaedin could not make out anything of the incoherent mumbles coming from her mouth.

"Bryna!" he yelled, tapping her shoulder with his boot.

She looked at him, shuddered, and then her eyes cleared. "Sorry about that…" she whispered. "I… don't know where I was…"

"What is it?" Jaedin asked. "Did you see something?"

She ignored him, reaching over and tightening her fingers around his arm.

"Be careful," she whispered.

She turned and left. Jaedin watched his twin as she walked

away. Something about her tone and the look in her eyes chilled him. Her grip was so tight it left marks on his skin. He could still feel it.

He considered pressing her about it – felt an urge to leap off his horse to ask her if she had experienced another vision – but then his mother came to say goodbye. She opened up her arms to embrace him, and Jaedin leant towards her.

"Travel safe, darling," she said, kissing his cheek.

"I'll be back, Mother," he promised.

"Is everyone ready?" Ne'mair called.

Jaedin nodded, as did the others.

"Then we will proceed," one of his companions announced.

Jaedin's horse seemed to need little direction. It spurred into a trot and followed the others, falling into line behind Baird. Miles guided his horse beside him, and Jaedin smiled – he was glad his mentor would be there to keep him company.

He took one last look at his sister and mother, standing arm in arm outside the Hall. He waved as his horse turned a corner, feeling something inside him wrench as they vanished from sight.

The procession rode down the street. It was morning, and the villagers were walking out of their homes to begin their daily routines. Many of them paused to wave at the men from the Academy and their Chosen as they passed. Seeing all the crowds of people made Jaedin realise he was going to miss the forthcoming Festival of Ignis, but he wasn't sad about that. The Festival marked the middle of summer, and it was the one night of the year males could invoke Ignis' fiery side and fight each other without being reprimanded. Jaedin usually sheltered in his room to hide from the other young men who liked to make sport of picking on him.

They passed the street where Kyra lived. When her house came into view, Jaedin felt wretched. He had not had the chance to say goodbye. He also felt guilty; in his excitement, he had not thought of her much that morning.

When he looked at her window, he thought he saw her face behind the glass, but he couldn't be sure because the room was dark. He raised his hand. Waved. But the silhouette vanished.

Chapter 4

The Elders' Request

Rivan yawned as he walked down the stairs.

Two days had passed since Sidry left for the Academy, which had given him enough time to start shaking off feelings of resentment. They were beginning to ease and become replaced with boredom. Not only was his closest friend gone but so was Baird, and thus, Rivan's routine of vigorous training had been broken. He was struggling to find ways to occupy his time during his mentor's absence.

Rivan had even attempted to fill Baird's boots the previous day and mustered some of the boys of Jalard to the training fields himself, but he soon grew tired of playing coach.

The truth was they irritated him. With their inane questions and need for constant guidance. He even grew weary of their endless praise. Which was strange: Rivan had always liked the way the other boys admired him but, in Sidry's absence, he'd begun to find all their validation a little empty. It made him realise that he had many cronies who applauded everything he did and agreed with every word he said, but he was short on real friends.

No, Rivan decided. *Sod them. Sod them all! I'm going to take a day to myself...*

Perhaps he could go hunting. Or borrow a horse and ride out to somewhere.

But first, he needed some breakfast.

He ventured downstairs for food, passing his mother, who sat at her loom. It rattled away as she pulled the bar back and forth. When Rivan reached the hearth he discovered the pot was empty and his parents had neglected to save him any porridge that morning. He grabbed an apple.

"Someone came for you earlier..." his mother yelled to him as he took his first bite.

Rivan looked over to her. "Uh huh?" he mumbled as he chewed. "Who?"

"The Elders," she said, pausing from her weaving. "They sent a message. They want to see you."

"The Elders?" Rivan repeated.

*What the blazes would the Elders want with **me**?* he wondered.

"Yes," his mother confirmed. "At the Hall."

"Did they say when?" he asked.

"On the tenth hour, I believe…" she said.

Rivan turned his eyes to the window. It was almost tenth hour already. "Why didn't you tell me before?" he asked.

But his mother didn't hear him. She was weaving again, and the loom drowned out his voice.

Rivan cursed, running to grab his boots and hurriedly fastening them.

He slammed the door behind him as a small act of rebellion, but he knew his mother likely wouldn't notice. Or if she did, she wouldn't pay it any mind.

Rivan despised his mother. Which was a strange way to feel about the person who carried you into the world, but it was true.

The feeling was mutual. Even in Rivan's earliest memories, his mother had always treated him like he was an inconvenience. Rivan had even figured out why; his father told him once, during an evening where he had indulged in too much ale.

Rivan was an accident of fate. When he was born, his two brothers – both of whom were considerably older than him – had almost reached the age of independence and his parents had been looking forward to being free from the burdens of raising children.

The arrival of their third son hardly stopped them living out that desire. Rivan's mother had suckled him and taught him to walk and talk but, once that infantile period of his life was over, she distanced herself and left him to his own devices. Rivan had always been provided with everything he needed – food, clothes, a bed, a roof over his head – but he never got what most children craved most of all from their parents. Affection.

That was what initially drove Rivan to work so hard in Baird's lessons. When he was young, he desperately wanted to be Chosen to prove his worth and make his parents notice him, but he eventually realised it was a fruitless quest and nothing would ever make his parents see him as anything but an inconvenience.

And that was when Rivan began to resent them.

Rivan still yearned for the Academy, but he no longer cared about making his parents proud. For him, the Academy was a means to escape a home where he had always felt unwelcome.

But now it seemed he was going to have to grit his teeth and wait another year.

As Rivan walked through the village, he wondered what the Elders wanted from him.

The Hall was the largest building in Jalard. Its white walls loomed over the village, and it was capped by a cupola which contained a bell which rang at different times of the day. Rivan had heard that the bell was used as an alarm in the event of an emergency too, but that had never happened during his lifespan.

As Rivan neared, he noticed that Kyra was there, slouched against the wall. He nodded his head at her, and she smiled back thinly. An awkward silence drifted between them.

"Hi…" he said, ending it.

He felt less hostile to Kyra than he usually did. Perhaps it was because, for once, he could identify with her on some level. Neither of them made it into the Academy, but their friends did.

"Hi…" she replied coolly.

"Why are you here?" he asked.

"I got summoned by the Elders," she yawned. "I hope I'm not in trouble again…"

"They've called for me too…" he murmured and began to wonder if it was possible they were there for the same reason.

"How are you doing?" she asked.

She didn't need to elucidate – they both knew what she meant.

He sighed. "I'm okay, I guess… there's always next year…" he said, trying to sound as optimistic as he could.

She nodded and then her gaze shifted to something behind him. Rivan turned around and saw Dion, an old friend of his, striding towards them.

"Hi Dion," he called.

"Hello Rivan!" Dion said, grinning in his usual jovial way as he crossed the space between them. "The Elders want to see you too?"

Dion patted Rivan on the back. It was a friendly gesture, but for Rivan it served as a reminder that Dion was still taller than him. A fact which had always nettled.

"Yeah..." Rivan replied. "They want Kyra as well."

"What in Lania's name would they want the three of us for?" Kyra pondered.

"Hi Kyra," Dion said, turning to her and waving.

"Hi," she replied, and their old rivalry could be felt in the cold, challenging stare she gave him.

"I heard you guys didn't get in to the Academy?" Dion said, looking between the two of them. "How in gods' names did that happen? I thought it was a sure thing. You guys are *good*!"

"You were too... it's a shame you don't train with us anymore," Rivan lied. He liked Dion but was secretly glad when he quit. Not only had Dion been decent with a sword but he had been popular too. It was only when he and some of the others left a year ago that Rivan finally became Baird's favourite. Dion was the son of a blacksmith, and thus, he had gone on to learn his father's trade full time.

"Yes. It *is* a shame..." Kyra added. "I could repay you for that very painful bruise you gave me..."

"Yeah, I have no doubt you would!" Dion laughed. "You two were younger than me and I could barely keep up with you back then!"

They were interrupted by the door to the Hall opening. A woman peeked her head out.

"Excuse me," she said. "The Elders are ready to see you now."

"All three of us?" Dion asked.

"Yes," she nodded. "Dion, Rivan, and Kyreena. Is that correct?"

Kyra bristled when the woman called her by her full name, and it took a lot of self-restraint on Rivan's part to not burst into laughter. He had not heard anyone call Kyra that for years.

"It's *Kyra*," Kyra said. "But yes..."

"This should be interesting..." Dion commented as they followed the lady inside.

She led them into the main chamber – a spacious room

where meetings and events were often held – and the three Elders were sitting behind a table at the far end.

Rivan, Dion and Kyra formed a line in front of them and the assistant left, closing the door behind her.

Rivan had heard that in larger communities Elders were drafted by election, but in a village as small as Jalard this was not necessary. At a time when a new Elder was needed the person most suitable for the role naturally slipped into place and, if enough people were ever unhappy with the way they conducted themselves, they were pressured into stepping down.

"Welcome," said the one in the middle. She was a small and frail woman with a wrinkled face, but her hair still retained its colour and there was a bright intelligence in her brown eyes. "And thank you for answering our summons."

The two men on each side of her uttered similar greetings.

"How may we please you?" Dion asked, smiling at them.

"As you no doubt already know, Baird left with the others for Shemet," she began. "We actually had in mind a task for him to fulfil, but since he is no longer here, we would like to ask the three of you to carry it out in his stead."

"What is it?" Rivan asked.

"We need some supplies," one of the men explained. He resembled Kyra a little in his features, and Rivan could vaguely recall hearing somewhere he was a relative of hers. "And would like you to venture to Habella. Is this possible for you? Or do you have other duties?"

Rivan shook his head, as did Kyra. With Baird not around there wasn't much for either of them to do.

"I'll need to ask the old man first…" Dion replied. "But it shouldn't be a problem."

They spent the minutes which followed discussing the finer details of the expedition and, at the end of it, the Elders gave Dion a list of items they needed to requisition and a bag of coins.

"Well… I think we've covered everything," the woman sitting in the middle announced. "Do you have any questions?"

The three of them shook their heads. They had all been on trading expeditions before, as Baird sometimes used them to teach navigation skills. Rivan always leapt upon them with great enthusiasm because they were an opportunity to get out of Jalard.

"You may take a fourth to accompany you if you wish," she added.

"Sounds good," Dion agreed. "When would you have us leave?"

"As soon as possible," one of the men replied. "Today, if you can."

The three of them made their way outside and, once Rivan had shut the door behind them and they were safely out of earshot, Kyra lunged her fist at the wall.

"Oh. Poor Kyra," she muttered sardonically. "She didn't get into the Academy, but let's make her feel like she is needed! This is just patronising!"

"I don't think it's like that…" Rivan reasoned. "With Baird away, we are the natural choice…"

"I think this is going to be fun," Dion grinned as he jingled the bag of coins. Money was a rare commodity for most villagers of Jalard, who primarily traded in goods and skills. "Shall we meet at the stables at noon?"

Rivan didn't know why, but the way Dion had taken it upon himself to be the bearer of the coins and was now calling the shots galled him. In the last year, *he* had grown used to taking charge of things.

"Sounds good," Kyra agreed.

"They said we could take a fourth," Rivan remembered. "What do you think of Aylen coming along?"

"Good idea," Dion nodded.

"Sure," Kyra said. "I actually don't mind him. Just make sure his friend Dareth doesn't tag along. He's an asshole."

*   *   *

Aylen stared at the target carved into the bark of the tree and rocked the dagger in his hand back and forth for a few moments. When it felt right, he let go, and the blade soared across the garden and struck the inner circle.

"I just can't believe that *soddy* got into the Academy, and I didn't!" a voice beside him exclaimed.

Aylen sighed.

It had been three days since the Academy made their

announcement, but Dareth was still in a foul mood and showing no signs of letting it go.

"He only got into the booksy part," Aylen said. "He's going to be reading boring scrolls about history and whatnot. Why are you jealous?"

Dareth made a grunting noise and turned away. Aylen knew better than to press him; after years of trying to placate Dareth's dark temper, he had learnt it was sometimes best to let him cool down in his own time.

Instead, Aylen got up, walked across the lawn, and retrieved his knives from the target. With Baird away, training was cancelled, so Aylen had spent most of the last two days in his garden, throwing daggers at the tree while Dareth sulked.

"Do you want a go?" Aylen asked, offering him his knives.

"I guess so…" Dareth muttered. He took them, shuffled around so he was facing the tree, and began hurling them at it. Aylen could tell his friend wasn't really concentrating. Two of the blades struck the target – but nowhere near the centre – while the third missed completely and landed on the grass.

"You're trying to do it too fast…" Aylen said.

Dareth got up to collect the daggers, muttering a curse under his breath.

"This isn't really my thing…" Dareth grumbled when he returned.

"You're not bad…" Aylen said. "Besides, you *always* beat me when we duel."

"It's just… I had it all figured out in my head…" Dareth said as he sat down again. He still had a sour expression on his face, but his bearing was calmer now. "This year Rivan and Sidry – or maybe even Kyra, if she was lucky – would get into the Academy. And then *we* would be Baird's favourites. And next year would be our turn."

You have a good chance of being Chosen, one day… Aylen thought. *But not me.*

Aylen didn't say that though, as Dareth's mood seemed to be cooling and he didn't want to fuel another outburst.

Aylen was good at archery, but when it came to hand-to-hand combat he was mediocre. He was smaller than most men his age.

Aylen began to throw his daggers at the target again. He considered missing one to make Dareth feel better but thought better of it. *That would just be patronising,* he thought. *And he would probably know.*

Besides, Aylen wanted to practise. Daggers were his forte – the one thing he was known for being skilled in – and he planned to stay on top.

"But now we're probably going to have to wait another *two* years," Dareth grumbled. "Plus we *still* have to put up with that annoying bitch. I was looking forward to seeing the back of her!"

Aylen sighed again. A few aeights ago Kyra defeated Dareth in a duel, and his friend had been bitter about it ever since. In Aylen's opinion, they both fought well, but to Dareth that didn't matter. He couldn't bear the fact he had been beaten by a girl.

Aylen could see why some of the boys found Kyra annoying. She was hot-blooded and brash. When she won she was smug and when she lost she was ungraceful. But still, Aylen could never understand why she stirred up so much hatred in his friend. He wished Dareth would chill out sometimes.

The way Aylen saw Kyra had changed recently, but he could never tell his friends about it.

He threw the last blade, and it hit the centre. Bulls-eye. He smiled to himself and got up to collect them.

When he returned, Dareth had another go. They all hit the target this time. But mostly the outer ring.

"Well done!" Aylen praised and patted him on the back. "You're getting better!"

Dareth winced, and Aylen withdrew his hand. A terrible realisation dawned upon him.

"He's hit you again…" Aylen whispered. "Hasn't he."

Dareth turned away in shame.

Aylen leant over and peered down the gap of his friend's tunic to see blue marks all over his back. "Gods…" Aylen gasped. "Dareth… you need to do something. What about your mother? Does she know?"

"She knows…" Dareth muttered.

Aylen stared at the bruises, his hand quivering in anger.

The man was not even Dareth's real father. How could he

get away with *this*?

"Let's go to the Elders," Aylen suggested. "They'll do something."

"No!" Dareth's eyes widened in fear and he shook his head. "It's none of their business!"

"Dareth…"

"No!" he yelled.

They sat in silence for a while. Aylen wanted to help his friend, but he didn't know how. He had no experiences of his own to compare Dareth's situation to. Aylen came from a happy family. His father was a gentle man. He couldn't even imagine what Dareth was going through.

But this did make Aylen realise one of the reasons why his friend was in such a foul mood.

With Rivan and Kyra to still compete with, Dareth's chances of getting into the Academy next year had just got smaller.

That meant another year of living in the same house as his stepfather.

"Aylen!"

It was his mother, calling to him from the house.

"I'm here," Aylen yelled back. He got up and ran to her.

"What is it?" he asked when he reached the house. His mother stood by the door.

"You've got a friend here to see you…" she said.

"Oh…" Aylen said. He wondered who it could be. Aylen had a few friends in the village but none of them made a habit of calling at his house all too often. Apart from Dareth, of course.

"Rivan?" Aylen said in surprise when he recognised the broad figure standing outside.

"Hi Ally," Rivan said. "Are you free for a few days?"

*   *   *

Sidry was in a sombre mood for the first two days of his journey to Shemet. He watched the hills roll by.

He had always loved the terrain of western Sharma, with its green meadows blanketed with wild flowers, interrupted by patches of woodland which offered brief periods of sanctuary from the sun, but now he knew he would not be returning for a long time it seemed different. A little greyer.

He thought about all the people he was leaving behind – his parents, who begged him not to go, and Rivan, who had hated him for being selected – and wondered if they would ever forgive him.

On the third morning, he was pulled out of these thoughts when Baird levelled his horse beside him.

"Cheer up kid!" Baird grunted. "You should be excited."

Sidry smiled weakly. He'd heard Shemet could fit a hundred Jalards in its borders and had buildings taller than thirty men standing on top of each other. The thought of such a place made him nervous.

He knew he should be excited. He should be grateful. Many from the village would have done anything to be Chosen in his place, including his closest friend.

"Are you going to tell me what's bugging you?" Baird asked. "It's been three days now, and you're still being a miserable git."

"It's just… my friends," Sidry mumbled.

"Don't worry about Rivan," Baird said. "He'll get over it. There's something else, isn't there? Tell me, why weren't your folks there to see you off?"

"They didn't want me to go."

"Why?" Baird pressed.

"I don't know," Sidry said. "They said it was the farm…"

"Only child, aren't you?" Baird recalled.

Sidry nodded.

"They were scared to let you go. I've seen it before. Don't worry. By the time you come back, they'll be proud of you."

"We were up all night arguing. At first, they were angry, but by the morning my mother gave up. She was just sat there… crying…" Sidry explained. The memory still upset him.

"When I get back I'll talk to her…" Baird said.

The thought of Baird attempting to bring his mother around made Sidry smile, briefly. "I don't fancy your chances, but good luck."

They rode in silence for a while. The men from the Academy were leading the way. Sidry turned to check on Jaedin and Miles and saw they were lagging behind, as usual.

"Baird?" Sidry said.

"Yes?"

Sidry hesitated. "Why was it me? And not Rivan? Or Kyra even?" he asked.

It was a question which had been plaguing him the whole journey.

It took a few moments for Baird to reply. "I don't know…" he admitted. "They both had glowing reports from me."

"Something strange is going on…" Sidry whispered.

"Do not think that you don't deserve your place," Baird said. "Your report was good. You *are* good. You could do with more confidence, granted, but if it had been down to me the three of you would have *all* got in. Together."

Sidry didn't know how to respond to that. He didn't consider himself worthy.

"And remember, the reports don't just come from me," Baird reminded him. "Maybe you had a better one from Miles than the other two… I've heard Rivan struggles with reading his letters. Is that true?"

Sidry nodded.

"So perhaps that's it," Baird said and stroked his beard. He leant closer to Sidry and lowered his voice. "Between you and me, I intend on finding out what happened… Rivan and Kyra *will* get in the Academy, one day. Don't you worry…"

Sidry nodded. He'd suspected as much when Baird made the decision to join them on the journey to Shemet.

He heard a voice behind them.

"Wait!"

Sidry and Baird drew to a halt and turned around to see Miles and Jaedin had stopped riding.

"Isn't it time we had a break?" Miles said.

Baird made no effort to hide his exasperation. He sighed heavily.

Sidry sighed too. He was more patient than Baird, but even he was getting irritated by their less-seasoned companions. Since the moment they'd set off, all Jaedin had done was whine. He and Miles were slowing them down.

"It's not even time for lunch yet!" Baird yelled back.

"I need to relieve myself," Miles said. "And look at Jaedin! He needs to rest."

Miles pointed to the young man beside him who was drooped over his horse and looking woefully sorry for himself.

Baird was about to argue back, but Ne'mair cut him short. "Fine!" he decided. "We will break for a few minutes."

Everyone dismounted, apart from Baird who stubbornly remained in his saddle.

"We aren't making very good progress..." Baird muttered to Sidry. He glared at Jaedin as the boy sat on a rock and rested his face in his hands.

Sidry pulled a carrot out of his pocket and fed it to his horse. "He might get used to it..." he said with all the optimism he could muster.

Ne'mair and the other representatives sat together in the grass, chatting merrily as they shared watered wine from a flask.

Sidry decided he might as well empty his bladder while he had the chance so made his way to the bushes. After casting a quick glance around to confirm his privacy, he loosened the chord of his leggings and began urinating against a tree.

He heard rustling a few feet away and looked around.

"Miles? Is that you?" he called, but got no answer.

Sidry shrugged. *Probably just a squirrel*, he thought as he finished his business and made his way back to the clearing.

When he returned, Baird was frowning.

"Did you see Miles?" he asked.

Sidry shook his head. "I thought I heard him though."

"He's taking a while..." Baird commented.

"Maybe he's having a–"

They were interrupted by someone yelling. Sidry turned around.

On the far side of the clearing, four figures appeared from the trees. They were clad in green robes. Sidry couldn't see their faces because they were wearing hoods, but he immediately knew – from instinct – they were hostile.

"Who are you?" Ne'mair called to them as he and his companions rose to their feet.

They didn't answer. They drew blades out from their robes and continued marching.

At first, all Sidry could do was stare as the Academy representatives unleashed their swords. He couldn't believe this was actually happening. Who were these men? Where had they come from?

He remembered the noises he'd heard in the trees.

Are there more? he wondered.

Baird was about to spur his horse into motion, but Sidry grabbed his saddle.

"Wait!" Sidry warned. "I think we're surrounded!"

Baird paused and they scanned the clearing. Sidry saw more figures on the other side of the glade emerge from the trees. "There!" he said.

They were closing in on Jaedin, but the young man did nothing. He just cowered against the rock he sat upon.

"Jaedin!" Sidry called, ushering him over with a motion of his hand. Jaedin got up and ran to him while Baird spurred his horse and galloped towards the pursuers at his heels. Jaedin was forced to dodge as the stallion whipped past him.

Sidry handed Jaedin a dagger so he could defend himself, but he didn't seem to know how to hold it properly. His hands were shaking.

He's not going to be any use... Sidry realised.

"Get behind me!" Sidry said, positioning himself between Jaedin and the incoming hostiles. Two of them were coming in fast. Sidry drew his sword.

One man dived at him, his sword swinging. Sidry deflected a blow and held his ground. A second man came in from the side, so Sidry parried his strike and spun around, sweeping his blade at both of the attackers to keep them at bay. They backed away slightly, recognising an adept swordsman and reconsidering their tactics.

Sidry knew he was outnumbered and they would likely coordinate their attacks if he gave them the opportunity, so he went on the offensive and thrust his blade at one of them. The man blocked, but his companion was caught off guard, and Sidry drove his foot into his belly, knocking him over. As he fell, the first man came at Sidry again, his blade whirling towards Sidry's neck. Sidry blocked, locked, and twisted, and his foe's weapon flew from his hand. He turned and fled.

"Watch out!" Jaedin warned.

Sidry turned. The man he'd kicked over was back on his feet and coming for him. He was so occupied with Sidry that he didn't hear Baird's horse gallop up from behind him and, as he raised his sword to strike, Baird had a free opening. His sword flashed.

Sidry gawped as Baird's blade tore into the flesh between

the man's neck and collar.

The man screamed, and Sidry's mentor yanked his blade free in a burst of red.

"Don't hold back!" Baird roared as the man fell, still screaming. "Aim to kill! They are doing the same!"

Baird pointed to the corpse of one of the Academy representatives a few feet away. Blood was pooling beneath him, and his eyes stared blankly at the sky.

Baird kicked his horse into motion again. Three more figures had just appeared, and he galloped to meet them.

Sidry took a moment to gather his wits and take in the situation around him.

Men were fighting. Some had fallen. All around him patches of grass were stained with blood. He couldn't see any of the horses, aside from Baird's. Where had they gone?

Sidry looked at Jaedin. One of the cloaked strangers was closing in on him. He held up the dagger Sidry gave him with trembling hands. Sidry gasped, knowing the boy's odds were not good.

Sidry didn't see what happened next. Two more men had just appeared and were running toward him, so he was forced to turn away. As they closed in, Sidry ducked, narrowly missing a blade, and then righted himself. Another sword flashed. Sidry skirted around it.

Someone came up behind Sidry and pushed him to the ground. He fell and then felt the end of a blade press into his back. He froze.

"Don't move!" a voice muttered into his ear.

Chapter 5

Captivity

Once Kyra had finished preparing for her journey, she swung her bow and a quiver full of arrows over her shoulder, picked up her bag, and marched towards the stables.

The last two days had been miserable for her and, despite originally suspecting this trading mission was nothing more than an orchestrated distraction, she was secretly glad she had something to occupy herself with. She hoped it would help take her mind off her failure to get into the Academy.

She tried not to think about it, but every time she had a spare moment she couldn't help herself. As she made her way through the village, she thought about how Jaedin was on the road to Shemet.

Kyra had always thought of Rivan and Sidry as her rivals for a scholarship at the Academy. The fact that her friend – who had spent all those years lazily sitting behind a desk reading books while she had been working so hard – was now being rewarded was hard for her to bear. She had always thought Jaedin's interest in history a hobby at best but, more accurately, an excuse to truant Baird's training.

The huts of the village passed her in a blur as she made her way towards the stables. She was tired of this place. Tired of walking on the same old pathways, seeing the same surroundings, and bored to death of the people. She wanted to get out of Jalard. She wanted to see the world. She wanted excitement. Adventure. That was why she had always worked so hard to be Chosen.

She had focussed all her will and determination on a dream which her friend fell upon by accident.

When she reached the stables, the boys were waiting for her.

"You're late," Dion commented.

"Not much," she shrugged.

Kyra then became aware that they were all staring at her. Dion, in particular. He had a devilish grin on his face.

"What are you wearing?" Aylen asked, his eyes wide.

Kyra blushed, only then realising that her new outfit was the reason they were all staring. "Just a little something I made," she said, trying her best to assume a casual manner. She had not been expecting a reaction as strong as this.

They studied her, looking her up and down. It was crafted from tanned leather which was both protective and durable, forming a bodysuit covering her from her shoulders to knees, with several pouches to serve as holders for tools and emergency supplies. The scabbard for her sword was attached to a girdle at her waist, and she even had a matching strap for her quiver of arrows.

"You do realise this is a *trading* mission," Rivan remarked when his eyes wandered to her sleeves. She had sewn pockets into the insides of them to conceal daggers for quick access. They were supposed to be hidden, but Rivan's warrior-eyes found them.

"Always be prepared," Kyra quoted Baird.

"Does it have to be so… revealing?" Dion asked.

Kyra sighed. She had fashioned the original design for purposes of practicality, but Meredith added some of her own finesse while they were making it, claiming it was to serve the purpose of keeping her cool in hot weather.

The twinkle in Dion's eyes when he looked at her sparked an unfamiliar feeling Kyra was not expecting.

Kyra had not seen Dion much over the past year – ever since he quit training – but in that time, he had changed. She couldn't help but notice how much broader his shoulders were, and how all those months he had spent working iron had made his arms thick with muscle. His face had matured, too. He looked more like a man now and less like a boy.

When Kyra turned around and made her way towards the stables, she found herself being very conscious of the way she moved. She could feel Dion's eyes on her.

She paused at the doorway and turned to discover that he and Aylen had not moved a step. They were both still staring.

"You coming to get horses?" she asked. "Or are you going to stand there gawping?"

"Get over yourself," Rivan hissed, already on his way to the stable doors. Dion and Aylen soon followed.

When they stepped inside, they spotted the stable master in one of the stalls grooming a horse.

"Can I help ye?" he asked.

"Yes, we need horses," Kyra announced, leaning over the bar between them.

"What ye be needin' horses for?" he asked, raising an eyebrow.

"Trading mission," Dion replied, unrolling the parchment the Elders had given them.

* * *

They left Jalard immediately. Kyra was glad to be outside again, with the wind running through her hair and the sunshine on her skin, but whenever she looked down she saw tracks on the ground which were not much more than two days old and knew they must have been left by Jaedin and the others, on their way to the Academy. They were a constant reminder of where she was not going.

Dion and Rivan kept the lead, and with them all being experienced riders they made good progress; by late afternoon they passed the remains of a camp where the others must have stopped for their first night on the road. Kyra rode beside Aylen, and they entertained themselves by seeing who could catch something for supper first; she with a bow, or him with his daggers.

Rabbits and deer were in abundance but hard to catch, as the heavy trotting of the horses tended to scarper them. Towards the end of the day, Aylen caught a rabbit at the end of one of his knives and it tumbled onto the grass.

"I still don't get why you use them so much..." Kyra remarked as he cleaned his blade and slung the quarry over his shoulder. "Knives have bad range, and they're not as accurate!"

"You're right about the range," Aylen conceded. "But accuracy comes with practice. You lost time loading your bow."

"And I bet they're expensive too..." Kyra said, gesturing to the sheath at his waist. It was divided into sections, and each one had the tip of a handle poking out from it.

"Not really..." Aylen shrugged. He pulled one out for her to see. "I rarely lose any... and they don't even have proper handles. They're cheap."

They look like they're fairly light, too, Kyra realised. *They* **are** *well made...*

"Easy for you to say..." Kyra muttered. "My Da ain't no fancy trader..."

"Can we *go* now?" Rivan grumbled.

"Is this how kids flirt these days?" Dion joked.

Kyra laughed, but Aylen was visibly blushing as he remounted.

What's the matter with him? she wondered. Out of all the boys from the village, Aylen had always been the one she felt most comfortable with, and she thought he would have been able to handle a gag between them.

They rode on for a couple more hours until they noticed that sunset was not too far away, and then pitched their tents. They built a fire, and a spit to roast the rabbit on. As the hills around them darkened, they sat around it and feasted on the meat, along with some of the bread and fruit the Elders gave them.

When they were finished, Kyra reached into one of her bags and drew out a bottle of mead she'd stowed away when packing, opened it up, and took a sip. It burned her throat a little, but it was pleasantly sweet and, after a few moments, left a warm feeling in her chest.

Kyra stared at the bottle in contemplation. She'd brought it with the intent of drinking it herself, but she'd bonded with Aylen and Dion a little that day, and even Rivan was being more agreeable than usual, so she felt inclined to share it.

"Want some?" she asked, offering it to Aylen.

"What is it?" he asked.

Dion reached over and grabbed it.

"Mead..." he answered. He held it up to his nose and then drank some. "My aunt's mead, no less."

"Grendeline is your aunt?" Kyra asked. She was surprised by this. Grendeline was an eccentric lady who lived alone in a little cottage away from the rest of the village. Kyra had come across it by accident once whilst she was out riding and befriended her.

Dion nodded. "Curious that you managed to get some," he pondered as he handed the bottle over to Aylen. "She hardly ever lets *me* drink any of the stuff as she doesn't like giving it to the young'uns..."

Kyra grinned at him. "I have my ways."

"Oh really?" Dion smiled back. "Tell me."

"I went there with my little sister," Kyra said. "But I told Grendeline she was my *daughter* and she traded me a couple of bottles for a deer."

"Cunning," Dion smirked. "But I think aunt Grendeline's eyes must be going funny. You look far too young to be a mother."

Kyra looked for the bottle and caught Rivan drinking from it quite generously.

"Stop hogging it!" she yelled, snatching it back from him.

*   *   *

Sidry pounded his fists into the door until he noticed smears of blood on the panels. He stopped, only then realising that his knuckles were bleeding but, almost on cue, they began to throb and ache.

He gave the door one last kick before turning away and continuing to pace the room.

He woke up inside this confined space a few hours ago. Before that, the last thing he could remember was the ambush. He had a painful lump on his head, so he knew he must have been knocked out. He had no idea how long he had been unconscious for.

The room he was in was bare. Just a bed, a chair, a chamber pot, and four grey walls. There was no window.

He had no idea why he had been imprisoned – he didn't even know who his captors were. He found it hard to believe that they were bandits, if only for the peculiar way they had all been clad in matching green robes.

He paced back to the door. Its wooden panels were thick. He couldn't see any locking mechanism, nor even a handle. It must have been built to only open from the other side. Whoever his captors were, they were organised.

"Let me out!" he screamed, kicking at the door. "Just tell me what you want!"

Still no answer. No one came. They hadn't even brought him any water or food.

He saw a chair in the corner and had an idea.

A few moments later he charged at the door with the chair

in his hands. The first blaring crunch merely dented one of the legs, with no damage to the panels, but this sent Sidry into a rage and he carried on smashing it until all the legs were broken.

The door opened eventually, and a man appeared on the other side of the frame. At first Sidry just stared, wide-eyed, at his unusual appearance. Just like the men who ambushed them, his skin was paler than most people from western Sharma, and he had bright blue eyes. The most distinctive thing about him was that Sidry had never seen someone so well groomed before; he was wearing an ornate tunic with a sash about the waist, and the moustache above his mouth had been carefully shaped. It was immediately clear he was wealthy.

"You won't get anywhere with that," he said. He was very well spoken and Sidry was already finding something about the tone of his voice infuriating.

Sidry didn't know what to say. This man was the strangest person he had ever met in his life.

"May I introduce myself?" the stranger asked, without waiting for a reply. "My name is Lord Shayam, and I am your host."

"You're Gavendarian, aren't you," Sidry realised, noticing the foreign accent.

"That, I am," Lord Shayam admitted with amusement in his eyes. His gaze then went to the mess Sidry had made of the room. "You figured that out quickly, so you're obviously not a complete barbarian…"

"Where's Baird?!" Sidry asked.

"Oh, that oaf," Shayam said, waving his arm in a dismissive yet ostentatious gesture. "Don't worry about him, he is being well looked after. Although, he is having some adjustment issues…"

Sidry decided that he had had enough of chatting. He ran at the man with what was left of the chair but, as he reached the doorway, a field of energy flashed before his eyes and sent him reeling back.

Shayam was not surprised. He merely chuckled and looked down at Sidry. "The doorway is Enchanted. You're not getting out that easily…"

"What do you want from me?!" Sidry said as he lifted

himself back up. "Are the others here?"

"The others are here, and you will find things much more pleasurable for yourself if you cooperate," the Gavendarian decreed and then closed the door.

*   *   *

Kyra took a few more gulps from the bottle, leant back, and looked up at the sky.

All three moons were present that night. The largest, Teanar, dominated the sky in its later stage of waxing, while its two brothers were crescents on each side of the horizon. She couldn't see many stars because the moons were too bright, but that was not unusual; nights where the sky turned black and the stars dominated the welkin were rare.

"What do you think stars are?" she asked as she passed the bottle of mead over to Aylen.

The stars were starting to blur now, and the number of them doubled whenever she let her eyes slip out of focus, but she didn't mind.

"Aren't they supposed to be the place where The Others came from?" Aylen remembered, taking a swig.

"That's just religious crap," Rivan grunted. "Who cares what they are? I prefer it when the moons are out anyway."

"Why? Are you scared of the dark?" Kyra teased.

"No!" Rivan replied indignantly. "You can just see better. It's more practical."

"Don't they have a special festival when all the moons vanish at the same time?" Dion recalled.

"Has that ever happened?" Aylen asked.

"It's very rare for all three to disappear," Kyra remembered. "I think the last time was about seventeen years ago... I was just a few aeights old, but my Mum told me about it."

"Since when were you all clever and stuff?" Dion asked, handing her back the bottle. Kyra thumped him on the shoulder.

"I'm not..." she said, looking back up. "Jaedin told me the story, once. About the moons. And the goddess Verdana."

"How are the moons connected to Verdana?" Aylen asked.

"You don't know?" Kyra turned to him in surprise.

Aylen shook his head. As did Dion. Whereas Rivan just made it clear he found the topic boring by making a huffing sound and turning away.

"Well basically," Kyra began. "Lania had an affair with Manveer. Oh wait, you do know who *Manveer* is, don't you?" she checked.

"Of course I do," Aylen replied. "He's the god of clouds, rain, and thunder."

Kyra nodded. "Anyway, where was I? Oh yeah... Once, Lania made love with Manveer, and with him she birthed three children. They were called Teanar, Lumnar, and Lunid," she explained, pointing to each moon as she named it. "Now... when Ignis found out about this he was pretty pissed off, as you can imagine. So he kinda got angry and threw them into the sky so that from then on they could watch over Lania at night and make sure she wasn't doing the nasty with anyone behind his back. You following me, so far?" she asked Dion and Aylen.

They nodded.

"Then..." Kyra continued. "Basically, one night, Lania had another affair. This time with Gazareth... Blah. Blah. Blah. You should all know *that* story... And with Gazareth, Lania birthed a child called Verdana... Now..." Kyra drew a deep breath as she tried to remember what happened next. "When Lania tried to hide the child of her dirty little secret from Ignis, it was Lunid!" she exclaimed, pointing at the smaller moon accusingly. "Who grassed them up! And thus, Ignis found out about Verdana, and they all had a big fight. The end."

"Really?" Dion said, stroking his chin. "Is that the *exact* way Jaedin told it to you? Because I've met that guy before, and I didn't really feel his personality in the telling."

He lifted the bottle to his lips and drank.

There isn't much left, Kyra realised, noticing how high Dion needed to tilt the bottle to drink. "Give that back!" she said, making to snatch it but he pulled it away from her reach.

"Hey, that's mine!" she exclaimed.

"It's my aunt's!" he laughed.

She leapt on top of him, but he placed the bottle to the side and grabbed hold of her wrists. She tried to free her arms but he was just that little bit stronger than her. She found herself involuntarily giggling as they wrestled.

"Aylen, help!" she called between fits of laughter, but no one came to her aid and she carried on struggling with him.

She eventually managed to roll herself off from him and scrambled for the bottle. She raised it to her lips and gulped the last of it down

"None left, idiot!" she proclaimed when Dion grabbed it back from her.

She was feeling very lightheaded now. Not only were the stars blurry, they were swaying. She felt a strange compulsion to lean back and rest herself against Dion. And not only did she *feel* it, but she discovered she also had the boldness to *do* it.

She tried to make it seem like an accident.

No one was more surprised than her when he didn't push her away – instead, he put his arms around her.

Kyra then noticed Aylen and Rivan had left the campfire and retreated to their tent. She and Dion were alone.

"Was it something I said?" she laughed.

* * *

Behind the fabric of the tent, Rivan tried to sleep but Kyra kept laughing. It was ear-piercing and seemed to echo all around him.

"Can't she be quiet?" he grumbled, shuffling onto his side.

"Did you see them?" Aylen asked. "Flirting! As if we weren't there!"

Rivan had to admit it made him uncomfortable too.

At first, he couldn't figure out why he didn't like the idea of Dion and Kyra liking each other. For it certainly wasn't jealousy. Rivan had known Kyra since she was a girl and seen her in the most degrading of tantrums. There was no way he could ever look at her in that way.

One of his friends seeing her that way felt like a betrayal. Kyra was his rival and, despite the fact she sometimes beat him, the one thing Rivan could always rely upon – the one thing he had over her – was she was outnumbered by gender, and the rest of the boys had his back. If Kyra managed to wrap Dion around her finger, the dynamics would change.

"I know," Rivan said. "What in Gazareth's balls would anyone see in *her* anyway?!"

Rivan waited for Aylen to reply, but nothing came, so Rivan assumed he had fallen asleep.

He turned over again and closed his eyes, but Kyra's laughter rang through the tent once more.

* * *

Kyra had never kissed a boy before, but she discovered she liked it. She wanted more. She pressed up close to him as his tongue circled her mouth and enjoyed the warmth of his body and the feeling of his hands on her back.

His lips parted from hers, and they looked each other in the eyes. She ran her hands over his chest and looked up to the sky as he kissed her neck, sending prickly waves of heat dancing through her insides. His hands wandered down her back and rested on her buttocks. They kissed again. She could smell the mead in his breath, and their tongues were wet.

She tried to unfasten the lacings of her bodice but was interrupted by him pulling her back down to kiss him again. She ran her hand down the trail of his stomach and caressed his hard member through his leggings.

"Calm down," he muttered, grinning.

She ignored him and tried to touch it again, but he grabbed hold of her wrist.

"Not tonight," he whispered into her ear.

"Why?"

"We should get to know each other first," he said. He gestured to the tent where Rivan and Aylen were sleeping. It was just a few feet away. "We're not alone, either."

* * *

That night, when Bryna was sleeping, she found herself witness to a vision.

She dreamt of men in green robes.

They were gathered around a bed which was covered in white sheets. At first, Bryna could not see much, because the flickering candlelight only brought to her vision distortions and shadows, and each time she tried to gaze directly at the men's faces, their features warped and blurred.

But, as the scene gained clarity, she saw that beneath the folds and creases of the bedspread, was the shape of a human body, lying still.

A woman in a black dress stood at the head of the bed with her face tilted towards the ceiling. Her lips moved without making a sound, but there was a clear purpose behind her silent chant and Bryna could feel dark power in the air. The room seemed to shake as a cold wind swept through the dark strands of the woman's wild hair, obscuring her features.

The woman opened her eyes and looked down at the figure laid before her.

"Uncover the body," she uttered.

Two of the robed men came forward and pulled back the sheets, revealing the person beneath. He was a grown man of muscular build.

"Shave him!" she ordered.

Another assistant appeared with a vial of white lotion, which he began to smear over the subject's chest, while a second man followed up by gliding a razor over his skin. With each stroke, a section of lotion and body hair was removed, and the blade was cleaned off in a bowl of water. A process which must have taken a few minutes seemed to be over in seconds.

The men in green robes then stepped away and retreated into the background while the woman began to dance, twirling in circles around the bed in a state of reverie, her arms swaying back and forth. Her mind was clearly in another place, but she moved with a graceful awareness of her surroundings.

She leant over the bed, and it was only then Bryna noticed she had a gilded dagger in her hand. The woman lowered the blade to the man's neck and pressed it into his flesh, drawing a line of crimson down to his shoulder. Blood oozed from the parting of his skin.

She continued carving upon him. The red marks she made formed an intricate pattern which covered his entire body. All the time, her eyes were closed, but she worked without pause or hesitation, until his arms, stomach, thighs, and calves were bleeding runes.

"Give me the Stone," she ordered, rising to her feet again.

One of the hooded men shuffled forward and unveiled a crystal. It was glowing, faint blue. He placed it in her hand.

"Uncover his head."

The last remaining sheet covering the subject's head was removed, but the woman leant over him and obscured his face from view. The scene was pulled away from Bryna's eye-line. Blackness swirled around her. It faded.

*   *   *

"Bryna!"

She jerked upright and from her throat rasped a faint cry which waned and died.

"Bryna?" Meredith repeated, shaking her by her shoulders. "Are you okay?"

Bryna opened her eyes and was relieved to see she was once again in her bedroom, but the dream lingered in her mind and it took her a while to gather her wits and adjust to the waking world again.

Her gown was clammy with sweat.

"Bad dream again?" Meredith asked.

Bryna nodded.

"Do you want to tell me about it?" Meredith asked as she sat on a chair beside the bed.

Bryna shook her head. She didn't even know how to begin.

Meredith put a hand on her arm. Bryna was grateful for the comfort, but a part of her yearned for solitude that moment. From an early age, she'd become aware that not everyone saw visions like hers, and it was a burden she'd learnt to cope with alone.

"Sorry," Bryna apologised. "I woke you, didn't I…"

"No," Meredith shook her head. "I had a dream as well."

"Really?" Bryna turned to her mother. "The dark room? With the men in green robes and that woman…"

"No," Meredith shook her head. "Mine was different."

"What was it?" Bryna asked.

Meredith leant back on her chair and looked to the window.

"It was about your father," she admitted.

Bryna was surprised to hear that word from her mother's lips. It wasn't very often Meredith spoke of her father; any mention of him usually brought her to tears, so Bryna and Jaedin rarely asked about him.

But that night, there were no tears in her mother's eyes. Her bearing was strangely equanimous.

Bryna never knew how to feel when her father was mentioned. He died shortly before she and Jaedin were born. She never knew him, so she didn't miss him. She sometimes wished she had known him so her mother would have someone to share his memory with. And the pain it stirred within her.

"I want to give you something," Meredith said, pulling at Bryna's hand and carefully pressing something cold and round into her palm.

"What is it?" Bryna asked as she examined it. It was stone with a gleaming nebula of purple colours in the centre. It was attached to a chain and clearly designed to be worn about the neck. Bryna could already sense that it was no simple adornment; just touching it alone was making her fingertips tingle.

"It was your father's," Meredith explained. "A family heirloom. In my dream he said it was time. He told me to give it to you."

"What about Jaedin?" Bryna asked.

"It chose you, Bryna," Meredith said. "Wear it. At all times."

* * *

Shayam looked up from his desk as the door swung open and Carmaestre swept into the room. She made a half-hearted bow before him, but Shayam knew that this was merely an act of courtesy. She smiled coldly, and her dark eyes betrayed her true feelings; that, even though he was in charge of this operation, she considered herself above him.

Carmaestre was a lavish dresser. That night she had clad herself in a black dress with tasselled sleeves which trailed all the way to the floor. She was beautiful and malefic. Her hair was as dark as her soul, and the garish makeup painted around her eyes made it impossible to guess her age. No one knew how old she was, nor where she was from, but they tolerated her secrecy because she was useful. She possessed the magic which made everything they had so far achieved possible.

"The procedure went to plan, my Lord," she announced. Her tone when she called him 'Lord' was almost mocking but Shayam ignored the slight.

"Magnificent!" he replied. "How is the subject?"

"He should recover," Carmaestre shrugged. "But there's no sign of any remarkable changes yet either…"

"Okay…" Shayam nodded. He was neither surprised nor disappointed. The ritual she just performed was the equivalent of an arrow shot into the dark; they had not been expecting to hit any particular target because they were not even sure if one existed. "Make sure he is kept under sedation until we can be sure."

She nodded. "While we have the other Stone, I think it might be worth trying the procedure on a younger subject."

Shayam shrugged. He thought it would likely be a waste of time, but he had learnt over the years that Carmaestre worked best when kept on a loose tether. "If you so wish. We do have a spare, after all. Would tomorrow morning leave you with enough time to prepare?"

"Yes, my Lord."

*   *   *

With no window to tell what hour of the day it was, time lost meaning to Sidry. He spent his hours in captivity dozing in and out of sleep or pacing about the room. He could not even hazard a guess at how long he had been there anymore, but it almost felt like a lifetime.

He knew now that bruising his knuckles by banging them upon the door and damaging the furniture wasn't going to get him anywhere and accepted that, at this moment in time, he was powerless. He conserved his energy and waited for something to happen. He ate the food they gave him and, after some good behaviour, they even replaced his chair. His knuckles began to heal.

While he sat, many things plagued his mind. He blamed Miles for insisting they break. And himself even more for not realising the foolishness of the location they chose for it. A clearing surrounded by trees was the perfect setting for an ambush. He, Baird, and the Academy representatives should have all known better.

But to be attacked by such a large group in the wilderness of western Sharma was unheard of. Occasionally there were bandits, but Sidry had long discerned that Shayam and his men were not bandits. They were too sophisticated and organised. No matter how hard Sidry wracked his brains, he could never fathom an explanation for who they were or what they could possibly want from him.

He had not seen Shayam again since their first encounter. Sidry's only human contact since then had been with the robed men who acted as the man's servants. They seemed a little docile, and they refused to speak to him, let alone answer any of his questions.

The whole scenario was so surreal to him that, in his many hours of confinement, he began to question the reality of it all. Sometimes Sidry even considered the possibility that this was all an elaborate setup by the Academy to test if he was worthy.

If it was, was he doing the right thing?

He'd had an idea to use the knife they gave him to eat one of his meals with to try to prise the door open. The food must have been drugged though because, after he finished eating, he felt mysteriously tired and could barely keep his eyes open. He stashed the implement under his pillow just before he fell asleep but, by the time he woke up, it had vanished.

He was not surprised. He knew it was a hopeless plan from the beginning and only attempted it out of desperation and boredom.

Sidry was lifted out of his thoughts when the door opened.

It was Shayam. His attire that day was shades of blue, but it was just as flamboyant and fancy as what he was wearing the last time Sidry saw him.

The fact that someone so small and frail had power over him was infuriating. Sidry knew that if he could somehow just get past that magical barrier in the doorway – what did Shayam call it? 'Enchanted'? – and it came down to a matter of mere physical strength, he could take Shayam down within moments.

"What do you want?" Sidry asked, trying to keep his expression and tone calm. Hoping that by doing so, he would get more answers this time.

"That will all become clearer in time," Shayam replied as he stepped into the room.

He's lifted the Enchantment, Sidry realised as he watched Shayam's feet cross the threshold.

This was it! Sidry finally had the chance he had been waiting for.

He leapt to his feet and dived at Shayam, but his body was suddenly gripped by an invisible force and pulled towards the ceiling. Sidry gasped.

"You really think I would step into this room unprotected?" Shayam asked. He opened up his hand, and red energy crackled within his palm, making it no mystery that he was the source of the sorcery.

Sidry looked down and saw he was floating several feet above the floor. He couldn't even move his legs. They hung limply from his body.

"Coward!" Sidry screamed. He kicked and thrashed and fought with all his will against the invisible force holding him in place, but all that his efforts achieved were slight twitches in his limbs. Magic was not something Sidry had much knowledge of, as very few people in Jalard were Blessed, but now someone was using it on him and it had rendered him powerless.

"Now, I suggest you start being a bit more cooperative," Shayam said. "Or one day you will find out how disposable you are, boy!"

Shayam flicked his wrist, and Sidry collided into the wall behind him. His feet touched the ground again, but he still couldn't move.

"Carmaestre?" Shayam called, turning his head to the doorway. "You can come now... He's ready."

A woman with long black hair entered the room. Sidry gasped when he first saw her because she bore such a strong resemblance to Meredith, the medicine woman from Jalard, but it didn't take him long to glean that it wasn't her. This woman was younger, and there was something sinister about her eyes.

She smiled as she closed in on him.

The last thing Sidry remembered was the feeling of her hand on his forehead.

Chapter 6

The Morning After

Dareth woke that morning to sunlight beaming through the window. He groaned and covered his eyes.

It took him a while to summon the will to get up that day. Not only was Baird away – and thus there was no training for him to go to – but now Dareth's only friend had upped and left too.

Dareth shut the drapes, lay back again, and stared up at the ceiling.

Aylen was probably on the back of a horse right now, enjoying another day of bonding with Rivan and Dion while on the road to Habella.

And Dareth was stuck here. Alone.

Dareth was familiar with being excluded. Most of the villagers looked down on his family, and he didn't make friends easily.

But it still hurt when it happened.

Dareth wasn't even sure he *liked* Rivan. And yet he always found himself craving the older boy's approval. He could never figure out why.

When Dareth worked up the motivation to get out of bed, he rummaged through the piles of clothes on his floor for something to wear. After finding a tunic and leggings which weren't too smelly, he put them on and ventured to the kitchen.

His home was a mess, as usual. The only food he found in the pantry was sour-smelling cheese and stale bread.

As he began to eat, he heard footsteps, and his mother entered the room. Her hair was bedraggled and her eyes were swollen and red, like they usually were when she had been up late drinking farmer's brew.

"You ate the food?!" she screeched at him.

Dareth didn't reply; the crumbs on the table spoke for themselves.

She huffed and stumbled over to the mirror to brush her hair. "You're still sulkin' aren't you?" she said, looking at him in the reflection. "Tarvek's already said he's sorry, okay! Just get over it."

"I've heard that one before," Dareth replied.

"He's cutting down on the suds," she added.

"Oh really?" Dareth asked sardonically. "That's funny, because last night I heard two pissheads stumbling around the house. Who were they?"

She ignored him and continued running the comb through her hair.

"Do you even know what today is?" Dareth asked, standing up and putting a hand on his hip.

She frowned.

Every year, it's the same day. Dareth thought. *But you always forget...*

"It's the day Dad died..." he reminded her. "Ten years."

She didn't even pretend to look guilty. She just shrugged.

Dareth left the house, slamming the door behind him.

He would be going to the graveyard to pay his respects alone that day. Just like the year before.

*   *   *

When Kyra woke up by the remains of the fire, the taste of stale mead burned her throat. She groaned, placing a hand to her stomach as the first wave of nausea hit her.

It was morning. She opened her eyes to sunlight glistening through the trees.

She was a little confused at waking up outside at first, but then she turned her head and saw Dion. The sight of his body beside her triggered hazy memories from the previous night.

He began to stir. Kyra panicked and got up. She ran away, feeling an urgency to make for the bushes, and it was not just her need to empty her bladder to blame. She couldn't face him. She couldn't even look him in the eye.

After she had relieved herself, Kyra went to the river to wash her face. She was stalling for time. Her distorted recollections were starting to gain more clarity.

She was relieved to remember she had not had sex with him. But she remembered the kisses and everything else.

And the fact that she had *wanted* to.

She couldn't hide from him forever and, when she

returned, she felt his eyes follow her as she packed her things away.

Dion opened his mouth, as if to say something, but she avoided eye contact and continued to busy herself.

Rivan and Aylen emerged from the tent, and the four of them cleared away the camp and loaded up the horses in silence. The atmosphere was awkward. No one seemed to be in the mood to prepare anything for breakfast, so they just mounted their horses and continued with their journey.

Kyra pulled out an apple as a snack, hoping it would settle her stomach. Dion was riding a few feet ahead of her, and she stared at the back of his head as she ate it. She found herself thinking about the way his body had felt pressed against hers and the feelings it had stirred.

She still found him attractive, but now she was sober she felt awkward. She didn't know what to say to him, or how to act. When it came to boys, Kyra was so accustomed to being defensive whilst in their company – so as to hold her ground with them – that she didn't know how else to be.

Jaedin was the exception to that rule, of course. But that was different. Jaedin wasn't like most boys.

This was uncharted territory.

Aylen was riding a few feet behind her, so Kyra reined her horse and levelled beside him.

"Aylen," she cooed, trying to get his attention. He seemed distracted that morning. He was staring at the hills. She waved a hand in front of his face, and he looked at her.

"Can't handle your mead, hey?" she teased.

He smiled, but it seemed forced.

"Well, you best have your daggers handy! Because my arrows will be the first to spill blood today!" she challenged. "Maybe we should up our game and hunt something bigger."

"There's no point," Aylen shrugged. "We have enough food. It would just be a waste…"

What is with everyone today? she wondered.

She looked at the ground and saw tracks left by Jaedin and the others on their way to the Academy. They didn't look much more than a day old. She was catching up with them. She realised that, if she and the other boys rode quick enough, there was even a chance they would run into them when they reached Habella. The town was on the way to Shemet, after all.

It was very likely the Academy representatives would want to stop there to rest up and gather provisions.

Kyra was beginning to feel guilty for the way she left things with Jaedin, but she was not sure if she wanted to see him again so soon.

She rode in silence. The hills rolled by and, with no conversation to distract her, Kyra found her eyes being drawn to the tracks. Her mood soured. They made their way down a hill, and the cornucopia of vegetation forced them to ride in single file. Kyra took the lead, following the trail until she found a gap between the trees and guided her horse through it. When she emerged into a clearing, she noticed something strange about the tracks on the grass ahead and immediately knew something was wrong.

She drew her horse to a halt, and Rivan stopped beside her. They turned to each other and then back to the ground before them. The scattered prints were confusing, but it was obvious something had happened there.

The tension between them dissipated immediately, and they leapt from their horses.

"What's going on?" Dion asked.

"Don't you know how to track?" Kyra said.

"Not very well…" Dion admitted, scratching his head.

"You don't need to be a scitting ranger to see something happened here!" she exclaimed.

Kyra tiptoed over to examine the scene in more detail. She was careful, as she didn't want to obscure the marks on the ground.

"Stay back," she warned, directing her voice to Dion in particular. "Unless you know how to tread properly… otherwise you'll ruin them."

The most obvious clues she could see were hoof prints left by a horse which had trampled around the clearing several times.

"Someone's horse got a bit excited…" Rivan commented beside her.

Kyra nodded. "It charged at some people over there," she concluded, pointing to three sets of tracks which intercepted those of the horse.

What happened here? she thought anxiously as she scoured for more clues. What she found did not bode well. It was clear some form of skirmish had occurred there. She began to worry about Jaedin.

She found a patch of flattened grass.

"Look!" she said. "Someone fell here."

"Maybe it was just bandits…" Aylen suggested, but the growing alarm on his boyish face betrayed him. "Baird and Sidry would've seen to them…"

"Come here!" Rivan yelled. "I found something!"

"What is it?" Kyra called back as she raced to join him. She sensed an urgency in his voice, and when she reached him she saw why. He was standing next to a patch of blood.

"Shit…" she breathed.

"It…" Aylen began hesitantly. "It… looks as if two people dragged a…"

Body, Kyra finished in her head the word which Aylen couldn't say. There were two pairs of footprints between the flattened grass which marked the dragged bulk, and it ran all the way down towards a row of bushes nearby.

"Let's have a look," Kyra said, walking over to investigate. Aylen followed her, but Kyra could sense he was reluctant.

Before they even reached it, Kyra smelt something foul. She clambered over some of the foliage and saw a twisted shape tangled within all the branches and leaves.

When she saw the face, she gasped.

Her initial shock was followed by a small wave of relief. It wasn't a pleasant sight – seeing those dead, lifeless eyes – but she was at least thankful it was not Jaedin. Nor anyone else she knew.

It was one of the Academy representatives.

"He's dead…" Aylen whispered in disbelief.

Kyra nodded. "Let's go, Aylen," she said, grabbing his shoulder and pulling him away. "We need to find out what happened to the others…"

*   *   *

When Jaedin heard the bolts clicking, he turned his eyes to the door expectantly.

The door opened and revealed Shayam. The eccentric man was the only person Jaedin had spoken to between his long periods of confinement.

"Hello Jaedin," Shayam greeted, smiling. "How are you feeling?"

Play along... Jaedin coached himself as he composed his expression to one he hoped hid his distrust. He prepared his wits for another battle of wills. *Don't let him see that you are on to him.*

Jaedin had accepted the vulnerable position he was in at a very early stage and, after careful consideration of his options, decided he was most likely to learn the truth or get a chance to escape if he feigned acquiescence. He had hoped that by probing Shayam with questions his captor would eventually let something slip, but it appeared the man was sharper than that and, so far, Jaedin had gleaned nothing.

"Better," Jaedin lied. "Is there any news?"

"Your friends are still recovering from their injuries," the man who couldn't quite disguise his Gavendarian accent replied coolly. "They should be well enough for you to see them again soon. We still haven't managed to track down those bandits who attacked you yet though, I'm afraid... but I did send a messenger to your village to let them know you are safe and being cared for."

Do you really think I am that stupid? Jaedin thought, but kept his jaw shut. He knew those men were no bandits, and he was Shayam's prisoner, but everything else was a mystery Jaedin was determined to solve.

"Thank you," Jaedin forced the words out of his mouth.

"You seem to be coping well," Shayam commented as he stepped into the room. "The other young man we are looking after has been quite boisterous... he doesn't seem to understand that our only wish is to help you during this time of need."

Jaedin peered down the hallway but he could not see anyone else there. Did that mean Shayam was alone this time? During his last visit, Jaedin caught a glimpse of a man in the corridor wearing a green robe which confirmed his suspicion that Shayam and the people who ambushed him were in league with each other.

If I can get past Shayam, I may be able to escape. Or at least find out where I am before they catch me, Jaedin thought to himself.

"Maybe if you let me speak to him..." Jaedin offered.

Shayam shook his head. "For the sake of your own safety, I'll have to say no. He has been violent to those I sent to care for him and I believe it may be due to a head injury. He's confused."

He doesn't look very strong, Jaedin thought as he sized Shayam up. Jaedin wasn't strong either, and he didn't know how to fight, but he *did* have his magic.

The only problem with that plan was that Jaedin's magical strength was limited; he could stun Shayam by casting a spark from his hand, but it would exhaust most of his *viga* and he would only be able to do it once.

I'll just have to make it count, Jaedin decided as he summoned his magic. Energy tingled in his palm and, when he had gathered enough, he raised his arm to direct the blast. Rods of blue light flared in the air between them but, at the last moment, a red sphere manifested around Shayam, blocking the spell.

Shit! Jaedin cursed, realising that, not only was Shayam Blessed, but he was likely more apt than him. For a moment, they just stared at each other, and then Jaedin panicked and ran for the door. An invisible force grabbed hold of his ankles and wrists. Jaedin struggled to free himself, but Shayam's magic held him tight and lifted him from the floor. Jaedin couldn't break free. He didn't have enough *viga* left.

He was then sent hurtling across the room, colliding into the wall and dropping clumsily onto the bed.

"Do you really think your little act of cooperation fooled me?" Shayam asked.

Jaedin glared at him. For so long now, he had bitten his tongue and not let his distrust show itself, but now that mask was gone.

"What do you want from me?" Jaedin asked. "Tell me! Now!"

"You are in no position to be making demands," Shayam said, looking down at him. "All will be revealed to you soon. Who knows, I could even let you be a part of this if you see the sense of our cause... I quite like your temperament."

"Where are my friends?" Jaedin yelled.

"Friends?" Shayam repeated, smirking. "It's funny you ask that because, speaking of friends, *I* have one whom I would very much like for you to meet. He has made a special request to see you too… I will go get him now. He is waiting outside. I am sure the two of you will have much to talk about."

Jaedin frowned as Shayam disappeared into the hallway.

He didn't have to wait long until another figure appeared at the door, and when Jaedin saw who it was, he gasped.

"*Miles?*"

* * *

"Kyra!" a voice called. "Wait!"

She turned and realised the three boys had drawn to a halt.

"What?" she called back, reining her horse.

"The sun's going down," Dion yelled.

Kyra looked up at the sky and noticed the dimming horizon for the first time. She had not realised time had passed so quickly. Kyra had not left her saddle since they found the corpse of the Academy representative. She'd been riding all day.

"And?" she shrugged, turning back to them. "Why have you stopped?"

"It's time to rest," Rivan yelled.

"Are you joking?" she screeched, her hands tightening around the reigns.

"No."

Cowards! she thought, as she watched Rivan and Aylen dismount. She couldn't even contemplate sitting still at a time like this.

"*You* can rest, if you like," she said, turning her horse around. "I'm carrying on."

"No Kyra!" Dion said. "That's insane!"

He's spurred his horse to catch up with her.

"Leave me!" she exclaimed, riding away.

"You won't be able to keep up with the tracks," he argued as he followed her. "And you know it!"

"What else am I supposed to do?" she asked, halting. "Make a cosy little fire and sit idly by? They could be dead for all we know!"

"Get some sleep," he suggested. "We'll leave again at sunrise."

"But I need to know what's happened to them!" she moaned.

"We don't have a choice," he said, gentling his voice as he moved his horse in closer. "If you carry on riding through the night you'll just wear yourself out, and you won't make much progress anyway – it's too dark. You won't even be able to see the tracks soon."

She knew he was right, but the thought of staying still at a time like this frustrated her. She was sick with worry.

"Come on, Kyra," he said. "You need to sleep. And then you'll be more alert tomorrow."

"I need to find Jaedin," she whispered.

"I know…" he grimaced. "Sidry is my friend too."

"I didn't even say goodbye," Kyra said. "What if something's happened to him?"

*   *   *

As Miles walked into the room, all Jaedin could do was stare at him in dismay.

"He said you were an old friend," Jaedin gasped, his lips trembling. "Why did he say that, Miles?"

"Jaedin…" he said. "There is so much I need to explain."

"You're with these people?" Jaedin realised as blood rushed into his face. "What have you done, Miles? Please tell me it's a lie…"

"There is little time," Miles said. "I can't explain everything yet. All I can say is that I am doing what's best for you. Best for everyone…"

He took a step closer, but Jaedin recoiled. His head began to hurt. It was all too much to take in at once. The one man he had always looked up to had betrayed him.

A realisation dawned upon him.

Miles was from Gavendara, and so was Shayam. Why had he not made the correlation before?

Jaedin put his hands to his face in a vain attempt to shut out the world. He couldn't make sense of any of it. Miles had betrayed him, and he had been kidnapped, but why? He was just a young man from a village most of the world had probably never heard of. What could they possibly want from him?

He felt a hand on his shoulder and flinched. Miles was sitting beside him now. His brows were drawn together in concern, and Jaedin saw guilt in his eyes. It made him want to believe that Miles still cared for him, but that just confused him even more. He didn't know what to think. Or trust. After all these years of pretending to be one of them, Miles was clearly a good liar.

"You're shaking," Miles said. He turned to the door and raised his voice. "Bring us wine!" he yelled.

A few moments later, a man in a green robe entered bearing a tray with two cups. Miles took them both into his hands, and the man walked away without saying a word. Witnessing Miles order Shayam's men around made Jaedin feel another stab of betrayal.

"Drink this," Miles said. "It'll calm your nerves."

Jaedin was in too much shock to object, so he accepted the cup and took a sip. It was sweet and warmed his chest. He drank more.

"Give me one good reason why I should believe anything you say," Jaedin said.

"Because I am not going to say anything," Miles replied. "I am going to *show* you."

"Show me?" Jaedin asked.

"I am going to let you *psycalesse* with me," Miles said.

Jaedin was surprised by that answer. He looked at his mentor suspiciously. Was he serious?

It was not often someone willingly offered to do such a thing. If Jaedin *psycalessed* with Miles, he would be able to peek into his mentor's inner psyche and glimpse his deepest thoughts. It would be impossible for Miles to lie to him.

"Meredith did teach you how, didn't she?" Miles said.

Jaedin nodded. His mother taught him and Bryna the technique when they were children. Most people who were Blessed, no matter how weakly, were capable of performing at least some of the arts of Psymancy and the ability to *psycalesse* was one of the most common.

But Jaedin's mother had also warned them to only use it in the direst of circumstances, and only when the subject was willing.

"Do you want to?" Miles pressed.

Jaedin worried this was some kind of trick, but he was also desperate for answers.

"I don't think I have enough *viga* left," Jaedin said. "I used most of it on Shayam."

"I think you should be okay..." Miles said. "The arts of Psymancy don't require as much *viga*. Just try."

"Okay..." Jaedin said, though he was not entirely convinced. It had been a while since he practised any Psymancy. It was a form of magic his mother had always tried to steer him away from. She warned him it was dangerous. "I will try."

Miles took a last sip from his wine and placed it on the table. "Shall we get this done, then?"

"Yes..." Jaedin said and shifted around, so he and Miles were facing each other. He closed his eyes and steadied his breathing, recalling the process his mother had taught him so long ago.

Once Jaedin had stilled his mind, he placed a palm on Miles' forehead. He closed his eyes again. His awareness of the room around him and his physical body faded away. Jaedin became a being of green energy. The same one he always became when he called upon his magic and sometimes when he dreamed. His *psysona*.

He could feel Miles' *psysona* too. His was grey. Jaedin's hand tingled as he slipped through the veil between and entered Miles' consciousness. He fell into a chasm of spiralling colours.

Welcome to my mind, Miles' inner voice said. Jaedin heard it echo all around him.

Jaedin steadied himself and took in his surroundings. All he could see were walls. He tried to breach them but they pushed him back. He was trapped in a box of energy.

He's shielding me from his thoughts! Jaedin realised.

The implication dawned upon him.

Only people who were Blessed could place barriers within their *psysona*. Miles had never told Jaedin he was magically apt. It was yet another secret he had kept from him.

But why?

And how many more did he have?

You are Blessed! Jaedin called out.

Guilty... Miles admitted. *But let's not get side-tracked, Jaedin. Let me show you what you came for.*

But you're hiding things... Jaedin said.

There are some things I do not wish you to see, Miles

89

replied. *We are all entitled to our secrets. Our private thoughts.*

The walls around Jaedin trembled as Miles sent him a wave of consciousness. They seeped into the prism Jaedin was encased in, and Jaedin felt them. He felt emotions, mostly. He felt that Miles deeply cared for him and wished him no harm. They were genuine.

Jaedin was comforted by this, but he wanted more.

These are just feelings, Jaedin said. *I want to know why we were ambushed.* **Why** *are we being kept here!?*

But Jaedin's grip on the *psycalesse* began to fade. He was being drawn back into his own body again. Why was he being pulled back? Jaedin desperately clung to Miles' *psysona.* He wasn't ready to leave yet. Not until he had what he came for.

Another one of Miles' thoughts slipped through the barrier, and Jaedin saw an image of the glass of wine he drank. And more.

The drink! Miles! You didn't...

But Miles didn't need to answer. Thoughts could not lie.

Jaedin knew that if his drink had been spiked he didn't have long left, but he held on to the connection with all of his might.

No! Jaedin screamed as he resisted the pull. *Tell me why you're doing this Miles!* **Why?**

He drew upon the very last reserves of his *viga* and directed a beam of energy at the walls around him in a last ditch effort to pierce through. They tore apart. A storm of Miles' thoughts swirled around him. Jaedin saw Shayam. He finally knew who he really was and Miles' connection to him. Jaedin finally knew why he had been kidnapped. Miles had a plan. They wanted him and Sidry. For... for...

But it was too much to memorise at once. They flashed through Jaedin's consciousness faster than he could comprehend them. He was slipping away. He felt a lurching in his navel as he was pulled back into his own body.

Jaedin opened his eyes – his real ones – as he fell back onto the bed.

"Miles..." he said. "I understand now... I can see... but... there must be another way..."

Miles was kneeling by the side of the bed. They stared into

each other's eyes. A part of their minds' were still connected. They could feel each other's thoughts.

"I'm sorry Jaedin…"

"Miles…"

The last thing Jaedin felt, as his eyelids closed, were Miles' lips on his.

*   *   *

Miles lifted his head away and looked down on the young man sleeping.

"It has begun…" he said, with a tear in his eye.

Chapter 7

The Zakaras

Carmaestre was noticeably tired when she returned from performing the third procedure. Sweat lined her brow, her eyes were glassy, and the glow of excess magic still seemed to cling to her like a hazy aura.

"It is now complete, my Lord," she uttered tiredly.

"How is the subject?" Shayam enquired.

She frowned. "I have already noticed some... peculiar things."

"Such as?" Shayam asked, leaning forward with interest.

"None of my incantations would make his forehead fuse with the Stone," Carmaestre explained. "I was forced to make an incision."

"The subject?"

"Still alive," she hurriedly added.

"Good," Shayam said. That was how he liked things done; cleanly. He was averse to mess.

"He has already fully healed," she added with a hint of surprise in her voice.

Shayam paused and considered the possible ramifications of this.

Past subjects of Carmaestre's rituals had sometimes come out of them with remarkable traits. These people were kept under close observation afterwards. Especially following an incident that happened years ago. Things got very messy, that time.

"Keep him sedated. Until we know more," Shayam said to her. "We will only wake him when we are sure he can be managed..."

"I have never seen anything quite like it, my Lord..." Carmaestre shook her head. "His wounds closed themselves up within seconds. Before my very eyes."

"Interesting..." Shayam said. "In that case, we should make sure all *three* of them are kept under sedation until we reach headquarters. They can be examined further then."

"As you request, my Lord," Carmaestre stiffly bowed. "Are

we still proceeding with phase two?"

"Yes. I would like you and the regiment to leave for Jalard immediately."

* * *

Dareth knew that Tarvek was drunk from the moment he stumbled into the kitchen. His clothes were filthy, and his red face was covered with a messy, neglected beard.

"Where's your mother?" Tarvek grunted.

"I don't know," Dareth said coolly. "I thought she was with you."

Dareth carried on with his task. He was making a stew. He hated cooking and he wasn't very good at it, but when he went into the village to collect their rations that morning they didn't have any bread so he walked away with only a sack of vegetables.

"Yer mother said y' were whining yester mornin'," Tarvek said, crossing his arms over his chest. "You upset her."

Dareth ignored him.

"You were talkin' about your Da, she said," Tarvek continued. "Wha' you go talkin' abou' him fer? A stiff's a stiff, kid. He ain't coming back, so why you go tryin' ter make yer mother all surly boots?"

Dareth chopped on the turnip he was cutting harder in a vain attempt to drown out his voice. Dareth knew better than to talk back. He didn't want to get into an argument with Tarvek when he was drunk. Dareth had made that mistake before. He knew the consequences.

"Look at me!" Tarvek bellowed, thudding his fist against the wall. "I'm talkin' to yer!"

"Look at you?!" Dareth asked. He dropped the knife on the counter and faced him. "*Why*? You're a ruddy mess!"

Tarvek smiled, and as soon as Dareth saw that smile, he knew he had made a mistake.

He shouldn't have argued back. That was what Tarvek wanted.

But he couldn't help it. He was *so* angry.

Tarvek squared up to Dareth. "Listen kid!" he muttered into his face. Dareth could smell the stale ale in his breath. "I want yer to stop botherin' yer mother. Stop whinin' ter her about yer

Da! Like I said, he's a stiff and he's ney comin' back."

"This is nothing to do with you!" Dareth yelled.

"Yer think so, do yer?" Tarvek made a loud, throaty laugh and turned his head to the ceiling. "Let me tell yer something, Dareth. Yer Da snuffin' was the best thing ever happened t' yer Ma. Do yer think I've only been puttin' it to her since he went? Me and yer Mam were at it fer years, Dareth! *Years*! So don't try to convince yerself it was all happy families b'fore!"

Dareth swung his fist into Tarvek's face and his knuckles cracked against his cheek.

The drunk pulled away in surprise and put a hand to his face. It was already red. A bruise was forming.

Dareth was even more shocked by what he had just done than Tarvek was.

He had never hit his stepfather before. He had done it without even thinking. It was like something had possessed him. Rage.

It felt *good*.

But he knew he was in for a beating now. When Tarvek was drunk, he didn't need much of an excuse.

Dareth tried to back away, but Tarvek closed in on him and punished Dareth with a blow to the temple which sent him dizzy. Tarvek then grabbed Dareth by the neck, and Dareth felt his feet lift off the floor, shortly followed by the back of his head slamming into the wall.

"Listen kid!" Tarvek screamed, holding him there. "Your Da' was a cunt and yer mother was screwing me all along! Get it?"

Dareth couldn't quite get anything. He was dizzy with pain and everything around him was swaying. He saw several versions of Tarvek's face leaning toward him. He tried to pull away, but Tarvek had him pinned to the wall. Dareth writhed, desperate to find a way to get out.

His hand slid across the counter and found the kitchen knife.

"Just ask your mother!" Tarvek taunted as he raised his fist to punch him again, but he didn't get the chance.

Dareth plunged the knife into his throat.

For a moment, Dareth was held still. He felt warm blood splash onto his hand. Tarvek's eyes widened in disbelief.

He dropped Dareth. Staggered away. The blade was protruding from his neck, and blood was streaming down his collar. A flap of skin pulsed around the exposed handle; an unmistakable sign that Dareth had struck an artery.

Dareth watched in horror as Tarvek shrank to the floor. He couldn't believe what he had just done.

"Me and yer mother…" Tarvek gasped. He looked at Dareth in a way he never had before. An entwining of fear, regret, and something else which Dareth could not place. "We were… b'fore y'… were born."

Dareth had an inkling of what it was the man was trying to say but he didn't want to hear it.

"I could b' your–" Tarvek began, but Dareth leant down and pulled the knife out of his throat before he could finish the sentence. The moment the blade was wrenched out of Tarvek's neck, blood belched from the opening in bursts of red. The first few were heavy, but each one got smaller. Tarvek convulsed, and it was not long until his eyes rolled back into their sockets and the room was filled with the wet sound of his death rattle.

Dareth stared. It had all happened so quickly. He couldn't believe what he had just done. Tarvek's eyes were still open, but there was nothing behind them.

Dareth looked at the knife he had used to kill his stepfather.

Maybe even his real father.

Liar!

He dropped it. The gravity of what he had just done finally struck him, and so did the consequences.

He didn't feel any guilt.

But he knew he needed to get as far away as possible before the body was discovered.

He ran to his room and hurriedly packed his things.

* * *

Before daybreak had even touched the horizon, Kyra, Rivan, Dion, and Aylen packed their tents away and set off again. Kyra studied the tracks on the ground to the finest detail in the hope of finding more clues. The four of them didn't speak to each other much. They travelled with haste and didn't pause for any breaks.

At about noon, Kyra was almost thrown from her saddle when Rivan's horse halted in front of her, forcing her to pull her own steed to a stop.

"What are you doing?" she screeched as she steadied herself.

"Just shut up and look ahead!" Rivan said.

It was only then Kyra saw the terrain of endless trees at the bottom of a hill below them. She had been concentrating so hard on keeping the tracks in sight that she had not seen what was right in front of her.

Kyra had never been to a forest before. Not a proper one. Western Sharma was covered in patches of woodland but most of them were relatively small; the majority of the terrain was dominated by copses, farms, and meadows.

The tracks are leading towards it, she noted.

Aylen whistled. "Now that's a big load of trees."

"It's the Forest of Lareem," Kyra realised.

"Really?" Aylen asked.

"Yeah," Dion nodded his head. "I've been here before. It was a few years ago, mind… Hasn't Baird ever taken you?"

Kyra shook her head. "We were too young," she reminded him. "I think he was planning a trip soon, though."

"We're going to have to leave the horses behind," Dion announced, and leapt from his mount.

"Why?" Kyra asked.

"They'll slow us down. Trust me. You'll see when you get there," Dion reassured as he guided his horse to a tree.

"I think he's right," Rivan agreed.

Kyra was sceptical but it seemed she was outvoted so she followed suit. She was anxious and just wanted to get going.

"Ready?" Rivan asked after they had finished securing their steeds.

Kyra nodded as she slung her bow and quiver over her shoulder.

They made their way down the hill at a jog and it wasn't long till they reached the bottom and entered the trees. Shadows formed around her as the canopy blocked out the sun. Kyra took a deep breath of wonder and looked up at the mighty trunks rising up to the sky.

"Be careful what you touch here," Dion warned. "Some of the plants are poisonous."

Kyra nodded. She didn't say it out loud but she could see now that Dion had been right about not bringing the horses; the ground was covered in mossy roots and vegetation, and there was no discernible path. It would have been difficult for them to negotiate.

She remembered something Bryna once told her.

"Wait," Kyra said and blocked Rivan's path with her arm.

"What?" Rivan narrowed his eyes.

Kyra ignored him and began searching her bag for something suitable as an offering. She turned to Dion. "Where's the bag of coins the Elders gave you?"

Dion seemed just as puzzled by her sudden interruption as Rivan, but he reached into his pocket all the same and drew out a leather pouch.

Kyra snatched it, loosened the knots, and pulled out a silver coin.

This will do, she thought to herself as she leant down and placed it at the base of a nearby tree.

"Lareem, daughter of Flora and descendant of Lania," she whispered. "We leave you this gift in thanks and ask for safe passage through your land."

Rising back onto her feet, Kyra hoped the goddess had heard her plea and entered the forest.

"Waste of money…" Rivan grumbled, while Aylen stifled a giggle behind his hand.

*　*　*

"Jaedin!"

He felt hands on his shoulders, shaking him out of sleep.

When Jaedin opened his eyes, Miles was looking down at him.

"Jaedin!" Miles exclaimed, a huge amount of relief in his face. "You're okay?"

Jaedin sat up and immediately knew that something was wrong.

He held his hands up to his face and looked at them. They were still his hands. They looked the same and yet everything about them and the rest of his body felt… *different*.

"What have you done to me?" Jaedin whispered.

"Now Jaedin–"

Memories of his last conscious moments came back to him, and Jaedin turned to his mentor.

Miles was a traitor. He had drugged him. He had been working with Shayam the whole time.

Jaedin grabbed Miles by the collar, possessed by anger more intense than he had ever known, and pushed his mentor away. Miles' feet left the floor and he flew across the room, colliding into the wall and falling to his knees.

Jaedin gasped. Did he really just do that? How was it possible?

"What did you do to me!?" Jaedin yelled. His voice faltered as his state of mind shifted from anger to despair. He could feel strange things prickling his senses which were new and alien to him.

"Don't you remember?" Miles asked. He warily got back on his feet but dared not come closer. Jaedin caught fear in his eyes.

*He's scared of **me**?* Jaedin thought to himself. The idea seemed ridiculous. Jaedin had never so much as thrown a punch in his entire life.

"Remember what?" Jaedin brought himself to ask.

"The *psycalesse*," Miles said. "What you saw."

Jaedin shook his head. His last conscious moments before he passed out were hazy. He could remember that Miles had some kind of secret plan but none of the details.

"I can't remember what you showed me," Jaedin said. "I know there was something, but…"

"So you don't remember what happened just before you fell asleep?" Miles asked quietly.

"No," Jaedin shook his head. "Why?"

"Don't worry," Miles seemed relieved. "It doesn't matter."

"It *does* matter!" Jaedin exclaimed.

Miles put a finger to his lips and crept closer.

"Jaedin…" he whispered. "We are getting out of here."

It was then Miles caught Jaedin's interest.

"You want to get out of here, right?" Miles asked.

Jaedin nodded.

"Then you will have to trust me," Miles said. "I don't have enough time to explain… I switched the potion which was keeping you asleep for a dud. If you want to escape, we need to go *now*. Shayam will notice soon."

Jaedin knew that to trust Miles right now would be foolish. He didn't even know what his motivations were. Why would he scheme his kidnapping only to help him escape?

But there was one thing that Jaedin *did* remember from the brief time that their minds were connected: he'd felt Miles' emotions, and he knew his mentor cared for him. That was not the sort of thing which could be faked during a *psycalesse*.

Jaedin looked Miles in the eyes. A fatal mistake, for there had always been something Jaedin found compelling about Miles' eyes.

"Come with me, Jaedin," Miles said. "There will be plenty of time to explain if we get out of here, but only if we leave now."

*   *   *

"So you think this is it?" Aylen whispered.

Rivan peered at the building through the leaves of the bush the three of them were crouched behind. Its grey walls of stone rose up almost as high as the trees around it and lay in stark contrast to the vibrant greens of the forest.

Is Sidry in there? he wondered.

"That is one ugly building," Dion remarked.

"It looks like it was built in a rush," Rivan said, eyeing up its crude structure.

"Why would anyone build something like this in the Forest of Lareem?" Aylen pondered out loud.

Rivan was not a very religious person but even he had to agree that it was all very odd. The Ancient Forests were protected by sacred law. It was said that Gavendara destroyed one of theirs hundreds of years ago and they had been cursed with barren lands ever since.

Another thing which bothered Rivan about the building – apart from its strange location – was that it didn't have any windows. He'd been hoping to be able to get a glimpse inside and gain an idea of what they were up against, or maybe even spot their friends.

"Why would someone build a place without windows," he wondered.

"I'm getting a bad feeling about this…" Dion muttered.

"What are we going to do?" Aylen asked.

"Take them by surprise," a voice behind them answered.

Rivan turned around, startled at the sound of her voice.

Kyra was back. She had an annoying ability to sneak around without being heard. He'd sent her to scout the area for that very reason.

And the chance to be free of her for a few minutes.

"What?" he asked.

"Take them by surprise," Kyra repeated as she crouched down beside them and pointed at the double doors at the front of the building. "We'll burst through the door."

"*That* one?" Dion asked. "Wouldn't it be better to find a side door or something?"

"No," Kyra shook her head. "There aren't any others. I looked."

"No windows?" Rivan asked.

"A couple…" Kyra said. "At the back. But one had a big thorny bush outside – they might hear us if we try to climb over it. And the other is too high. We could build something to climb it, but it would take too much time…" She shook her head. "We need to just charge in. If we do that we might catch them off guard."

"Kyra, we have no idea who they are!" Rivan hissed. "They could *kill* us!"

"They're probably just bandits…" Kyra muttered. "And Baird said they are usually spineless… Look at the place! It's a dump, and it's clearly not built to withstand an attack. They're hiding in the Forest of *Lareem* of all places."

"So you want to just burst through the door?" Dion asked flatly. "What then?"

"You two can break the doors open," she said, pointing at Rivan and Dion. "And me and Aylen will point our bows at the first two people we see. Tell them if they move, we kill them. They won't be expecting it, so I doubt they'll be armed. We'll demand our friends back."

"That's insane…" Dion remarked.

"Coming here in the first place was insane," Kyra pointed out.

Dion and Aylen turned to Rivan, both of them pleading with their eyes for him to protest.

He tried really hard to think up another plan – anything so

that Kyra was not in charge.

"I can't think of anything else…" he admitted.

*　　*　　*

Sidry awoke to Miles and Jaedin standing over him.

"What the fuck!" he gasped.

"We're getting out," Miles declared, tossing some clothes onto his lap.

"How did you get in here?" Sidry exclaimed.

"Just put those clothes on!" Miles said. "We don't have time!"

The two of them turned to give Sidry some privacy.

Sidry sat up and took a few moments to gather his thoughts.

The last thing he could remember, before this, was the encounter with Shayam. And the weird woman who came into the room and put her hand on his head.

Sidry realised his body felt sore. He pulled back the sheets and saw scars. Still fresh and pink. Lines and symbols. Spiral patterns. They had been carved into his flesh. They covered his chest. Arms. Stomach. Feet.

He choked for breath. He couldn't breathe.

*What did they **do** to me?* he thought.

He opened his mouth to scream, but Miles rushed to his side and covered his mouth with his hand.

"*Quiet!*" he urged.

"Look what they've done!" Sidry whispered when Miles pulled his hand away. To his shame, his voice broke.

"You want to get out of here, don't you?" Miles asked.

Sidry stared at the scholar. He wanted to scream but held it back. He took a few deep breaths to calm himself down, and then nodded.

"Get dressed then!" Miles whispered. "I'll explain *later*!"

Sidry took another look at what they had done to his body. *Try not to think about it,* he thought and swallowed a lump in his throat. He put his leggings on. As he was tying the cord around his waist, he caught Jaedin studying him.

"What are you staring at?!" Sidry growled, making Jaedin's face turn red.

Be angry later, Sidry told himself. *For now, you need to just get the fuck out of this place.*

He pulled his tunic over his neck and slipped into his boots. When he finished tying the laces, Miles handed Sidry his sword and Sidry hurriedly fixed the girdle to his waist.

"Are you ready?" Miles asked.

"Just about," Sidry declared. His legs felt a little stiff, so he stretched them.

"We need to go!" Miles said with urgency in his voice. "Come on!"

Miles opened the door. Sidry was just about to follow him when questions began to form in his mind. Ones he had not considered until then.

How was it that Miles managed to gain access to his room and free him?

Wasn't Miles from Gavendara? Like Shayam.

It was because of Miles that they stopped that day, just before they were ambushed.

When the implications of these thoughts crystallised, Sidry drew his sword and pressed the end of the blade to Miles' neck.

"You're with them, aren't you!" Sidry realised.

Miles slowly raised his open palms in the air. He didn't seem surprised.

"Sidry, stop!" Jaedin pleaded. He tried to intervene by stepping between them but Sidry pushed him away. He fell.

"We need to go!" Jaedin whined from the floor. "He's helping us!"

That kid's a moron! Sidry thought, deciding to ignore him. He turned his attention back to Miles.

"You're Gavendarian, too!" Sidry proclaimed. He forced Miles' head back into an awkward position with the end of his sword. "And you disappeared just before we were ambushed!"

With a shaking hand, Sidry pulled at the nape of his tunic, revealing some of the scars on his chest. "What have you done to me?!"

Miles tried to reply but couldn't because of the sword at his neck, so Sidry lowered it a little to allow him to speak.

"How is it you are awake?" Miles asked.

"What are you saying?" Sidry muttered impatiently.

"You were drugged," Miles said. "They were going to take

you away. You are only awake now because I swapped the potions."

"And *how* did you manage that?" Sidry challenged. "Because you're one of them!"

"Sidry, we need to go!" Jaedin said. He was back on his feet but maintaining a wary distance. "He's getting us out of here."

"Shut up, *soddy*!" Sidry spat before he turned back to Miles. "Give me one damned reason to trust you!"

"Because I'm going to help you get out of here," Miles said, indicating the doorway. "Look!"

Sidry stared at the empty corridor. The sight of an open door after all those days of confinement was like a dream come true.

Sidry sheathed his sword. He wasn't sure he had what it took to kill someone anyway. The ambush had been proof of that.

Sidry didn't trust the scholar, but this was his chance to escape and he was going to take it.

"Shayam and the rest are eating downstairs," Miles explained. "If we hurry we can sneak out from a window and make a run for it."

"Don't think you're off the hook," Sidry warned as he followed Miles. "I'll deal with you later."

*   *   *

"Ready?" Kyra whispered as they gathered outside the door.

Aylen's hands shook as he readied his bow.

Dion nodded, but his face betrayed his trepidation.

Rivan was trying to put on a brave front, but Kyra could tell that even he was deeply apprehensive.

All those years of training don't do much to prepare your nerves for the real thing, Kyra realised, feeling the knot in her own stomach. She was acting more confident than she felt to boost their morale, but the truth was that she didn't have a clue what was waiting for them on the other side of that door.

Probably just bandits, she hoped as she put a hand to her amulet and made a quick prayer to Briggan.

"I'm ready," Aylen said.

She turned to Rivan. "Now!" she uttered.

Rivan and Dion charged and thrust their shoulders into the door. The hinges cracked, and it burst open.

Kyra ran inside and did a quick scan of the room. It was a large hall. Around fifteen men were sitting at a table. Heads turned. They stared at her.

Kyra noticed they were all wearing green robes.

Who are these people? She wondered. They resembled a strange cult more than a gang of bandits.

She pushed her questions aside. She was here to rescue her friends.

Determining their leader was easy. A man was sitting at the head of the table and he was the only one not clad in green robes. He wore a blue tunic of elegant design and had a finely-shaped moustache which curled up at the sides of his mouth.

"Don't move!" she warned, pointing her arrow at the man closest to her. She tautened the string, ready to loose, and Aylen sidled up next to her and aimed his bow at another member of the table.

The man with a moustache rose from his chair, his lips curving into a wily smile. "Well my..." he said in a stately voice. "What an entrance!"

"Any of you come closer, and this one gets it!" Kyra warned.

"And for what do we owe this pleasure?" the leader asked her.

He's a smarmy bastard, Kyra thought. She found it strange he didn't seem worried.

"We've come for our friends!" Rivan said, drawing his sword.

"Collect their weapons, Dion," Kyra said over her shoulder.

"I wouldn't do that if I were you," the leader warned.

"We'll do what we bloody like!" Rivan retorted.

"Who the fuck do you think you are?" Kyra yelled at the stranger.

"I am Lord Shayam," he introduced himself, making a slight, almost mocking bow.

"Good for you," Kyra snorted. She turned back to Dion. "Get their weapons."

Lord Shayam just smiled. Kyra noticed something in his hand was glowing.

What is that? she wondered.

She was about to warn Shayam that she would start loosing arrows if he didn't cease whatever he was doing, but her eyes were drawn to the man nearest to her. He was foaming from the mouth.

Is he diseased? she wondered.

She realised it was something much more sinister when the man fell to the floor. He convulsed, let out a terrible wail, and his skin turned grey.

"What are you doing to him?" Kyra screamed. The crystal in Shayam's hand brightened, making it seem to her that the two phenomena were somehow connected.

Shayam ignored her. The man on the floor continued writhing. Kyra heard his bones creak as his limbs twisted and grew. She could barely believe her eyes. A new form seemed to be bursting from beneath the man's skin. His face swelled. His eyes turned bulbous and black. A pair of ridged mandibles clawed out from his mouth.

"What is that?!" Aylen gasped.

Kyra was lost for words. No matter how many times she blinked, the creature was still there.

It crawled towards her.

Fight now. Think later, Kyra told herself.

"Just kill it!" she yelled.

She loosed her first arrow. It struck, and brown ichor trickled from the creature's abdomen, but the monster merely flinched. It continued crawling towards her on its four rickety, black legs.

Aylen's arrow missed and struck the wall behind the creature. With shaking hands, he began to reload.

Kyra nocked another arrow. This time, she aimed for one of the creature's legs and struck true. The beast stumbled but righted itself again, continued crawling.

"It's *still* coming..." Kyra exclaimed in disbelief. Two of her arrows were now sticking from its body, but they didn't seem to have any effect.

Aylen missed again. "Screw it!" he muttered, discarding his bow and reaching for his daggers.

The monster was less than a dozen paces away. Kyra

nocked another arrow, but she couldn't get a clear shot because the creature was darting from Aylen's daggers. One of his blades struck the monster's head but bounced off and clattered to the floor. The creature flinched. Kyra saw her opportunity. She loosed.

Her arrow struck its eye, and the creature fell back, its arms flapping wildly. It screamed. A grating, ear-piercing wail. Kyra covered her ears.

Kyra thought the creature would die, but it somehow righted itself again. The arrow had gone all the way through its head, and the tip was sticking out from the back of its skull. Yellow puss oozed from the opening. But still, it walked. Its remaining eye locked on her and it made a sound of rage.

It bounded at her, flexing its mandibles. Its four leathery, black legs creaking. Kyra's heart thudded in her chest. She wasn't sure she had enough time, but she reached for another arrow anyway as the creature closed in.

She was saved by Aylen. He appeared by her side and, with a flick of his wrist, took out the remaining eye with one of his daggers. The creature fell back again with a shriek.

Rivan rushed past Kyra, sword in hand. As did Dion. The monster clawed at the air around it blindly. One of its pincers narrowly missed Rivan's neck, but he ducked.

Dion found an opening. He drove his sword into the creature's abdomen, but his blade didn't pierce its carapace. The creature shrieked again, and one of its claws grazed Dion's shoulder. He pulled back, bleeding.

Rivan came in from the other side, cleaved one of the monster's legs with his blade, breaking through. The monster fell. Roared. It righted itself and came after Rivan but the stub where one of its legs used to be dragged behind it, leaving a trail of blood.

Rivan ducked and dodged from a frenzy of mandibles as the creature limped towards him. Kyra nocked another arrow to her bow. She aimed for its head, but the creature swerved away and her arrow struck the wall.

Dion jumped back into the fray. His shoulder was wounded and he was still bleeding, but he hammered his sword upon one of the creature's remaining legs. It came off, and there was another ear-piercing scream. The creature kicked and thrashed and blood pooled the floor around it.

It writhed and raged for a few more moments, but its cries were brought to an end when Rivan hacked off its head.

The hall went silent.

Kyra turned to Shayam. He still stood at the head of the table. "What the fuck was *that*?!" she yelled at him.

The faces of the robed men around him remained impassive and uninvolved, but Shayam smiled back at her with nothing more than vague amusement.

"That was one of the things we created," he answered. "We call them Zakaras."

Kyra looked down at the sanguine mess of rawbone limbs and brown ichor pooling around the carcase of the creature. She couldn't believe her eyes.

We need to get out of here, she realised.

She reached into her quiver, reloaded her bow, and turned back to Shayam. "I don't know who you are, or what you have going on here, but we just want our friends. Give them back and we'll leave."

"That was a marvellous display," Shayam said, staring at what remained of his creature. "But I fear I will bore of you soon..."

"Did you fucking hear us?" Rivan yelled. "Our friends. Either you give them back or you die!"

"Well, you see," Shayam said, fondling his chin with his fingers. "There's just one small problem with that..."

Red light flared from his palm again, and the men at the table quivered in unison. Green robes fell to the floor. Their bodies' grew and stretched. Kyra's ears were filled with the sounds of flesh and bone tearing and creaking.

Some of them turned into beings like the one they had just felled – with crooked black bodies and pincers – but others took on entirely different forms. One shifted into a huge bestial creature with bulging arms covered in brown fur; it raised its head to the ceiling, opened its jaws, and roared, displaying razor-sharp teeth. Two grew so high they almost reached the ceiling, and several pairs of tentacles stretched out from their myriapod bodies. Their small heads were oval-shaped, and they had just two dark slits for eyes.

"You are outnumbered," Shayam finished, opening his arms out to the horde of monsters which now filled the space between him and the intruders.

The creatures shuffled towards them.

Kyra froze. She could see they were getting closer but couldn't bring herself to move her legs.

"Come *on*!" Rivan roared, grabbing her shoulder and pulling her back.

Kyra snapped back into reality and retreated. She and the boys huddled together as the monsters closed in on them. She considered making a run for the door but knew they would never make it. They were trapped.

"Any bright ideas now?" Rivan asked.

*　　*　　*

"Where are we going?" Sidry asked as Miles led them down the corridor.

"We need to get Baird," Miles explained. "He's being kept–"

He was interrupted by the floor trembling, and the three of them stopped and placed their hands upon the walls to stop themselves falling.

"What was that?" Sidry asked when it ceased.

Sidry heard a thud behind him and turned around. Jaedin had fallen to his knees.

"Jaedin!" Miles rushed to his side. He grabbed Jaedin by his shoulders and tried to lift him, but the young man went limp, and the most Miles could manage was sit him with his back against the wall.

"Get up!" Miles shouted as he shook him.

Jaedin was hyperventilating.

"What's the matter with him?" Sidry asked Miles. "Can't you sort him out? We're supposed to be getting out of here!"

Miles ignored him and continued shaking Jaedin by his shoulders. "What is it, Jaedin?"

It was only then Sidry noticed Jaedin had a scar on his face. A thick red line down the centre of his forehead. Sidry had been too preoccupied with the strange marks on his own body to notice it before.

It was unlike any scar he had ever seen. It was centred and precise. Like someone had cut Jaedin's forehead open with careful deliberation.

Why would they do that to him? Sidry wondered. The idea of carving someone's forehead open horrified him. Sidry traced his fingers over his own face to make sure they had not done anything similar to him. As far as he could tell, they hadn't.

Jaedin was in pain; Sidry could see that now. His entire body was trembling.

"What's happening to me?!" Jaedin screamed. Tears ran down his face.

"I will explain later," Miles said.

"They're inside my head!" Jaedin choked between laboured breaths.

"Can you see anything, Jaedin?!" Miles asked. "What are they *doing*?"

Jaedin's eyes snapped open and, to Sidry's shock, they were glowing. Red light shone from them.

"Kyra!" Jaedin yelled. "They have Kyra! And Aylen! I can *see* them!"

And then the light glowing from Jaedin's eyes faded.

"I have to help them!" Jaedin yelled and leapt to his feet. Miles tried to hold him down but Jaedin shoved him aside and raced down the corridor.

"Jaedin!" Miles shouted, chasing after him. "Wait!"

"What about Baird?" Sidry asked, realising that they were now heading in the opposite direction.

"Come!" Miles pleaded. "Quick! Baird can take care of himself!"

*   *   *

Kyra took another step back and felt a wall behind her. They were trapped.

"No!" Aylen cried out. "I don't want to–"

In an unlikely show of solidarity, Rivan put his arm around him.

"I'm sorry," Kyra croaked, as the creatures closed in on them. "I didn't think it would–"

She couldn't finish the sentence. As the first Zakara leapt at them, Kyra held up her sword in one last final act of defiance and closed her eyes.

Then nothing.

Silence.

At first, Kyra thought the gods had graced her with a quick and painless death, but then she heard one of the young men beside her gasp. She opened her eyes.

There was a field of energy between her and the Zakaras. Grey, yet translucent. Kyra could see the monsters through its haze. One of the creatures leapt again, and instinct made Kyra duck for cover, but there was a flash of light, and the monster tumbled back.

Kyra looked up and saw the field of energy was all around her. It formed a sphere between them and the monsters.

She knew that it must be some kind of sorcery, but where had it come from?

"Kyra!" a familiar voice called.

She squinted her eyes and saw Jaedin at the top of a staircase on the other side of the hall. Sidry and Miles stood behind him.

*   *   *

Sidry could scarcely believe it when he caught sight of Rivan on the other side of the chamber. How did his friend land himself here? And why were Kyra, Aylen, and Dion with him?

And the *creatures*. Sidry stared at them in disbelief. He did not know where they had come from – how they even existed – but Sidry instinctively knew they could only be the spawnings of something evil.

"How long will your shields last?" Sidry asked Miles.

"Not very long!" Miles uttered between gritted teeth.

Another monster leapt at them, but Miles' shield flashed and sent the creature tumbling back down the stairs. Sidry still didn't trust the scholar, but he was well aware that his sorcery was the only thing keeping them alive.

"I'll help," Jaedin said, putting a hand on Miles' shoulder. "I'll give you my energy."

This is a stalemate, Sidry realised. He knew little about magic, but he could guess that, even with Jaedin's help, Miles could not sustain the shields forever. The monsters weren't going anywhere.

Sidry looked to his friends on the other side of the hall.

Miles had cast a protective bubble around them too, but they were also trapped.

"I can't keep this up much longer!" Miles warned. His forehead was wet with sweat. He turned to Jaedin. "Jaedin, I need you to try something."

"My magic is useless," Jaedin said. "You know that. But I can give you my *viga*."

"Jaedin…" Miles gasped. "Those monsters. What Shayam did to you while you were sleeping… you can–"

The ceiling rumbled. Sidry looked up and witnessed it tremble. Cracks were forming.

"What th–" he began to say, but his voice was drowned, and Sidry ducked, covering his head as an avalanche of stones and rubble fell. The entire room shook.

*   *   *

When it ended, all Sidry could hear was the ringing in his ears. He cautiously unwrapped his arms from around his head and opened his eyes to see only a cloud of dust in the middle of the room.

"What did you do?" he whispered, turning to Miles and Jaedin, but they looked just as confused as he felt.

"That wasn't us…" Miles said.

The dust began to clear, and Sidry saw that the ceiling above them was gone. The entire upper floor had imploded. Chunks of ceiling, walls, and other debris now covered the hall. The monsters had been crushed. Sidry could see bloody limbs and other body parts sticking out from the wreckage. And blood. A foetid stench hit his nose.

Something was glowing in the middle of the room. A tall, humanoid figure with three horns on its head. It stood in the middle of the devastation.

Sidry gasped.

It was not one of the monsters, Sidry was certain of that; those creatures were morbid and misshapen, whereas this being was beautiful. Incandescent. Sidry was in awe of it. He felt that such a being could have only come from the realm of the gods. Its indigo body shimmered. Its oval face was mostly flat. It had no mouth, just two narrow slits where its eyes should be, and a blue gem in the middle of its forehead which beamed with light.

Everyone stared at it, and the being stared back. It turned its head and looked at each one of them.

"What is that?" Jaedin whispered.

Within the rubble, something stirred. Sidry turned and saw one of the monsters crawl out from beneath the wreckage.

The glowing, god-like being turned and faced the monster.

The monster leapt, but the horned being stepped out of its path. It moved almost too fast for Sidry's eyes to follow. The glowing being then raised its arm and the flesh of its fingers moulded together into one single, tapered limb. Sidry gasped. It had somehow turned its arm into a shimmering, celestial blade.

The being swung its gleaming blade down upon the monster and it passed through its body like a knife cutting through hot wax. The monster's organs wriggled out of its body like worms. Blood showered as the dead monster fell in two halves.

Sidry heard a noise below and looked down. The rubble was moving. Another monster was climbing out from the debris.

"Watch out!" Sidry called and then covered his mouth. He did not know why he was trying to help this mysterious being. He didn't even know *what* it was. For all Sidry knew, it would kill him and his friends once it had finished with the monsters.

Sidry's warning came too late anyway. The monster flexed its long, cirrus limbs and sent them spiralling towards the horned being. They coiled around its arms and wrists. The horned being jolted in surprise and tried to squirm itself free but the monster tightened its grip.

The horned figure bent its knees and launched itself into the air, stretching the monster's tentacles until they tore apart. The monster fell back and writhed, kicking dust and rubble as it tried to right itself again. The stumps where its elastic appendages used to be quivered.

The glowing, godlike being raised its foot and crushed the creature's head into the floor, ending its morbid existence.

Sidry gulped. The monsters were gone now. The only living things left in the room were him and his friends. If this being was going to kill them, it would happen now.

The being fell to its knees. There was a sudden flash of light. Sidry covered his eyes.

When it died, Sidry tore his hands away from his face and saw the horned being had vanished.

Baird knelt in its place.

Chapter 8

Interrogation

When the doors opened, Sidry saw sunlight for the first time in several days. He experienced a brief moment of euphoria as he drew in a breath of fresh air and, once his eyes had adjusted to the light, he looked up and saw an immense network of branches brimming with green leaves above him.

Sidry had always wanted to see the Forest of Lareem but never imagined it would be under such circumstances.

Kyra and Aylen ran into the trees, and he followed. He didn't look back.

Sidry felt a strange plethora of emotions as he made his way through the forest. Despite everything he had been through and the thousands of unanswered questions whirling through his mind, he knew that he was lucky to be alive and, at first, he was simply relieved about that. His thoughts did eventually wander to the marks on his body. And the monsters he'd just seen. He wondered where they came from.

He was careful to keep a watchful eye on Miles. He was determined to not let the traitor get away. Sidry had many questions he wanted to ask, but he knew it was not the time for interrogation or swapping stories yet. For now, he just wanted to get as far away from that place as possible.

Every time Sidry looked at Baird, he remembered the glimmering being which blasted its way from the upper floors and killed the monsters. He remembered the stunned way everyone had just stared at him when the being vanished.

It was Baird who had ended the silence. "Search the building!" he'd shouted, as if he had just remembered who he was. "Find Shayam!"

The sound of his voice snapped them all out of their stupor, and they scrambled to do as he said. None of dared to voice their questions. They were too scared.

They searched the entire building – or what remained of it, at least – and found no one.

Sidry was pulled out of his recollections when he noticed a

115

change around him. Bright sunlight shone beyond the trees in the distance. They were reaching the end of the forest.

Sidry was relieved to be clear of the place; he doubted he would ever be able to properly appreciate the Forest of Lareem after what happened to him there. They were finally back in the meadow; terrain familiar to him.

Sidry only realised just how tired he was when they ascended the hill. It was steep, and by the time he reached the top, his chest was burning.

Four horses were tethered to one of the trees. Kyra rushed to check on them while Sidry collapsed under the shade of its branches.

Everyone was exhausted. Dion rested his back against the trunk of the tree and put a hand to his bloodied shoulder.

"Are you okay?" Sidry asked him.

"I'll live," Dion said as he caught his breath. "Ruddy stings, though."

"Would you like me to look at it for you?" Jaedin asked.

Dion grinned. "You've just been *waiting* for an excuse to get your hands on me, haven't you?"

Jaedin scowled and began to walk away.

"Hey," Dion hailed, lifting his arm and ushering Jaedin back. "I was kiddin'! Just trying to lighten the air, you know… Can you? Please?"

Jaedin seemed far from amused, but he grudgingly tended to him anyway. "Kyra," he called. "Have you got any dressings or anything?"

"Way ahead of you," Kyra yelled back, returning with a burlap sack.

Jaedin knelt beside Dion. "Remove your tunic, please," he said.

Dion smirked, and for a moment it seemed like he was about to make another quip, but Jaedin stopped him.

"*Don't*," Jaedin said flatly. "If you *want* my help, just *do* it…"

Dion uncovered his shoulder, and Jaedin splashed some water over it from a flask.

The wound was about four inches long, and it snaked across the top of Dion's shoulder. Luckily, it didn't appear to be very deep.

Jaedin reached into Kyra's bag and drew out a pouch. He

opened it and sniffed the contents. Sidry suspected it was woundwort but he wasn't sure. Sidry, like most boys from Jalard, had been given very basic training in first aid by Baird, but Jaedin and some of the girls had been taught by Meredith and were more advanced.

Dion winced as Jaedin rubbed the ground leaves into his wound, but he didn't complain. Finally, Jaedin reached for a bandage and wound it tightly around his shoulder.

"That will stop it getting infected," Jaedin announced once he finished. "But I think my mother might want to stitch it when we get back."

"Thanks," Dion said. He looked at Jaedin's work and gave it a nod of approval. "I always look forward to an excuse to see lovely Meredith, the–"

Dion looked at Kyra – who was glaring at him – and stopped.

"*Used* to!" he corrected and sheepishly got up. "Where are my bags, anyway..." he thought out loud. "I'm sure I packed a spare tunic somewhere..."

"I think it is time for some explanations..." Baird announced once Dion had changed his clothes.

There was an uncomfortable silence, and everyone turned to each other. There were so many questions which needed answering. Who should tell their story first?

Sidry knew who *he* wanted some answers from. He glared at Miles, who was sitting on a rock a few yards away.

"I think we should start with you," Baird decided, turning to Rivan and Kyra. "Why aren't you in Jalard?"

Rivan rose to his feet. "The Elders sent us on a trading mission."

"A trading mission..." Baird repeated, raising an eyebrow. "How did that land you *here*?"

"We found your trail," Kyra explained. "While on our way to Habella... It was obvious something had happened... we found one of the Academy representatives... He was dead."

Sidry nodded sombrely. He knew that. His mind's eye flashed back to the day they were ambushed. The man's body sprawled upon the grass. Blood pooling from the wound in his chest. The thought of it still sent chills down Sidry's spine.

He had seen dead people before. Jalard was small, and

everyone knew everyone. When a member of their community passed on, most of the village would come to their funeral. The rite was tender and respectful. They were adorned in their finest clothes, laid with their most treasured possessions, and their loved ones would place gifts to be buried with them. Their eyes were always closed, not staring emptily at the sky.

They always died of sickness or old age. They were never murdered.

"What about Ne'mair?" Sidry remembered. "And the other one? Where are they?"

"We searched the whole building, didn't we?" Dion asked. "They weren't there. You think they were behind it all?"

"Why would they kill their own?" Kyra said.

"I can assure you that the Academy had *nothing* to do with this," Baird stated firmly. "So you can rid that from your minds! Anyway, back on topic..." he turned back to Kyra, Rivan, and the others. "You followed our trail?"

The four of them nodded.

"And then?" Baird pressed.

They went quiet and turned to each other. It was clear they were all reluctant to be the speaker. None of them wanted to bear the brunt of Baird's judgement.

"We burst in through the front door," Rivan replied.

"Through the front door..." Baird repeated ponderously. "Bit brash, no?"

"It was Kyra's idea!" Rivan pointed to the girl beside him.

Kyra squirmed. "It was the best plan we could come up with. We didn't have–"

"I will talk to you about plans later..." Baird cut her off. He exhaled audibly and shook his head.

They risked their lives for me, Sidry realised, feeling a wave of gratitude.

And yet, the four of them now stood with their heads hung low, staring at their feet to avoid Baird's condescending gaze. It seemed unfair.

"But I guess..." Baird's tone softened. "Despite your ill-conceived ideas of an attack plan, what you did today was very brave. If foolish."

The four of their faces went beet red with embarrassment. Compliments from Baird were few and far between. It was hard to know how to respond to them.

"So... what happened after you *burst in*?" Baird asked, placing a sardonic emphasis on the last two words. The moment of praise was over, and he once again composed himself into the role of their steely mentor.

"There were these men sat at the table..." Kyra said. "One of them was a snide little–"

"Shayam?" Sidry muttered.

"Yes!" Kyra said. "That's the one. The rest of them were wearing robes, and there was something not right about them..."

Sidry nodded. He always thought there was something odd about those men. When you looked into their eyes, they seemed lifeless and empty. They appeared to have no other purpose but to silently carry out Shayam's commands. Sidry could remember having a hard time getting any of them to even speak, let alone answer his questions. He wondered what happened to those men. And Shayam. Did they flee the building when the...

"They started shaking, and foaming at the mouth," Kyra said. "They... they turned into the monsters–"

"*What?*" Sidry exclaimed.

Kyra nodded at him. Sidry could see from her face that she hardly believed it herself. "Those *things*... he called them Zakaras."

"What do you mean, *they* turned into those things?" Sidry asked. "How did that happen?"

"How the fuck am I supposed to know?" Kyra exclaimed.

No one spoke for a while. Baird placed a hand on his chin as he considered the information he'd just been given.

He turned to Miles.

"I think it's your turn to explain yourself..." he decided, and the tone of his voice changed, becoming severe.

Everyone stared at the man who sat on a rock a few yards away. He hesitantly raised his head but avoided making eye contact with any of them.

"He's one of them!" Sidry pointed at him.

"What?" Kyra said.

"He's a Gavendarian, you idiot!" Sidry shouted. "Just like the rest of them!"

"Quiet down!" Baird yelled, silencing them. He turned

back to Miles and the look on Baird's face, as he glared at the traitor, made Sidry realise that all the times Baird yelled at them over the years, none of them had actually made him angry.

And, from the look in Baird's eyes right then, Sidry hoped he never would.

"You've got some explaining to do…" Baird said.

"Yes, I do…" Miles said. He stood up and rubbed his hands together. "I will tell you everything…"

"What are those things?" Sidry yelled. His outburst was rewarded with a glare from Baird, but he couldn't help himself. He needed to know.

"As Kyra told you, they are called Zakaras," Miles confirmed.

"That word sounds familiar…" Jaedin murmured.

"Yes, Jaedin. I imagine you have come across that word before… but none of the books you have read will explain what you witnessed today," Miles said to his pupil before turning back to the others. "And yes. Those men did turn into them…"

"How's that possible?" Baird asked.

"It's a long story…" Miles said. "And to explain it properly, I will need to start at the very beginning… Some of the things I say may seem irrelevant at first, but you'll need to bear with me…"

Baird nodded.

Miles hesitated before he began. He stared up at the sky, as if pondering. "Well…" he said. "First of all, I need to ask all of you something. Are you aware that there is a plague ravaging Gavendara?"

A plague? Sidry thought. *Is that what turned those men into those things?*

"Just as I thought…" Miles shook his head when nobody answered. "When I crossed the border, it came as a great surprise to me when I discovered most Sharmarians are utterly unaware."

"I had heard of it…" Baird admitted. "I think the Synod thought it best that our people were not troubled by the problems of our neighbours. Where is this going?"

Sidry was surprised by this. The Synod was the governing body of Sharma. Every village and town paid them taxes and, in return, the Synod protected their land from foreign enemies, provided aid for troubled communities, and education for the young. They also ran the Academy.

The idea they would consciously withhold information from the public shocked him. It made him wonder if they had any other secrets.

"You will see..." Miles said. "I just need to explain this to them first. I promise you it is all relevant..." He turned back to the others. "For those of you who don't know. The Ruena – as we call it – began about twenty-five years ago. It has no known cause and, unlike most other widespread diseases, it does not seem to be directly contagious. Bubbles of it never form. People seem to contract it at random, and we have still not discovered any pattern. It is thought that as many as one in seven have been infected so far, and numbers are growing. Not even our greatest healers and sorcerers have been able to find a cure. Many conventional medicines and methods have been tried and tested, but to no avail."

Miles let that last statement hang before he continued. "Then, about fifteen years ago, in an act of pure desperation, some of us began to turn to other places for answers. We looked in books and ancient annals to see if we could find any hints to a similar outbreak in our history, but there were none. We went back even further, and excavated ancient temples to the mountains of the north, whose walls are covered in runes so old that even Jaedin here would have difficulty translating them."

"Are those the ones–" Jaedin interrupted, but he was cut off by Baird.

He was going to ask about the marks on my body, Sidry realised as their eyes met. "Some of us could decipher them..." Miles said. "And they spoke of old rituals. Virulence. Ways of making people stronger. More powerful. And... well... in a country suffering from a fatal sickness... it appeared that we had found our answer..."

Mile's eyes darkened. "I do believe that, in the beginning, at least, the tests were carried out with the best intentions," he said solemnly. "Subjects were people dying from The Ruena anyway, and they willingly gave their lives in the hope of finding a cure. We even achieved some results, eventually. We managed to bring people back from the brink of The

Ruena, but it came with some peculiar consequences. Just as was written on the walls of the temples, these people became stronger... and... some of them became creatures like the beings you saw today."

"What?" Kyra exclaimed. "Your people *made* those *things*?"

"What were you in all of this?" Baird asked.

"I was just a scholar," Miles raised his hands. "They were investigating ancient temples and it made sense to have people with my knowledge at hand."

"But you were still a part of it..." Baird said.

Miles nodded. "Initially. But I began to have doubts..." he explained. "When some of the tests went wrong. And people were killed. I also discovered that they were secretly taking people against their will when they were short of volunteers. I didn't like any of that."

"So why didn't you stop it?" Baird asked.

"As I said, I was just a scholar," Miles reminded him. "I was powerless... If they knew that I was starting to have reservations about the work they were doing, they would have killed me. I wanted to stay alive. So I could keep an eye on them. So that, when the right time came, I could act against them. And today was that day."

"But you've been living with us for... what... ten years?" Baird frowned at him.

"Yes..." Miles nodded. "It has been almost ten years now... I was sent to Sharma to live as a spy."

Everyone stared at him.

It had been obvious for a while now, but they finally had a confession.

Miles had been living in their village for years. He had pretended he was a refugee, but it had all been a ruse.

"Why were *you* chosen?" Baird asked. "Of all people?"

"Well... there wasn't much left for me to do in Gavendara anymore..." Miles shrugged. "They had finished excavating those temples, so there were no more runes left for me to decipher... I am also Blessed. That was another secret I was instructed to keep from you. I am what they call a 'Blessed of Diammna' – the goddess of sanctuary and shelter – and thus my magical abilities are limited to defensive arts. I can manifest shields of energy to protect myself and others... but, more importantly, I can shield my *mind*. This makes me the perfect spy... Grav'aen, the man in charge – the one whose orders Shayam is following – is possibly the most powerful Psymancer in the world and he can see into people's minds. Except for mine, of course.

"Grav'aen has many moles in Sharma... he wanted me to be among them because, unlike most of the others, I can disguise my intentions if I ever encounter other people who can read minds. What Grav'aen considered my greatest strength turned out to be *his* downfall, because he never discovered my intention to betray him."

"How have you betrayed him?" Baird narrowed his eyes. "You *helped* them ambush us."

"I helped you escape, too," Miles said.

"No!" Baird's face turned red. "Don't lie to me! *I* was the one who got us out of there!"

"Yes, you did!" Miles agreed. "But you were all being drugged! I swapped the potions which were keeping you asleep for a harmless concoction."

"It's true," Jaedin said to Baird. "He was helping me and Sidry escape just before you appeared. Tell them, Sidry! Tell him it's true!"

He's a strange boy, Sidry thought, looking at Jaedin. *After all Miles has done... he still wants to help him...*

"It's true," Sidry admitted reluctantly. "He freed me and Jaedin. We were just on our way to get you as well... but then everything else happened."

"It was thanks to him you were taken in the first place!" Baird reminded them.

"I know," Sidry said. "I don't think it makes up for it either..."

Baird turned back to Miles with a stony expression.

"There *is* more..." the scholar said. "As to why I acted the way I did... Please... just let me finish. If by the end you want to kill me, then by all means do. But let me tell you the rest. Please."

Baird hesitated. Sidry could tell from the cold rage in his eyes that it was taking a great amount of restraint on his part to not run Miles through with his blade there and then, but they all wanted to know more.

He nodded.

"Over the last ten years, I have been a mole..." Miles admitted. "But, for the most part, a sleeping one... And for the first nine of those years, my only instruction was to integrate myself into Sharmarian society as much as I could. Please believe me when I say I came to genuinely care about many of you..." Miles looked at Jaedin and the young man sniffed. "Grav'aen always told me he had an important quest lined up for me... and, a year ago, he finally awakened me and told me the details of his plan... When I heard it, I knew my time to betray him had come. I had to stop him. Do you wish to hear what this plan was?" he asked Baird.

"Just out with it!" he said impatiently.

"The reason Shayam and his minions came to Sharma," Miles explained. "Was because Grav'aen wanted him to try some of their experiments on Sharmarian citizens... They wanted to find out what it is which is different about you..."

People gasped.

"For some reason, The Ruena has *never* crossed the border, no matter how many people, like myself, have migrated. Your people seem to be immune, and Shayam was sent here to find out why," Miles said. "Once Shayam had created enough Zakaras, he was planning to attack your village and use Jalard as a testing ground but, thanks to our intervention today, he never had the chance."

Sidry felt a knot tighten in his stomach at the mention of Shayam creating Zakaras.

Had *he* been turned into a Zakara?

Sidry looked at his hands. He didn't *feel* different.

But he had scars all over his body, so Shayam had obviously done *something* to him.

Would one of those creatures be aware of what they were? Or would it lay dormant inside them until it was somehow awakened?

"But that still doesn't explain why you let them ambush us," Baird said, crossing his arms over his chest.

"I am just about to come to that," Miles reassured him. "But I first need to explain to you the *second* reason why they came here..." he turned back to the others and continued his story. "For years, there were some... other experiments Grav'aen wanted to try... But these were considered so unconventional he wanted them done far away from the prying eyes of other Gavendarians. Grav'aen knows that not all of the people who originally got behind him still agree with some of the lengths he has gone to. Therefore, he wanted them conducted somewhere off the beaten track."

"What were these," Baird began, and then paused before he said the final word. "*Experiments*?"

"Kyra," Miles turned to her. "Did you see Shayam using a red crystal? Just before those men turned into Zakaras?"

Kyra glared at him

"I did…" Aylen said from beside her.

"Those crystals were found while they were excavating a temple dedicated to the god Zakar. Ten of them were found, in total, and it was discovered that those who possessed them could control the minds of those who had been changed into Zakaras. They became very useful after the later experiments because the subjects became bloodthirsty creatures with little remaining humanity."

It was starting to make sense to Sidry. The docile men in the green robes. The way Shayam seemed to have a silent control over them.

"It was thought, by someone, that these stones could be fused to a person through a ritual. That it would result in the amplification of the stones' powers. But the procedure was considered very risky, and no one came forward to be the first," Miles explained. He turned to Jaedin. "And that is what they did to you, Jaedin. You possess one of the Stones of Zakar."

Everyone stared at Jaedin. "Wha-what stone?" he asked, looking down at himself. "What do you mean? Where is it?"

He doesn't even know… Sidry realised, looking at the scar on Jaedin's forehead.

Everyone turned to each other, and Sidry could tell what they were all thinking.

Who was going to tell him?

Kyra rose to the occasion. She walked over to Jaedin, placed a hand on his shoulder and attempted a reassuring smile, but it was more of a grimace.

Kyra then pulled out one of her daggers and held it lengthways in front of Jaedin's face so he could see his reflection on its surface.

Jaedin's jaw trembled, and he ran his finger down the scar.

"What is this?" he croaked.

"I'm sorry, Jaedin," Miles whispered.

"What did they do to *me*?" Baird asked through gritted teeth. "What was that thing I became?"

Miles turned to Baird but did not dare look him in the face. "You were fused to a crystal they found in a temple dedicated to the god Gezra," he said, staring at his shoes. "The same thing was done to Sidry…"

Sidry felt everyone's eyes turn to him and a horrible feeling curdled in his stomach.

Sidry pulled up his tunic and showed Miles his scars. Everyone gasped but, during that moment, Sidry didn't care. He was beyond embarrassment. "You let them do this to me!?"

"Does that mean that Sidry could become that thing too?" Rivan gasped.

"I would say it is very likely he can…" Miles said.

Sidry pulled his tunic back down and turned away from everyone. Now his rage had subsided, he couldn't stand the way they were all staring at him.

Could he really turn into that being? He didn't believe it. He wouldn't know how to. He didn't know if he *wanted* to.

He heard gasps behind him and turned around to see that Baird had shoved Miles to the ground. The traitor was on his knees.

Baird pressed a sword to his neck.

"Give me *one* reason not to kill you!" he screamed.

Miles looked up at him. "Because I have only acted out of the best interests for you all."

"*Liar*!" Baird roared. "You admitted yourself that you were a spy! You helped them ambush us!"

"Baird! Please!" Miles raised his hands. "They were planning to use Jalard as a testing ground. We've stopped them!"

"You let them do those things to us!" Baird yelled. "We could have been killed!"

"But you *weren't*!" Miles said. "And Sharma is better for it!"

"What are you talking about?!" Baird retorted. "One of the Academy representatives is dead. Another two are missing! How can you justify that?"

"There is a war coming!" Miles said. "Baird… you are a

soldier. You remember the last war. Imagine if it happened again, but this time it wasn't a human army they sent across the border, but one of *Zakaras*!"

Baird's eyes widened.

"I was in a very difficult position," Miles explained, while he had the chance. "Yes, I could have just warned Sharma of what was to come, but Grav'aen would have found out. He would have attacked sooner. It wouldn't matter how much time you had to prepare! Can you imagine an army of that strength? It was a hard decision and I hate myself for it. Every day I lived in your village – I learnt to care for many of you – knowing that I had to betray you to help you!"

"What have you done to help anyone?" Baird spat.

"Grav'aen is going to make an army of Zakaras. It is inevitable," Miles prophesied. "He and his most trusted followers will use the Stones of Zakar to march those monsters into your nation. Can't you see what I have done, Baird? Sharma has one of those Stones now too. In him!" he pointed at Jaedin.

"Not to mention that thing you turned into!" Miles continued. "Shayam and the others. They ran away. Do you know why? Because they were scared. Years of experimenting and they have never created anything like what we saw today! That is another thing taken from the hands of the enemy and placed into ours."

"This is not some kind of game!" Baird screamed into his face. "Did you *see* what they did to Sidry!? You *let* them do that!"

"I'm sorry…" Miles whispered. He shook his head. "All I ever tried to do was what I thought best…" he cried. "Sharma was doomed. To an evil greater than the world has ever seen. I had to make some tough decisions…"

He is sick, Sidry thought to himself. *He knew what he was doing was wrong but he did it anyway.*

"You are *not* a god!" Baird screamed and pressed the sword to Miles' throat again. The scholar winced and a bead of blood streaked down his neck.

"Is there anything else you would like to say?" Baird asked him.

Miles looked at Jaedin. "I'm so sorry…" he whispered.

Jaedin was still crying. Sidry could see conflicted emotions in the young man's eyes. "Baird," Jaedin whispered. He looked at Miles again. "Please... don't..."

Sidry turned away. Miles was clearly insane, and he deserved what he was about to get.

But Sidry didn't want to watch this. He'd already seen too much bloodshed that day.

He closed his eyes and waited for the sound of Baird's blade severing Miles' neck, but it never came.

"Consider yourself our prisoner," Baird uttered. "If you try *anything*, I will kill you. I promise. The only reason I am keeping you alive is so I can take you to Shemet... The Synod can deal with you. Do you understand?"

"Yes..." Miles said.

Sidry uncovered his eyes and watched as Baird walked away. His sword was clean, and Miles was still alive.

* * *

They made their way back to Jalard and, with two people on each horse, it was an arduous journey. Sidry was sharing a steed with Baird, and they rode at the back of the group so they could keep an eye on Miles.

They travelled silently, and the horses were pushed hard. Their breaks were few and brief, but even Jaedin dared not to complain.

Two of the moons were full that night, so they travelled well into the evening and pitched their tents late.

Sidry could not sleep. He tossed and turned in his blanket while memories of the Zakaras haunted him. They lived behind his eyelids when he closed them and, even when he lay with his eyes open, the symbols they cut into his body throbbed. He eventually gave up and made his way outside – it was his and Rivan's turn to keep their watch soon anyway, and he wanted a chance to speak to Baird alone.

Baird was sitting by the fire, watching Miles' tent. Part of the purpose of keeping watch was to make sure the traitor didn't escape.

"It's not your turn yet," Baird grunted.

"I couldn't sleep," Sidry replied as he sat next to him.

The collar of Baird's tunic hung low, and Sidry saw some of the scars on his chest. They were identical to his.

128

"Baird…" he said. "I… think I want to stay in Jalard…"

It had taken Sidry time to summon the courage to say that. He thought Baird would rebuke him for it but his mentor didn't say anything. He just stared at the fire.

"All of this…" Sidry continued. "It has made me realise I want to be home. With my family. And my friends. I feel safe there…"

"Sidry," Baird said. "You do realise that being chosen by the Academy is not the only reason I want to take you to Shemet now, don't you?"

Sidry had not thought about that but, now Baird had said it, he had a horrible feeling it was something to do with the scars on his body. What they did to him.

"If everything Miles has said is true," Baird explained. "Sharma will have much more to worry about than running Academies. And if you and Jaedin have been given something that can help…"

"Whatever it was they did to us, it didn't work on me," Sidry shook his head. The thought of the Synod having an interest in him made him uneasy. "I don't feel… different. I don't think I can do that thing you did."

"How do you know for sure?" Baird asked. "Have you tried?"

"I wouldn't know *how*…" Sidry admitted.

And even if I did, I wouldn't try…

Out of the corner of his eye, Sidry saw Rivan emerge from their tent. He stretched his arms up to the sky and yawned.

At least someone managed to get some sleep, Sidry thought bitterly.

"I will give you some time to think about it," Baird finished as he got up. Sidry watched him leave, knowing his mentor was not going to give up easily.

Rivan sat by the fire and yawned again.

"Rivan…" Sidry began. "I never got the chance to thank you."

"Well, there's no time like the present…" Rivan grinned.

"Thanks."

Sidry realised there was a silver lining to everything which had happened to him; the ill-feelings which manifested between him and Rivan when he was Chosen for the Academy were gone now.

Sidry was glad to have his friend back.

"I think I am going to stay in Jalard," Sidry announced.

Rivan opened his mouth, and it seemed he was about to argue.

"No. Seriously," Sidry cut him off. "Not because of my parents. Or because of you. It's because of *me*. I just realised that there is more to life than that damn Academy."

"Well, I guess I will see you in a few aeights then..." Rivan scratched his head. "Because Baird asked me earlier if I wanted to ride to Shemet with you."

"What?" Sidry turned to him. "Why?"

"To help you keep an eye on that son-of-a-whore!" Rivan explained, pointing at Miles' tent. "Make sure he doesn't do a runner. And... well... it looks like things are going on and I want in on the action."

"Yeah... it's been quite the adventure. I've had the time of my life..." Sidry said dryly.

Rivan slapped his shoulder. "Sorry," he said. "But it ain't been all fun and games for me either... Even if you don't want to go to the Academy anymore, why not just come for the ride? Have you never wanted to see Shemet?"

Maybe I would have, once, Sidry thought. *But I'm not sure anymore...*

"I'll think about it," Sidry said.

* * *

In the morning, Kyra was preparing her horse when she felt two hands press against her buttocks. She jumped in surprise.

"You bastard!" she exclaimed, pushing Dion away.

She tried not to smile, but she couldn't help herself.

Dion grinned mischievously. "Sorry," he replied, putting his arms around her. "I missed you last night."

Kyra missed him too. She had nightmares about those monsters, and when she woke up she found herself wishing Dion was beside her. Her feelings for him were not scaring her as much as they used to. She was learning to embrace them.

"I know..." she said. She then lowered her voice and whispered into his ear. "But Jaedin has been through a lot... he needs me right now."

"Want me to back off?" he asked. Although his body was saying something else. He was pressed against her.

"Maybe for just a couple of days?" she suggested. "I'm Jaedin's only friend here... He doesn't get on with any of the others... and... well... he's scared of Baird..."

Miles used to be the only man he could look up to... Kyra thought to herself, and her jaw clenched as she thought about the traitor. She'd been fond of the outlandish scholar too, but he'd made fools of all of them.

"I understand," Dion said. "How is he coping?"

"Well... he's still alive..." Kyra shrugged. "But he's been betrayed."

"Everyone ready?" Baird yelled, interrupting them.

Kyra leant over and pressed her mouth to Dion's.

"Yes!" she called back before jumping onto their horse. Dion sat himself behind her and wrapped his arms around her waist.

"You know..." he whispered in her ear. "If I wasn't certain you'll be sent to that Academy next year, I would ask you to shack up with me."

Kyra laughed as she kicked the horse into motion.

*   *   *

Baird made them travel at a hard pace again that day in the hope they would arrive in Jalard by nightfall but, when evening struck and it became clear they were not going to make it, they found a place to camp.

Jaedin tried to help them pitch the tents, but the other boys kept finding fault in his every action and complained he was doing everything wrong. He felt like he was more of a hindrance than a help, so he gave up.

He wanted some time alone anyway, so he found a spot by a stream nearby and sat.

Usually, after a day of riding, Jaedin would be suffering from a whole range of aches and pains, but not anymore. Since his escape, his body had changed. It felt alien to him. His muscles seemed to no longer feel strain like they used to. He didn't even feel tired.

He still had not told anyone. He was doing everything he could to push it to the back of his mind and convince himself that there were perfectly reasonable explanations for what he was feeling. His body was just getting used to all the riding. He was becoming stronger because he was getting more exercise.

But, deep down, Jaedin knew there was something more than that going on.

He was pulled out of his thoughts by the sound of footsteps. Miles now stood beside him. They both stared at the sun, which was beginning to set and, for the first time that Jaedin could remember, they shared an awkward silence. Jaedin had never been short of anything to say to Miles; there had always been some engaging theory to discuss, some holes in a book Jaedin wanted to unpick. Apart from his sister and mother, there had been no one else in the world Jaedin was more comfortable around.

But now, the man felt like a stranger. Everything they had shared through the years felt like a lie.

And it hurt.

"How could you..." Jaedin said when he broke the silence.

"I'm sorry..." Miles whispered.

"It's not good enough..." Jaedin shook his head.

"Jaedin..." Miles hesitated. "You are a clever young man. You can see the bigger picture. Can't you see that I had no other choice? That I did what I believed to be for the greatest good for all?"

Over the last two days, Jaedin had had a lot of time to think about everything Miles had revealed to them. If it was all true, what Miles had done was logical. Ruthless, but still logical. Jaedin could see this, but he still couldn't find it within himself to forgive him.

Jaedin shook his head. "There is just one thing I don't get," he said. "Why did you choose me?"

Miles didn't reply.

"Why *me*?" Jaedin pressed. "Of all the people you could have abducted as part of your master plan? I could have died! They used the Stone of Zakar on me, and you want me to use it against them. I am not strong! I can't even help myself, let alone others!"

"It wasn't my choice—"

"*Liar!*" Jaedin hissed. "You think I don't know? It's obvious you did something! Tell me, Miles, why were Kyra and Rivan not Chosen for the Academy? How did you pull *that* one off?"

Miles' eyes widened.

"Yes," Jaedin said, knowing from his mentor's reaction that he had caught him out. "I figured it out. So tell me: how did you do it? How did you make the Academy choose me instead of them?"

"When I said it was not my choice," Miles replied. "I was telling the truth. The reports that are sent to the Academy... they all go from Baird to Meredith, and then me..."

"You scrapped them!" Jaedin realised, placing a hand over his mouth. "Kyra's and Rivan's reports! That's why they weren't Chosen!"

Miles' silence was as good as a confirmation.

"And what do you mean it wasn't your choice?" Jaedin added. "You did it! You had a choice!"

"I mean that..." Miles hesitated. "*She* came to me. In a dream."

The expression on Miles' face was one of reverence.

"I think it was Verdana," he added. "She told me to do it..."

"You let them do *this* to me because you had a *dream*?!" Jaedin pointed to his forehead.

"The choices of the gods are often strange..." Miles said softly. "But not to be questioned."

"Screw that!" Jaedin muttered. He looked away. "They turned me into a freak..."

"Jaedin..." Miles whispered. He placed a hand on his back "You are not–"

"Don't touch me!" Jaedin exclaimed.

Shadows of guilt darkened Miles' eyes. He stared at Jaedin in a way which begged for forgiveness, but Jaedin turned away and looked at the sunset. He knew if he looked into Miles' eyes for long enough, he would crumble into forgiving him.

"Jaedin," Miles said. "I'm sorry this has been chosen for you, but when the time comes–"

"No!" Jaedin hissed. "This is your mess! You can sort it out. I am going to the Academy and living a normal life!"

Miles opened his mouth to say something else.

"Shut up!"

Jaedin watched as the last crescent of the sun melted into the horizon, and its glow faded. The crimson haze of sunset shifted to a cimmerian curtain, streaked with beams of azure. Teanar and Lumnar were still large in the sky but beginning to wane.

Jaedin looked at Miles. Despite everything that he had done, he found himself unable to hate him.

And he hated it.

"I figured out where I have heard the word Zakar before…" Jaedin said.

"And?" Miles asked.

"Zakar was one of the Other gods," Jaedin recalled. "Only a minor one. That is why it took me a while to remember."

"That is correct," Miles affirmed, nodding his head in approval.

"It was said he had an army of demons," Jaedin added. He thought of the Zakaras. "You also said that the crystals they used on Baird and Sidry were from a temple of Gezra… Gezra was Gazareth's son. His bodyguard and henchman. Some accounts even claim that he was a triple god – and that Gazareth actually had three sons, all called Gezra – but that is heavily disputed. Scribes got carried away with the number three hundreds of years ago. It was fashionable."

"Very good, Jaedin."

Chapter 9

Returning to Jalard

The moment they reached the boundary of the village, Jaedin knew in his gut that something was wrong. The first thing he noticed was how unnaturally quiet it was. He didn't hear a single animal rustle in the undergrowth. There were no birds in the sky. The trees were still and silent, and no wind stirred their leaves. It seemed that even the force of Ta'al had abandoned them. One did not need Bryna's ability for precognition to feel the semblance of danger in the air when they reached the first building and no one came outside to welcome them back.

The street was empty.

"Where is everyone?" Kyra said as they dismounted.

Jaedin felt goosebumps on the back of his neck. He forced himself to carry on walking even though he was feeling a strong urge to turn and run.

Baird grunted and led them further into the village. Everyone turned their heads from side to side as they walked, searching for signs of life. They were beginning to realise that something dreadful must have happened but were all too scared to say anything. As if by mentioning it, they would turn it into a reality.

Then they saw the first body, outside the gate of someone's garden.

Jaedin looked and regretted it instantly. It was an image which burned into his mind. Blood everywhere. One arm was missing. The other limbs were bloodied and mangled. Jaedin recognised the victim's face but couldn't recall his name. It was one of the many farmers of the village Jaedin had never spoken to.

Baird rushed over to inspect, as did Kyra and Rivan. Kyra gasped. Aylen, too, gave in to morbid curiosity and ran over to peer over Rivan's shoulder only to recoil and empty his stomach on the wall of the victim's house.

Kyra was the first to transition from a state of shock to panic. She dashed into the village. It caused a chain reaction,

135

and everyone dispersed, running to their homes to check on their families. They left the horses behind. Forgotten.

Jaedin, however, continued walking. Slowly. Hesitantly. None of this seemed real yet. His legs felt heavy.

He turned a corner. Saw a torn-up pathway, sticky with blood. It had caked into the mud. Brown and red and black. The smell caught the back of Jaedin's throat. He covered his mouth. More bodies of dead villagers. Houses were in shambles. Gates hung lopsided. Doors ripped from their hinges. Windows shattered. Even some of the walls had fallen.

Jaedin tore his arm away from his mouth to say something to Miles, but he couldn't find any words. None of this felt real. The village he grew up in was a scene of devastation and corpses were everywhere, yet he found himself walking through it languidly. As if it was all a dream.

He heard a scream. Looked up. It was coming from Aylen's house.

Rivan was dragging Aylen out of the door by his shoulders. The younger boy fought to free himself, but Rivan was bigger than him. Rivan's face was a grim expression.

Jaedin did not need to ask what they had seen. The broken look in Aylen's eyes was enough.

The sight stirred up memories from Jaedin's childhood. He and Aylen had once been friends. It was back they were very young, so Jaedin hadn't thought about it for years. They had grown apart.

But, in that moment, it didn't feel that long ago. Jaedin looked at the garden where they used to play. He remembered Aylen's parents. Jaedin liked them. Aylen's mother had always been pleasant to him, even after he became estranged from her son.

It was then that the gravity of the situation finally struck him. Jaedin thought about his own mother. And his sister. Where were they?

Jaedin broke into a run. He could barely feel his legs. The huts of the village streaked past him.

"Jaedin!" Miles yelled. "Wait!"

Jaedin ignored him. All he could think about was Bryna and Meredith. The devastated village passed in a blur.

Jaedin never knew he could run so fast but he reached his home in seconds. He turned around, realising that Miles was no longer behind him. Had he outrun Miles? Or had the traitor taken the opportunity to escape?

Jaedin didn't care. The walls of his house were cracked, the windows were broken, and the front door tilted from its frame by a single hinge.

He gulped down his fear and climbed over the fence.

*   *   *

Kyra felt a pain in her chest. It felt as if her heart had ceased. Tears welled from her eyes. She moaned.

She had just found her father's body. It lay on the path outside her home. His neck was bent at an impossible angle. His eyes were open, but they stared into nothing.

She knelt beside him and covered his body with a blanket from her backpack.

The Zakaras had done this. She knew it. No weapon made by a human could make such lesions. Not even a bandit would gut a man and unravel his organs from his body.

She wailed again. Hot tears streamed down her face. She kept choking between her wails; she was struggling to breathe.

She leant forward and closed her father's eyelids so the harrowed look in his eyes could no longer haunt her, but they were stuck. Rigor mortis had set in.

"Kyra..." a soft voice said.

She looked up and saw her little sister in the doorway of her house.

*   *   *

Jaedin ran outside and threw up in the garden. He closed his eyes, but the sight of what they did to his mother would haunt him forever.

Bryna! he thought, once he'd spat out the last of the bile from his mouth. He looked back at the house but the thought of going back in there and seeing not only what remained of his mother again but also his sister, made his blood curdle. His lower lip trembled. No. He couldn't. He couldn't go back in *there*.

He then felt a surge of energy pass through the village.

Jaedin gasped and looked about himself. It was like a wind,

but it wasn't. It was like nothing he had ever experienced before. He didn't know what to compare it to.

It flowed through him. *Into* him. It grew stronger.

Something within Jaedin's forehead tingled.

Images filled his mind.

*   *   *

"Luisa!" Kyra wiped tears from her face. "Are you hurt?"

She ran over, wrapped her arms around her sister, and clung to her body tightly.

Kyra didn't want to let go her go at first – almost as if she was afraid that, if she did, Luisa would disappear – but eventually she pulled away and looked at her.

Luisa's hair was messy and tangled, and her dress was dirty and clung to her skin, but she didn't seem hurt. It was a miracle.

And, despite everything Kyra had just seen, her heart was filled with joy. She thought she had lost everything, but her little sister – the most precious person to her in the world – was alive.

"What happened?" Luisa said, her eyes misted with confusion.

"I don't know, Luisa…" Kyra mumbled. Her lips were still trembling. She found it hard to speak. "Something bad."

Kyra mustered the bravest smile she could and ran her fingers through her sister's blonde hair. "I'm sorry! I couldn't help them, but we are alive, and I'm going to take care of you."

*   *   *

Jaedin fell to his knees and pressed his palm to his forehead. Images were flashing through his mind. None of them lingered long enough for him to comprehend. His temples were palpitating, and sweat fevered his brow.

He could *feel* the dead people of Jalard. In his head. Something was calling out to them.

And they were awakening.

Jaedin felt them open their eyes. They were no longer human.

Jaedin trembled.

Something was terribly wrong.

* * *

Dion ran across the village to reach his home. He already knew from what he had seen on his way that the odds of his father surviving were not good, but he had to be sure.

Blacksmiths always lived on the outskirts. They posed a fire hazard. When Dion reached the smithy, there was no smoke clouding from the chimney. It was a bad omen. In Dion's entire life, his father had never let the fires completely die.

But he saw movement.

His father was standing in the doorway of their house.

"Dad!" Dion yelled. The terrible feeling in his gut eased a little. He ran to his father and wrapped his arms around him. "You're okay!"

His father remained as still as a tree.

Dion pulled back and took a closer look at him. There was no recognition in his father's eyes. They were empty.

He must be in shock, Dion realised. He recalled the training Baird had given them in dealing with traumatised people and snapped his fingers in front of his father's face but his eyes didn't even flicker.

"Dad! Wake up!" Dion shook him.

"Dion?" the blacksmith's lips moved, but the way he said his son's name was odd. It was as if it was a word he had never uttered it before.

"Yes!" Dion exclaimed. "It's me."

His father didn't say anything else. Dion wondered what horrors he must have been through for him to come to this.

He stepped past him and inspected the house. There didn't seem to be any damage. There were even embers still glowing at the hearth, deep within a pile of ash.

I'll get the fire going and make him a drink, Dion decided as he reached for some kindling. *That will help bring him round.*

And then Dion hoped he could get some answers.

* * *

Jaedin tried to muster control of the visions invading his mind, but he was lost as a passive victim of them. He felt the minds of the dead awaken. He felt their hunger. He saw familiar places of the village through their eyes as his perspective flickered between them.

He saw Dion. He was building a fire. His back was turned to the being whose perspective Jaedin shared. It was watching Dion.

It was creeping towards him.

No! Jaedin's inner voice screamed as the image of Dion's wavy blond hair and shoulders gained clarity. Jaedin could sense the creature's intention as it approached the young man bent over the hearth. It was going to kill Dion. Jaedin could see through the hunter's eyes. He could feel a set of claws where a hand should be. It reached for the young man. *Dion! Run!*

Dion must have heard a sound because he turned around, but it was too late. The monster struck, drove its claws into Dion's chest, and Jaedin felt them tear through his ribcage.

No!

But the monster continued. Dion fell. He tried to scream but the monster jumped on top of him and sank its teeth into his throat.

"Dion!" Jaedin yelled.

The vision was over, and Jaedin became aware of his surroundings again. He was outside his home.

He looked at his hands; they were his own, but only a few moments ago it felt like he had claws. He had been inside the mind of another being. He witnessed it kill Dion.

It was like *he* had killed Dion.

Another image entered Jaedin's mind. He gasped.

He saw Kyra's face. Something wanted to hurt her.

*   *   *

"They're not dead..." Luisa whispered into Kyra's ear.

Kyra blinked. *She doesn't know what's happened*, she thought. *How can I explain it to her?*

She put her arms around Luisa's neck. "I'm sorry, Luisa... but they are. You still have me... I will protect you."

"Kyra!" someone yelled.

Kyra turned and saw Jaedin sprinting towards them.

"See!" Kyra turned back to Luisa. "Jaedin's here. You remember Jaedin, don't you?"

Luisa's head rolled back. An inhuman groan wheezed from her throat.

Kyra stepped back in horror.

It was only then Kyra noticed that black spines had grown from her sister's back. They flexed, curling outwards, like a spider stretching its limbs.

"We are not dead!" Luisa said. Her voice was rasping and coarse. Inhuman.

"Kyra!" Jaedin yelled, grabbing her arm. "Run!"

"What's happened to her?" she cried as Jaedin pulled her away. "Luisa!"

Luisa's eyes were no longer alive. They didn't glow with youthful innocence and naive joy like they once did. They were cold.

"Let me go!" Kyra screamed, trying to free herself from Jaedin's grip.

"That is not your sister!" Jaedin yelled as he dragged her away. His strength, during that moment, was unbelievable. Despite Kyra's resistance, he somehow managed to pull her all the way to the gate. Kyra had always been stronger than him; how was it he was now overpowering her?

Luisa tilted her face up to the sky. Her body quivered as a new form burst from beneath her flesh, twisted and grew. Her skin thickened, turned black. The tentacles protruding from her back stretched and fanned out like wings. Kyra screamed as her sister's once angelic face turned into a bruised purple and her eyes bulged out from her sockets. Kyra no longer recognised her.

The monster who had once been Kyra's sister smiled.

Kyra had no choice but to flee. Jaedin grabbed her hand. Led her through the village. She tried to keep up but he was too fast. He almost yanked her shoulder out of its socket.

"Jaedin!" she gasped. "Slow down!"

"Sorry!" he mumbled.

She stared at Jaedin in disbelief. Not only did he just manage to drag her across her garden, but now, as they were fleeing for their lives, he was outpacing her.

Kyra saw movement in the corner of her eye. One of the corpses twitched.

"It's *moving*!" she gasped. "Oh my gods! Jaedin! What's happening?"

"I don't know!" Jaedin cried over his shoulder.

"Where are you taking me?!" Kyra asked.

"The others!" he yelled. "They're outside the Hall!"

Kyra brushed tears from her eyes. Something changed in her at that moment. She brushed away her anguish and fear too. Survival instinct took over.

As they approached the Hall, she caught sight of Baird and quickened her pace. Aylen, Rivan, and Miles were there too.

"My sister!" Kyra screamed when she reached them. Hot tears poured from her eyes. "My sister! She's–"

She stopped when she noticed one of the corpses was moving. A woman covered in blood. She rolled over and looked at Kyra with hallowed eyes.

All around them, more of the dead were beginning to stir.

"What do we do?" Rivan gasped, turning to Baird.

"They are Zakaras," Miles said. "You must kill them."

"Kill them?" Kyra repeated in disbelief.

She looked around them. Some of the corpses had risen to their feet and were staggering towards them. Many were missing limbs or had entrails dangling from their bodies, but they didn't seem to acknowledge they were in any pain. They slumped forward. One was just a head, torso and hands. He dragged his body through the dirt, caked in his own blood.

They all had familiar faces.

"They are already dead!" Miles yelled, his voice breaking from its usual composure. "These things are not your friends or family anymore!"

Kyra knew he was right. She'd just she watched her sister turn into a monster.

Kyra heard a rumble behind her and turned. The doors of the Hall burst open, and a humongous feline creature emerged from the opening. It opened its jaws, and a long, dark, tapered tongue stretched out of its mouth, darting towards Rivan. He ducked and rolled from its path, unleashing his sword as he righted himself, but the monster jerked its head and its tongue came hurtling towards him again. This time Rivan stood his ground and swung his blade at the appendage.

There was a flash of light; Kyra covered her eyes. When it was over, she turned to its source to see that Baird had summoned the shimmering, horned being again.

Baird charged at the Zakara, forming his new blades, the stone at his forehead glowing.

Kyra turned away. She did not see what happened next in that skirmish. She didn't have time to watch Baird.

The undead villagers were closing in.

"Rivan!" she yelled, nocking an arrow to her bow. "Help me! Baird can take care of himself!"

"Don't..." Sidry whispered. He was sitting on the grass a few feet away with a lost look in his eyes. It was like he had given up.

"We kill or we die!" Rivan concluded as he brandished his sword and raised it between himself and the villagers.

Aylen wiped the tears from his cheeks with the back of his hand and reached for his daggers.

Kyra's first arrow struck a villager through the chest, sending him falling back with arms flailing. More were advancing. One of them was only a few feet away; Rivan charged at her and ran his sword through her neck.

Kyra reached into her quiver for another arrow. The villagers began to tremble. She paused in dismay, choking on her breath as a terrible realisation hit her.

She knew what was happening. Both her sister and Shayam's men had done the same thing when they turned into Zakaras.

Rivan retreated, falling back beside her as the villagers twitched and contorted. Grew. Warped.

Aylen tried to take advantage of the situation and continued throwing his daggers, but they seemed to have little effect. The villagers his blades struck just fell to the ground and continued to shift form.

Baird appeared, charging to their aid. He circled the space around them, swinging his blades. He moved almost too fast for eyes to follow. A shimmering blur of light, followed by showers of blood and body parts dropping.

Baird held back most of the onslaught, but he was alone, and some of the monsters were slipping through the cracks. Kyra loosed more arrows, but most of her hits failed to impede them; the Zakaras just continued. Some of them didn't even seem to notice they had arrows stuck in them.

She heard a thud beside her. Jaedin had fallen to his knees.

"Jaedin!" she yelled. She crouched beside him and lifted his head. Gasped.

The scar on Jaedin's forehead had opened. A red stone shone from it. Crimson light. His eyes were glowing too.

Kyra then became aware that everyone else had turned silent. She looked about herself.

The monsters had stopped moving. They had frozen in mid-motion. As if time, for them, had paused.

Kyra, Rivan, and Aylen turned to each other and shared confused expressions.

Jaedin groaned and the light shining from his eyes faded. The Zakaras spurred back to life.

"What's happening to me?!" Jaedin gasped. He placed a hand to his chest and caught his breath.

"You can control them, Jaedin," Miles said, rushing to his side and placing a hand on his shoulder. "Don't fight it!"

"I *can't*!" Jaedin screamed.

The circle around them was becoming smaller, and there was no way out. Kyra got back to her feet and reached for an arrow. One of the Zakaras was dangerously close, so she shot at it, pierced its eye. The Zakara let out a coarse scream and fell back, clawing the air blindly.

A flash of blue light came from behind her. Kyra turned to see that Baird had changed back to his normal form.

"I can't hold them off!" Baird gasped, resting his hands on his knees. "Too many!"

Kyra looked at Jaedin. If what Miles was saying was true, Jaedin was their only hope of getting out of this situation alive. The crystal at his forehead was shimmering again. It glowed with the same kind of light as the one Shayam wielded in the Forest of Lareem.

"Focus, Jaedin!" Miles urged. "You can do it!"

"I don't know how!" he yelled back at his mentor.

"Jaedin!" Kyra screamed as she reloaded her bow. "They're going to *kill* us!"

Her arrow missed. The monsters were too close for ranged combat now, so Kyra dropped her bow and unleashed her sword. She knew that she wouldn't last long against these things, but if she was going to die, she would do it fighting.

She was just about to charge in when she heard a scream behind her. She turned to look.

144

It was Jaedin. He had risen to his feet. His eyes and the crystal at his forehead were glowing again, and his fists were clenched by his sides. Kyra could tell, from the look on his face, he was in pain.

But the monsters had halted again.

Jaedin's whole body shook with violent determination. The wound in his forehead widened. The crystal burned with light.

"What the fuck!" Rivan gasped. He looked from the circle of frozen monsters around them to Jaedin's glowing eyes.

"He's holding them off!" Miles explained, pointing at Jaedin. There was something about the mad joy in his eyes that Kyra found unsettling. "That's the Stone of Zakar! It's working!"

"I don't know how long I can do this!" Jaedin groaned between gritted teeth.

"We should run!" Baird decided and scanned the area around them. He pointed to a gap between all the frozen Zakaras. "There! Get up! Everyone! We need to go!"

"Where's Dion?" Kyra asked, realising he was missing.

Everyone turned to each other, dumbfounded.

"I think he went to his house..." Rivan responded.

"Then we'll get him!" Kyra said as she picked up her discarded bow.

"Kyra..." Jaedin gasped from beside her. "Dion... he's..."

She turned to him. Jaedin's face bore a grim expression. It was not just from the effort of holding the Zakaras at bay. He was trying to tell her something.

"No!" she shook her head before he could finish. *No! Not another one!*

She refused to believe it.

"Kyra," Jaedin uttered as he struggled to maintain control. "I saw it... but I was too late. I'm sorry..."

"You *what*?!" she screeched.

Jaedin opened his mouth to explain but his faltering attention caused the Zakaras around them to become disturbed. Some of them twitched. One of them began stumbling forward again, but Jaedin turned his glowing eyes to it and it halted.

"What do you mean you saw it? Why didn't you–" Kyra asked, but someone came up behind her and closed a hand around her mouth. It was Miles.

"Don't break his concentration!" he uttered into her ear. "Or we *all* die!"

"Kyra!" Baird roared. "We are leaving! *Now!*"

It was an order. And the urgency in Baird's voice snapped Kyra back into the reality of their dire situation. She nodded, feeling a heavy weight in her chest.

"Can you hold them off, Jaedin?" Baird asked.

"Not for long!" Jaedin whispered, shaking his head. "I think someone else is trying to control them!"

"Try," Baird said. "Can you keep that up while walking?"

"I don't know…"

Baird walked over, carefully placed his hands on Jaedin's shoulders, and began to guide him through a gap between the monsters. Kyra made to follow them but noticed Sidry still sat on the grass.

"Sidry!" she yelled.

At the sound of his name, Sidry slowly turned his head and looked at her. His eyes had lost their inner light and his face wore a resigned expression.

"Leave me here," he whispered. "I want to stay…"

"Gazareth's balls, you are!" Kyra screamed. She ran over and grabbed his arm. He was a dead weight and made no effort to help himself back to his feet.

"Get up and stop wasting time, you cavecrawling twat!" she yelled as she struggled to lift him. "I'd chop off my own hand before leaving another person to these fucking things! Even if it's just *you!*"

"Get up, you idiot!" Rivan roared as he appeared. He grabbed Sidry's other shoulder, and together, he and Kyra lifted him.

They escorted Sidry through the gap in the monsters. The Zakaras remained still, apart from the occasional twitch of their ghostly, confused eyes. They were so close Kyra could smell them. She gulped. If Jaedin lost his hold on them for a mere moment, they would all be killed instantly.

After creeping past the last monster, they broke into a run. Kyra breathed a sigh of relief as they built some distance between themselves and the creatures. It was not long until they were nearing the outskirts of the village.

* * *

Kyra ran. Her chest burned, and her legs became heavy, until each stride became agony. Her entire body cried out for her to stop, but she couldn't. Not when she knew what was behind her. She kept on with iron-willed determination.

Despite all the pain, she only began to comprehend just how much time had passed when she saw the dimming sky and realised the day was coming to an end. They had been running all this time but, somehow, it didn't feel that long ago since they escaped the horrors of Jalard.

Aylen was the first to collapse. He fell onto the soft ground of the meadow, and the others followed suit, falling and burying their fists into the grass. Breathless and traumatised.

"That's enough," Baird announced.

Kyra looked over her shoulder. They had run so far that she couldn't even see Jalard anymore. It had disappeared. It was a memory.

And then she saw Miles. His head and shoulders appeared as he crested the hill and finally caught up with them. The scholar had lagged behind the rest of them the entire way.

Their eyes met. The sight of the traitor following at their heels, as if he was one of them, made Kyra's blood stir.

She squared up to him and drew a dagger to his neck.

"Tell me why I shouldn't slit your throat you cavecrawling cunt!" she challenged through gritted teeth. "Tell me!"

The pupils of Miles' eyes dilated. The point of Kyra's blade had already drawn a bead of blood. Her hand shook with the temptation to do away with him. With just a flick of her wrist, she could put him out of her misery.

"Kyra!" Baird yelled from behind her. "No!"

But not even Baird's commanding voice would quell Kyra's anger.

"It's his fault!" she screamed. "*He* did this to us!"

"No Kyra!" Jaedin appeared beside her. "He didn't know!"

"He didn't warn us and now everyone's dead!" she moaned.

"Miles would never do this! My mother was there! Please, Kyra!" Jaedin cried. "Just put the knife down!"

The sight of her friend in tears made Kyra's conviction falter. She stared at Miles, and she could see sorrow in his eyes. A resigned acceptance.

But no guilt.

Kyra realised she believed it. She didn't want to, but she did.

It would be much easier for her to just kill him. It would make her feel better for a moment, but she couldn't bring herself to do it.

She withdrew the blade from his neck.

"Don't speak to me!" she hissed when he opened his mouth to say something. She pointed the dagger to his face "Don't look at me. Don't even breathe the same air as me."

He looked down.

"If you ever lie, or cause harm to me or anyone else I know ever again, I'll kill you," she promised and stepped away.

Kyra always thought that anger was a state of mind, but now she knew different. It was visceral. She could feel its manifestation in every part of her body. A stabbing pain in her chest. A pang in her heart. A burning in the pit of her stomach. The way she was clenching her jaw so hard that her teeth were grinding. She could feel it in the tightening of her every muscle.

She brought the dagger to her arm and drew its edge across her skin. Blood ran. A ragged gasp ran from the group as they saw what she was doing. "I will find who is responsible," she whispered through trembling lips and watering eyes. "And I will kill them."

She drew the dagger across her forearm again, making another cut. It was strange. She could barely feel it as it bore through her flesh. And she wanted to feel *something*. Anything different to what she was feeling now. "Shayam. Grav'aen. All those Gavendarian cunts responsible for what has happened. I will not rest until they are all dead!" she vowed.

And then, as she drew her own blood one last time, she added.

"I swear it. On my blood."

A hand grabbed hold of her wrist. Kyra looked up. It was Baird. His expression was stern. It tore into her soul.

She let go of the dagger.

*   *   *

While Jaedin treated Kyra's wounds, she barely seemed to

notice his presence. She just sat with a haunted expression. The only movement she made was the occasional shudder.

Jaedin applied a salve of herbs. It would help her arm heal and stop it from becoming infected, but he knew her arm would most likely scar. There was nothing he could do about that. He wrapped a bandage around it, and while he did it, he thought about what Kyra had just done. The implications.

Kyra had just made a *bloodoath*.

Everyone from Jalard knew what a bloodoath was. Legendary characters in tales they were told as children often made such pacts with the gods. By drawing one's own blood whilst speaking a vow, people became 'Bloodsworn'.

And in every tale where the oath was broken, the ending was always the same. The Bloodsworn died.

Most of the other villagers probably thought bloodoaths nothing more than a myth, but they feared it just enough to never try it. Jaedin had never known anyone who had made a pact before, so he wasn't sure how much truth there was to the legends.

But one thing Jaedin did know, was that his mother, Meredith, had sternly warned him against ever making a bloodoath.

And Jaedin's mother had always been rather scathing about the 'petty superstitions' many of the villagers had.

Once Jaedin finished tending to Kyra, he rubbed her shoulder for a while to comfort her, but she ignored him.

Jaedin looked around him. Most of the others were in a similar state to Kyra. They sat quietly. They didn't even look at each other. None of them spoke. There were no appropriate words for what they had just experienced.

Sidry, in particular, was in such a sorry state it seemed he was dead to the world. He just stared up at the sky. Only the weak expanding and contracting of his chest was reassurance he still breathed.

Jaedin only felt a vague sense of despair. He was strangely numb to emotion. Nothing that happened seemed real to him yet. It had not quite sunk in.

When Baird finished building a fire, he asked Jaedin to brew a potion which would help them sleep. Jaedin obeyed silently, opening the bag his mother packed for him and searching for some garanwort.

When he found it, he crawled over to the fire and brewed the concoction. Baird had already suspended a pot of water over the flames.

Once it was finished, Baird made each of them drink the mixture. None of them had the strength to argue. Some of them did not even have the will to hold the cup to their lips, but Baird did it for them. They were all forced to drink.

* * *

Jaedin woke a bit earlier than the others. While the sun was still rising. He was confused for a while when he saw all the others sprawled out on the grass nearby but then, with a sinking heart, he remembered the events of the previous day.

He got up and walked down the hill. He wanted to be alone. He sat and stared into the distance, thinking about everything that had just happened. It still didn't feel real to him.

He reached into his pocket for the last remaining slither of a tunic he had used to make bandages the night before and placed it upon his forehead, so it covered the scar. He tucked the two other ends of it under his long curtains of hair and tied it around the back.

It was a simple thing, but it felt cathartic. It marked a transition in his life. He had a terrible feeling he had not seen the last of Shayam or the Zakaras, and he didn't want people to see the scar. Or the crystal, if he was ever forced to use its powers again.

When he had finished tying the second knot, Jaedin noticed a dark shape below him, crawling up the hill. He looked down, his eyes focussing.

Jaedin gasped when he recognised who it was. He leapt to his feet.

When he reached her, she collapsed into his arms and caught her breath. "I told you I would find you, Jaedin," she whispered into his ear as they embraced. "We are connected."

Jaedin stared at her, barely believing his eyes.

It was Bryna.

Chapter 10

The Journey Begins

"Jaedin! Get away from her!" Baird exclaimed when he saw them.

The twins jumped at the sound of his voice and looked up at him like a pair of terrified mice.

"Why?" Jaedin asked.

"Jaedin!" Baird repeated, adopting a sterner tone of voice. "Step away from her *now*!"

It was an order. It had taken years of leadership for Baird to perfect that tone, and it was rare someone had the gall to disobey it, but the blind love for the thing Jaedin seemed convinced was his sister prevailed, and he held onto her.

Baird considered his next action carefully. A few days ago, he would not have greatly cared about Jaedin's life. For he had always been a feeble, useless boy. Baird had heard, from the mouths of others, that Jaedin was intelligent – how else would he have been Chosen for the Academy? – and there was a certain kind of intelligence Baird appreciated because it made better warriors, but Jaedin's acumen was not of any form useful in the field. And he had never shown any interest in the arts of combat.

Jaedin had always been a hindrance to him. Baird strived to achieve his challenges. If he was set a task, he met it with precision. His task in Jalard was to mould its youths into the most apt warriors possible, and one feeble young man who barely had the strength to hold a sword, let alone wield it, was, to him, a failure.

But after seeing what Jaedin could do yesterday, this feeble young man held new value. Baird had just spent the entire night considering the odds of their survival if they were attacked again. Premeditating the likelihood of them all reaching Shemet with Shayam in pursuit. He even pondered a rough calculation of how Sharma's defences would fare against a Gavendarian invasion aided by Zakaras, and Shemet defending itself from an army of those beasts crossing the northern border.

Many scenarios ran through his mind and, in all of them, this feeble young man from Jalard – his failure – held a crucial role.

The bitter irony vexed him. Why couldn't the Stone of Zakar have been fused to Rivan, or someone else more worthy? What kind of sick joke were the gods playing on the world?

"She's my sister!" Jaedin said.

"We don't know that yet!" Baird said.

Baird studied the girl. She resembled Bryna, but Baird analysed her every detail, searching for any which would indicate she was no longer human.

She had not done anything suspicious so far. She hadn't spoken a word, but she had always been a quiet girl. She was the stranger half of Jalard's outlandish twins. Her skin was pale – almost unnaturally so – and her black hair had a peculiar purple hue which matched the unique colour of her eyes. She had a haunted expression on her face, but that was no different to the other people around him who had survived yesterday's horror. None of them were ready to face the world yet. The things they had seen were too harrowing.

It was too bad they had no choice.

Baird felt some remorse for what had just happened, but it was numbed. He wasn't from Jalard. He had never come to think of it as 'home'. His experiences during the War of Ashes hardened him; he had witnessed comrades die, civilians slaughtered. He'd seen villages burnt to their very foundations.

Baird had not just lost his entire family, like these kids had. Baird had never even had a family, so the idea of it was somewhat alien to him. He was an orphan, raised within the Academy itself, and it had therefore never been instilled into his nature to get too attached to people.

He felt a sense of loss over the fate which befell a village in which he had dwelt for the last ten years, but Baird learnt long ago to deal with grief by concentrating on his goals. He was no longer teaching youngsters to wield swords – they were fighting for survival – and, unless Baird stayed focussed, they would be the next to die.

He was not going to let that happen.

Kyra appeared, next to Baird. "Bryna…" she whispered in disbelief.

Baird turned to Kyra in surprise. It was the first time her lips had uttered a single word since she made that bloodoath the previous day.

"Stay back Kyra," Baird said, blocking her path. "She might be one of them."

Baird got no joy out of crushing Kyra's newfound sense of hope, but he needed to put her safety first.

Kyra seemed to listen to him. She stopped, and eyed Bryna suspiciously. This was good news to Baird. It seemed Kyra's sense of reason was not completely lost.

"She's not!" Jaedin said.

"We can't be sure, Jaedin!" Baird said.

"I *know* she isn't!" Jaedin replied. He pointed to his forehead. "I can sense Zakaras. And she *isn't* one of them."

Baird considered this. He had no idea how Jaedin's new powers worked. He had only seen their application the first time a day ago. Could the boy really sense them? As well as control them?

"What about yesterday?!" Baird realised, feeling a wave of fury. "Why didn't you warn us?"

"I didn't know how to back then..." Jaedin mumbled, his voice laden with much regret.

"How can you be sure now?" Baird asked.

"Stop it!" Jaedin cried. "I just *know*."

Baird turned his eyes back to the young woman next to Jaedin. She had still not spoken for herself.

If she was a Zakara, she could have killed him by now... Baird realised. *But that could just be a ruse... A plot to gain our trust, so it can maximise damage to the whole group...*

Baird pondered whether he should trust Jaedin. The young man had always been cowardly, so it seemed very plausible he could be convincing himself that thing was his real sister because he couldn't bear to accept a grim truth.

"How did you survive, Bryna?" Baird said, shifting his focus back to her.

Bryna met his gaze but then turned away. She opened her mouth to speak but nothing came.

"I will ask again," Baird said, adopting a sterner tone. "How did you survive the attack on the village, Bryna?"

She turned her eyes down to her feet.

"Leave her alone," Jaedin put an arm around her. "Can't

you see she's been through enough?"

But she might be a Zakara! Baird thought. What were the chances that the one survivor of a massacre was this cowering young woman before him? Baird had heard she was Blessed, but was she really strong enough to outstand Zakaras?

"Bryna…" Kyra whispered. "Is it really *you*?"

Kyra walked to Bryna. This time Baird didn't stop her, but he watched warily as the two friends reunited. They shared a warm embrace.

What else could Baird do? He could scarcely send Bryna away into the wilderness just because of his suspicions. Jaedin had personally vouched for her.

As moments passed, and nothing of alarm occurred, Baird relaxed a little.

So… we have another survivor… he mused, and his mind began to ponder the ramifications of this. Kyra and Jaedin both had a new light in their eyes. Baird realised this turn of events was good for morale. To them, Bryna's survival was a glimmer of hope they had found in the darkness.

Despite this, Baird couldn't help but worry. Jaedin was inevitably going to slow them down already and, like him, Bryna didn't have any survival skills or know how to fend for herself. Baird was of the understanding she had been given some training in the arts of healing from her mother, but he wasn't sure how extensive they were. Or even how useful they would be in their situation; if they were overcome by Zakaras, chances were they would all be dead anyway. *She's going to be a burden…* Baird thought. *But she's **your** burden now, so you'll just have to make do. Pull yourself together, Baird. These people need you.*

*   *   *

After an arduous day of marching under the hot glare of the sun, Baird finally called for a stop in the afternoon and told Rivan, Sidry and Kyra to hunt for something to eat while the rest of them set up camp.

It was clear that Kyra and Sidry were still shell-shocked and lacked the resolve – the thought that they even needed to eat had probably not even occurred to them – but it had been ingrained into them from a young age that when Baird gave you an order, it was wise to carry it out, so they reached for their bows and made their way into the woodland.

Rivan, however, was eager. He welcomed any task he was given. It helped keep his mind away from his grief. Besides, he had not eaten a proper meal for over two days, and his belly was growling.

As he crept silently through the trees, with his bow in hand, he did begin to worry about his friend though. The three of them had split up – as they were more likely to catch something that way – but Rivan realised in hindsight that it may have not been so wise to let Sidry be on his own yet. Since they escaped Jalard, Rivan had not left his friend's side once, until now. Nothing he did or said consoled him.

Rivan seemed to be coping much fairer than the others. He was suffering, but not to the same extent they were. He did mourn. He had liked and loved many people from Jalard and, even though he had never been close to his parents, it had been surprisingly heart-wrenching to find them dead; the truth that Rivan could barely admit to himself, let alone anyone else, was that a part of him had always craved excitement and adventure, and now – in a very twisted way – his dreams had come true. His quiet beginnings in a humble village were over. He had slain monsters. Most of his friends and family were dead. They were on the run.

And he had never felt so alive in his life.

After initially worrying if this meant he was heartless, Rivan was pushing guilt aside. He was trying to be pragmatic. What happened had been and gone, and the most important thing now was the survival of himself and his friends. And to do that he needed to keep his mind in the present.

He heard something rustle; he pricked his ears and shifted his head. It was coming from about twenty paces away. A thicket was obstructing whatever it was from view though, so Rivan crept silently to avoid alerting his prey, nocking an arrow to his bow.

But then he heard Sidry's voice.

"Dion?"

Silent approach was abandoned. Rivan rushed to find his friend. Sidry had not spoken much sense over the last two days, but why would he call out the name of one of their deceased friends? Had he lost his sanity?

Rivan caught sight of Sidry's wavy blond hair between the branches of trees and raced over to him. When he reached him, he saw something else in the clearing which made him question his own sanity.

Dion stood before them.

"I found you!" Dion said. "See! I told you my tracking wasn't that bad."

Rivan blinked several times, but he still stood there.

Sidry took a step forward, but Rivan grabbed his shoulder and pulled him back. "No! Stay back!"

"What's going on, guys?" Dion asked. "Chill out. It's me."

"I'm sorry, Dion," Rivan said as he raised his bow and pointed an arrow at his friend. "But we can't be sure you're not... one of them."

Dion seemed mildly shocked, at first, but then his mouth curved into a smile.

"You're scitting me, right?"

Rivan shook his head grimly.

"Chill out Reev," Dion said, holding out his open palms. Rivan noted that he wasn't armed and he was still wearing the same clothes from last time they saw him, only bloodstained and torn. "It's me. Dion."

"Bryna survived," Sidry whispered. "Dion could have as well?"

Rivan ignored his friend. He was still in trauma. He wasn't capable of making rational decisions.

Dion took a step forward.

"Stay back!" Rivan yelled, pulling the arrow back so that it flexed the cord of his bow. "I'm sorry, Dion, but we can't take any chances. Jaedin said you were dead."

"You're listening to *him* now? What's wrong with you? You always said he was a useless sodd," Dion smirked.

Something didn't quite ring true about that statement coming from Dion. Rivan could vividly remember a conversation they once had where Dion admitted that he did not have anything against sodds. *Why would I care what they get up to?* he had said, as he raised his shoulders. *If they want to hump at each other, it just means there's more girlies for me!*

They were interrupted by a disturbance a few feet away. Rivan turned to the source and saw Kyra emerge from the trees. She froze, and her jaw dropped open at the sight of Dion. A small deer cradled in her arms – the prize of her hunt – fell to the ground with a thud.

"Kyra…" Dion implored her. "Tell them it's me… you know it's me, right?"

"Dion…" Kyra whispered. She stared at him as if she could barely believe her eyes.

She walked to him.

"Kyra!" Rivan called. "Stay back! We don't know what he is."

But she ignored him and carried on walking.

"I am so glad we are alive, Kyra," Dion said as she drew near.

Kyra smiled.

"I thought I had lost you," Dion said, opening up his arms to embrace her.

Rivan noticed that Kyra was holding a dagger behind her back. Before he had time to shout a warning, there was a flash of steel, followed by red.

Dion flopped to the ground, flesh hanging out from his throat and blood rushing. Rivan raced towards them and grabbed Kyra's wrist.

"What the fuck are you doing?!" he shouted, forcing back a compulsion to hit her across the face.

"He's one of *them*!" she yelled.

"We didn't know that yet!" Rivan screamed.

She clenched her jaw. He could see a well of emotions in her eyes; too overwhelming for her to control. A tear welled out from one of them and rolled down her cheek.

Rivan knew Kyra had only done what she thought best, but that could have been the *real* Dion she just killed!

"That wasn't Dion…" her voice croaked. "I could see it in his eyes."

Rivan wanted to argue further, but he couldn't find the words. They should have reached a decision together. Not brashly acted on gut instinct.

"Err, Rivan…" Sidry said, pointing to the ground behind them.

Rivan and Kyra both turned and gasped simultaneously.

Dion had vanished, and only a patch of blood remained where his body had been.

* * *

Jaedin looked up when Kyra returned from the hunt. She had a small deer slung over her shoulders and wretchedness in her eyes. It was clear, from her posture and the air which surrounded her, that something terrible had just happened.

"Are you okay?" he asked.

She ignored him, dropped the deer onto the grass, and began to skin it.

Jaedin's suspicions were confirmed when Rivan and Sidry arrived a few minutes later and informed the group about the incident with Dion. Baird listened to their stories gravely and motioned that extra care was to be taken during the watch that night. Everyone was instructed to sleep in their clothes in case of a sudden awakening.

The incident caused Jaedin much worry, for he had not sensed it coming. Wasn't it just a day ago he had felt all the Zakaras in Jalard come alive? That he had controlled them? Why had he not sensed Dion?

Jaedin hoped that it was because Dion had been out of his range – whatever his 'range' was – but it did make him wonder how quickly he would be able to warn the others if they were ever in danger again.

He considered relaying his worries to Miles, who had always been someone he could talk to about his anxieties without reprisal or judgement, but Jaedin no longer trusted his former mentor. Jaedin could not talk to any of the others about it because he feared they would react badly and Baird might start suspecting his sister again if he knew he was having doubts over his ability to detect Zakaras.

Once the deer was cooked, they sat around the fire and ate in silence. Jaedin thought he would never be able to stomach food again when they escaped Jalard, but was surprised – and slightly guilty – when his insides were very welcoming to his first proper meal for days. Afterwards, Jaedin once again tried to comfort Kyra, but she shrugged him away. It was the third time she had rejected his company since they had escaped from Jalard, but Jaedin had seen her talking to his sister a few times. It made him jealous. It felt like his best friend and his sister were excluding him – even if Kyra's conversations with Bryna were a bit one-sided. It sank Jaedin's heart to accept the truth, but he suspected the real reason Kyra was distancing herself from him was that a part of her blamed him for Dion's death. For not learning to use his power quick enough to save him.

She and Aylen were keeping the first watch that night, so Jaedin left her by the fire and retreated to his tent. Baird never placed Jaedin or Bryna on watch duty. Jaedin didn't know whether to feel insulted or relieved.

He entered the tent that he and Bryna shared and found his sister meditating. She often did this. Their mother taught them and, for Bryna, it was especially important to keep her mind clear so she could control her powers.

"Bryna…" he whispered and tapped her shoulder.

She opened her eyes.

"What happened to you at the village?" he asked.

She turned away.

"Bryna… please… tell me," he pleaded.

She smiled faintly and placed a hand upon his.

How can she smile like that? he thought. *After all we've been through?*

Her hand felt cold. Unnaturally cold. But she wasn't shivering.

Jaedin worried about her. Baird and the others believed she would not speak because she was traumatised, but he knew better. Something about her had changed. He was surprised no one else had noticed it.

He looked into her eyes. He no longer recognised them. He used to be able to read Bryna's thoughts through her eyes, but now he only saw flickers of things which scared him.

"What happened to you, Bryna?" he asked. "You have changed. I can feel it."

It was as if she carried a great darkness with her. He wished she was not so reluctant to share it.

She brought a finger to her lips. Behind it was a smile that chilled him to the bone.

"Don't be scared, Jaedin. I will protect you."

* * *

At sunrise, Jaedin was awoken by Baird. They packed away the tents and, after a quick breakfast eaten in silence, continued with their journey.

Baird marched at the head of the group. He was alert – constantly craning his neck from side to side to scan their surroundings – and there was a tone of urgency behind everything he said as he yelled orders at them. The little breaks he allowed them were brief.

They certainly had much to fear. Dion was undoubtedly a Zakara, and the fact that he tracked them down once meant he could likely do it again. It made Jaedin wonder if Shayam was aware of their location too.

Everyone felt the pressure Baird placed upon them, but it seemed most were obeying his orders not because they shared his sense of urgency, but rather because they had no will to argue. Last night, Baird had to force Sidry to eat. Jaedin was beginning to wonder whether the boy's mind had been permanently damaged from what he had been through. Aylen had taken it upon himself to look after Sidry and never left his side, but it was obvious he was suffering too.

The only member of the group who seemed to be coping was Rivan. Baird had even entrusted him with the task of covering their backs. He was just as alert as Baird. He kept stopping to scan their surroundings whenever he heard the slightest sound.

Kyra walked alone. You could see the tension in her body in the way she marched. She still accepted the comfort of no-one but Bryna, and any attempts at conversation were spurned.

But the one who disturbed Jaedin most was still his sister, walking beside him. She didn't seem traumatised, like the others, only distracted. She strolled along in a manner one would on a leisurely day out walking along the hills, but Jaedin could tell something was on her mind.

Later in the afternoon, Jaedin felt a tingling sensation in his forehead and drew to a halt.

"I can feel something…" Jaedin said. He closed his eyes. "I think there are Zakaras nearby."

"Where are they?" Rivan asked.

"I don't know yet…" Jaedin uttered. "It doesn't work like that."

"How *does* it work then?"

"Give me a moment!" Jaedin snapped. "And I will *try* to find out."

Rivan said something else, but Jaedin blotted out his voice. He closed his eyes. Focussed. The crystal in his forehead began to hum. He listened. Tuned in to its energy.

Jaedin's mind was suddenly engulfed in a furore of sensations. Fleeting images flashed through his consciousness. He saw a terrain of green hills rolling by. The Zakaras bounded towards their prey. He felt their hunger.

Jaedin tried to assimilate his mind with them – like he had done back in Jalard – but something was blocking him. He felt the presence of another. Shayam. *He* was their overlord. He was fully immersed within their minds. Controlling them. There was no space for Jaedin to interfere.

"They are coming from that way," Jaedin said, pointing as he opened his eyes to a hillock covered with trees.

Rivan and Kyra reached for their weapons.

"There are three," Jaedin added.

"Just three?" Baird said. He smiled to himself and marched to face them.

There was a flash of light. Jaedin covered his eyes but peered through the cracks between his fingers. He saw Baird as a dark shadow in the centre of bright, radiant light, his limbs stretching and moulding into a new shape.

The light ceased, and where Baird had been now stood a being over eight feet tall and glimmering. Jaedin took in its magnificence. Its shining armour. The three horns protruding from its head. Jaedin remembered Miles saying that the crystal they had fused Baird with was from the temple of Gezra. He wondered what he would find if he looked up a description of this deity. Could it be that Baird was now an avatar of Gezra himself?

Jaedin was pulled out of these thoughts when three figures leapt out from behind the trees. Kyra nocked her bow. Baird charged at them.

"Jaedin!" Miles urged. "Help him!"

Jaedin nodded at his old mentor and focussed on attuning his mind with the crystal in his forehead again. It had already become activated by the proximity of the Zakaras. The power was still strange to him. It was not like drawing upon his magic. The energy he used when he controlled Zakaras was not *viga*; it was not his own. It felt alien to him.

Jaedin directed his will upon the Zakaras – tried to still them, make them stop – but Shayam's will was strong, and he had a firm hold upon his creatures. Jaedin struggled to overcome it.

As Jaedin battled with Shayam, he watched Baird face off the incoming Zakaras. Baird summoned his blade, and his arm reshaped itself. The first Zakara leapt at him. He sidestepped. The creature twisted around and leapt again but Baird met it with his blade. It shrieked. Drew back.

Baird was just raising his blade when Shayam's walls crumbled, and Jaedin tumbled into the minds of his creatures.

"I've got them," Jaedin announced as he assumed control of their consciousness. The Zakaras froze. Jaedin held them there.

Shayam was already fighting back for control. His willing for the Zakaras to attack and kill conflicted with Jaedin's efforts to restrain them. The creatures began to tremble. They were confused.

Jaedin clenched his fists. Focussed all his will. He had the upper hand, for now.

Meanwhile, Baird squared up to one of the inert monsters. He raised his arm and brought it down upon its neck but, as soon as his blade bore through its flesh, green liquid erupted from the opening and the action became obscured by smoke.

There was a sizzling sound, like burning grass. Baird backed away. He held his blade-arm to his face and it melted in a cloud of grey fog. Everyone gasped. Within moments, Baird's arm was no more than a stump, and the grass around the felled Zakara was burning.

"What's happening?" Jaedin asked.

"The blood is melting his arm! It's corrosive!" Miles realised.

Jaedin gulped as he watched the ground around the monster's corpse turn black. How many of those things could Baird defeat before his weapons withered away to nothing?

One of the two remaining Zakaras came for Baird, swiping its claws, and Baird recovered just in time to dive out of its way.

Jaedin felt a hand on his shoulder.

"Stop staring and *do* something!" Rivan roared as he shook him.

Jaedin turned his attention back to the skirmish, cursing himself for getting distracted. *Only two left,* he thought, *this should be easy...*

He called on the power of the crystal again. Baird was on the ground now. One of the Zakaras was preparing to leap at him. Jaedin strained to control it. Pushed with all his will.

Jaedin managed to draw the creatures to a halt again, but Shayam fought back. The Zakaras quivered.

Baird rose to his feet, smoothing his remaining left arm into another blade.

Jaedin didn't manage to see what happened next. He suddenly became aware of a presence beside him. At first, he thought it was another Zakara, but it was a distinctly different sensation.

It reminded Jaedin of the time he performed the *psycalesse* upon Miles. But in reverse. Someone was tugging upon *his psysona.* Trying to enter his mind.

Jaedin drew upon his *viga,* awakened his magical senses.

What are you? he called out to the being.

But Jaedin felt his grip upon the Stone of Zakar slipping. Activating his *viga* to perform Psymancy took Jaedin's focus away from the Zakaras. He realised it was not going to be possible for him to concentrate on both at the same time. He struggled. He didn't know what to do. Baird was wounded. He needed his help.

Jaedin turned to Miles, but his former mentor was staring at the ongoing fight before him and did not notice Jaedin's plight. Jaedin opened his mouth to cry out, but the person who had entered his mind seized control of his vocal cords.

You will stop. Now! a voice reverberated through Jaedin's mind. It was male.

Jaedin summoned all of his *viga* and cast a beam of energy at the psychic attacker to try to push them away, but it dissipated, and Jaedin felt the barriers of his mind crumble as his physical body dropped to the ground.

*   *   *

"What the fuck is he *doing*?" Rivan roared.

Miles grabbed Jaedin by the shoulders and turned him over. His eyes were closed. He had lost consciousness.

Miles face wrinkled into a frown. "I don't know…"

Rivan snarled. He was not at all surprised. *Of all times he could choose to faint!* he thought, bitterly angry.

He cursed and turned his attention back to the fight so he could analyse the situation.

There were two Zakaras left. One of them was a similar creature to one they encountered in Shayam's base in the forest; it had a gangling, myriapod body with several long tentacles for limbs. But Rivan was much more worried about the monster on the other side of Baird: its paunchy, dark form was covered in a thin layer of yellow fuzz, and it looked remarkably similar to the one that Baird had just felled at the cost of his arm. Did it also have acidic blood coursing through its veins? The kind which dissolved Baird's armour?

The myriapod flexed its tentacles. Baird fled, but one of the appendages caught hold of his leg and he toppled over, his body dropping with a massive thud. Another five tentacles soon followed, coiling around his arms, and Baird struggled as the beast tightened its limbs.

Rivan gripped the hilt of his sword, considering whether charging in to help would be an act of suicide.

He was interrupted from these thoughts when Kyra loosed an arrow. It pierced one of the Zakara's tentacles, and the creature shrieked. Baird managed to free himself. He leapt back to his feet; charged at the other Zakara with his blade-arm raised high. Before the monster knew what was coming, the weapon flashed towards its head. The creature tried to duck but was too slow. Baird's blade tore into its shoulder, and the air was filled with an abominable wail.

Rivan's heart sank when he saw smoke. It was as he feared; this beast had the same corrosive blood which seemed to dissolve anything it touched.

Baird lifted his one remaining arm. The blade was melting away. Soon, it would also be just another withered stump.

Baird turned the narrow slits which were his eyes back upon the beast and struck, making one last fatal blow before his blade-arm was gone. The Zakara had no chance to react. Baird's blade cleaved its head clear from its body.

Green blood pulsed from its neck. Baird tried to retreat but was too late. His head and upper body were already covered in the corrosive ichor and layers of his glimmering armour melted away. He clutched his head. He didn't make a sound, for he had no mouth, but to Rivan it appeared his mentor was in agony.

As Baird fell to his knees, the remaining Zakara wrapped two of its tentacles around his arms.

Rivan forgot about the danger. Instinct took over. He ran in to aid his mentor. Kyra appeared beside him. They charged, side by side. Rivan watched the cloud of smoke billowing around his mentor, wondering if the acid would get past his armour and kill the real Baird beneath.

When they reached the scene, the Zakara still had its tentacles wrapped around Baird's arms. Rivan dived in and hammered his blade on them. The hilt jilted in his palms as it met the tough tendrils of flesh, but he drove down with all his might until they snapped.

The beast fell back, and its dismembered limbs dropped to the grass like a family of dead snakes.

Baird collapsed. There was a flicker of light and, when it was over, he was human again.

Rivan rushed to him, scanning his mentor for injuries and noting with some relief that his body seemed to be intact.

"Lift him," Kyra yelled, reaching down and grabbing one of Baird's shoulders. Rivan gripped him from the other side, and they hauled him to his feet. They carried his heavy weight down the hill and dropped him to the ground next to Jaedin.

"Make one of your shields!" Rivan shouted at Miles, and the scholar began to summon grey energy from his palms.

While Miles cast the shields, Rivan turned around to check on the last Zakara. It was back on its feet, but only two of its tentacles remained. The stumps, where the others used to be, quivered.

Rivan then noticed Kyra running towards it. He cursed.

She had rushed back in to challenge it alone.

"Kyra! Get back!" he yelled, but he knew he was too late. It was a brash and foolish move, but Kyra had always been impulsive. She would never back down now. She was too stubborn.

The monster's two remaining tentacles jutted out towards her. She ducked from the first and swung her blade at the second, but missed.

The monster's tentacles then closed in on her from each side. She tried to brace herself but was too late. The impact knocked her sword out of her hand.

No sooner had her weapon fallen, the other tentacle wrapped around her waist. The monster reeled her in. She reached for the rubbery limb and tried to prise herself free, but her efforts were useless. She struggled as her feet were lifted from the ground, biting down upon her lip. Rivan recognised that habit; she always did that when she wanted to stop herself from screaming.

The Zakara pulled Kyra in closer, toward its gaping mouth lined with yellow teeth. Another tentacle coiled around her neck.

Something changed within Rivan at that moment. He wanted to help her. He drew his sword. He was about to charge to her aid, but a voice stopped him.

"I wouldn't do that if I were you..."

Rivan looked for the voice and saw Dion leaning against a tree several yards behind Kyra and the monster.

This time the Zakara which had taken over Dion's body was not even pretending to be the real Dion. The look in his eyes was austere and menacing. It had Dion's voice, but the tone and pronunciation were utterly wrong.

"You see..." Dion said. He clicked his fingers, and the other Zakara tightened its tentacle around Kyra's neck. She gargled for breath. Squirmed against its scaly body.

"If you come one step closer, my servant here will rip her head off."

Rivan trembled with anger. He looked at Kyra as she struggled for breath and, to his utter disbelief, he was *concerned* for her.

The girl he had loathed his entire life had turned into his comrade. When did that happen?

Rivan wanted nothing more, during that moment, but to slaughter the being which had the guile to impersonate his friend.

But he couldn't risk Kyra's life for that.

"We will leave you now..." Dion said, turning away. "But don't worry, you will see us again. Very soon."

Chapter 11

Close Your Mind

Jaedin was disturbed from sleep by a damp cloth smothering his forehead. When he opened his eyes, his sister was looking down on him.

"He's awake," she announced to the others.

Jaedin sat up. It was dusk, and the sky was red and dimming. He was surrounded by pitched tents, and there was a fire burning a few yards away.

Everyone was staring at him.

"Take this, Jaedin," Bryna whispered into his ear as she placed a steaming cup into his hand.

He took a sip of his sister's concoction. It tasted vile, and he could not recognise any of the ingredients by taste, but Bryna's knowledge on herbs surpassed his own by far so he trusted it would help clear his head.

"What happened to you?"

Jaedin knew that was Rivan's voice from the deprecating tone before he even turned to face him. He was scowling.

"Baird!" Jaedin exclaimed as post-sleep delirium ended and he remembered his last conscious moments. He looked around but couldn't see their leader. "Where is he? Is he okay?"

"No thanks to you..." Rivan muttered.

"Why can't you *ever* just shut the fuck up!?" Jaedin snapped and threw the steaming cup in a wave of fury. The contents splashed across the fire, making it sizzle. "You don't have any fucking idea what I just went through!"

Even Rivan was taken aback by Jaedin's outburst. It wasn't often he lost his temper.

"At least I've been *trying*! Which is better than your two cronies here," Jaedin pointed to Sidry and Aylen. "What did *they* do to help?"

Sidry and Aylen shifted uncomfortably.

Someone tapped his shoulder. He looked and met his sister's eyes. She handed him a new cup of her potion. He was sorry for dropping the last one in his rage, but he didn't need to say it. Bryna knew.

"I think that is enough blaming for today..." Baird said, and all eyes turned to him as he emerged from the shadows, carrying a stack of firewood under his arm.

Everyone shifted guiltily. Their leader had just returned.

Baird placed the wood next to the fire and sat at the head of the circle.

"But you still owe us an explanation..." Baird said to Jaedin.

Jaedin hesitated. How could he explain when even *he* wasn't quite sure what had happened?

He scanned the faces sat around the fire. They read as hostile, confused, scared. They had questions to which they yearned for answers.

There was one exception. Miles. The traitor. Unlike the others, his eyes were warm and understanding. Despite everything, years of habit took over, and Jaedin turned to his mentor for support.

"Miles..." he began and paused as he tried to find the right words. "I think someone attacked me... not physically. They attacked my mind. It felt strange. It was like the time we *psycalessed*. But someone else was in *my* head."

He saw recognition in his mentors' eyes, but he could tell that everyone else around them was baffled.

"I know, Jaedin," Miles replied gravely. "It's just as I feared..."

"Feared?" Baird repeated, turning to Miles.

Miles was quiet for a few moments, which Jaedin guessed was him taking time to think of a way to explain something arcane to the uninitiated.

"I mentioned before that Shayam's leader, Grav'aen, is a remarkable Psymancer," Miles began. "I believe he has been targeting Jaedin."

Even Jaedin was surprised at learning the identity of his psychic attacker. He cringed at the memory of experiencing another person probing his *psysona* and invading his consciousness.

"He targeted Jaedin..." Baird considered. "Does this mean he can do it to any of us? At any time?" he asked.

"Hard to say, really..." Miles pondered. "What we just experienced was a systematic attack: Shayam attacked us with Zakaras while Grav'aen attacked Jaedin psychically to lower our defences. But, for him to attack Jaedin today, from all the way in Gavendara, means that he must have *psyseered*. '*Psyseering*', for those of you who are not aware, is a Psymancer technique where the magician leaves their body behind and projects their *psysona* to reach other places and people. Gavendara is a long way away, so this would have been draining, even for him. I can imagine he would need time to recover his *viga* before it was possible for him to make another such attack."

"How long?" Baird pressed.

"It is hard to say…" Miles pondered. "A couple of days, I would guess."

"But he can turn on any one of us again after that…" Baird thought out loud as he stared at the flames.

Miles shook his head. "A person needs to be Blessed to be open to the attack of someone who is *psyseering*. And, as far as I know," Miles finished, glancing at the twins. "In this group, that is just Jaedin, Bryna, and myself."

Everyone's eyes lingered between Jaedin and his sister.

"But," Miles continued, breaking the silence. "As I said before; psychic defence is one of my specialities. It is usually one of the first things someone learns when they are taught to harness their Blessings, so I am surprised they have not been already," he said, as his eyes turned from Jaedin to Bryna. "I can teach them."

Initially, Baird's eyes lit up at the prospect of a solution to the problem, but just as quickly, he frowned. Jaedin could guess what he was thinking; Baird was remembering that Miles was their prisoner. Baird was weighing up his options. Considering whether he should trust Miles to aid them against their common enemy.

"How long would it take?" Baird grunted.

"Considering their aptitude…" Miles said. "I guess they would pick it up fairly quickly. There would be some results almost immediately, but proficiency would come with time."

"Could you begin tonight?" Baird asked.

Miles shook his head. "After what just happened, Jaedin will be drained. He needs to recover. Tomorrow should be sufficient."

Baird nodded.

Jaedin felt a bit incensed. That whole conversation took place as if he wasn't even there. Nobody asked *him* if he wanted lessons. Or if he was feeling too drained for them.

Even if it was true.

"I do not need your help, Miles," Bryna announced.

Baird stared at her in disbelief. It must have been the first time he had heard her speak since she joined them.

"*I* will decide what you need..." Baird replied coolly. "It's in the interest of our safety."

"I do not need it," Bryna repeated. "I can take care of myself."

"I will decide–"

"In all respect, Baird," Miles cut in. "This is an area you know little... I happen to know that Bryna has received more magical guidance than Jaedin. Her mother told me, on more than one occasion, that she is both intuitive and very competent. I believe her."

Her words echoed in Jaedin's mind. *I don't need it. I can take care of myself.* Something about the knowingness in her voice chilled him. Behind it lurked a hint that she knew something he and the others didn't.

"Where's Kyra?" Jaedin said, realising she had not spoken yet. It was rare for the group to have a discussion without her having something to say. He looked around but couldn't see her.

None of the others would look at him. They all turned away.

"What's happened to her?" Jaedin asked, feeling a lump in his throat.

"They took her," Baird said.

"Took her?"

"Yes," Baird nodded solemnly. "They took her away. The Zakaras."

"Which way did they go?" Jaedin asked.

"We can't go after them, Jaedin," Baird shook his head. "We don't know where they are. And even if we did, it would be unwise."

"You guys did it before. Right?" Jaedin turned to Rivan. "So we can do it again."

No one said anything.

"Kyra risked her life for us," Jaedin reminded them. He

turned to Sidry, who was still staring at the fire – Jaedin couldn't even tell if he was listening. "And now we won't do the same for her?"

"Do any of you remember what Dion's last words were?" Miles asked. No one responded but he continued anyway. "He said, 'you will see us again very soon'. They will come for us when they are ready."

Jaedin shuddered.

"One thing you need to realise, Jaedin," Baird said. "Is that even if we do find Kyra, she might not be the same."

She might be one of them, Jaedin realised.

"It seemed like they wanted to keep her alive when they took her," Miles said. "I know how these people work. I think that, considering their situation, she is much more valuable to them as a hostage. We have things that they want, so they have taken something of value to us."

"Believe what you will…" Baird muttered. "I grew to care for that girl as well, despite all her insolence," he admitted. "But if she is one of them, I will kill her myself."

* * *

The following morning, Baird announced they were heading to Habella, the nearest town. He made them walk at a fast pace, and the day was long. They dared not stop, for fear of something following them, and every unseen corner or shadow was met with unease. The terrain of southern Sharma which they had grown up in and adored had turned into a death trap. Bushes were cover monsters could hide behind, hilltops were places they lay exposed and could be seen for miles, and woodlands were the perfect setting for an ambush.

When the day came to an end, Baird called for a stop and everyone began to prepare for the night, pitching tents and gathering wood for fire.

Jaedin was just about to help Bryna prepare supper when Miles approached him.

"Jaedin," he said. "Will you come with me, please."

It was time for his first lesson in psychic defence.

Miles led him away from the camp so they would be free from any distracting noises, and they sat together upon the trunk of a felled tree.

"I am going to teach you how to protect yourself from Grav'aen," Miles said.

Jaedin nodded.

"To do that, I will need to teach you how to shield your *psysona*," Miles began, assuming his tutorly manner which Jaedin remembered all too well. "The kind of manifestation this shield will take will be more similar to what you encountered in my mind when we *psycalessed*, rather than what you saw the other day when we escaped from the Forest of Lareem. Do you understand the difference?"

"Yes," Jaedin said. When he and Bryna lit fires with their hands, they were manipulating the elements around them, but this was another kind of magic. One which transcended the physical world. "This is Psymancy."

"Yes," Miles nodded. "How much did your mother teach you of Psymancy?"

"Not much," Jaedin said. His gut twisted at the mention of his mother; it kindled memories from his childhood. "When Bryna and I were little... we shared a room, and sometimes, when mother put us to bed, this strange thing used to happen... I think it was what you mentioned the other day. '*Psyseering*', wasn't it? We would lie in our blankets, but another part of ourselves floated out from our bodies and we flew around the room together. Sometimes, we even passed through the walls of the house like they weren't even there..." Jaedin shook his head. It seemed like a childish game at the time, things they had made up, but, looking back now, he knew it had been real.

Miles' eyes widened. "That part of you which left your body was your *psysona*... Indeed, what you were doing was *psyseering*. Which is a dangerous thing for children to attempt. When people *psyseer*, they wander the *aythirrealm*."

"The spirit world?" Jaedin asked.

Miles shook his head. "Not exactly... but that is a common misconception. The *aythirrealm* isn't the actual spirit world, but a dimension which exists *between* the mortal world and the spirit world. People who wander the *aythirrealm* while *psyseering* will occasionally come into contact with lingering spirits and other beings, but it doesn't occur as often as you would think. It is thought to be just as taxing for the dead to journey into the *aythirrealm* as it is for the living, and not much is known about the *actual* spirit world which exists beyond the *aythirrealm* as all the souls who have ever crossed from there and communed with us have been very cagey about speaking of it..." Miles paused and placed a hand on his chin. "The easiest way to understand the *aythirrealm* is to think of it as a boundary which exists between the worlds of the living and dead. It is certainly not a place children should venture... I am quite frankly surprised your mother didn't properly warn you about it."

"She *did,*" Jaedin said, feeling defensive of his mother. "Once, Bryna and I were floating around the village and saw two men below us fighting outside the tavern," he reminisced. Jaedin and Bryna used to see lots of things which seemed strange when they explored the village at night that way. "We flew back to our bodies, got out of bed, and ran to tell Mum that one of the villagers was bleeding and needed her help. She thought we were just sharing nightmares again and told us to go back to bed. But then someone knocked at the door...

"When she found out how we knew, she was furious," Jaedin recalled. "She told us all these horrible things which could happen to us if we did it again... but I don't think she stopped Bryna... Bryna has always been more gifted than me... I think, to her, things like that come naturally so there wasn't much Mum could do about it.".""

"You must both be strong in Psymancy if you can *psyseer,*" Miles said.

"But I thought that all people who were Blessed are Psymancers?" Jaedin asked.

"Yes... to a certain degree," Miles agreed. "Almost all people who are Blessed are capable of performing a *psycalesse*, for example, but not many can *psyseer*, Jaedin. And what I said yesterday was also true: everyone who is Blessed – no matter how small that Blessing may be – is vulnerable to attack from other Psymancers. This is because their *viga* is active, and we shine brighter than people who are not Blessed, whose *viga* lays dormant."

"People who are not Blessed have *viga*?" Jaedin asked.

Miles nodded. "What do you think *viga* is, Jaedin?"

"It's just the energy I use when I do magic," Jaedin shrugged.

"It is more than that, Jaedin," Miles said. "*Viga* is the energy – the force, if you will – of your *psysona*. Think of our physical body and your *psysona* as twins. Now, what happens if you do too much exercise – or, more likely, in your case, stay up too late reading?"

"I get tired," Jaedin replied.

"Your *physical* body gets tired," Miles corrected him. "Not your *psysona*. Your *psysona* only becomes tired if you use too much of your *viga*. Because that is the energy it uses. People who are not Blessed still have a *psysona*, and thus they also have *viga* too, it is just that they both lie dormant while they live a mortal life... I am surprised Meredith didn't teach you more about all of this," Miles frowned.

"She taught me a few things..." Jaedin said. "Like how to *psycalesse*. But she told me to only ever do that if I had to... she said I should stay away from Psymancy because it wasn't safe," Jaedin's voice croaked towards the end of that sentence as he thought of his mother.

"Psymancy can be very dangerous..." Miles conceded. "But, now you are being targeted by Grav'aen, you have no other choice but to learn some of its techniques. Like it or not, it is a part of your world now. I respect your mother's wishes, Jaedin – you know how fond I was of her," Miles placed a hand on Jaedin's shoulder. "But circumstances have changed. Terribly. And it is essential, for your own sake, that you learn to protect yourself."

When Miles touched him, Jaedin almost shrugged him away. But he didn't. It was the first time Jaedin had not rejected a gesture of his friendship since his betrayal; he didn't have the strength to anymore. He needed the comfort. With everything that had happened since his mother died, Jaedin had been forced to bury the pain to survive, but now he was suddenly overwhelmed by emotions. A tear rolled down his cheek, and then another. Jaedin covered his face. He tried to quell them but he couldn't. Miles pulled him into his arms.

"I miss her," Jaedin croaked.

"Me too," Miles breathed into his ear.

It finally got the better of him, and Jaedin released all the pain and grief that he had been holding back. He had not forgiven Miles for what he had done, but in that brief moment, it was forgotten.

Jaedin became conscious of himself again when he realised that his tears had dampened Miles' tunic. He lifted his head, and they looked into each other's eyes. It made Jaedin's heart race.

But Miles turned away. Cleared his throat. "Are you ready to begin now?" he asked.

Jaedin felt strangely flustered, but he nodded.

"First, we will meditate – to open up your mind for this exercise – and then I will guide you through a process to help you connect with your *psysona*. After that, *if* we get that far today, I will then teach you how to protect it," Miles explained, asserting his tutorly voice which brought back to Jaedin many memories. "Throughout this session, I will occasionally try to reach into your mind, so I can test how strong your defences are and give you a better idea of how you can stop others from doing so. Is this okay with you?"

Jaedin nodded again, but this time more hesitantly. He was not sure he liked the idea of Miles seeing his thoughts, but he knew he had no other choice. So, he leant back and closed his eyes.

"Now. I would like you to breathe slowly. Concentrating on each breath–"

"I know how to meditate," Jaedin muttered.

He inhaled deeply with his nose, expanded his chest outwards, and then breathed out slowly through his mouth. He repeated. Became aware of Miles matching him breath for breath. They were in synch. It became a rhythm, and Jaedin no longer needed to concentrate. Each breath came to him automatically. He began to focus on clearing his mind.

He could see Jalard. The way his home looked after the attack. His mother's corpse. Blood everywhere.

He shivered, suppressed that memory.

It was replaced by the face of his sister. Jaedin had still not got to the bottom of what happened to her. Had no one else noticed how different she was? He wished he could tell someone without raising suspicions. Could he trust Miles?

His thoughts were disturbed by a peculiar feeling. Jaedin realised it was Miles' *psysona* probing at his own. It came as a surprise, as Jaedin had not been expecting Miles to start so soon and he hadn't been given any warning. He pushed thoughts of his sister aside. He didn't want Miles to see them.

He tried to clear his mind, focus on the task at hand, but Bryna's face was replaced by Kyra's. They had taken her, and it was partly Jaedin's fault. Was she still alive? Would they turn her onto a Zakara?

"You need to clear your mind, Jaedin," Miles said.

"Sorry..."

"Let me guide you," Miles said and softly began to guide him through a visualisation. A green meadow. A stream running by. Fishes gliding through the shimmering waters, dodging the beaks of birds on the hunt. The birds took off for their nests, in the trees. The trees were spreading their leaves out to the sun. Their roots were firmly anchored in the rich earth.

For the first time in days, Jaedin's mind was at peace. He felt the wind in his hair and the sun on his face.

But he was snapped back to reality by the uncomfortable sensation of Miles trying to penetrate his mind again.

"I am just on the outside. At the moment," Miles said, beginning the lesson. Jaedin could hear his voice, but it seemed distant. He could feel Miles' *psysona* against his own, tapping against it. It was almost like knocking at a door. "Can you feel that?" Miles asked.

"Yes," Jaedin felt his lips move, but the rest of his body remained perfectly still.

"That is the edge of *you*. Your boundary. If I tried hard enough right now, I could force my way in. Just like Grav'aen did yesterday."

The presence faded.

"We need to work on strengthening your defences," Miles concluded.

"I am ready..." Jaedin agreed.

"First you need to summon some of your magic," Miles began.

Jaedin was already fully attuned with the core of his *psysona*, so drawing upon his *viga* came to him naturally. A fountain of green energy, deep within him.

"Gather a sphere of it," Miles instructed. "Make it yours to command."

The energy was wild. It sometimes seemed to have a mind of its own but, thanks to years of practice, it did not take

Jaedin long to muster control over it. He channelled it, so it coursed to a single point between his hands. Not his real hands; the hands of his *psysona*.

"Expand it outwards," Miles said. "Make it grow. Until it forms a bubble around you."

As Jaedin carried out this action, the sphere of energy became faint, so he fed it more of his *viga*. He cast his hands outwards. It expanded. Magic poured from his palms. He felt a peculiar sense of security he had never felt before. That he had not even realised he had been missing, until that moment.

"And now," Miles finished. "Solidify it. Think of a stone, one that is special to you, and let the sphere take on its attributes."

He thought of jade. The stone his mother named him after when she saw his eyes for the first time. The sphere around him already had the right colour, so it was just a case of feeling it crystallise into that form.

"Are you done?" Miles asked.

"I think so…"

Jaedin felt Miles' psyche press against the boundary of his own again, but this time it didn't feel as invasive. If Jaedin wasn't in such a sensitive state of trance, he possibly would not have even noticed.

"Very good. You seem to have taken to this quickly," Miles complimented. "You can come round in your own time."

Jaedin was feeling peaceful in this state, but he knew he couldn't stay forever. He let his mind drift back into reality – and he once again became grimly aware of his situation.

He was sitting on a tree stump. His village had been laid ruin. His best friend was missing. They were on the run.

He and Miles both opened their eyes at the same time, and Jaedin found himself mesmerised by the opia. The patterns of blue and grey in Miles' irises. He experienced that strange feeling again. A warmth in his chest. Like his insides were melting. Alarm. His heart raced.

They both leant forward, and their lips met. It was slow and hesitant. Jaedin had never kissed anyone in such a way before. His knees began to tremble.

And then Miles pulled away.

"I think…" Miles said.

Jaedin stared at him in disbelief.

"It's best we forget that happened, Jaedin."

*   *   *

They walked back to the camp side by side, but neither of them could look at each other. Miles spoke to him in an aloof manner – about how he would need to practise the shielding technique in his spare time and feed it more of his *viga* on a regular basis to keep it strong – but Jaedin was only half listening. The moment they returned, Miles retreated to his tent without a word of parting.

Jaedin sat by the fire and stared at the flames. He didn't feel like sleeping yet.

He thought about what had just happened.

Just who was Miles? There were so many different versions in Jaedin's head. The Miles he had known as a child. Miles his teacher. Miles his friend. Miles the Gavendarian. Miles the betrayer.

Which one was the real him?

That moment had changed Jaedin's relationship with him forever.

Jaedin knew now that he had been burying his desire for Miles. He had buried it so deeply he even hid it from himself. He didn't even know at what point these feelings began because, for a long time, he had misinterpreted them for others he had for Miles, as his mentor, his tutor, and friend.

The Gavendarian spy. The man who turned his life upside down.

Jaedin was pulled out of his thoughts by Bryna's voice.

"What happened, Jaedin?" his sister asked him.

Jaedin looked at her. He had not even noticed that she'd sat down with him until that moment. She had caught him unawares.

She knew something was on his mind. That something had just happened. She could see it written all over his face.

If Jaedin let her look into his eyes for much longer, she would probably leach it out of him.

He turned away, and a deep silence lingered between the two of them which transcended words. That was the first time Jaedin had ever shut his sister out from his thoughts. He had always let her know everything.

But a part of his life had just been awakened which he didn't want to share with her.

"Tell me," she pleaded.

He shook his head. "No. I can't."

Another silence.

"Now you're not the only one who is keeping secrets..." he muttered, feeling almost smug.

She looked into the flames. Was she hurt? Jaedin could never tell these days.

"I *will* tell you... One day," she whispered. "About what happened to me... but not yet. It isn't time."

*　　*　　*

Kyra fluttered out of sleep, gradually becoming aware that there was a warm body pressed against her and her face was nestled into someone's shoulder.

When she opened her eyes, a familiar face smiled at her.

"Morning, beautiful..." he whispered.

She was in Dion's arms. They had slept like this a couple of times before. It almost felt familiar.

But, when she looked into his eyes, she realised something was not quite right, and memories came flooding back. She screamed. Tore herself away from him.

That was not Dion. Dion was dead.

He smiled at her from beneath the blankets they spent the night under together. Kyra looked down. She was relieved to find that she still had her clothes on but, when she reached for her daggers, the sheaves within her sleeves were empty.

She cast her eyes around them. She was in a tent. Not one of the small, easily dismantled ones that she had been sheltering within during her travels recently. This was a larger one, made from white canvas and held up with high wooden beams. The kind of tent someone pitches with the intention of an extended stay.

"What's the matter?" he asked.

"Stay away from me!" Kyra screamed. She crawled to her feet and ran to the opening, drawing it aside.

Outside were four men in green robes. Shayam's men. They stared at her.

"Don't worry," Dion tried to reassure her. He smiled, but there was something empty about it, and it sent chills through her. "You are safe here,"

Kyra cursed under her breath. If there was one word to describe her situation, it was not 'safe'. Behind all those men standing guard outside, she had seen other tents. This was some kind of base, and it was swarming with Zakaras. How was she going to escape?

Dion rose from the blankets. Walked to her. She tried to back away, but he pursued her until she felt the canvas of the tent against her back. He had her cornered.

"They won't harm you," he said and reached for her face. He ran his fingers through her hair.

"Stop it!" she screamed, slapping his hand away. "You're not Dion!"

He looked away. As if he was hurt.

Could a Zakara even *be* hurt?

"I am still me," he said, but she knew it wasn't. His expression, his posture, the way he spoke. Everything was wrong.

"I am me. And so much more," he finished.

"What do you want from me?" she asked.

"I want to rekindle our relationship," he replied, his eyes wide with madness.

*　　*　　*

When Dareth stumbled into the streets of Habella, he knew he must have been a sorry sight. He was weary. His clothes were dirty and torn. His hair was matted and grimy. It must have been clear, to all who saw him, that he had just made an arduous journey.

After killing his stepfather, Dareth knew it was very likely people would come looking for him, so he avoided all roads. He left Jalard and took a route through an untrodden wilderness of dense forests and craggy hills.

The first two days were direful. Dareth couldn't rid his stepfather from his mind. It haunted him. He could still remember the sound the knife made when he sank it into Tarvek's neck. The feeling of warm blood on his hands.

Dareth tried to distract himself by keeping busy. Each day,

he had obstacles to cross, and at the end of it he had to build a shelter to sleep. He foraged. Hunted. Gathered wood.

But, once night came, his belly was full, and all the work was done; there was nothing left for him to do but stare into the flames of his campfire.

Those were the hardest times.

Being alone, Dareth had a lot of time to think. After a few days, his recollection began to blur. The details lost clarity. It took on the quality of a hazy dream. It began to feel distant. Like something which happened long ago.

Tarvek deserved what he got, he told himself.

What else could Dareth have done?

Having never navigated on his own before, Dareth got lost many times during his journey, but he managed to find the way to Habella eventually.

He was back in civilisation now, and looking forward to a hot bath and sleeping in a real bed.

He spotted an inn which looked suitable and stepped inside.

The bar was empty, which Dareth thought unusual, but it suited his purpose. He was on the run, after all, and needed to be careful. Dareth chose this establishment because it was on the outskirts, and thus, it probably needed all the business it could get and was less likely to ask questions.

A man stood behind the counter cleaning glasses. "Do you have a room?" Dareth asked him.

The innkeeper raised an eyebrow. "Bit young t' be travellin' alone, lad?" he muttered.

Dareth put his hands on his hips, hoping that, by appearing confident, he would curb this man's suspicions. "Do you have a room or not?"

"Ye," the innkeeper said. "But it will not be ready for a while yet, lad. Do ye have money?"

Dareth brought out a bag of coins from his pocket. The innkeeper raised an eyebrow again.

Maybe I shouldn't have shown him how much I have... Dareth thought and made a mental note to find a discreet place to hide his more valuable coins.

Dareth had been surprised how much money he found when he raided his mother's room just before he left. It was far from a fortune, but it was still much more than he had been expecting.

"Two lannies a night," the innkeeper said. "Pay upfront."

Dareth handed him the coins. "I will be back in an hour," he declared. "Will it be ready then?"

The innkeeper nodded.

Dareth turned, smiled to himself, and walked away.

He knew coming to Habella was a risky idea, but he couldn't resist a night of comforts after being in the wilderness for so long. He had worried that words of his deeds may have already travelled here and people would be suspicious of a young man his age travelling alone, but it seemed his act of confidence had paid off.

And while Dareth was here, he may as well take a look around the market.

"I need a name. For t' room," the innkeeper said when Dareth reached the door.

Shit! Dareth thought, realising that he hadn't prepared one. He tried to think of one on the spot, but all that came to mind were variations of his own name and those of people he knew. He didn't want to name any of his friends and risk getting them into trouble.

"Jaedin," he found himself saying.

Dareth was surprised by that choice.

But then he smiled to himself. Now, if he *did* make any trouble here, it would be even more fun.

"Jaedin of Jalard."

Chapter 12

Sidry's Awakening

That night, as Sidry lay in his blankets, Jaedin's words echoed in his mind over and over again.

At least I've been trying! Which is better than your two cronies here. What have they done to help?

And the terrible thing was that Sidry knew it was true. Jaedin had dealt much more fairly with their trauma than he had, and he had been instrumental in ensuring the survival of the group.

Ever since they escaped from Jalard, all Sidry had done was replay the things he had seen there in his mind over and over again in a tormenting cycle. He could not believe that his entire life and everything he had ever known had been snatched away from him so abruptly. So harrowingly. He was angry with the world. With the gods who had let such things happen. He could never shake off the knowledge that the last time he saw his parents his mother was weeping over him leaving and his father refused to say goodbye. They were dead now, and he would never be able to reconcile with them.

At least I've been trying! Which is better than your two cronies here. What have they done to help?

That moment changed it all.

The worst thing about those words was that they had come from Jaedin. *Jaedin* – the boy that Sidry and his friends had mocked for years for being frail and cowardly – criticised Sidry for not pulling himself together.

Before that moment, Sidry could only feel despair. He couldn't imagine any future for himself when his entire past had been ripped away so grimly, but Jaedin had dragged his mind back into the present. He made Sidry realise he was deeply ashamed of himself.

*   *   *

Sidry woke the next morning with a newfound sense of determination. It was time to buckle up. Be alert. Be alive. Be useful.

And not be outdone by Jaedin, of all people.

He climbed out of his tent just after sunrise and went to the river to wash his face. It was cold and refreshing, and it startled him into a state of wakefulness that he had not felt since this nightmare began.

*   *   *

They arrived at Habella that day.

There was a pervading feeling of apprehension as they approached its outskirts. Usually, one felt a sense of solace when returning to civilisation again after some time spent in the wilderness, but recent experience had tainted any sense of security. Sidry was far from forgetting what happened the last time they reached a human settlement expecting safety.

As they entered the first neighbourhood, Sidry looked around. He found the style of the tall buildings a little overbearing. He was used to the single-storey cob huts of Jalard, and this was his first time seeing other kinds of architecture. Rows of houses towered on each side of them. There were all identical and joined to each other, blocking out the sun. Their roofs were made from slate instead of thatch, which appeared more solid but gave them a rather grey and dismal quality.

Sidry's anxiety eased when he saw the first signs of life. A man stepped out of his front door and made his way into the town. Sidry then saw children playing in an alleyway. A woman was hanging laundry out to dry from her window. She waved.

Baird led the way. Sidry could tell by his posture and the way he kept craning his neck as he scanned their surroundings that he was on high alert.

An elderly man appeared at the end of the street. He seemed to be someone of high esteem, judging from his appearance. The billowy blue cloak he wore seemed very regal for someone from rural Sharma, and he had a presence about him. He walked with the aid of an oaken staff.

"Greetings travellers," he said, and they drew to a halt. "I am Frih'dra. Where has this fine group travelled from?"

"Jalard," Baird replied.

"Oh, Jalard..." the Frih'dra recalled, stroking his white

beard. "A village to the south of here, I believe? I trust you are here for trading?" he asked and looked at each of them. Sidry realised it must have been clear to him there was something unusual about this party: none of them had the bright eyes rural Sharmarians typically had when they were getting to see the world outside their village.

It was not so long ago that Rivan, Aylen and Kyra had set off for this very same town on a trading expedition. And Sidry and Jaedin should have passed through here on their way to the Academy.

It was not so long ago, and yet they had lost so much.

"But you do seem a large group for that..." Frih'dra said. "Can I ask of you what your business would be?"

"We bring sad news. And a warning of danger..." Baird replied gravely.

Frih'dra turned back to Baird. He didn't seem surprised. "I had feared thus, for you do have the air of someone who carries a heavy burden. Come," he said, turning around and beckoning them to follow. "For you seem weary. I will provide you with baths and a meal. And then we will discuss this matter."

Sidry could tell from the tightening of Baird's shoulders that he did not want to waste time on such trivial things, but the man had just offered them hospitality and it would have been considered rude to turn it down.

"Yes, we will come with you, but please don't go arranging any baths. We cannot stay long, and all that hot water would be wasted," Baird replied carefully. "Can I have a moment, please? I wish to discuss something with these two young men here?" he said, pointing to Rivan and Sidry.

"Of course," Frih'dra said. "Take your time."

Baird motioned for the two of them to follow him and they walked away a little so that they were out of earshot.

"Rivan," Baird said. He reached into his pocket and drew a bag of coins. "I have a feeling that man is going to waste much more time than we have and I want to get out of here and on the road to Shemet as soon as possible. Can the two of you go to the market while I talk to him? We need food, blankets... maybe some new leggings for Jaedin – those things he's wearing look ruddy ridiculous – oh, and ask around for a good place to find horses."

"Sounds good to me," Rivan smiled. "I'm not so keen on sitting down and swapping stories. Where shall we find you?"

"The square. In about an hour," Baird suggested. "That'll be good... a deadline to meet you will also give us an excuse to get going."

"Okay," Rivan nodded. "Come on, Sidry. Let's go."

* * *

Jaedin watched as Rivan and Sidry walked away, deeper into the town, and Baird returned.

"Are you going to accept my offer of a meal, then?" Frih'dra asked.

"Yes," Baird said. "Although, can you summon the other Elders, please? There are some very urgent things I need to discuss with you, and they all need to be there. It cannot wait."

"That is agreeable," Frih'dra dipped his head. "I believe two of your group have left us though," he said, pointing his staff in the direction Rivan and Sidry had just wandered. "Will they be returning shortly?"

"They're taking a look around the market," Baird replied. "I'll be meeting them there in an hour."

"I see..." Frih'dra replied, stroking his beard in contemplation. After a short pause, he turned and began to walk, ushering them with his hand. "Well, I guess we best make our way to the Hall then. Follow me."

As they walked, Jaedin thought longingly of the hot bath Baird had just turned down. He was still not used to life on the road, but he was trying his best not to complain. He knew it was silly to worry about a bath after all they had been through yet couldn't help it. He had never gone so long without washing. His body felt sticky and clammy. He had tried to wash parts of himself in a stream that morning but it wasn't quite the same. His hair was still greasy, and his scalp itched.

He then became aware of a tingling sensation in his forehead, and all those trivial thoughts were instantly forgotten.

It was the Stone of Zakar warning him that Zakaras were nearby.

Don't panic, Jaedin told himself, drawing a deep breath to calm his nerves. He was conscious of the fact that he was in a very public place; he didn't want to attract any unnecessary attention. If there were Zakaras here, the last thing Jaedin wanted was to make a scene.

He closed his eyes and connected to the crystal. Not so much to make his eyes glow, but enough for him to find out more. The Zakaras felt distant. Jaedin guessed that meant they were not in any immediate danger.

But what were they doing here?

I've got to tell Baird, Jaedin decided, quickening his pace to catch up with him.

"They're here," Jaedin whispered as he sided up next to Baird.

Baird's eyes widened, and his hand went to his sword.

"Not here!" Jaedin hissed. "Somewhere further."

"Where?" Baird whispered back once he'd composed himself. They continued walking.

"Not sure," Jaedin shrugged. "Probably on the other side of the town."

"How many?" Baird asked.

"I don't know," Jaedin shrugged. He then noticed Frih'dra was staring at them; the aged man was trying to eavesdrop and being none too subtle about it. "They aren't close enough."

"Tell me if they get closer," Baird whispered. "Don't... do anything yet. Hopefully they won't spot us. Tell me if anything changes."

"Is there a problem?" Frih'dra said, walking to them.

Baird gritted his teeth, not quite able to mask his annoyance at the interruption. "Yes. And we need to talk to you about it as soon as possible. How much further are you taking us?"

"Not far," Frih'dra reassured. "We're almost there."

They continued walking. Jaedin turned around and caught the eye of his sister. He knew, from the unspoken language the two of them shared, that she was stressed about something.

"What's the matter?" Jaedin asked, walking over to her. Her face was even paler than usual and her hands were trembling.

"I don't trust him," she whispered, and Jaedin followed her gaze. She was staring at the back of Frih'dra's head.

"Are you both okay?" Miles asked, joining Jaedin and his sister.

"Bryna doesn't trust him," Jaedin answered for her.

"Why?" Miles asked Bryna.

Bryna shook her head. Whatever her reasons, she was not going to voice them.

"Don't worry Bryna, I'll keep an eye on him," Miles said, putting a hand on her back. "I am sure Baird knows what he's doing... That man is the town Elder. We are just going to tell him what happened to us and then we will leave."

Jaedin nodded encouragingly, but Bryna didn't even seem to hear.

They wound their way down another street, and Jaedin saw a large open area with an elevated stone platform ahead. He guessed it to be a gathering place for the citizens, like the one they had outside their own Hall in Jalard.

Baird noticed something behind them and frowned.

"*Bryna*?!" he yelled. "What are you *doing*?"

Jaedin turned around and saw this sister had halted and was staring at her feet.

Baird yelled her name again but louder. She flinched at the sound of his voice.

You're not helping, Baird! Jaedin thought.

"What is it, Bryna?" Jaedin said and softly tip-toed to her. He knew his sister. When she went off into her own little world, she was easily startled. All Baird was going to achieve by shouting was flustering her even more.

"There is an Enchantment here," she whispered, eyeing the ground before her. "I can feel it."

"What?" Baird called.

"She thinks there's an Enchantment here," Jaedin yelled to him.

Jaedin scanned the cobbled road beneath his feet to see if he could spot any runes. He didn't see any, but he knew that didn't mean much because there were ways of hiding them. Enchanting was a complex form of magic involving much preparation and ceremony. Jaedin had read a fair bit about it in the books in Miles' study but never seen it in practice. Enchanted objects or places could lay dormant for years, centuries even, before they were activated and they could be triggered by almost anything: a word, a spell, an event, or even just a person.

"It's just a ward to provide a safe haven for the town's

people," Frih'dra explained. "If need be... it is not active at the moment."

"And I think you are going to shortly learn just how useful it could be," Baird nodded his head with approval. He turned back to Bryna. "Bryna. Come on! We can't waste any more time!"

Bryna looked up at Baird when she heard her name, but she didn't move.

"Follow me, Bryna..." Jaedin coaxed her softly.

Please Bryna, just come... he added, looking her in the eyes.

Jaedin was worried that if his sister kept acting up, Baird would decide to leave her behind somewhere and they would be separated. He saw the way the former soldier looked at her; he knew Baird saw her as a hindrance. Jaedin was useful to Baird because he possessed the Stone of Zakar, but his fey sister, with her foggy consciousness and outlandish behaviour, was a different story.

Bryna gave in, but her fear was palpable in her tense posture as she stepped across the threshold.

"See," Frih'dra said. "Not so bad, is it?" He turned and continued walking, stepping up onto the elevated platform in the centre of the square.

Jaedin heard his sister gasp.

"*Hiberkis!*" the old man said as he slammed his staff against the base of the stone.

"No!" Bryna screamed.

Jaedin's heart lurched. Pale white light spiralled around them. Baird reached for his sword, and Aylen's hands went to his daggers. Jaedin's reflex was to just close his eyes and cover his head, for he could not fathom what was coming. The temperature around him plummeted so rapidly he knew that there could only be some form of sorcery at work.

When Jaedin dared to open his eyes again, he looked up to see Baird was still in front of him. The burly soldier had been frozen in the motion of unleashing his sword. Jaedin stared in disbelief. It was like someone had turned him to stone.

Frih'dra still stood on the platform with his staff held against the gigantic rock he had used to activate the Enchantment. Aylen and Bryna also stood frozen in place, but Jaedin was somehow free from the chilling air Frih'dra had conjured. There was a sphere of grey energy around him.

Jaedin turned to Miles, realising his former mentor was the one behind it. The scholar had cast a shield around himself too. The two of them were the only ones yet to be frozen by Frih'dra's spell.

"Quick, Jaedin! Run!" Miles yelled. Jaedin could tell from the urgency in his voice that his shields would not hold for much longer. Miles was using the last of his remaining *viga* to hold out against Frih'dra's magic.

"Jaedin! Go!"

There wasn't any time for Jaedin to think. He could feel some of the icy energy from the ward seeping in through the cracks of Miles' shield and knew he only had a few moments left to make an escape. He took to his feet and ran.

*   *   *

The market place was noisy and crowded. Sidry asserted his way through the throngs of people as men and women loudly touted their wares from behind their stalls. Most of them were merely trading in grains, wine, cheeses, fruits and clothes, but there were a few selling weapons and household items too. There was even a shifty man who claimed to be selling Enchanted jewellery. Sidry knew very little about magic but guessed he was a fraud.

Rivan approached one of the booths and was soon engaged in an animated discussion on the price of a pair of leggings with a stern-faced merchant who shook his head firmly at Rivan's opening offer. The seller seemed stubborn, and Sidry knew his friend well enough to guess that he had likely just met his match. They could be arguing for a while yet.

There was a woman selling weapons at the stall next door, so Sidry decided to have a browse while he was waiting. He admired the workmanship of the daggers. They were never Sidry's weapon of choice – he, like Rivan, preferred fencing – but he did like to have one handy in case something happened to his sword.

They made him think of Kyra. She had always liked daggers. Sidry wondered if she was still alive. He had never liked her, but she was still one of them. One of the survivors from Jalard.

"See any you like?" the woman behind the stall asked.

Sidry looked up, and she bared her teeth in a seller's smile.

"Just looking," he said.

But the woman was no longer paying attention. Her gaze shifted to something behind him.

Sidry turned around and caught the sight of Jaedin sprinting down the street.

Oh shit... Sidry thought.

What was he running from? Where were the others?

"Rivan!" Sidry yelled, grabbing his arm and pointing.

Rivan's eyes widened. He slammed some coins upon the counter and snatched something from the trader. He and Sidry took to their heels.

"What the blazes is he doing?" Rivan asked as they ran out of the market place. They were forced to push their way past the crowds of people dawdling their way through the stalls and received many scathing looks in return. Sidry was too busy trying to keep Jaedin in sight to pay them any heed. By the time they fought their way through, Jaedin was at the other end of the street and about to turn a corner.

"Jaedin!" Rivan called out as they ran after him.

Jaedin skidded to a halt and turned around.

"What's going on?" Rivan shouted as they raced to catch up with him.

"No time!" Jaedin panted between laboured breaths. "*Run! They're coming!*"

"Who's coming?!" Rivan asked.

But Jaedin was already running again. Sidry was about to yell another question when he caught sight of three men in green robes sprinting towards them.

They were Shayam's men, which could only mean one thing.

The Zakaras were here.

Sidry rushed to catch up with Jaedin but somehow couldn't. The young man was too fast. "Wait up!" he called. Since when could Jaedin outrun him?

Jaedin stopped by the entrance of an alleyway and ushered them to follow. "Come! Quick! Down here," he yelled.

He disappeared between the buildings. Sidry chased him, eventually reaching the end of the alleyway and finding Jaedin waiting at the corner. The three of them paused for a moment to catch their breath, and Rivan took the opportunity to peer down the lane to check for their pursuers.

"I think we've lost them," Rivan announced. "What the blazes is going on?" he asked, turning to Jaedin.

"Frih'dra," Jaedin panted. "He–"

"Shit! They're coming!" Rivan interrupted him, and the three of them started to run.

"This way!" Rivan yelled as he led them down a street.

A few of the townspeople stared as they fled. A man tried to cut their path. "What are you scits playing at?!" he yelled, stretching his arms out.

"Mind your own ruddy business!" Rivan roared, landing a blow to the man's stomach. They continued running. Sidry turned around guiltily, saw the winded man fall to his knees with his hands on his gut. Not far behind him were Shayam's men. They were getting closer.

"Oh no!" Jaedin muttered under his breath.

"Just run!" Rivan yelled. "We can outpace them."

"There's more ahead," Jaedin shook his head. His face was pale with terror. "They're going to surround us!"

"I can't see any..." Sidry muttered. He scanned the street ahead of them. There were no men in green robes, just normal people. Some of them were staring.

"I can *feel* them!" Jaedin said. "They're getting closer!"

"Can you hold them off?" Rivan suggested. "With that thing you can do?"

Jaedin shook his head. "Not while running."

"You did at the village..." Rivan reminded him.

"That was *walking*! Baird was guiding me!" Jaedin shouted back.

"We'll guide you," Sidry decided, grabbing Jaedin's shoulder. "Just try!"

Rivan grasped hold of Jaedin from the other side and, together, they guided him as the three of them ran. Jaedin closed his eyes. A faint red glow radiated from beneath the band on his forehead.

Sidry turned his attention back to what lay ahead of them, remembering that he and Rivan were going to have to be Jaedin's eyes if they wanted to escape. Ahead of them were three men in green robes. Jaedin had been right; they were surrounded.

"They're ahead of us!" Rivan muttered to Jaedin.

"I *know*!" Jaedin uttered, even though his eyes were screwed shut.

Men from both sides were charging. Sidry knew that they didn't have long left. He looked around for any side streets or alleyways they could run down to buy themselves more time, but there weren't any. They were trapped.

"If you're going to help, do it now!" Rivan shouted into Jaedin's ear.

"If you let me concentrate, I *will*!" Jaedin screamed.

The Zakaras were just a dozen paces away. Their bodies began to tremble. Sidry recognised the motions; they were beginning to transform. Claws, talons, scales and razor-sharp teeth grew from their bodies. Sidry considered unleashing his sword.

Jaedin stretched out his arm, facing his palm towards the Zakaras, and they fell back as if pushed by an invisible force. Rivan howled in victory as they ran past the toppled monsters.

"Keep that up, Jaedin. I can see a way out!" Rivan yelled, and Sidry helped him lead Jaedin around a corner to the next street.

*　　*　　*

Dareth paced through the streets of Habella, his heart hammering against his chest as he made his way back to the inn. He didn't dare look back.

He had just seen Rivan and Sidry at the market.

He went there to buy provisions – as he was planning to leave Habella the next day and there were a few things he needed – but then he saw their faces in the crowd. At first, Dareth had been so shocked to see them that all he could do was stare. He was baffled as to why Rivan and Sidry were in Habella together. Didn't the two of them part on not-so-great terms when Sidry left for the Academy over an aeight ago? Shouldn't Rivan be on his way back from a trading mission right now?

Dareth couldn't think of any explanation for it, but he knew he couldn't let himself be seen by them, so he fled. If the two of them were here, there was a chance others from Jalard were. It was even possible they were there because they were looking for Dareth.

I need to leave, he realised. *Now.*

But where could Dareth go?

The road to Shemet was not an option. It was too busy. There was a risk Dareth would bump into someone he knew.

Perhaps he should head north. He had heard that the coast up there was fairly remote. He could find a small, inconspicuous village there and start a new life for himself.

Yes, he decided. *I'll go north.*

Once Dareth reached the inn and was back behind the safety of walls again, he took a moment to catch his breath and recover his nerves. The owner glanced at him and frowned, but Dareth avoided eye contact. He made his way up the stairs.

When he opened the door, a man was sitting upon a chair in the middle of the chamber. At first, Dareth thought he must have entered the wrong room. He opened his mouth to begin an apology, but the man smiled at him. Knowingly.

Before Dareth had any time to react, two more men appeared from each side of the doorway and grabbed him, pulling him inside. Dareth struggled to free himself but his captors were unusually strong.

He knew his game was up, but he had to try. He didn't know what the penalty would be for killing his stepfather, as Dareth had never heard of someone committing such a crime. Would they believe him when he told them of the years of abuse he suffered?

Dareth fought with all his might, but the outcome was inevitable. They forced his arms behind his back and pushed him to his knees.

Dareth looked around to see if he could spot any familiar faces, but none of these people were from Jalard. Who were they?

"You're not Jaedin…" the man in the chair said.

Dareth spat on the floor, deciding that if he was going to go down, he might as well do it properly. "Of course not," he muttered. "Do I look like a soddy to you?"

"Take him away."

* * *

A shiver made its way down Kyra's spine when a shadow appeared at the entrance of the tent.

He was back again. No matter how many times she told him to go away, he always came back.

She ignored him as he placed the meal upon her lap. Like every action towards her, it was done with simulated tenderness. There was no genuine warmth behind it.

This thing had Dion's face, but it was just a monster imitating the actions of a human. Sometimes, Kyra wondered what his monstrous form was beneath his skin – was he bearlike, or gangly and covered in scales? Did he have talons or fangs? Or was he some other kind of hideous variation she had not seen yet? – so far, she had been spared finding out.

Although, sometimes she thought she would prefer to see it in its true form. At least then it wouldn't have Dion's face.

She could feel its eyes looking down at her.

"Why do you keep pushing me away?" he whispered.

"Because you make me feel sick..." Kyra muttered. She didn't even look at the food he placed on her lap. She tossed it aside. She wasn't hungry.

"You must eat," he said, leaning down and placing a hand on her shoulder. She cringed. "You haven't eaten since you got here."

"What about you?" Kyra asked, finally looking at him. "Do Zakaras need to eat?"

"If we wish," he said. "But not as often as your kind..."

His drew his hand away from her shoulder and held it up before his face. Stared at the outline of his fingers. "I wish you could understand..." he said. "If only you could *experience* this. You would then... I have never felt so pure. So free. There is no pain. No loss. No regrets..."

"Well, fuck off then!" she screamed. "You are *free* from me! You can let me go and have no regrets!"

"It's not as simple as that..." he said.

She looked at him. "What do you want from me?"

He sat before her. "We are still a new race," he said. "We are in our infancy. Not much is known about us. Not even by ourselves. We come from humans, but we are... different."

Kyra shuddered when he referred to Zakaras as a 'race'. He said it so coolly. Like they were a perfectly agreeable addition to the world.

Did this mean they were planning to spread throughout the whole of Sharma? Or would they remain a dark secret of the Gavendarian aristocracy?

"We were created from the runes of Zakar himself," he explained. "Zakar is our God. We are his Chosen, and he is our master. It was not known, until the accident at Jalard, that when humans are relieved of their mortality by our hand that, somehow, their bodies are reborn and they become *one* of us."

'Accident'. 'Relieved of their mortality'. His words echoed through her mind. Kyra's stomach turned over at the lighthearted way he spoke of the massacre of her village.

"Stop speaking of yourself as if you're natural!" she said, anger rising as a heat in her chest. "You are an accident! There is no place in this world for you!"

"We all came from the gods…" Dion said.

"You are a *defect*!" she screamed. "An experiment which went wrong! Nothing more!"

"Stop it!" he warned her.

Kyra broke into laughter. She had to. She knew that if she didn't laugh, right then, she would start crying instead. And, this way, at least she kept some of her strength.

"Why are you laughing?" he asked.

"The irony!" she chuckled to herself. "They were trying to find a cure for a disease, and they just created a new one!"

For the first time, she incited a reaction from the monster sitting in front of her. It wasn't pain, for they could not feel that.

It was offended.

"You are a disease," Kyra continued, while she had the upper hand. "A virus. You said so yourself! *I* was born from my parents!" Kyra said, and her voice quivered at the mention of them. It almost brought her to tears, but she held them back. "Carried into the world by my mother, who loved me! *You* are created through the death of others. Not through love! You are nothing more than a disease, and using fancy words won't change that."

Dion turned away, unable to argue back, and Kyra knew she had won.

Zakaras are simple creatures, she thought. She guessed this one was merely repeating the lies that Shayam had told it. It had no intellect. No imagination. No ability to form ideas of its own.

"That is what you are here for..." Dion said, ending the silence.

"What are you waffling on about now?" she asked irritably.

"You say that you were born from an act of love," he looked at her. "We do not know if that is possible for us yet... it has never been tried."

Kyra had an idea where this could be going, but she knew that she must be wrong. The idea was something too foul to even bear contemplating.

"But we would like to try..."

At those last words, Kyra's entire body became possessed by hot rage. She became barely aware of herself and unable to consider her actions. She had never felt so repulsed in her entire life, and the only way she could deal with it was to inflict as much pain upon him as she could.

She leapt on top of him. He struggled against her, but she pinned his arms to the ground with her knees. She pounded her fists into his head. Over and over again. Eventually, she heard his skull crack, but she didn't stop.

When Kyra became aware of herself again, her knuckles throbbed and were covered in blood. She landed a few final blows to expel the last of her fury and repair her torn dignity.

Then, she got up and turned away from him, not wanting to see what she had just done to the face of someone who had once been a friend. More.

She heard him get up, as she knew he would. She had seen those things crawling along the ground when they had no limbs, chase their prey when they had no eyes to see, walk on two feet even though their entrails dangled from their bodies. She knew it would take more than fists to kill it.

"The choice is yours," Dion said before he left the tent. "But there are ways of getting around your objections."

She heard him laugh as he walked away. "Remember, you wouldn't object to it if you became one of us, and that is something which could be arranged easily. I would rather not take that path but we will if we have to... I will see you soon. My love."

* * *

"So... you just ran away?" Rivan asked.

Jaedin sighed, already sensing from Rivan's tone that he was somehow going to blame him for what had happened.

After running for hours to clear some distance from Habella, they had stopped in the middle of a forest.

"I had no choice…" Jaedin said, feeling defensive and not even knowing why.

"And Miles saved only *you*?" Rivan asked.

Jaedin paused. He was unable to explain that one.

Just *why* had Miles used the last of his *viga* to save Jaedin, rather than himself? That question had been in the back of Jaedin's mind ever since he escaped, and now Rivan had voiced it too.

All Jaedin could do was nod.

"I'm *very* suspicious…" Rivan said, folding his arms.

"Why?" Jaedin asked.

"*Miles*," Rivan uttered the name with venom. "*Miles* – the one who caused all this shit – only saved *you*. You think none of us have noticed that you've been all chummy with him again recently? Have you forgotten what he did to us? Do you have any bloody backbone!?"

"I didn't *ask* to be saved," Jaedin snapped. "He just did it! What would you have preferred I do? Let myself be captured? If it wasn't for me running away and finding you, they would have got *you* as well!"

"He's right, Rivan," Sidry intervened. Until that moment, he had stayed out of their altercation.

Rivan grunted and turned away. His own friend had supplied him with the voice of reason. He let out a curse and expelled his frustrations by lungeing his foot at the trunk of a tree.

Jaedin sighed with relief. Although his respite was short-lived.

Now that Rivan's interrogation was over, the silence which followed gave him time to reflect on the direness of their situation.

There were only three of them now.

Rivan pressed his forehead against the tree, leaning upon it while his anger subsided.

"So what do we do now?" Rivan asked.

Jaedin realised just how very alone he was. The only members of the group who cared for him were gone. He felt lost without his sister. If he'd been given a choice, Rivan and

Sidry would have been the last people in the entire world he would have chosen to be stuck with.

And, with Baird gone, it seemed that Rivan was now their leader.

"Sun is setting," Sidry said. "We're probably safer here in the wood than out in the open."

"What about night watch?" Rivan pointed out. "There are only two of us."

Two? Jaedin thought, as neither of them even seemed to register he was there. *Do I not even count?*

"There are three of us!" Jaedin said.

Rivan sneered at him. "You have never–"

"What? Stayed awake and kept my eyes open?" Jaedin said. "Sounds really hard!"

"It's more than that–" Sidry began to explain, but he was also cut off by Jaedin.

"Please, remind me. What are we watching out for at nights, these days?" he asked.

Rivan and Sidry glanced at each other, not quite sure where the question was leading but guessing from Jaedin's tone it was a trap.

"Zakaras," Jaedin answered for them. "And which one of us can not only see and hear them but *control* them as well?"

"And what if you go all woozy and pass out again?" Rivan recalled. "Remember what happened the *last* time we relied on you?"

"That was not my fault!" Jaedin said.

Rivan didn't respond. The argument had gone as far as it could go.

"So," Jaedin ended the silence. "Who is going first?"

The two friends turned to each other.

"You know what?" Rivan decided, turning back to Jaedin. "Fuck it. No watch tonight. We just won't build a fire. As long as we have no fire, they won't be able to find us in the middle of this damn place anyway."

Jaedin opened his mouth to object.

"No arguments!" Rivan exclaimed.

"But what are we going to do?" Jaedin asked.

"What do you mean?" Sidry said.

"I mean, where are we going to go now that Baird and the others are gone?" Jaedin said.

"We are heading to Shemet," Rivan said. "Just as Baird planned."

* * *

When it began to get dark, they ate the last of their provisions. None of them spoke.

Sidry fought back against despair.

It was hard to not go back into that dark place again. It seemed all hope was lost, but Sidry was determined to pull himself together for Rivan's sake.

Sidry didn't like Jaedin either, but a part of him felt sorry for him right now. He thought that Rivan was unfair to him sometimes.

The tents they usually slept in had been with Baird and the others, so the only possession they had to get them through the night was the blanket Rivan snatched from the merchant in the market.

Rivan spread it upon the mossy ground, and he and Sidry looked at each other.

Sidry could tell his friend was having thoughts similar to his own: the two of them had shared bedding and slept beside each other many times. They were comfortable with it.

But Jaedin was a different matter. He had been the object of many jokes between the boys of Jalard over the years, but was there truth to the rumours? Was Jaedin really a sodd?

And, if so, was Sidry comfortable sleeping beside him?

But what else could they do? It was going to get very cold soon and, without a blanket, the boy would suffer.

"Jaedin," Sidry said, the words sounded forced even as he said them. "Come here… you will–"

"No way!" Rivan exclaimed. "I'm not sharing with a sodd!"

"Get over yourself," Jaedin muttered. He lay on a patch of leaves a few yards away from them. "I would rather freeze to death than share that rag with either of you."

Another awkward silence. How many would the three of them share before they reached Shemet?

Sidry got into the blanket with Rivan. The woods began to darken. Sidry tried to sleep but he couldn't because, deep down, he knew that this was very wrong. He could hear

Jaedin shivering. The other boy might get ill just because they couldn't bring themselves to share a blanket.

If Baird could see them right now, he would have been appalled.

Eventually, Rivan cursed. He sat up, removed his cloak from his shoulders, and tossed it at Jaedin.

"Take this," he said. "Should be enough to keep you warm – it's bigger than you are anyway."

*   *   *

Sidry came around in the morning to Rivan shaking him by his shoulders.

"Sidry!" he shouted.

Sidry opened his eyes. It was daylight, but he felt darkness in the air.

The next thing Sidry heard was Jaedin's voice. "They are coming!" he said. He was standing a few yards away.

Rivan cursed and rose to his feet. "Get up, Sidry!"

Sidry stumbled to his feet. His head swayed as blood rushed into his brain. He was just about to scramble for his belongings when he remembered he didn't have any.

"Where are they?" Rivan asked, running over to Jaedin.

Jaedin's eyes began to glow as he summoned the power of the crystal. Sidry could already tell from the look on the young man's face that the news wasn't going to be good.

"Everywhere…" Jaedin whispered. "They're coming from all sides!"

Rivan cursed again.

Sidry took a look around them. They were enclosed by trees and he couldn't see anything beyond them.

"How many?" Sidry asked, feeling rubatosis as his heart rate escalated. There were only three of them, and there was no escape.

More importantly, Baird wasn't there to guide them.

"Many…" Jaedin answered, his lips trembling.

The branches of a nearby tree snapped, and they turned to see a Zakara sliding its scaly body between the trees.

"Stand back!" Jaedin yelled. He stepped forward, trying to seem bold, but Sidry could tell from his posture that he was terrified.

Jaedin clenched his fists, and the crystal on his forehead glowed. The Zakara froze. Jaedin's legs trembled as he fought to control it. Sidry heard sounds from behind them and turned around to see another monster.

"Stay here!" Rivan yelled as he drew his sword and charged to meet it. "Cover Jaedin!"

"No! Don't!" Sidry yelled, but his friend ignored him and squared up to the beast alone. There was no going back for him now.

Sidry swore and turned his attention back to Jaedin. He knew their only hope of getting out of this situation alive was if he could somehow muster control of the Zakaras.

Sidry ran to him. Jaedin was trembling, and his eyes were scrunched tightly together. He let out a gasp and his knees buckled. Sidry caught him as he fell.

"Too many," Jaedin whispered. "And Grav'aen... he is... I am trying to fight *him* off! As well as Shayam. I can't control them... I'm sorry."

"It's okay," Sidry said, for he could see from Jaedin's pained expression that he had truly done all he could.

There were Zakaras all around them now. They filled the gaps between every tree. With a sinking heart, Sidry realised that their situation was hopeless. They were going to be either captured or killed, and he was powerless to stop it.

Sidry looked at the scars on his arm. Ever since he'd escaped from Shayam's base, he had dreaded the thought of being a freak, but now he wanted the powers Baird possessed more than anything.

Why was it that Baird could transform into that glowing being, yet Sidry couldn't? They had both been the subjects of the same ritual, had they not? They both had the same runes carved into their flesh.

Sidry touched his forehead. Was it true? Was there really a Stone of Gezra in there?

Please, he called to something within himself. *Please. If you do work... please let it be now. I want to fight. I want to protect my friends.*

He opened his eyes, and nothing. The only difference was that the Zakaras were now closer.

Sidry tried again. One of the Zakaras was now just a few feet away. Sidry could tell from the tensing of its muscles it was about to leap.

Please!

His sense of dread left him. Something outside of himself, yet at the same time within him, awakened.

Everything around him vanished. Sidry was no longer in the woods and surrounded by Zakaras. He was encased in a dimension of pure white light. His body felt like it was melting. He looked down and watched his arms changing shape. His body became encased in celestial armour, a glimmering blue membrane of skin.

He now knew there was a crystal inside his forehead because he could feel it pulsating as it sent waves of energy coursing through his body, changing him, transforming him into something else. He felt his forehead open as the crystal emerged to the surface of his skin, but it wasn't painful.

He had never felt so powerful in his life.

The white light abruptly faded, and Sidry found himself back in the woodland, but he now stood taller before the horde of monsters.

The Zakaras paused. Stared at him with their black eyes.

Do they realise that I am now something they should fear? Sidry wondered.

His eyesight was enhanced and, despite the wider parting of his eyes, everything was clearer and more three dimensional. Sidry could see everything around him to the tiniest detail; the veins in the leaves of the trees, the particles of dirt on the ground, the pores in the Zakaras' scaly armour, the tips of their protracting talons. Sidry looked down at his body for a moment in amazement and saw he was in a similar form to the one Baird assumed, only Sidry's biological armour had a tinge of green.

Looking at his hands, Sidry recalled what he had seen Baird do many times and moulding his fingers together – turning his arm into a blade – came to him as naturally as breathing.

A Zakara leapt at him, but Sidry reacted quickly and swung his new blade into its path. When his blade met the monster it carved through it, and Sidry felt a string of peculiar sensations as the sharp edge bore through its flesh – he could *feel* the creature's muscles and guts tearing through his blade. It was sensitive.

The two halves of the beast's corpse fell, and Sidry roared in triumph only to hear a strange polyphonous ringing sound resonate from where his mouth should be.

His roar of victory was short-lived. Another Zakara jumped upon him, but luckily Sidry's quickened reflexes shirked its attack, and he dived out of its reach. A third Zakara tried its chances, but Sidry lifted his foot and slammed it into the creature with such force its body sprawled through the air and crashed heavily against a tree several yards away.

Sidry looked around. Four more were scurrying towards him. How could he take on so many?

One at a time.

He launched into the air, plunging into the middle of the cluster and slicing one of them in half as he landed. The rest of them scattered. Another creature leapt at him, but Sidry ducked and circled his blade, cutting through several legs while he was down. They all fell back, blood pouring from the stumps where they once had limbs.

Sidry rose again, tall and powerful, and moulded his other arm into a second blade.

The beasts were coming at him from all sides now, and he knew he must not let them enclose him. He drove forward, sweeping his blades to keep them out of his range. They ducked and dodged around him, but his attacks were so frequent he always found an opening to spill more blood.

He darted from side to side, taking out attackers from every direction to prevent them from closing in on him.

But, no matter how many of them he took down, there were always more.

Sidry was interrupted by an odd sensation in his back. He turned his head and saw that he had been struck. He also felt an awareness that he had been damaged, and it was an unpleasant sensation, but not painful.

Tentacles coiled around his legs. Sidry tried to turn, to kick himself free, but two more banded around his arms and shoulders.

Chapter 13

The Encampment

Dareth opened his eyes, but all he could see was darkness, and when he tried to move it was only to discover that his hands had been bound behind his back. After a few moments of disorientating confusion, he remembered the men who seized him at the inn, and cursed.

What had happened to him?

He guessed from his blistering headache that he had been knocked out. He turned his head from side to side, but the darkness lingered; something was covering his eyes.

Although he was lying still, Dareth felt an odd sensation in his stomach – as if he was somehow moving. He realised he could hear the trotting of horses, coupled with a spindling noise he soon recognised to be wheels.

The walls around him lurched as the wheels went over a rock and he bumped the back of his head against something. Agony enflamed his bruised skull, and his instinct was to clutch his head, but his wrists burned against the ropes that bound them behind his back.

He kicked out in fury, but his foot met another barrier and he realised just how small a space he was contained in. His knees were pressed against his chest. He began to feel claustrophobic.

"Where am I?" he called.

There was no answer.

"What's going on!?" he yelled, but all he could hear was the trotting of hooves as the carriage moved on.

He realised they must have dumped him in the luggage compartment, and anger swelled up in him at this indignity. He swore, screamed out demands for answers to his unknown captors, and their lack of response only infuriated him further. He knew there must be someone at the reigns, guiding this carriage to its destination. Why was no one answering him?

His anger gave way to fear and he writhed in his cell for a while, searching for a way out, but it was useless. He gave up, giving the wall of his prison one last kick to expel his rage.

In the cramped isolation, his mind wandered. He fretted over what was going to happen to him. He didn't know where they were taking him, or how long he had been unconscious.

He cursed himself for being so foolish. He knew venturing into Habella was risky. Why did he do it? He would have to be wiser in the future.

If he still had a future.

The confinement made his body ache, and he lost any sense of time. He drifted into sleep for fleeting periods but found himself repeatedly awoken by the cart going over a bump or a sudden lurch as it turned a tight corner.

Eventually, the cart stopped. He heard muffled voices and pressed his ear against the wall but couldn't make out any of the words.

"Where am I!?" he called out.

They didn't reply.

The door above Dareth swung open and tempered light glowed through the strands of his blindfold.

"You have two choices," announced an epicene, patronising voice with a peculiar accent that Dareth couldn't place. "You can either come out willingly, or you can make this difficult for yourself."

Dareth clenched his fists and took a deep breath to calm himself. That voice was irritating, but he knew threats would get him nowhere so he did as he was told. For now, Dareth had to accept he was powerless, no matter how much he hated it.

Several pairs of hands lifted Dareth out of his confinement. His limbs were stiff, and he stumbled a few times when his feet touched the ground; it took all his will not to cause a struggle as they got him to walk.

Dareth was guided somewhere and then pushed to his knees. The blindfold was removed. Light stung his eyes, and Dareth turned them to the ground, blinked a few times as they adjusted.

When Dareth looked up, he saw a man sitting before him. It was the same man who had been waiting for him in his room at Habella. He had a delicate face and a finely groomed moustache. He was small and almost dainty, which made the situation all that more unbearable for Dareth; he knew that if he was not bound, and the two of them were alone, he could overpower this man in moments.

Dareth looked around himself. He was in a white tent, and there were men in green robes all around him. Staring at him.

"It wasn't my fault!" Dareth exclaimed. "He was going to kill me!"

The man raised his eyebrows, and a confused yet amused expression gave shape to his features.

"Who the fuck *are* you?" Dareth asked. Why wasn't anyone from Jalard there? Surely they would need to confirm his identity before they punished him for his crimes? Where was his mother?

"I am Shayam," the man introduced himself. "But that is not the real question. For I am much more interested in who *you* are…"

Dareth was rendered speechless. He was Dareth of Jalard. The boy who killed his stepfather. Surely they knew who he was or why else would they have taken him?

"Now…" Shayam leant forward, narrowing his eyes. "I have met Jaedin, and you do not look much like him to me…"

Dareth sneered. "I would bloody hope not."

"So why do you choose to travel by that name?" Shayam asked.

"Stop these fucking games!" Dareth said. "We all know why I am here. I killed Tarvek. Yes! I admit it! I'm not ashamed either! The world's better off without that cunt!"

"I believe it is you who is playing games…" Shayam chuckled.

With every word uttered from this man's mouth, Dareth's confusion grew. Who was he? Why did he have such a strange accent?

For the first time, Dareth began to consider the possibility that he was not here for the reasons he initially thought.

"Did they pay you to travel by that name?" Shayam accused. "Are you a decoy? A friend helping them escape?"

"A friend of who?" Dareth asked.

"Jaedin, of course," he replied.

Dareth laughed. "Me? Help *Jaedin*? Are you scitting me?"

"Just answer the question!" Shayam snapped. He seemed to be getting impatient now.

"I *hate* Jaedin!" Dareth replied. "That's why I travelled by that name. Makes it more interesting if I cause trouble."

Why is he so interested in that worthless sodd anyway? Dareth thought to himself, noticing Shayam had just shifted in his seat. For some reason, Dareth's cry of hatred had caught the man's interest.

"Is he your boyfriend or something?" Dareth asked, laughing again.

It made sense now. The man before him seemed like a bit of a soddy himself.

"Are you from Jalard?" Shayam asked.

"Of course I am!" Dareth replied.

"How long has it been since you were last there?"

Dareth didn't even know the answer to that question. Two aeights ago? Maybe three? He had lost track of time.

"Fuck knows," Dareth shrugged. "Who cares?"

Shayam raised himself from his chair. "That will be all, for now," he said and walked to the opening of the tent. He drew back the curtain, revealing daylight outside.

The conversation was over, and Dareth was more confused now than he had been before it began.

Dareth glanced at the men around him. They were all clad in matching green robes. None of them had uttered a single word or even twitched a muscle throughout that whole confrontation. Who were these people? Was this some kind of cult?

"I advise you to not make any trouble," Shayam warned as he closed the curtain behind him. "These men here are stronger than they look."

*   *   *

In the early afternoon, four of Shayam's men came and collected Bryna from the post to which she was tied. They unbound her and escorted her through the encampment. She was obedient. She walked with them silently, her face betraying no emotions.

They guided her to one of the tents and ushered her inside.

A woman was waiting for her. She was dressed in exotic

finery of black silks with tinges of dark reds and purples. Her face held a startling resemblance to Bryna's mother, but her hair was darker, and she had a pointed chin.

They stared at each other. Neither of them said anything at first, but their eyes spoke volumes.

The similarity between them was uncanny. The dark hair. Pale skin. And they both had distinctively rare violet eyes. There was an unspoken acknowledgement, between them, that they were connected somehow, but there was distrust too.

The guards left, and Bryna stood at the opening.

"Come in," the woman said. She motioned with one of her long, finely shaped fingernails for Bryna to sit upon the chair opposite her.

Bryna just stared at her.

"Sit down," she said and, although her voice was pleasant, Bryna could tell it was an order.

She sat. On the table between them stood a bottle of wine, two cups, and a bowl filled with blueberries and apples. Blueberries were a rare delicacy, and even the apples must have come from afar because Bryna had only ever previously seen green ones.

"Would you like some wine?" the woman asked. She smiled, but it lacked warmth.

Bryna shook her head.

"Some fruit?"

"I am not hungry," she replied.

The smile faded from the woman's face. It was clear she was merely trying to soften Bryna with pleasantries before she began the interrogation.

"I am Carmaestre," she introduced herself. "And I know who *you* are, but I do not know your name."

Bryna stared at her.

"What did your mother name you?" Carmaestre said, her voice hardening.

"Bryna…" she whispered.

Carmaestre turned away for a few moments. Her face was hard to read, but Bryna sensed that distant memories were running through her mind. "Bryna…" she muttered under her breath. "Bryna and Jaedin…"

She turned back to Bryna. "Born together?" she asked.

Bryna nodded. "Twins."

There was a silence. Bryna sensed that many questions were racing through Caemaestre's mind, but she was considering them all very carefully before she spoke.

"You are the one who caused all this..." Bryna broke the silence. Her voice was soft and monotonous, despite the gravity of what she was saying. "I saw you. You did those *things* to those people..."

Bryna caught a flicker of guilt in the woman's eyes, but she swiftly suppressed it.

"Can you not see how much damage you have done?" Bryna finished.

"So you can *see* things..." Carmaestre changed the subject. "That is interesting... your grandmother had that gift."

"What do you want from me?" Bryna asked.

Carmaestre gulped wine from her glass. It was evident Bryna's presence was having a profound effect on her. "When I first saw your brother. Back in the forest of Lareem," she said. "He almost brought me to tears. He seemed so familiar... like someone I knew from long ago."

From the look in her eyes, it was clear that this someone was very significant to her indeed.

"But I thought the resemblance was just a coincidence," Carmaestre's voice changed. It went colder. Bitterly so. She shifted on her seat, and her body language became defensive. "But it still pained me to do the ritual. To cut runes onto the flesh of a young man who looked so much like him... but, when I saw you," her eyes locked with Bryna's with intensity. "I knew it had to be true. You *had* to be my sister's daughter. You have her face, her aura – everything about you is truly her. Except for the eyes..."

She took another sip of wine. "You have his eyes..."

Bryna said nothing.

"Where are they?" Carmaestre asked.

"Dead," Bryna replied.

Carmaestre's eyes darkened. It was clear her emotions were conflicted. Grief was the most distinctive. But grief for what? The lives of ones precious to her? Or for something left unresolved?

"How?"

"My father, shortly before I was born," Bryna replied, and

Carmaestre flinched at the mention of him. "And my mother was killed by the monsters you created."

If guilt was the desired outcome, Bryna failed.

"Do not speak as if I am the one in the wrong!" the woman snarled. "Do you even know what your parents did to me!?"

Bryna shook her head.

"Your mother was a thief!!" she said. "She took *everything* from me, and from the day she ran away our family was doomed! The entire legacy has been lost! And all because your mother couldn't keep her legs together..."

Carmaestre put a hand to her chest and took a few deep breaths to calm herself. She drank more wine. Stared at Bryna.

"Not much of a talker, are you?" Carmaestre smirked. She leant over, placed her elbows on the table. "No, matter... I just have *one* more thing I would like to ask you..." she said.

This was the big question. The one she had summoned Bryna here for.

"What is on that chain around your neck?"

Bryna's heart froze in her chest.

"I see..." Carmaestre smiled to herself. "So she gave to you what she stole from me... Well! I'm taking it *back*!"

She reached for it, grabbing hold of the chain with greedy fingers and pulling upon it. When the purple stone emerged from beneath Bryna's collar, Carmaestre's eyes lit up. She parted her dark lips, longingly. She touched it but, as soon as her fingers made contact with the stone, it glowed.

There was a flash of light, and Carmaestre retracted her hand. The tips of her fingers were blistered; Bryna could smell burnt flesh.

She looked at Bryna. "It has already *claimed* you?!" Carmaestre gasped what seemed a terrible revelation. Her pupils dilated. "How can this be?! You weren't even supposed to be born! You were never part of the plan!"

Bryna didn't move nor say anything. The stone at her chest glowed, as did her eyes. An ominous power beset a dark haze of energy around her, which enwreathed her skin.

"Give it to me!" Carmaestre snarled.

Bryna shook her head. "I can't. It has chosen me. You said so yoursel–"

She was interrupted by a slap to the face.

"Take her away!" Carmaestre screamed, and Shayam's men were there in moments, grabbing Bryna roughly by her arms.

"I will find a way of getting that back, you bitch's bantling brat!" she howled as they dragged Bryna from the tent. "I *will* reclaim what is mine!"

* * *

Aylen watched as Bryna was escorted back to her post. She obediently placed her hands behind her back as the robed men – her escorts – tied her to it again.

"What did they do?" Aylen asked her once the men walked away, and they were alone.

Bryna shook her head. Whatever happened, she was not going to talk about it.

Aylen sighed. During their time held captive together, Bryna had barely spoken more than a few words to him; every attempt he had made to converse with her had been met with either cold, short, and distant replies, or nothing at all.

He was at least relieved to see that she had not come to any harm.

The two of them had been in captivity for two days now, bound to wooden beams with their hands tied behind their backs. Occasionally, they were allowed brief periods of respite, and their hands were untied so they could relieve themselves and eat, but always under close watch of their captors. At night they were covered with blankets and forced to sleep in the same uncomfortable position. Aylen's wrists were painfully sore now from his binds chafing.

He had not seen any of the others, and none of the questions he yelled at their captors were ever answered. The last thing Aylen remembered, before being here, was Frih'dra slamming his staff upon a platform, activating the spell, and Bryna screaming. Aylen had found himself engulfed by cold air which froze up his entire body. After that, he could only recall the moment Frih'dra brought him back to life by placing his hand on Aylen's forehead, just before they tied him to the post.

Aylen missed his daggers. They had been taken away from him.

Not that they would make much difference anyway, he thought to himself. The encampment was swarming with men who could transform into Zakaras. Even if Aylen had his blades, they wouldn't get him very far.

Sometimes, Aylen saw Shayam wandering around the camp. And once he spotted a garish woman in a black dress who stared at Bryna for a few moments before retreating to one of the tents. Apart from that, Aylen had not witnessed anything of note. Just endless streams of men in green robes walking around and performing errands. They were all Zakaras, Aylen was certain of it. With nothing else to do but observe them, he began to gain a sense for telling the difference between them and normal humans by studying the subtle disparities in their behaviour. When they talked, there was a lack of animation behind it, and their facial expressions only went from deadpan to sombre. They seemed to possess some of the intelligence of their former selves, but they lacked that special, indefinable spark which made somebody a *person*.

But Aylen also knew it was very possible he was only noticing these things because he was already aware of what they were. He suspected people fortunate enough to have never acquainted themselves with Zakaras would probably have no idea.

Aylen wondered why Shayam was keeping him here. He understood that Baird and Jaedin were a threat, and Miles was a traitor to his people. Now they had been captured, their prospects were grim.

We are the leftovers... Aylen thought, looking at Bryna. Neither of them were important in Shayam's schemes. Or a threat. He was surprised they hadn't been killed already.

He had seen no sign of Kyra, which made him worry. Was it because she was already dead?

He couldn't bear the thought of it. He wanted to see her. Talk to her. There were so many things he had wanted to say to her but had never had the chance.

Aylen was interrupted from his thoughts when he caught sight of someone being escorted towards him by Shayam's men. Someone limping.

As they came closer, Aylen recognised it was Rivan. His older friend had a sour expression on his face, and his wrists were bound together. A part of Aylen was happy to see him – he always felt safer when Rivan was around – but another part of him was sad that Rivan was now doomed to the same fate as him, whatever it was going to be.

He had never seen his friend look as defeated as he did that moment when he was tied to a post next to Bryna. He couldn't even look Aylen in the eyes, and Aylen knew it was because he was ashamed.

"Where's Sidry?" Aylen asked him, wondering what had happened to him. Had at least one of them managed to escape from Shayam?

"I don't know," Rivan shook his head. "He did it though," he said, turning back to Aylen. "He *changed*."

It took Aylen a few moments to realise what his friend was talking about.

"You mean like Baird?" Aylen gasped. "I thought he couldn't! He said–"

"He did," Rivan confirmed. "When it was needed, he did it," and, despite the hopelessness of their situation, his face lit up with pride.

Will I ever cause him to be as proud of me? Aylen thought, feeling a twinge of jealousy. He immediately scolded himself for having such a thought. Who knew what terrible fate lay in store for Sidry now.

"What happened?" Aylen asked.

"He fought well," Rivan replied. "He took many of those bastard things down… it just wasn't enough…"

Bryna sat between them and, throughout that whole exchange, the impassive expression on her pale face remained apathetic and uninvolved. She stared at the sky, seemingly unconcerned about their situation. Aylen scowled at her.

But his attention was soon drawn elsewhere when he realised a group of figures were walking towards them. In an encampment filled with men wearing green robes, it did not take Aylen long to deduce that the man at the front – the one in the red tunic and shiny black leggings – was Shayam. His presence loomed towards them like a black cloud.

"Afternoon," Shayam greeted once he reached them. Several of his henchmen stood on either side of him, expressionless. "I trust your passage here was pleasant?" he asked Rivan.

Rivan scowled, and Aylen could tell from the bruises on his face that his journey had been far from that.

"Where's Sidry?" Rivan yelled.

"The Avatars of Gezra are being watched closely," Shayam replied. "Thanks to Frih'dra's sorcery, they are much more manageable now. They will not be causing any more problems."

"The *what* are being watched?" Aylen asked.

"The Avatars of Gezra," Shayam repeated. "The crystals your friends were fused with are from the Temple of Gezra, so therefore it is only apt that the being they summon with its power be known as an avatar of this deity."

"What do you want from us, Shayam?" Rivan asked.

"Well you don't think I am going to let two Avatars, a boy who can meddle with my Zakaras, a vile traitor, and a group with some very sensitive information slip my grasp, do you?" Shayam answered.

"You killed our families!" Aylen yelled. "Isn't that enough?"

Shayam turned to him. "Did you just say that *I* killed your families?" he asked.

Aylen struggled against the binds as uncontrollable anger consumed him. Did this man feel no remorse for what he had done?

"What happened to your village was an unfortunate accident," Shayam stated, narrowing his eyes at Aylen as one would a child having a tantrum. "It was never my intention to hurt innocent people."

"We saw it ourselves!" Rivan snarled. "Your fucking monsters did it!"

"I am afraid that part of the blame must rest on you for what happened," Shayam said.

"This is bullshit!" Rivan hollered.

"I sent a group of my men to your village on a reconnaissance mission. No more," Shayam stated. "It was never our intention to harm them. But you quickly changed that."

Shayam opened the palm of his hand and revealed a red crystal. The one he used to control the Zakaras. Aylen noticed something strange; surely, at the angle Shayam was holding the gem, it should have fallen out of his hand? Aylen looked a little closer and saw that the skin surrounding the crystal was scorched, as if it had been melted. The artefact had somehow been fused into Shayam's palm.

Not brave enough to have his skull opened, like he did to Jaedin, Aylen thought bitterly.

"By utilising this, I have complete control over these men," Shayam explained. He turned, facing the palm of his hand in the direction of his henchmen a few yards away, and then red light glowed from his hand.

"Unlike Jaedin, I know such secrets as controlling them from a distance, and summoning several of them at once," Shayam said, as the men drew their swords in perfect unison. "His efforts have been a slight nuisance but, as he is not one of us, he will never be given the secrets to achieving his full potential."

He turned back to Aylen, and the light glowing from his palm faded. The men behind him sheathed their swords and reassumed a normal posture.

"I had full control over the men I sent to Jalard. I was doing so from my base in the Forest of Lareem. But when *intruders* came, I was distracted. I was forced to escape."

He looked Aylen in the eyes.

"When you forced me to flee, I lost control. If you want to blame someone for what happened to your village, you need look no further than yourselves."

*   *   *

"They're all dead…" Dareth murmured.

Even after saying it out loud, it still didn't sound real.

Carmaestre nodded gravely.

After Shayam's interrogation, and hours spent in confinement, Dareth had been brought before the presence of this woman.

On first appearances, he didn't think much of her. Everything about her, from her extravagant black dress to the long eyelashes that surrounded her cryptic eyes and her finely combed black hair, screamed out flamboyance and vanity. There was something about her Dareth didn't trust. Sometimes her facial expressions and body language did not entirely match what she was saying. As if she was hiding something.

But she was the first person to have treated him with respect for several days and, for this, he was willing to give her the benefit of the doubt.

She explained to him the terrible fate which had befallen his village. How she and Shayam were conducting important work which was for the benefit of all mankind; work which was disrupted by Baird and the others, who, in ignorance of their actions, caused the deaths of everyone in Jalard. She told him about the measures she and Shayam were now implementing to repair the damage Baird and the others had caused.

It was a lot to take in at once.

Dareth wasn't heartless. The news did stir some feelings within him, but they were numb and distant. It was a shame that so many innocent lives had come to an end, but Dareth had already turned his back on Jalard and, in many ways, never really felt like he belonged there. Most of the villagers had looked down on him and his family, and no one, apart from Aylen, had ever done anything to help him through those years of abuse he suffered.

The people of Jalard didn't deserve to die, but there was nothing Dareth could do to change it. It was out of his hands. It had happened. There was no point in him dwelling over something which had been and gone.

Dareth's heart sank when he thought of his mother. Despite all the things she let Tarvek get away with over the years, there was once a time she had been caring and responsible. Dareth didn't feel remorse for his mother as he knew her now; he felt remorse for the woman he remembered from his childhood. That woman had been dead for years, and he had been dealing with that loss for quite some time.

There was also a part of him which felt great relief. Dareth could not help but realise that this was convenient for him. No one knew he had murdered his stepfather. He was now free from the burden of his crime. He could live a normal life.

He felt guilty for having such thoughts. Shouldn't he be grieving for all those lives lost?

"And Aylen?" Dareth asked. "Is he here?"

Carmaestre nodded.

"Can I see him?" he said.

She shook her head. "Not yet. I'm sorry, but this is a very sensitive situation. Your friends have caused a lot of trouble, and we are yet to decide how we are going to deal with them."

"They are not my friends," Dareth shook his head. "Only Aylen was… Are you sure he was really involved? And not just… with them? Baird probably made all the decisions…"

When he talked, she seemed to actually listen to him. Dareth couldn't remember the last time someone of her years had taken him seriously.

"That is a possibility…" she pondered out loud.

"Could you talk to Shayam for me?" Dareth asked. "Maybe get him freed?"

"I will try…" she promised, smiling.

Dareth sighed. He guessed that was all he could do for now. He wondered how his friend was faring. Aylen had always been too sentimental, and Dareth could imagine he wasn't coping well with everything he had been through since they last saw each other. His whole village and family were dead, and he was partly to blame.

Aylen was the only person from Jalard who ever really cared, so Dareth was determined to do everything within his power to help him. He wasn't all that bothered about the others.

"But you should think about yourself, too," Carmaestre said, placing a hand on Dareth's knee. "You are in pain… grieving… is there anything I can do for you?"

She traced her fingers up and down his thigh, which aroused a stirring in Dareth's loins. He looked up at her, and she fluttered her eyelashes at him. Pursed her dark lips.

His eyes went to her cleavage. She was older. And Dareth had never been all that fond of people who dressed extravagantly, as it had always seemed to him that they were trying too hard to draw attention to themselves.

But she was quite attractive, for an older woman.

He wondered what she expected of him. How far she wanted to go.

Dareth didn't really have any experience with women. Some of the girls in Jalard had been nice to look at, but he'd never had any patience for them.

His penis, however, was already alert and throbbing

between his legs, and one of her hands ventured to caress it through his leggings. By this point, Dareth was too excited to give this turn in his fortune any more consideration. He didn't stop her when she unfastened his belt.

She kissed him, and the harrowing fate which had befallen the people of Jalard was soon far from Dareth's mind.

*　　*　　*

Kyra knew Dion was returning when the men standing guard outside her tent walked away. They only ever left when he visited her.

His shadow appeared at the opening, and he drew back the curtain.

She turned and smiled at him as he stepped inside.

"You're back," she said welcomingly. The way a wife would greet a husband who had just returned from a hard day's work.

Whatever she had done to Dion's face last time she saw him, it seemed Zakaras healed quickly, for there was not a single mark or blemish.

"You are happy to see me?" he asked.

Kyra looked down, feigning regret. "I am sorry for how I've been. It's just everything that's happened recently has been so overwhelming... and I pushed you away..."

She smiled at him. In the same way she used to smile at the real Dion. "But I have come round now. Dion, please don't be angry with me. You are all I have left."

He smiled back, and she noted, with satisfaction, that she must be putting on a good act.

But she was also surprised by how stupid these beings were. She hadn't been expecting this to work. Are these creatures *really* that gullible? Or was he also playing a game?

Either way, there was no going back now; this was her only chance to escape.

"Come to me, my love," she said, opening her arms out to him, forcing the last two words out despite the unpleasant feeling they brought to her insides.

His face lit up greedily, and he was on top of her in moments, pressing his body against hers and brushing his lips upon her neck.

She lay down on her back and reached into her leggings. This was it. This was her final chance. Her last resort.

She was glad that he didn't seem to want to kiss her mouth. She didn't think she could have brought herself to do that. She had to bite her lip to stop herself screaming as his hands explored her body.

Her outfit had many hidden pouches. Once, each one of them had contained a blade, but when she woke up in this encampment they had been taken away from her.

All except for one.

As part of its design, a tiny dagger had been sown in between the layers of the leather itself so that even the most stringent searches could not find it. Kyra had spent the last few hours picking at the stitches concealing it, with her fingers. The blade was barely three inches long, but very sharp – she wondered how much damage she could do with it.

She was about to find out. She had to act now. His hands were on her back, trying to remove her bodice. She couldn't bear this any longer.

He grunted when she slammed the blade into the back of his neck and, for a few moments, quivered against her like a stuck pig.

Then he stopped moving.

There was a brief silence. Kyra wondered if it was enough. Could she make her escape?

No. It wasn't. His eyes snapped open. He looked down on her.

Before he had a chance to react, Kyra drew the blade across his throat. Dark blood gushed from his neck. He tried to restrain her by grabbing her wrists, but she rocked herself onto her upper back and pushed her elbows against the ground to flip herself up – it was an old trick she often used to get herself back onto her feet quickly during duels but, with Dion on top of her, it worked to turn the tables: knocking him back. He fell to the ground, and now, she was on top of *him*.

She drove the dagger into his neck, tearing through his windpipe and severing as much of the flesh there as she could. He wheezed. Squirmed. And when he stopped squirming, she jumped off.

She knew it was probably not enough to kill him, but for now he was immobile, and she needed to get away before anyone noticed.

She ran outside and quickly scanned her surroundings. There were tents all around her and a few of Shayam's men in sight, but none of them seemed to notice her.

She fled, her heart hammering in her chest. This encampment was almost like a maze. She could not seem to find a way out. Every time she turned a corner, all she could see were more tents. She tried to avoid coming into contact with Shayam's men, but they were everywhere. Some of them were now giving her suspicious glances. She knew it wouldn't be long until Shayam saw her through their eyes.

She wound between the tents. Frantic. This was her final chance to get away and she was wasting it. She scanned her eyes across the encampment, looking for something. Anything.

"Kyra!" a voice called.

She turned to the source and caught sight of three people tied to posts. She rushed to them, recognising them immediately. They were bound to large wooden beams with their arms behind their backs.

"You're alive, Kyra!" Aylen exclaimed with much relief in his eyes. "They got us! In Habella. They got us all!"

"Where are the others?" Kyra asked, fearing the worst.

"In one of the tents!" Rivan said. "I think!"

"They've been frozen," Aylen added. "It's some kind of spell!"

Shayam's men had noticed her now. They were marching towards her. Kyra was running out of time. She knew she couldn't escape. It was useless. There was nothing she could do.

She wrapped her arms around Bryna. Tears streamed from her eyes. Bryna could not return the gesture as her hands were tied her back but, when Kyra broke away, her eyes spoke volumes to her. They said: *don't give up, Kyra.*

Kyra heard footsteps behind her. She knew she only had a few moments until Shayam's men reached her.

She scrambled over to Aylen, holding the blade she had used to stab Dion up in front of his eyes for him to see and then jamming it into the ground next to where his hands were tied. Hidden. Aylen may be just able to reach it and pry it out from the soil when Shayam's men were gone.

"I am sorry," she whispered. "It's all I can give you."

She heard Dion's voice.

"Kyra!"

She turned around.

Dion was standing behind her with a cohort of Shayam's men on each side of him. He had finally shifted into his true form. His body was covered in scales, his teeth were fanged, and his eyes were two tiny dots. A span of black tentacles emerged from his back and flexed. Each one of them squirmed and moved independently.

Kyra turned to Bryna, Aylen and Rivan one last time.

"The next time you see me, I will either be one of them or he will have done something to me so horrible that I will no longer want to live. Either way, if you can, please kill me."

Arms grabbed her. She was pulled away.

"Kyra!" Aylen yelled.

She held back tears. She had never realised that she thought of Aylen as a friend until that moment.

"Bye Aylen," she said. "Be strong. Don't let them break you."

Chapter 14

Blood is Power

Dareth listened to Carmaestre breathing beside him.

It was enjoyable, but it didn't live up to all those times he imagined it. He always thought that, after his first time, he would feel different – more like a man, perhaps – and he was a little disappointed.

Her sheets were soft, so different from the coarse linen that he was used to sleeping in. Just who was this woman? Dareth had heard that some Gavendarians were rich nobles who hoarded money. Possessed more of it than they would ever need. More than someone from Sharma could even comprehend. Was she one of them?

He looked at her, but she was facing away from him and all he could see was her black hair strewn across the pillow. He wondered what he should do. He considered leaving the bed and her tent, but he didn't know if he was allowed. He had been escorted there by guards, would they come back to collect him as well?

He didn't like the thought of being pulled from the bed and dragged outside naked when Shayam's henchmen came back for him, so he decided to dress in case that moment came. He climbed out of the bed carefully, so as to not wake her. The two of them had just pleasured each other but, now the moment was over, he doubted he and this oddball of a woman would have much to chit-chat about.

Shayam appeared at the entrance to the bedchamber, and Dareth turned away guiltily when the Gavendarian man's eyes wandered from Dareth's half-dressed body to the figure of Carmaestre lying on the bed.

"Hope I haven't disturbed anything…" Shayam commented. His mouth curved into a knowing smile.

"For the love of Gods!" Carmaestre moaned from beneath the sheets as she turned over. "Can't you let a woman rest?"

"Resting seems to be the last thing you've been doing…" Shayam snorted.

"What do you want, Shayam?" Carmaestre grumbled,

lifting her head to scowl at the man who intruded upon her.

"Actually, it is not you I came here for…" Shayam said and looked at Dareth.

"Well take him away and leave me in peace!" Carmaestre replied, dismissing Dareth with a flick of her wrist.

Dareth put his tunic back on and followed Shayam out of the tent.

Shayam led him through the encampment and, to Dareth's surprise, there was no escort this time, which he guessed meant the Gavendarian was beginning to trust him. It was strange to think that not much more than a day ago Dareth had been dragged here bound and blindfolded.

"Can I see Aylen?" Dareth asked.

Shayam shook his head. "Not yet I'm afraid, young man. This is a very delicate situation… we are yet to decide how we are going to deal with your friends."

"They are not my friends," Dareth shook his head. "I just want you free *one* of them. Aylen."

"I will think about it," Shayam replied. "We are not monsters. We will be fair."

Dareth wanted to argue further, but he knew it was useless. For now, he must wait.

"What about you?" Shayam turned to him. "You don't have a home to go back to, thanks to *them*. What are you going to do?"

Dareth almost told him he ran away from Jalard anyway but held his tongue. That was his secret now.

"I'm not sure," he replied. "I'm going to wait for Aylen."

"Your loyalty to that young man is surprising," Shayam commented. "I must say, I would not be so forgiving in your shoes. They are responsible for the destruction of your village…"

"I never belonged there," Dareth said, shaking his head. "Aylen was the only one who ever gave a shit."

"I remember you voicing your hatred for one of them in particular…" Shayam recalled. "In fact, that is why I have brought you here."

Shayam halted outside one of the tents and gestured to the entrance.

"What's in there?" Dareth asked.

"Go in and see," Shayam said.

Dareth stepped inside. It was a smaller tent than most of the others, and its only feature was a wooden table with a body laid upon it. Dareth looked at the face.

It was Jaedin.

"What happened to him?" Dareth asked. "You didn't tell me he was dead."

"He's not dead," Shayam shook his head. "He's just... let's call it a very deep sleep. I have a mage with me who has some interesting abilities in that regard... I have many interesting friends..."

Dareth stared at him. Jaedin's face was even paler than usual, and there was a faint glow around him. Dareth guessed that must be something to do with the spell keeping him asleep. Jaedin didn't even appear to be breathing. His chest never rose nor fell.

"Why bring me here?" Dareth asked.

Shayam's hand went into his pocket and, to Dareth's surprise, he brought out a dagger.

"Here," Shayam offered it to Dareth. "Take it."

Dareth hesitated.

"Take it," Shayam repeated, placing it in Dareth's hand.

Dareth gripped the hilt and examined the blade. It was much larger and sharper than the one he used to kill his stepfather. It even had a jewel upon its hilt. It was probably very valuable.

"You said you hate this boy," Shayam said. "Would you like to kill him?"

Dareth looked at Shayam. At first, he was sure that the Gavendarian must be joking, but the man seemed to be serious.

"Why?" was all Dareth could say.

"He destroyed your village! It's thanks to *him* your friend is in trouble!" Shayam responded. "Don't you want revenge?"

"But why *me*?" Dareth asked.

He wants me to take the stick for it, Dareth realised. *Either that or this is some kind of test.*

"You said yourself you hated him!" Shayam said. "Don't you want to do it? End him. I know you have killed before, Dareth. You can do it again, can't you?"

"I don't want to get done for murder!" Dareth muttered.

"You won't be," Shayam reassured. "You have my permission."

Dareth looked down at the Jaedin. Was it true? Could he

really kill him *and* get away with it?

It was tempting. There had always been something about Jaedin he despised. Dareth hated his delicate features. That girly black hair. Jaedin grew up in one of the biggest houses in Jalard just because his mother was some fancy medicine woman. And he had *always* looked at Dareth with his nose turned up. As if he was inferior. Since Dareth last saw him, he had taken to tying a band over his forehead. Why? Why did Jaedin and his barmy sister always feel the need to make a show of themselves by being so peculiar?

Now was Dareth's chance. Dareth could kill Jaedin.

And, apparently, get away with it too.

But Dareth found himself hesitating. He couldn't bring himself to do it.

And he didn't even know why. What was stopping him drawing the blade across Jaedin's neck? After all these years, he could *finally* win.

He kept thinking about Tarvek. The way the blood felt on his hands. The sound his skin made when the blade slit it open. It was not a pleasant memory.

Dareth handed the dagger back to Shayam. The Gavendarian seemed disappointed.

"No," he said. "I can't."

*   *   *

Rivan watched as Aylen pried his fingers into the ground and tried to pull Kyra's dagger free only for his hand to slip.

"Dig more," Rivan said.

Aylen winced but did as he was told.

He had been doing this for an hour now and was clearly in pain. Straining against his binds had chafed his wrists so much they had turned bloody and red. Rivan felt bad for making his friend do something which caused him pain, but he suppressed this guilt. They had no other choice.

He focussed upon his own duty: keeping watch. If Shayam or any of his men caught wind of what Aylen was up to, they would confiscate the dagger from them.

If Aylen managed to get hold of it, they would be able to cut themselves free from their binds, but what Rivan had not told his friend yet was he didn't have any idea what they were going to do once they got past that stage. He was still to come up with a plan.

The place was swarming with Zakaras. Rivan knew trying to fight them would be suicide. With a sinking heart, he realised rescuing the others was not an option. Rivan and Aylen's only hope of getting out alive was to flee.

They were going to have to leave their friends behind.

*But I **will** come back!* Rivan promised, to try and make himself feel better about it. *If we can get away, we **might** be able to find help... That is the only way we can possibly save the others.*

Even though his reasoning was logically sound, it didn't make the decision any easier. Rivan still felt guilty.

Bryna was another moral dilemma. Rivan knew that if the three of them escaped together, Shayam would send Zakaras after them once he discovered their absence. Would Bryna be able to keep up? Or should Rivan leave her behind too so that he and Aylen had a better chance?

"Got it!" Aylen announced. The dagger was in his hand, coated in dirt.

"Cut your binds," Rivan instructed. "And be subtle."

Aylen turned the blade upwards and lined the edge with the rope around his wrists. He squinted as he nicked away at the threads. Rivan kept an eye out for Shayam's henchmen.

"I'm free," Aylen announced, stretching his arms out and rubbing his sore wrists.

"Put your arms back behind your back!" Rivan hissed. "They might see you!"

Aylen grimaced but returned his arms to their original position.

"Now toss me the dagger," Rivan muttered.

Aylen flicked his wrist, sending the implement spinning. It landed next to Rivan's post. He grabbed it.

As Rivan cut at his binds, he looked at Bryna and once again considered what they should do with her in the equation. He felt terrible about it, but he knew she would slow them down. He would probably have to cut her binds for her – as he doubted she would be able to do it for herself – which might draw attention to them before they managed to get a head start.

Rivan came to the conclusion that he was going to have to leave her behind.

His thoughts were interrupted when he saw red flames flicker between Bryna's palms, followed by a puff of smoke. The charred rope which once bound her wrists together fell to the grass.

With a trick like that she could've freed us all! Rivan thought. *Why didn't she do that **before**?!*

He glared at her as he finished cutting through his binds, but she continued staring at the sky, seemingly oblivious that she had done anything wrong.

Once Rivan was free, he gave in to temptation and – like Aylen – rubbed his sore wrists before placing them back behind the post.

"What do we do now?" Aylen asked.

Rivan shook his head. He couldn't think of any better plan but for them to simply flee. And he knew they must do it soon. How long would it be until it was noticed they were no longer bound?

"We're going to have to run," he decided.

"But what about the others?"

"We can't do anything for them," Rivan shook his head. "We'll be lucky enough to escape... but *fighting* those things..."

"We have the dagger..." Aylen said.

Rivan held it up for his friend to see. It was tiny. The blade was barely three inches long. In combat it would be near useless. You would be dead long before you got close enough to kill a Zakara with it.

"Thanks a lot, Kyra..." Rivan muttered.

"It *did* free us," Aylen reminded him.

"Give it to me..." Bryna whispered.

"Why?" Rivan asked, looking at the girl. He was baffled as to why she would make such a request.

For the first time Rivan could remember, Bryna looked into his eyes. It sent tremors down his spine. He had never looked into the eyes of a witch before. It felt intrusive. Like she was burrowing into his soul.

"In the memory of the people of Jalard, give me the dagger. Please," she said, with surprising firmness.

Fine. He tossed it, and it landed on the grass beside her. *She can have it if it means so much to her*, he thought. *It's useless anyway...*

Bryna rose to her feet.

"Get down!" Rivan gasped. He cast a wary glance around them to make sure none of Shayam's henchmen were watching.

She ignored him and brought the blade to her wrist.

"What are you *doing*?" he hissed. Was she going to try to end herself? Rivan leapt to his feet to intercede. He didn't think much of the girl, but he didn't want to watch her bleed to death.

She drew the blade across her wrist, but there was no anguish in her expression, instead, she seemed oddly serene. A stream of blood evaporated from her wrist. Shimmering. Red.

Rivan paused mid-stride, suddenly wary of taking another step. He turned to Aylen in disbelief, almost as it to make sure that his friend was seeing the same thing.

Bryna's purple eyes darkened, turning black. During that moment, even Rivan could tell she was harnessing arts beyond common sorcery. Something darker.

For the first time, he was scared of her.

The red cloud pouring from her wrist swirled. A thread of it pulled towards Rivan. He would have fled in terror if he could find a way to move his legs. The energy pricked against his skin, seeped into him.

"What are you doing?!" he gasped.

He closed his eyes as her magic drowned him in a sea of crimson. He felt his muscles stretch and constrict. Dark energy surged through his limbs. His arms bulged and his fists tightened. The energy prickled its way up his neck, and he felt it work its way into his mind.

And then Rivan opened his eyes. He felt more aware. Alert. His senses were heightened.

He was under Bryna's spell, and there was nothing he could do about it.

"Hurry..." she whispered, with the voice of an old crone. "Do not waste my blood!"

He wanted to make her cease whatever it was she was doing to him, but his heart was beating fast and adrenaline was pounding through his veins. He felt stronger than he'd ever felt in his life. He couldn't stay still any longer. He wanted to strike down anything which dared to cross his path. *Everything* that crossed his path.

His sharpened senses heard the footsteps. Something coming for him.

Rivan knew what he had to do.

He looked for a weapon. The only thing he could see was the post he'd been tied to. He pulled it out of the ground with a single tug. It was almost five feet long and four inches thick but, somehow, in his hands, it felt as light as a feather now.

As Rivan charged at the attacker, his feet moved across the ground faster than he could have ever believed possible and the tents of the encampment streaked past him in a white blur. Before the guard even knew what was coming, Rivan slammed the post into his head. Blood and fragments of his skull showered.

For a moment, Rivan just stared in amazement at what he had done, but then he heard the footsteps. Two more men were coming for him.

One of them had drawn a sword, and the other was armed with a spear. Rivan bent his knees and launched himself into the air. As Rivan came down, one of the men thrust his spear into his path, but Rivan shoved it aside and landed a blow to his face with his boot. The man fell, and Rivan stamped upon his neck. It snapped.

He heard a sword breaking air and ducked, narrowly avoiding the incoming blade. Rivan cursed himself for being careless and righted himself. Turned to face his attacker. He was just about to strike him when the man suddenly jerked and the end of a spear burst out through his stomach.

What the fuck? Rivan thought.

Someone had finished the job for him.

The man collapsed, facedown, and Aylen stood behind him. The younger man yanked the spear out of the man's back.

Rivan stared at his friend. The outline of Aylen's body was glowing, which Rivan knew could only mean that he was also under Bryna's spell.

The witch was standing just a few yards away. She still had the dagger in her hand and her wrist was covered in lesions. As much it made Rivan uncomfortable, he couldn't resist the puissant effect it was having upon him. He felt ready to take on the world. Destroy anything that came in his way.

He grabbed the sword of his felled foe. The pole had served its purpose, but now Rivan had armed himself with his weapon of choice.

"Come," Bryna whispered, her voice sounded hoarse. "We must find Jaedin…"

She led them through the maze of tents. Rivan had no idea how this mysterious girl knew where her brother was, but it seemed that there was much more to her than he had previously thought, so he followed.

On their way, they were interrupted by a roar and heavy footsteps. Rivan turned to the sound and saw a large monster emerge from behind one of the tents. It raced towards them on its gigantic paws, baring teeth. When it drew close, Aylen drove his spear into one of its legs, and it howled, toppling over. Rivan knew that it would not take the creature long to recover itself, so he wasted no time and hacked off its head.

Aylen pulled his spear from the carcase. They heard another morbid groan from nearby and turned to see three more Zakaras bounding towards them. They were coming in numbers now, which could only mean one thing.

Shayam knew what they were doing and was trying to stop them.

Rivan raised his sword and charged to meet them. He heard the whoosh of Aylen's spear hurtling past him. The beasts staggered away from the incoming missile, and it was just the distraction Rivan needed to catch one of the monsters at the end of his blade. The Zakara shrieked as Rivan's sword tore through its chest. One of its companions leapt in, sweeping its claws, but Rivan back-flipped out of its range.

When Rivan landed back on his feet again, both of the Zakaras were closing in on him. He stood his ground, arched his sword above his head, and let out a battle cry. One of them leapt again, but Rivan danced out of its path. His blade became a whirl of grey, and he slashed the creature across its back, tearing a red, fleshy line into its pelt. The monster wailed. Rivan brought his sword down again and severed its head.

Aylen dealt with the other foe, kicking it to the ground and driving his spear into his eye. The creature jerked one last time and went still.

"Hurry! We must find Jaedin!" Bryna uttered.

She was beside him, and her sudden presence made Rivan jump. He turned and bore witness as she drew another red line across her wrist. He received another hit of her energy and took a deep breath as it coursed through his body, tightening his muscles.

She continued leading them through the encampment. It seemed to Rivan that they must be getting close because Bryna's black eyes were fixed intently on a tent ahead of them. They raced towards it, but Rivan heard screeching. He cast his eyes around, discovering that Zakaras were coming at them from all sides now. He and Aylen had fared well thus far, with the aid of Bryna's magic, but they had drawn far too much attention to themselves. Rivan knew it wouldn't be long until they became seriously outnumbered.

He grabbed Bryna's sleeve. "Come on!" he yelled. "Aylen! You hold them back!"

He sprinted towards the tent, pulling her with him. *Let's hope her instincts were right*, he prayed.

He tore through the opening. Jaedin was there, lain upon a table. The young man had his arms by his sides, and his face was white and still. There was a hazy blue aura of energy around him, but Rivan grabbed hold of him anyway and shook him by his shoulders to try to wake him. His body was cold and stiff.

"Jaedin!" he yelled. "Wake up!"

He heard a shriek outside the tent, making Rivan ever more aware that Aylen was out there alone.

"How do we wake him?!" he asked, turning to Bryna.

"I'll do it," Bryna whispered as she leant over her brother's body and pressed the blade into her wrist again. Her blood shimmered and flowed into her brother. Jaedin's white skin glowed, and his chest expanded as his lungs breathed life again.

Jaedin's eyes snapped open, and he lurched, gasping for breath. He looked at his sister.

"What are you doing, Bryna!" he gasped. He tried to snatch the dagger from her hand, but she held it away from him.

"I am getting us out of here…" she whispered.

Jaedin opened his mouth to speak, but Rivan ran out of patience and grabbed him by his shoulders. The noises from outside the tent were getting louder. He knew Aylen wouldn't be able to hold them off much longer.

"Use your power!" he screamed.

But Jaedin was too concerned with his sister. He stared at her bloody wrist. "But she's–"

"There's no time!" Rivan yelled into his face, shaking him again. "Stop the Zakaras!"

"Okay! Okay!" Jaedin screamed. His eyes began to glow, and his body trembled. Rivan held his breath. Praying this would work.

The noises outside the tent eased and, a few moments later, Aylen appeared at the opening. He put a hand to his chest as he caught his breath.

"They've stopped moving," he said.

*   *   *

Carmaestre grabbed Dareth by the hand and led him through the encampment. Chaos had erupted all around them. The men in green robes were running around frantically, and Dareth could hear screaming and other sounds of commotion.

"What's going on?" Dareth yelled at two of the men as they passed, but they ignored him.

"Quiet!" Carmaestre said. "You won't get any sense out of those damned things!"

She continued guiding him. The noises grew louder. Some of the sounds Dareth heard barely sounded human. He wondered what could be making them. Carmaestre told him earlier that Shayam's men were shapeshifters, but until that moment, Dareth had considered it a fancy exaggeration.

Carmaestre pulled him in through the opening of a tent. Shayam was inside it. Sitting in a chair and with his eyes closed, seemingly in a state of trance. The stone in the palm of his hand was glowing with red light.

"What the fuck is going on?!" Carmaestre demanded.

"Jaedin is awake," Shayam replied.

Carmaestre's face turned red with anger. "Frih'dra!" she screamed, calling out for the ageing sorcerer. He wasn't there.

"It's not Frih'dra's fault," Shayam said. The light in his palm died, and he opened his eyes. "Jaedin has had some assistance."

"*Who*?" Carmaestre asked.

"The girl with the dark hair–" Shayam began. He was about to say more but Carmaestre interrupted him.

"*Bryna*?" she gasped in disbelief. Her expression shifted from anger to mortal terror. "She's using her power?"

"What do you know of this?" Shayam frowned.

"There's no time!" Carmaestre exclaimed. "We have to leave!"

"Jaedin does not know how to use the Stone of Zakar as well as I do," Shayam said. "I can handle this–"

Carmaestre shook her head violently. "The girl! She changes everything!"

Shayam narrowed his eyes at Carmaestre. "Do you know of these powers she has?" he asked.

Carmaestre nodded.

"Why didn't you warn me?" Shayam said between gritted teeth.

"Because last time I saw her, she was a just cowering girl!" Carmaestre exclaimed. "I thought she was too afraid to use it."

"I believe there are other reasons you chose to not tell me…" Shayam accused, and the way Carmaestre lowered her head made it clear it was true. "And you will explain to me that foolish decision later… but, for now, what would you advise we do?"

"Leave!" Carmaestre replied, without a moment of hesitation. "Now!"

"You mean she is that powerful?" Shayam asked. "That we should flee?"

"I do not know the extent of her power," Carmaestre admitted. "But I don't want to stay here to find out, either!"

A piercing scream rang through the tent, and Shayam cast his eyes around them in alarm. When it finished, he rose to his feet. "This was only a temporary headquarters anyway…" he said. "I think it is time we moved on to somewhere a little more robust."

"Let's go!" Carmaestre uttered anxiously. "Now!"

"But what about the boy?" Shayam asked, looking at Dareth.

They both stared at him with calculated expressions, and Dareth realised they may consider it within their best interests to kill him. His body tensed. He wasn't going to go down without fighting.

"Do you want to come with us?" Shayam offered, making Dareth's jaw drop.

Dareth's initial instinct was to say no.

But when he actually considered it, he realised he was

tempted. There were two sides at war and, even though Bryna and the others were currently fighting back, it was clear to Dareth that the two people standing before him were going to triumph in the end. They were wiser, more prepared, and had resources.

But what would they want from him? Would they try to turn him into their pawn? Did Carmaestre want to lock him away for her pleasure?

Dareth was not going to be anyone's underling.

"Where is Aylen?" Dareth asked, remembering his friend. He couldn't leave Aylen behind, either.

Shayam shook his head. "He is fighting for them. He's the enemy."

"I will stay then," Dareth decided.

Shayam opened his mouth to object, but Carmaestre interrupted him.

"Leave him," she said, placing a hand on Shayam's shoulder and whispering into his ear deviously. "This could prove interesting…"

Interesting? Dareth repeated in his mind. What did she mean? Did they have some long term plan for him he didn't know about?

Shayam looked at Dareth thoughtfully.

"We will see you again, Dareth."

*   *   *

Kyra had not moved since Dion threw her back into the tent. She just lay there in the same position that she collapsed in. A static heap of despair, with the side of her face pressed against the dead grass.

She knew that the next time she saw Dion, he would kill her.

And in doing so, he would turn her into a Zakara.

She wondered what would happen if she became a Zakara. Would her spirit return to Verdana's womb? Or would she be trapped inside the body of a monster? Silent and powerless as Dion got what he wanted from her.

She now wished she had used the dagger to kill herself.

At first, Kyra was too lost in her despair to notice that something strange was going on in the encampment. She was dimly aware of sounds of commotion going on outside, but it just didn't register.

She was finally pulled out of her anguish when a shriek rippled through the tent so loudly she squirmed and covered her ears.

That snapped her out of it.

Kyra looked to the opening. The guards were gone. She was alone.

She pulled herself to her feet, her survival instinct reignited. Kyra didn't have a clue what was going on outside. She only knew that fortune had presented her with a chance to flee, and she wasn't going to waste it.

She ran to the opening and almost collided into Dion.

"Kyra!" he yelled, grabbing her by her arm. "Come with me! Now!"

"What's going on?" she yelled.

He tried to respond but choked on his words. It was like he had become possessed by something. He trembled. His face turned purple.

He fell to his knees, convulsing, tearing at his face with his hands. Kyra stared, wondering what was wrong with him, but swiftly realising she didn't care.

She needed to get away.

She fled, bursting out of the tent. There was blood everywhere. It was streaked across the tents and caked into the mud. It oozed around her boots. She almost slipped and fell. Bodies, both human and Zakara, lay everywhere. Too many for her to count. She tiptoed around them. Ran.

She turned a corner and saw a group of people marching towards her. Her heart leapt with joy when she saw their faces. Rivan, Aylen, Bryna and Jaedin.

"Kyra!" one of them yelled.

She ran to them, colliding into Aylen's arms. They embraced. He felt warm. Unnaturally so. When Kyra placed her hand upon his back, prickly heat radiated from his skin. She gasped and pulled away to take a look at her friend.

Aylen's entire body was lambent with a sable haze. Kyra had witnessed magic enough times to recognise its presence, but she had never seen anything like this before.

And she knew, in her gut, there was something beyond ordinary witchery afoot here.

She looked at the others. Rivan was also shrouded in the

same unsettling aura, and Bryna was holding a blade to her wrist.

"Bryna!" Kyra gasped. "What are you *doing*?"

Bryna ignored her and drew the blade. Blood streaked into the air like a cloud of crimson miasma and drifted towards Aylen. As it seeped into his body, a spasm ran through him and his eyes rolled into the back of his head. When they returned, his pupils dilated, swallowing his irises and turning them black.

She's been hiding something from us, Kyra realised.

The wall of one of the tents nearby tore apart, making them jump. A claw emerged from the opening, and then a body behind it.

It was Dion.

"Kill him!" Jaedin yelled, turning to face him. His eyes began to glow.

Dion trembled as he fought against Jaedin's telepathy.

Kyra turned to Rivan. "Give me your sword!"

"Don't worry," Rivan uttered as he stepped forward. "I'll do it…"

"No!" Kyra blocked his path. "Let *me* do it!"

"He was my friend!" Rivan exclaimed.

"He was my–"

Kyra heard something and turned around. Her heart leapt.

Jaedin had lost control. Dion was running at them. She backed away, but she knew it was too late. He was too close.

Dion leapt at her, his clawed arm swinging.

A spear flew into Dion's path and burst through his chest. Dion's body jerked like a ragdoll, his limbs flailing as he fell.

Before Kyra could register what had just happened, Aylen ran past her. He jerked his spear out from Dion's jittering body and stabbed him again. This time in the neck. Dion stopped moving after that, but Aylen yanked his spear out again and drove it into Dion's head. He stabbed him a fourth time. And then a fifth. He stabbed him over and over, with mania in his eyes.

When he pulled the spear out of Dion's corpse for what must have been the twelfth time, Kyra grabbed his wrist.

"That's *enough*!" she screamed, wondering if he could even hear her. "He's dead already!"

It took her a while to wrestle the spear out of Aylen's

hands. When she finally calmed him down, Aylen looked at her and his eyes cleared. He stared at what he had just done, as if he could barely believe it.

"Shayam's gone..." Jaedin announced.

Kyra looked across the encampment. It had gone still and silent.

"Where?" she asked.

"I don't know," Jaedin shrugged. His eyes were no longer glowing. "I think they must have fled... I was wondering why it was getting so easy for me to still the Zakaras. Usually, I have to fight Shayam to control them."

"You didn't still him very well..." Rivan grunted, gesturing to Dion's corpse.

"That's the weird thing..." Jaedin scratched his head. "He was harder to control than the others... there was something... different about him."

Kyra shook her head. She'd thought she knew what Zakaras were – just monsters with empty minds which could be controlled by those who possessed a Stone of Zakar – but now, after her experiences with Dion, she knew it was not quite as simple as that.

*   *   *

By the time they found Sidry and Baird, the effects of Frih'dra's hibernation spell were waning and they were beginning to wake. After stretching his limbs, Baird was quick to reassert himself as their leader and take charge of things. He ordered them to search the rest of the encampment for provisions and make sure none of Shayam's men had been left behind.

As the others began their search, Bryna took Jaedin by the hand and, without a word of explanation, guided him through the encampment. Jaedin tried to think of something to say to his sister, but no words came to him. What he had seen her do that day disturbed him. It felt like his twin had turned into a stranger.

She halted outside one of the tents and parted the opening.

"He's in here," she said, ushering Jaedin inside.

Jaedin entered the tent expecting her to follow, but instead she closed the curtain and walked away, leaving Jaedin alone with his former mentor – and wondering if his sister knew more than she was letting on.

Miles sat upon the end of a table rubbing his eyes and, at the sight of his mentor alive and well, Jaedin forgot about everything Miles had done; none of it seemed to matter any more. He ran to him.

"Jaedin?" Miles mumbled as Jaedin embraced him. His body was still cold from the effects of Frih'dra's spell, but he returned the gesture, placing a hand on Jaedin's back.

"You're okay?" Jaedin asked.

"I'm fine, Jaedin," Miles reassured. "What happened?"

"Shayam and the others are gone," Jaedin explained. "Bryna saved us."

"Bryna?" Miles said with surprise. "How did she–"

"I'm not sure," Jaedin replied. He didn't say anything more, but he was deeply troubled by what he'd just witnessed. He'd thought he knew what Bryna was capable of but what he'd seen her perform today were arts his mother would have never even dreamed of teaching her.

Jaedin changed the subject. "Why did you save me, Miles?" he asked. It was a question which had been in the back of his mind ever since he escaped from Habella.

Miles was about to answer when the curtain opened and Kyra stepped inside. She almost jumped in surprise at the sight of them.

"Gods!" she exclaimed, putting a hand to her chest. She had an assortment of bags and baskets hanging from her shoulder and a bunch of grapes in her hand. "You wouldn't believe some of the shit we've found! Miles, your friends are really fucking weird... want some of their poncey fruit?" she asked, and stuffed a grape into her mouth.

Jaedin shook his head. "Where did you get them from?" he asked.

"The tents are *full* of stuff!" Kyra exclaimed. "Lania knows where it all came from cause half of it's fodder I've never *seen* before. What you two doing cooped up in here, anyway?" Kyra chuckled. "Why don't you come outside?"

The bubbly mood Kyra was in made Jaedin smile because he hadn't seen her like this for a long time, but a part of him wondered; was she *really* on a high from surviving another ordeal, or was she wearing it to disguise her trauma?

He and Miles followed Kyra back to the centre of the camp, where the others were busy organising the loot they'd found. Everyone seemed to be having a good time stuffing their faces with Shayam's food and mocking some of the strange items they found. Jaedin was surprised to discover he was actually *glad* to see Sidry alive and well; the two of them even smiled at each other.

He noticed his sister sitting away from the others. Their eyes met, and she smiled thinly. Jaedin could tell she was anxious. He knew why too: once they'd finished celebrating their victory, the others would likely want answers for what she did that day.

Jaedin was just about to give Miles an account of what happened after he escaped from Habella when he became aware that everyone had gone quiet. They were all staring at something behind him.

Jaedin turned around and gasped when he saw the figure standing outside one of the tents nearby. Jaedin knew that face.

It was Dareth.

"Jaedin," Baird said cautiously. "Is he one of them?"

Jaedin called out to the Stone of Zakar, but the artefact didn't respond.

It doesn't work on him, Jaedin realised, and the ramifications of what this meant hit him.

The thing stood before him was not a Zakara. It was the *real* Dareth.

How was this possible?

Jaedin turned back to Baird. The leader was waiting for his response.

I could have them kill him... Jaedin realised.

Never before had Jaedin believed himself capable of such wicked thoughts, but the temptation was there.

Dareth was the person Jaedin had been the most glad to see the back of when he left Jalard. He thought about all the things the boy had said to him over the years. All of the bruises. The names. The public humiliations. The cruel laughter.

Jaedin could finally have his revenge.

But could he really *do* it?

"No," Jaedin shook his head, trying to hide how disappointed the words made him feel. "He's not one of them."

Chapter 15

A Stranger

Sidry stared at Dareth as Baird questioned him, barely believing his eyes. It was like seeing a ghost.

"I ran," Dareth replied. "I had to…"

"No one blames you," Baird said. "We saw what happened to Jalard. Did anyone else escape?"

Dareth shook his head. "Not that I know of."

"How did you end up here?" Baird asked.

Dareth hesitated and looked at his feet. Was it sorrow, which Sidry caught in the young man's eyes before he downcast them, or something else?

"I realise it's been traumatic…" Baird said gently. "But I need to know, Dareth."

"I went to Habella to find you," Dareth gritted his teeth. "But Shayam found me… they must've followed my trail… they kept me prisoner. I couldn't escape!"

"How long have you been here?" Baird asked.

"I… don't know," Dareth shook his head.

Baird stared at him for a while. Dareth's account had many gaps, but filling them seemed to be causing him distress. Sidry could understand that. Recent times had been painful for all of them.

For Baird, though, Dareth's brief account seemed to be enough. His shifted his attention to the more dubious member of the group, Bryna, and his expression went from friendly to hostile in the transition. "In my years I have seen many things, Bryna," Baird said. "But I have never come across anything like what you did today."

All eyes turned to the sullen young woman kneeling on the grass. Yet again, Jaedin's elusive and mysterious twin had surprised them.

Rivan had given Sidry a brief account of what she had done, and Sidry found some of the details deeply unsettling. Could it be true that this small, timid woman had saved them all?

"We deserve an explanation, Bryna," Baird pressed her. He

pointed to Rivan and Aylen – they both sat nearby on the trunk of a felled tree, with weary expressions – it seemed the effects of her sorcery had repercussions which they were currently paying. "*They* deserve an explanation for what you did to them."

Rivan lifted his heavy eyelids to glare at her.

Bryna turned her head down.

"Say something!" Baird yelled. He stormed over to her with his fists clenched and, for a brief moment, Sidry thought he was going to hit her. "Talk to me!"

She curled up into a ball and quivered like a terrified animal. "I can't…"

"Baird! She's–" Jaedin stepped in to defend her, but Baird pushed him aside.

"Stay out of this!" Baird roared. "I've been a fool to let her get away so far! It's time for answers!"

Bryna was still cowering below him, her dark hair covering her face. Baird grabbed hold of her wrist.

"Show me what you did to yourself!" he said, forcing back her sleeve.

But the sight of her exposed wrist stunned him to silence. Baird stared and, within his expression, Sidry read both confusion and fear. Sidry peered closer, to ease his curiosity, and saw why; there was not a single mark nor blemish on Bryna's arm.

Baird let go of her wrist like it was an abomination. She began to cry.

Sidry felt an overwhelming urge to comfort her – run to her side, put his arms around her and protect her – and it confused him, for he barely knew her. He had scarcely uttered a word to her in his entire life, but there had always been something about her he was drawn to, and that part had been growing recently. She was an enigma. A mystery. There was so much he found he wanted to know about her.

Sitting there, like a scared little girl, with tears flowing down her cheeks, she seemed so delicate and fragile, but they knew now that something dark and arcane lived within her.

"What is this?" Sidry drowned out the sound of her tears because he could bear it no longer. Baird looked at him challengingly – almost making Sidry lose his nerve – but he stood his ground. "She just saved our lives!"

He turned to Rivan and Aylen, who grudgingly looked away. No matter what their feelings were on the arts she used on them, they could not deny the solid fact Sidry had just spoken.

"What does it matter how she did it? Or where she learnt it?" Sidry carried on. He pointed at her as she sobbed. "She saved us! And you do *this* to her!?"

"He's right..." Aylen admitted.

Sidry looked at Baird from the corner of his eye. Now that his outburst was over he was expecting to be punished – that was the first time he had ever spoken out against their leader, and he had a feeling he was soon going to regret it – but instead, Baird turned his attention back to Bryna. His eyes were like fire. "I'll get it out of you, eventually..." he said.

He stormed off, and Sidry breathed a sigh of relief.

"Just one thing, Bryna," Rivan uttered, as Kyra sat next to her and placed a protective arm around her shoulder. "Don't *ever* do that to me again."

* * *

The drowsiness was beginning to wear off, but Aylen was spent, and every part of his body felt heavy. The feeling Bryna's spell had given him was one of indescribable power and the things he did while under it now seemed like a dream. He could remember slaying the Zakaras vividly, but it was like he had seen it through someone else's eyes instead of his own.

It was near sunset now. Most of the others were searching the rest of the camp for provisions and claiming beds for the night, but Aylen was too exhausted for that.

So many unexpected things had happened that day and, of all of them, the most shocking was being reunited with a friend he thought dead. When everyone else dispersed, Dareth walked over to him, and the two of them were finally alone.

"You left me there..." Dareth said.

Aylen had a feeling something like this was coming. Dareth had always been very jealous by nature. When Aylen went off with Rivan and the others on the trading mission, all those aeights ago, he knew his friend would feel bitter about being excluded. Aylen knew that, but he went away with them anyway because the opportunity to go to Habella was too good to resist.

"I had no way of knowing what was going to happen to Jalard," Aylen said.

"That's not the point," Dareth muttered. "You still chose *them* over me."

Aylen knew that is what it must have looked like, but it wasn't the truth. Not exactly.

Aylen had always cared a lot for Dareth, but his friend was a difficult person to be around sometimes. His erratic moods were exhausting and Aylen welcomed the occasional break from it all. He would never admit it, but one of the reasons he agreed to go to Habella was to get away from Dareth for a while.

That, and an excuse to spend some time with Kyra.

"The Elders sent us. It was for the village," Aylen said. It was a weak excuse, but he couldn't give Dareth the real one.

"The village…" Dareth muttered. "Shayam told me everything, Aylen. He told me what you did to Jalard…"

Aylen shuddered. From the moment Shayam had told him about the hand he and the others had in Jalard's fate, a knot had tied itself in his stomach. He kept trying to ignore it, but it was always there, and Dareth words had just tightened it.

"We had no way of knowing," Aylen mumbled as tears welled up behind his eyes. He did his upmost to suppress them. He didn't want to cry in front of Dareth of all people. "Shayam took Sidry and Jaedin! They were ambushed, and we found the trail. We couldn't leave them! It was the only thing we could do…"

Aylen could hear his conviction was weak in his own voice.

"You just keep telling yourself that…" Dareth muttered.

*   *   *

"Keep telling yourself that," Dareth repeated as he walked away, leaving Aylen to stew over his parting words. "Maybe eventually you'll believe it."

Once he was out of earshot, Dareth breathed a sigh of relief.

He panicked earlier when Baird questioned him. He realised he had not prepared a story. He was sure he was going to be caught out, but it seemed that Jaedin's deranged sister had drawn the scent away from him. There were many holes in Dareth's tale, so he needed to think through some of the details in case he found himself questioned again. He didn't want them to know what he did just before he fled Jalard, and he certainly did not want them to know about some of the interactions he'd had with Shayam and Carmaestre.

It surprised Dareth to discover that none of them seemed willing to acknowledge the part they played in Jalard's fate. They never spoke of it, but Dareth could sense the guilt some of them felt. It lingered over them like a dark cloud.

Dareth still didn't know how he felt about the situation. He did not like Shayam, but he could tell that the man was clever and powerful; a good man to have on your side. Dareth would have stayed with him and Carmaestre if it wasn't for his loyalty to Aylen.

The people Dareth was now stuck with were just a rat pack fighting a losing battle and causing unnecessary bloodshed along the way. Carmaestre and Shayam – although some of their methods seemed callous – were trying to achieve things which were for the greater benefit of mankind.

"I know what you did, Dareth."

He jumped in surprise at the sound of that ghostly voice and turned to see Bryna's shadow looming a few feet away.

"What do you mean?" he asked, acting bemused.

She was in the village when it happened, Dareth remembered.

"Tarvek," she whispered. "You killed him..."

Dareth held back a tremor.

"Are you going to tell them?" he asked, realising there was no point in denying it.

She shook her head.

"How did you–" he began to ask, but she walked away without another word.

Damn that girl is weird... he thought. Both of them had somehow walked away from Jalard unscathed. Dareth's survival was due to a peculiar trick of fate, but what was her story?

Dareth worried over whether Bryna would keep her promise, but he couldn't think of a way to dispose of her when there were other people around. He didn't want any more blood on his hands, either.

Bryna had been discreet and promised to keep Dareth's secret. Despite disliking her, he respected her for that.

He would let her live, for now.

*   *   *

The following morning, Dareth awoke in Carmaestre's luxurious bed for the second time but, on this occasion, he was alone. He could still smell her scent on the sheets. He knew he would see her again. He wasn't sure how he felt about that.

He went outside and joined the others. They were busy cramming as much of Shayam's food as they could into their bags and doing a final sweep of the camp to make sure they were not leaving anything behind. Dareth soon got impatient.

Much of the camp was strewn with rotting remains of Zakaras which were beginning to fester and smell. They had to step around the corpses as they left, and Dareth laughed when he witnessed Jaedin daintily pinching his nose between his fingers as he tip-toed past them.

"Leave him alone," someone said.

Dareth turned and found himself face to face with Aylen.

They had still not spoken since the previous night when Dareth had blamed Aylen for what happened to Jalard.

Aylen opened his mouth to speak, but Dareth stopped him.

"It's okay," Dareth said, hoping he could avoid them having to apologise to each other. He hated the awkward motions people went through to clear bad air. All forms of sentimentality made him uncomfortable. "I know you didn't mean for it to happen,"

Dareth then leant towards Aylen and whispered into his ear. "But you've got to stop listening to these idiots. You can't trust them."

*   *   *

There was not a cloud in the sky, and the sun was hot. The

terrain was unfamiliar, filled with steep hills of grassy reeds and the occasional trickling spring. Woodlands were sparse. They walked north for an entire day and did not come across a single road or pathway.

Baird decided to end the day early and, once they pitched the tents and gathered enough firewood, he announced that they were going to practise duelling.

Most of them grumbled about being tired, but Rivan was looking forward to a decent spar to lift his spirits.

They warmed up by practising a series of stances and lunges and then Baird called them up to duel each other.

Sidry and Kyra were first. Rivan watched the bout critically but, no matter how much of a bias he had towards his friend, he couldn't deny Kyra had fought well and deserved her victory. The two of them were almost equal in strength, but she was just that little bit more skilled and agile.

But on a different level, it no longer mattered. Sidry was now stronger than the rest of them could ever dream of being when he summoned his Avatar. Rivan wondered why he and Baird were even bothering to practise combat in human form; was it out of habit, sustaining an old hobby, or were they just trying to maintain a semblance of normality?

Sidry gracefully accepted Kyra's hand, and she helped pull him back onto his feet. Rivan was about to clap with the others over a well-fought duel when he noticed Jaedin approach them.

What's he doing here? Rivan wondered. Jaedin was supposed to be helping Bryna and Miles prepare supper.

"Yes?" Baird asked Jaedin.

Jaedin mumbled something, but Rivan didn't catch a single word of it.

"Speak up, Jaedin," Baird barked with a hint of impatience in his voice.

Something odd was going on. Everything about Jaedin's body language suggested apprehension. His lips were trembling, and he was fidgeting with his hands.

"I want to learn how to fight," he said.

Dareth giggled, and Rivan put a hand to his mouth to stifle his own laughter. He could still vividly remember the last time they witnessed Jaedin trying to wield a sword. They made jokes about it for aeights.

"Don't you have lessons with Miles?" Baird asked.

"Miles says I have learnt enough," Jaedin replied. He placed his hands behind his back and turned his gaze to his feet. "I can shield my mind from Grav'aen now… You don't need to worry about that anymore."

"Jaedin…" Baird hesitated. It was now clear that the last reason he gave had been a polite excuse. "We do not have any training swords–"

"I have a sword!" Jaedin said, pointing to the scabbard dangling from his waist. Rivan had noticed him walking around with it earlier that day and thought it strange. He must have found it somewhere in Shayam's encampment.

"That's not a training sword," Baird shook his head. "It's a real one… It would be too dangerous–"

"I want to learn to fight!" Jaedin repeated, surprisingly firm. "Please."

*   *   *

Rivan took measure of the figure before him.

Jaedin was tangibly nervous. He held his sword awkwardly. When most people held a sword it became a part of them but, with the timid young man before him, it was a foreign object. He couldn't even hold it up straight. It quivered in his hands.

Were circumstances different and this a proper duel, like the ones they used to have in Jalard, Rivan would have felt insulted at the pairing. But, things being what they were, he could only look at Jaedin and smirk.

Time for some much needed comic relief, he thought, sharing a derisive sneer with his friends.

"Go easy on him," Baird muttered as he walked past.

Rivan nodded. They were wielding real weapons. Ones a novice like Jaedin wouldn't even be allowed to touch usually, let alone practise with.

Rivan knew Baird's reasoning behind this unbalanced pairing: Rivan was the most skilled swordsman, and thus Baird was entrusting him to make sure neither of them came to any harm.

"Are you ready, Jaedin?" Baird asked.

Jaedin nodded at him and raised the sword again.

"Go!"

They both stood still.

Come on, you soddy! Rivan thought, steadying his grip on his sword. He didn't want to be the one to make the first move. He had no idea what Jaedin was capable of defending himself against.

Jaedin's footing was already clumsy, and they hadn't even begun. Rivan resisted the temptation to advise him to place one foot in front of the other to better hold his balance.

Guess it will have to be me then... Rivan sighed. *You are the one who wanted to learn so much!*

Rivan advanced and swerved his sword at Jaedin, in a simple, slow, and controlled strike.

Their swords met. Rivan stepped back, acknowledging that Jaedin was at least capable of basic defence, but he did not follow up with any counter.

Guess it'll have to be me... again... Rivan thought, realising just how tedious this was going to be. He thrust his blade at Jaedin's side, putting more speed behind it this time but preparing to halt the action if needed. Jaedin dodged, and they circled each other. Rivan was just about to raise his sword to make another strike when he saw, from the tell-tale signs in Jaedin's tensing muscles, that he was about to make an attack of his own. Rivan sidestepped, and Jaedin's sword flashed past him, so he countered. Jaedin backed away.

Playing the dodging game, are we? Rivan smiled to himself as he skirted around the confused young man who was barely holding his balance. *Too bad I'm faster than I look!*

Jaedin's side was exposed so Rivan swung for it, but the younger man ducked and brought his sword veering towards Rivan's legs as he turned, forcing Rivan to jump away.

He has good reflexes, Rivan realised, surprised by Jaedin's speed. He lost his train of thought when Jaedin's blade veered towards his abdomen. He arched his sword and blocked.

Rivan took a step back and considered. Jaedin had surprised him so far, so it was time to try something more advanced. Rivan's few extra inches of height gave him an advantage, so he raised his sword over his head. Jaedin braced himself, raising his own weapon. Their blades met.

Rivan ducked, circling his sword low, but Jaedin deflected and their blades clashed again. They both stepped away. Jaedin lost his balance for a moment, and his arms waved around wildly. Rivan resisted the temptation to nudge Jaedin with his foot to bring him toppling over – it would have been amusing, but Baird *did* say to go easy on him…

Rivan charged in to revive the duel. Their swords met and locked in the centre between them.

His grip is too loose, Rivan thought as his opponent's blade jittered against his own. Jaedin gripped the handle with both hands to strengthen his hold.

Rivan smiled. A sword lock. Now it was just a question of strength.

Rivan applied more pressure, and Jaedin backed away a little. Rivan was just about to end the lock when a sudden force propelled him backwards. Rivan's feet parted from the ground, and he flew. He swung his arms out to help catch his balance, and after he landed, he stared at Jaedin in disbelief. Everyone gasped.

Jaedin had just overpowered him.

There was no way Rivan was going to let the duel finish with Jaedin getting the better of him, so he charged. It was time to end this nonsense. He leapt at him, swinging his sword, putting all his weight behind it and catching Jaedin's blade at an angle he knew would knock it out of his hands.

Jaedin's sword fell. The duel was over.

Rivan heard the others muttering to each other. He didn't catch any of the words, but he knew what they were talking about: they had just witnessed Jaedin overpower him in a sword lock. Aside from Baird, no one from Jalard had ever been able to match Rivan's strength.

"Jaedin…" Baird uttered in disbelief.

Jaedin was markedly embarrassed. "What Shayam did," he said, his face turning red. "It changed me…"

*   *   *

After another four days of walking, they finally spotted a trail which appeared to be a pathway between two settlements. It was the first sign of civilisation they had come across since they escaped from the encampment, but they still had no idea where they were. Baird decided its north-easterly direction would be the most likely to lead them closer to Shemet.

Every evening, they trained with Baird while Bryna and Miles cooked supper. Although Jaedin held back from making any more displays of his abnormal strength, Kyra noticed some other tell-tale signs that the Stone of Zakar had changed him. Every now and then he made a movement which was almost too fast for the eye to see and, even though he was clumsy, his reflexes were abnormally swift. None of this made up for years of neglect though, and he would always experience a swift defeat once the person he was sparring with grew bored of humouring him. Eventually, Baird taught him a series of motions and stances to practise on his own.

For the rest of them, their training became focussed on devising tactics and methods for disposing of Zakaras. They had spent most of their lives learning how to fight against humans but many of those techniques were redundant now and needed to be adapted.

On the fifth day, they finally reached the end of the trail and found themselves looking down upon a settlement in the valley below.

Kyra halted beside Baird and surveyed the place. It was probably twice the size of Jalard but its features were similar. Most of the houses had thatched roofs, and she could tell, by the fields surrounding it, that it was a farming community. She could see signs of life too; sheep were grazing in the pastures, and smoke was wafting from the chimneys.

"I don't recognise this place..." Baird admitted.

"Only one way to find out," she commented.

"No," Baird shook his head. "It might not be safe. We will camp here tonight and take a closer look in the morning."

Kyra sighed. She knew that Baird had good reasons to be cautious after what happened in Habella, but this was a village in the middle of nowhere. What were the chances Shayam had come here?

Jalard was a village in the middle of nowhere, she reminded herself wistfully.

As the others pitched the tents and made a fire, Kyra felt restless. She didn't want to sit idly around a fire all evening. She wanted to do something.

"Can I go hunt?" she asked.

"Good idea," Baird nodded. "Take someone else with you though…"

Kyra cast her eyes around for volunteers and swiftly remembered the only people she was friendly with out of this bunch barely knew how to hold a bow. Most of them would never spend time with her out of choice.

There was one exception though; Aylen. She caught his eye and smiled. "Want to hunt something?" she asked him.

"Sure," Aylen said.

*   *   *

Aylen suspected he was going to be given a hard time from Dareth later but the chance to spend some time alone with Kyra was irresistible.

In truth, Dareth was irritating him. Aylen was eternally grateful that by some miracle he had been reunited with a friend he thought dead, but he was also beginning to remember how tiresome Dareth could be. He was once again finding himself having to constantly reason with him and curb his bad temper. It was a strain sometimes, and Aylen welcomed brief relief from it all. Even if it meant he would likely be punished for it later.

He looked at Kyra as they strolled into the woodland side by side. She smiled at him. Something had changed between them since they escaped from the encampment. It was only when they thought they were going to die that they realised they were friends.

He'd been meaning to catch a moment with her alone. She seemed to be in good spirits most of the time, but Aylen couldn't help but wonder if that was just a façade. What she'd said to him back at the encampment, just before she gave them the dagger, lingered in his mind. What exactly had happened to her there?

He was about to ask her but was pulled out of his thoughts by her voice.

"Aylen?"

"What?" he asked.

She opened her mouth again but hesitated. This coyness was very unlike the Kyra he knew.

"Have you ever had sex?" she asked.

He turned away. He couldn't look at her. He opened his mouth to reply but stammered. What should he say?

"It's okay," she said. "I haven't either…"

He smiled nervously. He wondered where this conversation was going. Was this some kind of mind game?

"Do you want to try?"

*   *   *

It was over in minutes that seemed like moments, and the whole thing felt like a strange dream that Aylen had no control over.

When she unfastened him, his member was already alert in excitement over something he could barely believe was happening. He was on his back. He wanted to say things to her, he wanted to do things, but he found himself immobilised and speechless. She was in control. She straddled on top of him and guided his organ inside her.

His body shook with disbelief.

She started to rock back and forth, but his body suddenly quivered with uncontrollable spasms and he reached a hasty climax.

It was over.

They both went silent for a few moments. He looked up at her breasts. They remained concealed beneath her bodice. He had imagined this moment so many times, but none of his fantasies had ever been like this. He wanted to reach and touch them. He loved the shape of them. He had wondered so many times what she looked like beneath her clothes. He wanted to touch her nipples and kiss her mouth. But why did he hesitate? Why did he feel like he wasn't allowed to when a part of him was inside one of her most precious places?

But not for much longer. He felt himself go flaccid, and he slid out of her.

She rolled off and lay down on the grass beside him.

They both stared at the sky.

"I'm sorry–" he began to apologise.

"Don't worry," she said. "Meredith told me it happens to a lot of boys their first time."

Aylen didn't know what to say. He could barely believe

that it had happened just a few moments ago. It already felt like a distant memory.

He remembered what he had been about to ask her before it happened.

"Kyra," he said, swallowing a lump in his throat as he plucked up his courage. "Are you okay?"

She frowned at him. "What do you mean?"

"I don't know..." Aylen said. "It's just... at the encampment, when you gave us the dagger... you said something about Dion. Did he hurt you?"

Her eyes darkened for a moment, but then she smirked. "No," she shook her head. "He didn't. *You* made sure of that, didn't you!"

She grinned and patted Aylen's forearm.

Aylen felt a huge wave of relief. "Still..." he said. "It must have been horrible... being stuck with him all that time..."

"I don't want to talk about it..." she said flatly.

"I just want you to know that I am here," Aylen said. "If you ever do want to talk..."

Kyra turned her head and looked at him. "You're not getting all sentimental on me, are you?" She chuckled, but there was something about it which sounded a little forced. "Just because you got to deflower me."

She reached for his hand and held it. But it wasn't passionate. It was in a platonic, friendly way.

"We aren't going to die virgins now," she said.

* * *

Jaedin retreated to his tent early that evening so he could spend some time reinforcing his shields. It had been a while since Grav'aen last attacked him psychically, but Jaedin was still strengthening his protections on a regular basis. It had become habit to him now, and he found he enjoyed the fleeting periods of peace he got from sitting down and tuning in to his *psysona*. It became his escape.

He heard the flap of his tent open, followed by the sounds of someone snuffling around noisily.

"Jaedin?" Kyra said. "Oh... sorry. Have I disturbed you?"

He opened his eyes and pulled himself back into reality. "No," he lied, shaking his head. "I was just finishing..."

He yawned and stretched out his arms. "How was hunting?"

"It was okay," she shrugged. "We didn't catch anything though…"

She sat down, got out some of her tools, and busied herself fletching arrows. Bryna joined them sometime later, and she was surprisingly coherent that evening. She even had some unexpected news.

"It is our birthday today," she said, patting Jaedin's shoulder.

Jaedin looked at her. "*Really?*" he exclaimed, then paused and realised it was certainly the right time of the year – their birthday fell exactly three aeights after the Festival of Ignis.

Jaedin had not even thought of it. Ever since they escaped from Jalard, they'd been too busy to keep track of the days. Apart from the brief interval when they visited Habella and were subsequently captured, each day had been exactly the same. It all rolled into one endless journey; they walked, made camp, trained, ate, and slept. Sometimes Kyra and some of the others would hunt. Always, they lived in fear of the Zakaras.

"Are you sure?" Jaedin asked.

Bryna nodded.

"How?" he asked, wondering if she had been marking the days down somewhere.

She shrugged.

"For many more cycles may you thrive," Kyra congratulated them and then sighed, dropping the arrow she was fletching. "I'm sorry…" she said. "I didn't even think…"

"It's okay," Jaedin said. "I didn't either… it's just…" he shrugged. "The way things are now…"

He thought of his mother and felt a pang in his chest. She had always made a big thing out of his and Bryna's birthday. She would invite Kyra and Miles over and cook a lovely meal for them to eat together. She gave them gifts.

"And we're stuck *here*…" Kyra muttered, shaking her head. "Shall we just go outside and tell the others," she suggested. "Perhaps Baird will–"

"Gods, *no!*" Jaedin said. The thought of Baird forcing the others to mark his and Bryna's birthday made him cringe. He knew most of them couldn't stand him and his sister. It would just be a chorus of empty felicitations.

"We should still do *something*!" Kyra said. "It would feel wrong not to…" she seemed to have a thought and smiled mischievously. "I know…"

"What?" Jaedin asked.

She put a finger to her lips, leant forward, and whispered in his ear. "I'll bet there's a tavern in that village down there. Let's go there later."

"But what about Baird?" Jaedin asked. "He would never–"

"Don't worry about Baird," Kyra shook her head. "I'll deal with him… Just be ready. When it's my turn to keep watch I'll come get you."

"But–" Jaedin began.

"No buts," Kyra shook her head. "It's your birthday! And who's he to tell us what we can and can't do? I think it is about time we got to have some fun."

* * *

Kyra came to get them later that night, and they sneaked out of the camp. As they tip-toed their way past the fire, Jaedin saw Aylen sitting there, and the young man watched them leave with a guilty expression.

How did Kyra convince him to agree to this? Jaedin wondered. He was being struck by nerves now. He knew if Baird caught them, he would make them suffer for this.

How did Kyra convince **me** *into this?*

It was dark. Jaedin crept silently behind Kyra's silhouette. He bumped into her once, and they both paused to stifle giggles behind their hands. Despite how anxious Jaedin felt he was also excited. He had never done anything like this before. He turned to his sister for reassurance. She smiled faintly.

Once they'd put some distance between themselves and the camp, they quickened their pace. The lights of the village drew closer.

Kyra cast her eyes around the first street they reached. "There must be a watering hole *somewhere* here!" she thought out loud.

As they got deeper into the village, a few strangers paused to stare at them. Jaedin began to worry. Baird had very valid reasons for being cautious.

He activated the Stone of Zakar for a brief moment to see if he could sense the presence of any Zakaras. He felt nothing, so it seemed this village was safe.

"I think I've found our first clue!" Kyra giggled as she pointed at a drunken man stumbling down the road.

They turned down the path he had just come from and saw light glowing from the windows of a large building. They stopped outside and read the sign – 'The Tarrey Joller'.

"What the fuck does that mean?" Kyra commented.

"I smell hops," Bryna whispered.

Kyra smirked and placed a hand on Bryna's shoulder. They walked into the tavern. Jaedin squinted as his eyes adjusted to the bright lights. At first, all he heard was a cacophony of loud chatter, but it soon died down, and a group of men paused behind their tankards of ale to gaze at the newcomers. Some of them whistled at the sight of two young women entering the premises.

Bryna blushed, covering her mouth with her hand as she passed them, while Kyra waved. Jaedin watched, realising how much his friend had come out of her shell recently. Back in Jalard, Kyra had always hated male attention, and the boys she grew up with had rarely given it.

It concerned him though. Ever since Kyra escaped from the encampment, she seemed to have gone to great efforts to present a cheery persona, but Jaedin couldn't help but suspect it was all a front. He'd tried to coax her into sharing what had happened to her, but each time she laughed him off and changed the subject.

And even now, as they rebelled against Baird by sneaking into the village – supposedly to celebrate his and Bryna's birthday – Jaedin couldn't help but feel that was just an excuse and the real reason they were there was because *she* wanted to.

"What'll you ladies be havin'?" the barman asked from behind the counter.

"Mead please," Kyra replied, reaching into her bag of coins.

"And for the gentleman 'ere?" he asked, glancing at Jaedin. "Ale?"

"Do you have wine?" Jaedin asked.

"Yes!" Kyra laughed. "Please can we have a glass of your finest red for this brute of a man here!"

Jaedin scowled at Kyra and went to claim one of the tables nearby. Shortly after, Bryna joined him with a glass in each hand, and they sat in silence for a while, which allowed Jaedin's thoughts to wander. He was worried someone would notice they had vanished from the camp. He didn't like the prospect of being on the receiving end of Baird's wrath.

His sister calmly sipped from her drink, as if she had not a care in the world. Jaedin eyes wandered to her wrist, where not a blemish or mark remained from what she had done to herself.

She saved us, he reminded himself when distrustful thoughts crept into his head. *We are lucky to be alive…*

Kyra joined them, and he took a big gulp of his wine to calm his nerves, causing her to raise an eyebrow.

"Thirsty?" she asked.

Jaedin nodded and smiled back. He realised he needed this. Time to let go and relax. Time away from the pressure of Baird and the others. Time away from Miles; a man who felt increasingly like a stranger recently.

"So there is something I need to tell you both…" Kyra said, placing her cup back on the table.

"What is it?" Jaedin asked.

Kyra pulled back the sleeve of her coat and bared her forearm for them to see. Just as Jaedin suspected, that time she had taken her dagger to it – after they escaped from Jalard – had left her covered with scars.

All of them had healed and turned white, apart from one. It stood out from the others. The wound had closed, but it was still fleshy and red. As if it was only a few days old.

"Is that new?" he asked. "I am sure Bryna can make a–"

"No…" Kyra shook her head. "It is not new… I did it the same time as the others. And it also just happens to be the cut I made the moment I spoke the oath… so let's not prattle. I think we all know what this is," she said, running a finger along it.

Jaedin looked down at the table.

"I think the legends are true. I am Bloodsworn…" Kyra said. "And… I want to know if the two of you can tell me anything. You *are* Meredith's children, after all."

Jaedin shook his head. "No…" he said. "I know just about as much as you do, I'm afraid. Just the things we were told in those stories when we were kids…"

"I can barely remember what it was I even *said* as I made it…" Kyra muttered and ran a hand through her hair. "I think I said something about not stopping until everyone responsible was dead. Does that I mean that if ever have a bad day – a morning where I am a bit tired and just think 'fuck it, I'm going to give up' – I will suddenly die?"

"I don't think it would be as sudden as that," Bryna said, placing a hand upon Kyra's.

How would **she** *know*? Jaedin looked at his sister.

"And I think I personally named Shayam and Grav'aen…" Kyra added. "I remember that… what happens if someone else gets to them first and kills them before I manage to? Would *that* break the oath?"

"I think the question you need to ask yourself…" Bryna said. "Is what did you *feel* when you said the words? The pact is one you made between you and the gods. They would understand what it was that you *meant*. And if there any ambiguities in the terms of the *oath*, the consequences for breaking them would be just as flexible. That is my opinion, and it is all I can give you…"

The three of them drank for a while in silence, and then Kyra changed the subject. She complained about Rivan. About how much he had been vexing her recently. Jaedin responded by bringing up how much he felt the atmosphere had soured since Dareth appeared. Bryna silently sipped at her wine.

Kyra got a second round of drinks. And then a third. The evening began to get hazier, and Jaedin relaxed a little. He found his eyes kept wandering to a man sitting at one of the other tables. He was wearing a dark cloak, and its hood shadowed most of his face, but Jaedin could tell he was watching them. There was no mistaking it.

Eventually, Kyra noticed it too.

"He's handsome," she commented quietly.

"And almost old enough to be your father…" Bryna added.

"Doesn't mean I can't *look*…" Kyra said and waved at him.

The man waved back and then got up and made his way

over to their table.

"Hello, stranger…" Kyra said. She fluttered her eyelashes, which almost made Jaedin choke on his drink.

The man pulled back his hood, and Jaedin caught a first proper look at his face. He had devilish, mischievous brown eyes and had a dimpled chin covered in dark stubble. He seemed like the sort of man who never groomed himself and cared little about his looks but was handsome in a rugged way. Jaedin sensed he was not native to this village. He had a wayward appearance, and his clothes were travel-worn.

"Would you like a drink?" he asked in a gravelly voice.

"Oh…" Kyra gazed at her cup, which was still almost full. "Haven't finished this yet… hold on just one moment…" She tilted it to her mouth and gulped down in one. "Now I'm ready!"

He smirked. "What would you fine ladies like?"

"You're not fooling me," Kyra said flatly. "You ain't no gentleman. Don't pretend to be all courteous for us."

He raised an amused eyebrow. "Ale for the lass, then?"

Kyra grinned. "The mead was just to warm myself up."

"And for the young man here?"

It took Jaedin a few moments to register the man was talking to him. He didn't know why, but he felt nervous.

"He will have a cup of red wine," Kyra answered for him.

The stranger turned to Bryna.

"I do not need," she replied.

He made his way to the bar, and Kyra's flirtatious eyes followed him all the way there.

"What are you *doing*?" Jaedin whispered.

"Getting us free drinks," she muttered through the side of her mouth. The stranger turned and looked at them as the barman poured their drinks. She waved.

"Do you have to be so…"

"Oh, that was just being friendly…" Kyra said. "He ain't interested in me. I could tell."

Jaedin wasn't convinced. The man seemed roguish and could be expecting something from Kyra that she wasn't prepared to give.

"I agree," Bryna said. "He seemed more interested in–"

"You noticed it too?" Kyra interrupted, turning to Bryna with knowing eyes.

"Notice what?" Jaedin asked.

"Oh, don't worry…" Kyra said. "Finish your drink before he gets back."

Jaedin downed the last dregs of his wine.

"Thank you," Jaedin said when the man returned and placed the drinks on the table.

"Cheers!" Kyra tapped her tankard against his. They beamed at each other as they took their first gulps.

Jaedin felt left out. He had never liked the taste of ale much. Wine had always been more pleasing to him.

Why was it that, during that moment, he wished he *did* like ale?

"So…" the man said, his eyes shifting between the three of them with scrutiny. "You don't seem like typical village striplings to me?"

"How so?" Kyra asked.

"Worldly," the stranger replied. "You have the eyes of people on an adventure. On the hunt for something."

Jaedin felt a bloom of sadness. It wasn't so long ago that they *were* just kids, from a village more remote and even smaller than this one.

"Where you on the road to?" he asked.

"Who said we were?" Kyra grinned.

"I can tell…" he smirked.

"Really?" Kyra said. "Because we're not the ones who felt the need to bring our worldly possessions out for a drink…"

She gestured to the large travelling pack tucked under his seat.

"I'm on the hunt for something myself…" he responded.

"And what would that be?" Kyra enquired.

"Maybe soon you will find out…"

The man stared at Jaedin. It was an intense stare. Jaedin couldn't place it. It made him uncomfortable.

"Where's the latrine?" Jaedin asked, turning to Kyra.

"In a cabin outside…" the stranger replied. "Can show you if you–"

"I'll find it!" Jaedin mumbled as he withdrew from the table.

He left one uncomfortable situation only to find himself in another; as Jaedin made his way across the bar, he felt the eyes of the village locals stare at him. Jaedin knew why.

When he'd entered the tavern earlier, they'd been too distracted by Kyra and Bryna to notice him, but now he was a young man with long black hair and wearing a billowy robe, walking alone. Jaedin was paler-skinned than most Sharmarians. He had been in the wilderness for so long he'd forgotten the effect his appearance had on people sometimes.

He avoided eye contact and rushed to the door. Once outside, in the cool night air, Jaedin breathed a sigh of relief. He didn't know why, but something about that man made him nervous. And he didn't like the way Kyra flirted with him either.

He made his way to the privy around the back, pinching his nose as he entered. After relieving himself, he stepped outside again. He decided to take a few more moments to gather his wits before he re-entered the tavern. Strangers made him feel uneasy.

As he walked back around the building, he almost bumped into someone and jumped in surprise.

"Easy lad!" a pair of hands caught him.

Jaedin looked up, and there was no mistaking that distinctive face.

It was the stranger from the tavern.

"Just making sure you found it alright," he explained, smiling.

All Jaedin could do was nod.

"Wanted to see you're okay," he continued. "You seemed… uneasy."

"I'm fine," Jaedin croaked. "Thanks."

Jaedin wanted to run back into the tavern, but the man stood in his way. His hands were still on Jaedin's shoulders, and they weren't moving.

"I find you intriguing," the man said.

Jaedin blushed. Confused longings stirred within him. He didn't want the man to notice them. He wanted to get back into the tavern. Back to safety. But the man was still talking. Jaedin tried to listen but the words drowned in his ears; the wine had begun to fog his brain.

He looked at the man's face. He was handsome. Very handsome. Jaedin watched his lips as he spoke.

The next thing Jaedin knew, the man's lips were pressed against his.

"What?" Jaedin gasped as he remembered himself and pulled away. He took a deep breath; his chest heavy with nerves.

The man smiled devilishly and pulled Jaedin in again, pressing their bodies together. It was enticing. Alarming. Jaedin didn't even know this man. Their lips met again. He was taking control, and Jaedin was letting him.

"Jaedin!" a voice yelled.

Jaedin's heart jerked in his chest. He knew that voice.

He looked over his shoulder and saw Baird storming towards them. His face red with rage.

"Stay away from this boy!" Baird hollered at the stranger as he pulled Jaedin away by his collar. Jaedin gasped for breath.

"Who are *you*?" the man retorted and bared his teeth. It was the first time Jaedin had ever met someone who didn't find Baird intimidating.

Jaedin was more embarrassed than he had ever felt in his life, but a realisation struck him; this stranger seemed to be under the impression Baird was his jealous lover.

It sent Jaedin into a fit of laughter. This, and all the wine he had drunk. He covered his mouth and tried to stifle it.

"I'm his *guardian*!" Baird uttered as he dragged Jaedin away.

Jaedin took one last look at the stranger. He gave Jaedin a wily smile and waved.

Baird hauled Jaedin to the street outside the tavern, where Miles was waiting.

Jaedin and his former mentor looked at each other, and there was something in Miles' eyes which Jaedin could not place, but he knew meant Miles had witnessed the whole thing. Jaedin turned his face to the ground in shame.

"The others must be in there," Baird said, gesturing to the tavern. He pushed Jaedin at Miles and made his way inside. "Keep an eye on this one for me!"

Jaedin and Miles were alone. Neither of them said anything. At one point Jaedin looked up at his mentor's face, but Miles ignored him and watched the entrance of the tavern. Jaedin would have preferred it if Miles screamed at him for what he had just done. Any reaction would have been better than this.

As they stood there, in silence, Jaedin felt the rift between him and his former mentor deepen.

Baird emerged from the tavern a few minutes later, dragging Kyra by an ear and Bryna by her wrist. "Stupid ruddy kids!" Baird roared. "Come on, Miles! Bring that one along!"

Miles grabbed Jaedin's shoulders and dragged him. Jaedin and Kyra looked at each other, and shockingly, despite it all, she was laughing. It was infectious, and Jaedin burst into a fit of giggles too. It was strange; he knew he was going to regret this in the morning but couldn't stop himself.

Kyra's laughter abruptly turned into a shriek when Baird pulled at her hair.

"Let me go!" she screamed. "I'm not a child, and *you* are not my father! You have no fucking right to–"

"Kyra!" Baird shook her, making her head roll back and forth like a doll. "Be quiet! We're in the middle of the street!"

He let her go, and Kyra staggered for a moment. When she recovered, she put a hand to her eyes and tears came. She sobbed.

"Why, Kyra?" Baird asked, with the sting of betrayal in his voice. "Don't you see how dangerous this was?"

"I wanted to have fun," Kyra whispered. "I could be dead tomorrow."

Chapter 16

Daylight

"I want the three of you out of that tent sharpish!"

It was morning, and Jaedin was startled awake by Baird's voice. He suppressed a groan and, when he raised his head, was swept with a wave of dizziness coupled with nausea. He remembered the events of the previous night.

He turned to Kyra, but she was still sleeping. She had collapsed on top of her blankets in the early hours with her clothes still on. He nudged her shoulder but she didn't respond.

"You have twenty seconds..." Baird warned and, at the sound of his voice, Kyra bolted, sitting up. The incoherence in her eyes cleared as her mind spluttered from being half asleep to painfully aware, and she stared at the outline of Baird's shadow upon the fabric of their tent; he stood outside, imposingly, with his hands on his hips.

Kyra checked her bags while Jaedin scrambled for his tunic. He had a blistering headache, and his stomach was threatening to empty itself, but he suppressed it all. He knew Baird was going to give them a hard enough time today as it was so he needed to avoid giving him any more excuses.

"Ten!" Baird began to count down.

He and Kyra looked at each other in shared torment. His voice rang through the tent again.

"Nine!"

Jaedin had no desire to find out what would happen if they were not out of the tent by the time his countdown finished. He searched for his boots, trying to remember where he had kicked them off.

"Eight!"

He was saved by Kyra – she passed them to him from under her blanket. His hands were trembling, and he dropped the second boot as he tried to slide his foot into it.

"Four!"

Jaedin managed to get his foot into the boot but didn't have time to fasten it, so he stumbled to his feet as Kyra opened the curtain of the tent.

As he stepped out into the daylight, the sun hurt his eyes and his head spun. He stumbled dizzily for a few moments until his eyes got used to the brightness and then looked up and saw Baird glaring at him.

"Now get ready!" Baird hissed. "Do you think you could do that for me?"

Jaedin knew that any reply would merely stoke the flames, so he turned his head down and resisted an urge to place a hand on his stomach.

*   *   *

Sidry felt no sympathy for Kyra as Baird berated her that morning. Last night, she had not only endangered herself, by neglecting her watch duties, but the safety of the entire group.

Not to mention the fact she was also to blame for his lack of sleep: Sidry and Rivan had to take an extra-long shift keeping watch while Baird stormed into the village to find them and, even after they returned, they were kept awake even longer by the sound of them arguing.

But now, Kyra and Jaedin stood before Baird with their heads hung low like disobedient children and, even though Sidry was tired, he couldn't help but feel grimly satisfied.

"Where's Bryna?" Baird yelled as he peered into their tent.

Sidry then, out of the corner of his eye, saw Bryna emerge from the trees. She strolled into the camp with her usual dreamlike content, cradling a basket beneath her arm.

"Where have *you* been?" Baird roared when he noticed her.

She looked at their leader airily.

"Garfeldens," she mumbled.

"What?"

She lifted her basket and indicated the flowers she gathered. "Garfeldens," she repeated. "They will be out of season soon. I–"

"When did you leave your tent?" Baird interrupted her.

Bryna shrugged.

Sidry had to cover his smirk with his hand when he saw the dismay on Baird's face. He knew the *real* reason Baird was vexed. In every respect, Bryna had achieved what Baird expected from them each morning – she had risen early and was promptly dressed and ready for the day ahead – the only reason Baird was irked was that she had left her tent during his watch, and he had not even noticed.

He glared at her, red-faced, his fists clenched at his sides.

"*Don't* stray from the camp without telling me!" he yelled. "*Ever!*"

*   *   *

After packing away their tents, they left the glade and walked to the village.

Kyra and Jaedin seemed to be bearing the brunt of Baird's anger, but Aylen would have almost preferred that to the cold silence the leader was putting him through.

It was like Aylen no longer existed. Baird was still yet to declare what his punishment was going to be. Aylen feared Baird would never trust him with the nightly watch duties ever again; thus demoted to the ranks of Jaedin and Bryna.

Aylen had never felt so isolated in his entire life. Everyone was angry with him. Rivan kept glaring at him. Dareth had been feeding him salty comments for helping 'the bitch' all morning. Even Kyra was ignoring him for some reason.

Aylen didn't know how Kyra managed to talk him into letting her sneak off. From the moment she asked, he'd known it was a stupid idea, but there was something about the way she looked him in the eyes and smiled which made it impossible for him to say no. Aylen was a bad liar. When Rivan and Sidry came to the fire to begin their shift and noticed Kyra wasn't there, Aylen tried to make an excuse for her, but they saw straight through it.

As they passed through a field of cows, Aylen began to feel nervous. They were getting close to the village now and, in recent times, Aylen had come to associate such places with danger.

*   *   *

It was just as they were entering a neighbourhood on the outskirts of the village that Jaedin felt their presence.

The place was the very picture of normality. An elderly woman sat outside her house knitting something. A man was wheeling a barrow down his pathway. Children were playing. They seemed to have not a care in the world.

But Jaedin knew that somewhere, in the further reaches of this village, Zakaras were lurking.

"They're here," Jaedin whispered, and everyone stopped.

"Why didn't you tell us earlier?!" Rivan hissed. "You were here last night, weren't you?"

"They *weren't* here then…" Jaedin said.

"Spare it you two!" Baird grunted. He cast his eyes about them to make sure their squabbling had not drawn any attention. "I'm getting tired of all this childish bickering."

"If Jaedin is right…" Miles said measuredly. "We should wonder why it is that they are here now but weren't last night."

Jaedin was glad to hear that at least *someone* had faith in him, but the manner his mentor spoke about him then was as if he wasn't even there. Miles had not even so much as looked at him since the incident the night before. Part of Jaedin hoped it was because he was jealous, but he knew that was probably just wishful thinking.

"Shayam could know where we are…" Baird mused but shook his head. "No. He would've attacked us in the night…"

"Or this is another trap," Miles said.

"I doubt it," Baird muttered. "Jaedin was probably just too grogged up last night to notice."

Jaedin clenched his fists behind his back, incensed. He *knew* there was no Zakaras here last night. It was one of the first things he made sure of when he sneaked into the village.

It angered him that Baird had such little faith.

"Where are they?" Baird asked him.

You have no faith in me, but you don't mind using me… Jaedin thought bitterly as he closed his eyes. His forehead started to tingle when he activated the crystal.

"They're on the other side of town," Jaedin announced.

"How many?" Baird asked.

"Five," Jaedin guessed. "I could reach into their minds and find out more if you wish… but if Shayam is controlling them, he might sense me."

Baird paused and pulled the face that Jaedin had come to recognise as his calculating expression; he was weighing up the risks and ramifications.

"Is it wise to go after them?" Miles pondered. "When we could possibly pass through here undetected…"

"No," Baird shook his head at the Gavendarian. "I'm sick of running! This time, we are going to confront *them*."

"We need to stop them multiplying," Kyra pointed out. "They could take over the whole village…"

Jaedin felt uneasy. Up till this moment he had only ever used his cursed powers when faced with no other choice, but now he was being obliged to protect the people of this village. Strangers. Did he want such responsibility? In his heart, all Jaedin wanted was to get out of this mess. To live a normal life. He had no illusions that he had what it took to be a hero.

He looked at Kyra and noticed she was subconsciously stroking the hilt of her sword. She was itching for a fight. She had always possessed a propensity for excitement and adventure; it worried him, but he knew there was nothing he could do to change her. Would he eventually have to choose between leaving her behind and living a peaceful life?

Would Baird even *let* him choose? It seemed Jaedin was regularly a part of his strategies now. A piece on his chessboard.

Jaedin looked at his sister. Her eyes were unreadable, like they usually were these days. She didn't even seem to be aware of the peril they were in.

"Lead us to them," Baird said.

Jaedin broke away from his thoughts and regarded their leader.

At least this escapade is distracting him from making my day a misery, he thought. *Okay, Baird. I will be your pawn, for now. But once we reach Shemet, I am taking me and my sister out of this mess.*

Jaedin marched towards the village. Everyone followed him. None of them spoke, but they strode purposefully, and the apprehension in the air was so heavy Jaedin wondered if the native villagers could feel it. Many of them stared as they passed.

It doesn't matter if they notice us, Jaedin thought grimly. *Soon, we are going to make a scene this place will never forget…*

They walked past a small market, and Jaedin caught the

scent of fresh bread, spices, and the yeasty odour of a brewery nearby, which did not help the queasy sensation in his stomach. They were now within the heart of the village. Jaedin made a silent plea to the gods that none of the civilians there would come to harm in the inevitable skirmish that was about to happen.

There are only five of them, he reassured himself.

They turned a final corner, and Jaedin looked down a busy street. The Zakaras were close now.

He activated the crystal and his eyes beamed with light, illuminating everything before him in different shades of red. This was a new ability he'd discovered when they escaped from the encampment. With it, Jaedin could spot Zakaras by sight.

All of the humans within Jaedin's field of vision became faint shadows within a dominion of red spectres but, ahead, five figures stood out, shining brighter.

Three men, a woman, and boy not much younger than Jaedin. They stood huddled together, seemingly normal villagers in the same drab brown attire as the other people around them, but Jaedin recognised that glassy look in their eyes. They were Zakaras.

He pointed to them.

"No..." Sidry muttered, shaking his head. "They are just..."

He looked at Jaedin in disbelief, and Jaedin could see his thoughts clearly in his eyes because they mirrored his own. Zakaras had so far been just Shayam's henchmen – they wore green robes and had Gavendarian faces – but these people were different.

One of them looked at Jaedin, and their eyes met. Jaedin wondered if it knew. If it could sense that he possessed a Stone of Zakar. He wondered if Shayam was controlling them this very moment and seeing Jaedin through its eyes.

He would soon know.

"They are not people anymore," Baird reminded them. "And unless we eliminate them they will kill others. They will multiply."

Jaedin called upon the crystal's power and focussed its energy upon his targets; the five Zakaras before him. He reached into their minds.

One of them suddenly broke away, leaping into the air. Its body jerked as it shifted form and, when it landed, what was once a boy had turned into a gargantuan creature covered in red bristle. It tilted its neck to the sky and shrieked a battle cry just before it rushed towards a group of civilians.

Jaedin mustered all his will into controlling that creature alone, only just managing to pull it into a halt when it was a scant few feet away from the villagers.

The scene erupted into chaos. Jaedin heard screams from all around him, and a stampede of terrified children ran past. He was blinded for a moment by a bright flash of light. It was Baird summoning his Avatar.

A woman bumped into Jaedin, breaking his concentration and causing him to lose control of the monster, but Baird was already on the beast, cleaving through its body with his bladed arm. Blood sprayed as the two halves of the creature dropped to the ground, and Baird rose above it like a god; mighty, towering and horned, his armour glimmering.

The villagers were still fleeing, flooding down alleys and roads and hiding behind buildings. Some of the braver ones watched from afar, staring with disbelieving eyes and agape mouths at the mighty sight of Baird in his Gezra form.

The four remaining Zakaras were the only villagers who had not yet fled the scene. They stared at Jaedin, and Jaedin could feel Shayam's presence within their minds.

Kyra nocked an arrow into her bow, Aylen whipped out his knives, and Rivan unleashed his sword, placing himself in front of them protectively. After a moment of hesitation, Dareth drew his blade too. With a second flash of light, Sidry transformed and ran into the fray.

Shayam willed the other Zakaras to shift into their true forms – Jaedin felt it before he saw the signs. Their crooked limbs quivered, their bodies bulged, and their flesh turned dark. As Zakaras, they were all of similar form; reptilian, covered in scales, and with dark oval eyes.

Baird and Sidry charged at them, and the four monsters split and dispersed. Baird thrashed at one, but the creature dodged his blade with ophidian speed. These Zakaras were faster than most of the ones Jaedin had encountered before.

I need to help them! Jaedin reminded himself. He closed his eyes and focused on the Stone of Zakar. He kept feeling the cyclone of Kyra's arrows whizzing past his ears, but he ignored it, focussing all his attention on channelling the crystal's energy. Everything turned red again. Jaedin saw Baird as a shadow, slashing his blades at the Zakaras, who stood out as four luminous slithering shapes.

Jaedin clenched his fists. Shayam still had a hold over these creatures, but Jaedin was determined to break through. He strained with all his might.

The walls crumbled, and Jaedin grabbled into their minds. It was disorientating at first. Their monstrous thoughts engulfed him. Jaedin felt their thirst for blood and killing.

He righted himself.

Fuck you Shayam, Jaedin thought as he stilled their movements. *Your beasts are mine!*

Baird vaulted one of them and cleaved its neck with his blade. Jaedin witnessed its luminescence fade away as its body dropped. Sidry dealt with the other, thrusting his blade into its skull. Its limbs made an involuntary spasm, and it fell.

There were now only two Zakaras left.

Shayam fought Jaedin to assume control over them again. Sweat gathered on Jaedin's forehead; he knew he couldn't keep his hold much longer.

"There's another one!" Rivan yelled. "Jaedin! Look!"

Jaedin looked in the direction Rivan pointed and saw a dark figure sprint across the rooftops. It leapt upon one of the other Zakaras, landing on its back. Jaedin gasped. This new creature looked like a Zakara, but it was attacking its own kind.

Jaedin tried to reach into its mind to find out why it was behaving in such a way, but nothing happened.

This Zakara was immune to the crystal's power.

When it had finished ravaging the other Zakara with its claws, the creature jumped away, leaving a sanguine mess behind. It sprang at the final Zakara.

"Well done, Jaedin!" Miles grinned. "You–"

"No," Jaedin shook his head. "That wasn't me. I'm not controlling him. I can't! He's different… He's not a Zakara–"

Jaedin stopped. He noticed Baird was racing to the new creature with his blades drawn.

No! Jaedin thought. *It was trying to help us! What are you doing?*

But Jaedin realised that, to Baird, it was just another Zakara. He was going to kill it.

The creature sprinted away, and Baird pursued it, chasing it down the street.

Jaedin pushed his weariness aside and broke into a run, following them. Miles yelled an objection, but Jaedin ignored him. He needed to save that creature from Baird. He wanted to find out what it was.

Ever since Jaedin woke up in Shayam's base in the Forest of Lareem, he had been too self-conscious to find out how fast he could run.

The others already knew he was a freak now. It was time to find out.

He felt the wind breeze past his face, and the buildings of the village streamed past him in a blur.

*   *   *

Only a few minutes had passed since the chase began, but the town was already behind him. No matter how fast Baird ran, the monster had always managed to stay a few feet ahead of him. Jaedin's superhuman speed was just fast enough to keep them in sight.

"Baird!" Jaedin yelled when they reached the top of a hill, but it seemed their leader either couldn't hear or was ignoring him.

"Baird!" Jaedin repeated.

Eventually, the monster halted and turned to face them. Its form began to shift. Its dark, leathery skin turned pale, and its bones creaked as they realigned. It assumed a human appearance and, within moments, all that was before Baird was a defenceless, naked man with his arms raised.

Baird raised his blade-arm to make a fatal blow.

"Wait!" Jaedin yelled.

Baird paused and looked down at the helpless man before him, seemingly only just realising he was making a gesture of surrender.

There was a flash of light and, when Jaedin opened his eyes again, Baird had also reverted to human form. He drew his sword.

"You see now why what you did last night was so stupid?!"

Baird yelled as he lowered his blade to the man's neck. "See how you almost got yourself killed?!"

Jaedin looked closer and gasped. He recognised that face.

It was the stranger from the previous night.

"He isn't one of them!" Jaedin yelled.

"Don't be ridiculous!" Baird looked down at the man and narrowed his eyes. "You saw what he was just then! He is one of *them*. Don't let this disguise fool you!"

"Didn't you see what he did back then?" Jaedin asked. "He *helped* us."

Baird's eyes widened. "That wasn't you? You weren't controlling him?"

Jaedin shook his head.

"Then what is he?" Baird said, looking upon the stranger again.

"I don't know," Jaedin admitted. "He's... different. I couldn't detect him, and I can't control him. I want to know why."

Baird lifted the sword from the man's neck, and the man tilted his head up. He looked at Jaedin. Their eyes met, and he grinned, making Jaedin blush.

He looks even better in the daylight, Jaedin thought as his eyes wandered over his body. He was muscular, and there was a faint spread of dark hairs across his forearms and chest.

Baird tossed the man his coat. "Cover yourself with this!" he said.

The stranger gave Jaedin a devilish wink before he placed the coat over his shoulders.

"Now explain yourself," Baird said, holding his sword just a few inches away from his nose.

The way the man smiled at Baird was almost mocking. Jaedin had never met anyone who did not fear Baird.

"Where would you like me to start?" he asked.

"Name," Baird replied.

"Fangar."

Baird raised a sceptical eyebrow. "Where are you from, *Fangar*?"

"No-where."

Baird brought the sword closer to his neck.

"Don't be hasty!" Fangar said, raising his arms. "Truth is, I don't know my real name. Or where I'm from."

"Because you're one of *them*?" Baird asked.

"Depends what you mean by 'one of them'…"

"Zakaras," Baird said, emphasising his impatience with his voice. "Shayam's men. The monsters. Don't pretend you don't know."

"If you mean, am I one of *those* diseased little wretches…" Fangar said with a hint of contempt. "Then, no! If you are asking if I am not quite human anymore, then yes; I *am* guilty… like yourself, may I add…"

"You're going to have to explain," Baird said.

"Explain *myself*?" he repeated, grinning. "I don't know how to really…" He shook his head and shrugged. "Ten years ago, I woke up like this. A man. With no name. And not quite human anymore. That is all I remember. I do not know who I am or what I am. All that I know is that they did something to me. And I want revenge."

"Ten years ago?" Baird asked.

"Call me an early experiment. I was one of the first Zakaras," Fangar lifted his head and brought a hand to his chest. "But do not worry, I am not contagious."

He winked at Jaedin, but then Baird's smacked his shoulder with the flat of his blade.

"Stay *away* from him!" Baird grunted.

"Not allowed to make his own choices, eh?" Fangar said.

"He's *sixteen*," Baird prodded Fangar's neck with the edge of his sword. "And under my care."

"Actually, I'm seventeen," Jaedin said without thinking. "It was my and Bryna's birthday yesterday…"

Baird looked at Jaedin in surprise.

"He's different," Jaedin said, keen to change the subject. "I can't control him with the Stone, so he's not a Zakara."

"But that doesn't mean we can trust him…" Baird said.

Jaedin couldn't help but agree. He *was* attracted to this man, but he also sensed something dangerous about him.

"How did you find us?" Baird asked him.

"I could smell him," Fangar gestured to Jaedin. "He has a rather interesting scent…"

Jaedin felt his cheeks turn red.

"I told you to stop–" Baird began to chastise, but Fangar cut him off.

"I know he has one of the Stones of Zakar," Fangar

explained. "That is why I can smell him. And also why I killed those things... I wanted to show you I'm not one of them."

Baird raised an eyebrow – he was clearly impressed by how much this man knew – but then his face creased into a frown again. "Why? What do you want from us?"

"I want the same thing you want," Fangar replied, meeting Baird's eyes. "I want revenge, you want to save humanity. Both of these things mean killing the men who did this to me."

"Why should we trust you?" Baird asked.

"What if I told you that I know where Shayam is headed right now?" Fangar asked. "And that he poses a great threat to Sharma?"

This news seemed to catch Baird's attention, but his expression was still laden with suspicion. "I don't trust you..." he said flatly.

Fangar shrugged. "It's your choice... I've answered your questions. Now, how about you answer some of mine? What would happen if Gavendara sent armies of Zakaras to attack Shemet not *only* from the northern border but also from the other side? Somewhere within Sharma itself. What if Shayam was, this very moment, heading towards a town where he plans to assemble an army from its citizens?"

Baird's mouth gaped in horror.

"Shayam is going to make a stronghold," Fangar said. "And I know where."

Chapter 17

Shayam's Plan

Baird spent an hour interrogating Fangar, gleaning more details about his story and the news he brought.

He didn't trust this man sitting before him, but he could not dismiss what he was saying because, if he was telling the truth, and they ignored him, the consequences could be dire.

Eventually, the others caught up and, at the sight of Baird sitting with a stranger who wore nothing but a cloak around his shoulders, they stared.

"What is *he* doing here?" Miles exclaimed when he recognised him. His face turned red with anger, and he turned to Baird for an explanation.

Baird could already feel the hostility in the air – and he knew he needed to take control of the situation before it got out of hand – so he rose, standing between them and Fangar.

"You *know* him?" Sidry asked.

"Oh yeah, we know him..." Kyra smirked. "Don't we, Jaedin..."

Jaedin's face turned beet red.

"Less of that, Kyra!" Baird muttered, giving her a glare which he hoped made it clear she was not to mention *that* matter again. He did not want Rivan and the others to know what happened between Jaedin and Fangar because it could reignite the feud between the two social groups in his care. Baird was having a hard enough time uniting this pack of survivors as it was.

Sidry, Rivan, Aylen and Dareth stared at the newcomer with suspicion, maintaining a wary distance from him.

"Is *he* the thing you chased?" Rivan asked.

When Baird nodded, Rivan's hand went to his sword.

"No, Rivan!" he said. "It's more complicated than that..."

"It's a Zakara!" Rivan said. "Why let it live?"

Fangar bared his teeth at the young man; he was clearly not in the least intimidated by him.

"He's right!" Miles agreed. "Baird, what is this madness?"

"Will all of you just *shut up*!" Baird yelled, silencing them all. He waited for a few moments, to make sure he had their undivided attention, and then turned back to Fangar. "This man here's got a story to tell you, and I want you *all* to listen!"

Fangar raised himself to his feet like a wolf standing to attention. Even when he was in human form, the way that he carried himself was unnatural. His posture, movements, and mannerisms all reminded Baird of a predatory animal, something carnal.

It's probably the Zakara in him, Baird realised. *I am placing these kids in danger by having this monster here. I should kill him now.*

But Baird couldn't do it. Because if there was even just some smallest truth to Fangar's claims, they needed him.

"Just in case you haven't noticed I am a 'he', and my name is Fangar," he began, and glared at Rivan. "And considering I helped you back there, I am quite frankly disappointed in the hospitality I've got so far! A simple 'thank you' would have cut it..." He turned to Miles. "And no. I am not a Zakara. I was an early experiment, and no-one with any damned crystal can control me."

"That's impossible!" Miles raised his voice. "The early experiments are all accounted for!"

"How do you know about the experiments?" Fangar asked, tilting his head to him. His fingers grew, became dark and tapered. Talons. Within moments, they were over a foot long.

He sprang at Miles.

"No!" Baird yelled.

He leapt between them, brandishing his sword, and Fangar halted before him. They stared at each other. Face to face. Baird saw the mad rage in his eyes.

He's either a good actor or he's telling the truth... Baird realised. He had seen that look in a man's eyes before. It was the look of a man who lived for one purpose only. Revenge.

It made sense. If Fangar had no memory of his previous life then what else would he have to live for?

Despite beginning to believe Fangar, this revelation concerned him. A man with such a strong desire for revenge could be dangerous to have around. They were often blinded by their rage. Some even hurt the innocent if they stood in their path.

"Miles has his own story. Just like you do," Baird said firmly. "And he has turned against our enemies at great risk to himself."

Fangar glared at the Gavendarian for a few more moments before he stepped away.

"I want to hear this story sometime..." he muttered as his claws shrank back into fingers. "And... Miles – is it?" he asked. "You say that all the early experiments are accounted for. What about the facilities which were destroyed?"

"The experiments went wrong," Miles recalled. "Causing–"

"No," Fangar smirked. "That is probably what they told you. But the truth is *I* destroyed them."

"No..." Miles muttered. "That's... impossible..."

"It was not. I assure you."

Miles gasped, and his expression became disconcerted. It seemed to Baird that the scholar's initial assertion that it was impossible had been merely a gut feeling which, in hindsight, he was unable to justify.

Miles was now realising that it was, in fact, very possible Fangar did it.

"You killed all those people?" Miles breathed.

"No, *they* had already done that job for me," Fangar replied, with the first hint of tender emotion Baird had noticed from him so far apparent in his voice. "I just put those poor wretches out of their misery..."

Miles opened his mouth as if he was about to say something back but then reconsidered.

"Fangar has some troubling news," Baird announced to advance the discussion. They all stared back at him with expectant expressions. "And he is familiar with Shayam–"

"How do you know he's not a spy?" Rivan asked.

"Do you think that *hasn't* crossed my mind?" Baird challenged.

"No," Rivan muttered, turning his face down. "I... just..."

"This man has information which we cannot ignore, for if he is right, the cost would be too great," Baird announced, pointing to him. "Tell them, Fangar."

Fangar circled the group with his eyes, looking at each of them. "I have devoted the only ten years of my life I can remember to hassling these men in every way I can. I have travelled around Gavendara, destroying their bases, killing those I could get to, and finding out as many of their secrets as I can. But, when I found out what their new plans were, I crossed the border."

His placed a hand on his waist. "Grav'aen wants to create an army of Zakaras to invade Sharma with. Baird has already told me you suspected this was the case – it was the reason he was leading you to Shemet. But their plans have changed. They now aim to attack Shemet not only from across the border, but *also* from the inside. Shayam is preparing to take over a city and create an army from its citizens."

This revelation was followed by gasps. Fangar had their attention now.

"As you know," Fangar continued. "Anyone killed by a Zakara turns into one – your village was proof of this – and anyone who is turned into a Zakara can be controlled by the Stones of Zakar. There are nine Gavendarian nobles who possess these Stones, including Grav'aen and Shayam. *Human* armies need training, food, shelter and, most of all, volunteers; people who offer their lives to protect their country, but all Grav'aen would need to invade Sharma is a small army and a few of these Stones... anyone they kill along the way will only add to their numbers!" He turned to Jaedin. "When I discovered someone had stolen one of the Stones of Zakar from them, I had to find him. I have been following your scent, Jaedin, and I couldn't believe it was true until I saw you with my own eyes. However small, you have given us a chance against them!"

Jaedin turned away with a flustered expression. Baird could tell the young man got no thrill from the prospect of such a grave responsibility.

"I need you to join me against them," Fangar finished, turning back to address them all. "I saw, back there in the village, that some of you have powerful abilities... if we are going to take on Shayam we need everything we can throw at him."

They all stared at Fangar as their minds took in everything he just said. Baird could tell most of them were still deeply suspicious of him, but he hoped they also realised they couldn't ignore what he was saying.

"I'm in," Kyra announced.

"Where is this so-called town?" Rivan asked.

"By the way that hammy hand of yours hand is crawling to your weapon," Fangar eyed up Rivan's blade. "I suspect you have in mind to try killing me once I told you. Here's a friendly warning, kid; you ain't no match for me."

"You'd stake your life on that?" Rivan asked between gritted teeth.

This is turning to chaos... Baird thought, feeling the energy in the air rising. He needed to take control.

He stepped forward and pointed to Fangar. "*No one* is to harm this man!" he decreed. "Unless he does anything untoward and you are *certain* he is a threat to you!"

Baird then turned to Kyra. "And yes," he said to her. "Fangar *is* going to join us."

And then, finally, Baird looked at Fangar. "But there are some terms... You have my word that no one here will harm you but, at the first hint of *any* suspicious behaviour from you, I will kill you myself! We will be keeping a very close eye on you... I am sure you can understand why we cannot completely trust you yet."

"That's fair. I wouldn't if I were you," Fangar shrugged.

"Now, what is the name of that town?" Baird asked.

"Shayam is heading to Fraknar."

Fraknar, Baird recalled. He had been there once when he was a young man. It was a large town west of Shemet, beside the river Marleena; not too far from the forest of Jilan'ur.

"On the journey to Fraknar, you will sleep with your tent at least twenty paces away from the rest of us," Baird added. "We will leave in the morning."

*   *   *

That evening, Baird observed his pack of survivors as they pitched their tents and collected wood for fire.

He knew it was a cruel fate which had placed people so young in this dilemma, but he was also aware that, for them to have any chance of getting out of this situation alive, they needed to be obedient to his orders. Kyra's escapade last night worried him. They were beginning to rebel.

Baird knew most of them did not like the idea of Fangar joining them – he felt the same – but he hoped they understood they had no choice but bear his company until they reached Fraknar and discovered the truth. Baird also knew that, despite Rivan's protests, he could count on the young lad to abide by his orders. And most of the others would act accordingly because they looked up to him.

On the other hand, Jaedin and Kyra seemed to welcome the newcomer. Although this made life somewhat easier for Baird, it concerned him. Kyra had always had a rebellious streak and Baird worried the presence of another maverick in the group would rub off on her.

Bryna seemed apathetic to the situation, as usual. Baird glanced at her a few times throughout the heated debate that the newcomer had stirred earlier and, while everyone else's faces revealed a whole spectrum of feelings and anxieties at the news Fangar brought with him, her expression remained impassive. For a good duration of the discussion she had even stared at the sky. As usual, Bryna was physically present, but her mind was on another plane.

Baird was still suspicious of Jaedin's twin. What she did at Shayam's encampment disturbed him. It was now a certain fact that something strange was going on with her, but, unless she became willing to open up about it, Baird was still far from discovering what it was. The most frustrating thing about the situation was that Baird could do nothing without seeming like a bully because all she had done so far was help them.

He was pulled out of his thoughts when Fangar approached him.

"I need to go back to the village. Get my clothes and things," he said.

Baird nodded. Fangar was still wearing nothing but Baird's cloak draped over his shoulders.

"It will be dark soon," Baird reminded him.

"I won't be long…" Fangar replied. "And I can see in the dark anyway."

Baird raised his eyebrow. Accelerated strength, speed, scent *and* sight. What else was there to this man?

"What is that village called?" Baird asked

"Not sure," Fangar shrugged. "Travel as long as I have, you seldom remember the names of these small places…"

Baird frowned. "If you don't know where we are now then how are we going to find our way to Fraknar?"

"I found Jaedin with my nose," Fangar reminded him. "And Shayam's a stinker."

Fangar dropped Baird's cloak to the ground. His skin darkened. His body changed. In all their shapes and sizes, Baird had never seen a Zakara which was not hideous and unsightly and, when Fangar was transformed, he was no exception. His body was covered in a dark shiny carapace. His back was curved. His hind legs were built for sprinting, and his mouth was filled with large fangs. He was smaller than a lot of Zakaras, but he had a bone structure Baird guessed to be very agile, and his long, tapered claws appeared to be lethal weapons.

His transformation finished, he leapt away, sprinting towards the village on four legs.

"Where's he going?"

Baird turned around. It was Jaedin. He was watching Fangar as he scampered into the distance.

"Just to the village. He'll be back soon," Baird replied.

"I need to talk to you," Jaedin said, placing his hands behind his back. Baird could tell he was nervous.

"What is it, Jaedin?" Baird sighed.

"I want me and Bryna out of this mess..." he said.

Baird frowned. He had been waiting for Jaedin to make such a request for a while. From the very beginning, he'd thought the young man was going to be useless, and Baird was quite frankly surprised how valuable he had proven himself since then.

Jaedin had already surpassed Baird's low expectations of him, but it was not enough.

"We need your help, Jaedin," Baird said, though it pained him to admit it. "You are the only one who can control the Zakaras."

"We both know that I am not cut out for all this," Jaedin said. "And neither is my sister."

"And what do you plan to do? Go hide in a village somewhere? Where would you stay? You have no family, no connections, no money, and you have some very powerful people after you," Baird pointed out. "Face it, Jaedin; you need us just as much as we need you."

"I want to offer you a deal," Jaedin said, meeting his gaze levelly.

Baird realised that, whatever Jaedin had in mind, he was resolute and determined. Baird had never witnessed him be so assertive.

"I am listening," Baird said.

"I will use this cursed crystal to help you defeat Shayam when we reach Fraknar. I owe you this much. But only on the condition that when we reach Shemet, you let me and my sister leave this mess behind us."

Baird pondered this. He didn't care much for Bryna; he found her unnerving and could never get any sense out of her. She had helped them escape from Shayam's encampment, but apart from that one, isolated incident, she had hardly lifted a finger.

But Baird needed Jaedin. Well, not Jaedin specifically, for he was once again proving himself a coward. Baird needed that Stone of Zakar he possessed.

"Here is *my* deal: I will arrange a safe place for your sister to live comfortably when we reach Shemet," Baird decided. "On the condition that *you* continue to help me."

"I am not your pawn!" Jaedin crossed his arms, bolder and more defiant than Baird had ever seen him. "When we reach Shemet, I am going to the Academy, and there is nothing you can do about it!"

* * *

Sidry rose early the next day. As he fastened the buttons of his tunic, he remembered the previous morning when he had done the same thing while looking forward to the prospect of sleeping in a real bed when they reached the village, maybe even purchasing some supplies. Their diet on the road had become quite limited, and he was starting to miss certain things.

They didn't even get the chance to *speak* to any of the villagers, let alone purchase anything. After the skirmish, the streets had lain deserted. The only signs of life were the few bystanders who were bold enough to watch from afar. Sidry tried to get close enough to them to explain but they fled from him in terror. They didn't seem to have any idea that he had likely just saved their lives by ridding them of a Zakara infestation; in their eyes, a group of strangers had entered their seemingly peaceful village and brought disaster with them.

Sidry sighed. It would be a while before they had such an opportunity again. After yesterday's disturbing news, Baird was going to push them harder than ever to reach Fraknar as soon as possible. It was unlikely they would be stopping at any settlements along the way.

He stepped out of his tent. It was still early in the morning, and Baird and Fangar were conversing by the remains of the fire. Sidry narrowed his eyes at the newcomer. Baird had decreed that he would be travelling with them from now, and Sidry would abide by his mentor's decisions out of loyalty, but that did not stop him from being cautious of the stranger now in their midst. He didn't trust him.

He sat down on the other side of the smouldering embers. Aylen was there. Their eyes met, and Sidry felt a thread of the awkwardness recently woven between them.

Sidry had not spoken to Aylen since he had tried to cover up for Kyra sneaking into that village. He couldn't understand what could have driven him to do something so stupid. He noticed the young man had become friendlier with Kyra recently but never realised just how much influence she had over him.

The truth was, Sidry had always thought of Aylen as part of his and Rivan's gang. Aiding their rival felt like a betrayal.

Sidry realised that was a poor reason to be annoyed with someone. Who was he to tell Aylen who he could or couldn't be friends with?

"Morning," Sidry said. "Sleep well?"

Aylen's eyes lit up.

The two of them engaged in small talk. It was a little awkward at first, but the ill-feeling between them gradually unwove itself.

"I don't trust him," Aylen whispered, looking at Fangar.

Sidry nodded. "But Baird is right. We have to find out if he's telling the truth."

"I know..." Aylen muttered. "But something's not right about him."

"I think the others met him before," Sidry said. "On the night they sneaked to the village."

Aylen nodded. "Do you know what happened?"

Sidry shook his head. "Rivan asked Baird about it, but he went all strange and told him to mind his own business."

"That's weird…" Aylen commented.

"I think something happened that Baird doesn't want us to know about," Sidry concluded.

"Did you notice Kyra winking at him yesterday?" Aylen asked. "I think she's got a shine on him…"

"Why don't you try and ask her what happened?" Sidry asked.

"No," Aylen shook his head. "She isn't talking to me at the moment. I think she's pissed off."

"Why?" Sidry asked.

"I don't know…" Aylen shrugged. "'Cause she got caught, I guess… Maybe she blames me."

Sidry tsked. "Remember that next time she asks you for a favour. Don't worry about her, Aylen," Sidry advised. "Maybe after this is over she and that freak of nature will run off together."

He laughed but, for some reason, Aylen didn't seem to find it funny.

*   *   *

Fangar led the group through the wilderness. His path did not follow any roads and trails. He never paused nor skirted around the hills or woodlands. He led them over arduous hills, cascading streams, and rocky outcrops, and he crossed such obstacles with the ease of a wild animal.

For Aylen, it was a particularly difficult journey. Now Jaedin was no longer hiding his physical capabilities, Aylen was pressed harder than ever to not be the straggler who held them back.

Dareth's mood had improved a little. The wedge between them had not fully healed, since Aylen aided Kyra in her escapade, but he had ceased giving Aylen such a hard time about it. They bonded through sharing their hatred of the new stranger in their midst.

At around midday, Fangar led them up a steep mountainside. He pulled his nimble body up the rock like a cat climbing a tree and was at the top within moments, whereas Aylen and Dareth had to slowly labour their way up, gripping upon the cracks and crevices to haul themselves one step at a time and, once they reached the top, they were exhausted. But Fangar did not give them any time to catch their breath; without a moment's pause, he was once again leading them on his wayward route down the hill.

"Where is this freak leading us!" Dareth muttered.

"He said it was the fastest way to Fraknar…" Aylen mumbled tiredly.

"And to *what*?" Dareth asked. "If he's telling the truth Shayam will slaughter us…"

"Baird seems to think we have a chance," Aylen said.

"Baird is placing too much faith in a soddy," Dareth hissed, glaring at Jaedin who was several paces ahead, as he usually was these days. "How is *he* going to be any use to you?"

"What else can we do?" Aylen asked. He could not see any other option they had but to follow Baird.

"Baird is sending us on a suicide mission just 'cause he's a soldier and thinks it is the right thing to do," Dareth whispered. "But we are not soldiers, Aylen, so why drag us into it? He hasn't even given us a choice!"

He does have a point… Aylen realised. Ever since they escaped from Jalard, when had Baird given them any choices?

But Aylen knew he had to stay with the group. He had nothing else left. Nowhere else to go. Everyone he cared about who was still alive was with him right now and, although he was scared of what was to come, Aylen needed to stay with them.

"It is just something we have to do…" was all Aylen could say.

* * *

Even though Midsummer had passed, and the days were getting shorter, they usually had an hour of daylight left after they set up camp, which they used to practice fencing, plan drills, and discuss strategies.

Baird often left the others to their own devices and focussed his attention on Jaedin. Nobody could deny the young man's determination. His elevated strength and dexterity gave him an advantage, and he improved considerably in a short amount of time.

Sidry watched one evening, as Baird demonstrated a series of manoeuvres to him. They were pretty basic, but he imitated them almost perfectly. Jaedin was still far from a swordsman, and nothing would ever make up for years of neglect, but he could now at least hold his blade with a grace which gave the impression he had an idea how to use it.

"It's your go, Sidry," Aylen said, waving a handful of daggers in front of his face and pulling him out of his thoughts.

"Or would you rather carry on staring at Jaedin," Dareth joked.

Sidry took the weapons. Aylen was helping them all improve their dagger slinging that day; it wasn't an art Baird had ever taught them, so Sidry had little experience. He could see the merit in learning something new, though.

And besides, Aylen seemed to enjoy giving guidance to people who usually bested him. It wasn't often he got a chance to shine.

As Sidry was aiming his first throw, he became aware of a shadow watching him. It was Fangar.

What's he doing here? Sidry thought. The man's presence made him uncomfortable.

"Don't mind me, kids," he said, seemingly oblivious to their scowls. "Carry on…"

Sidry sighed and turned his attention back to the target. He raised the first dagger again and swayed it back and forth a few times, getting his aim.

Once it felt right, he hurled it. It hit the tree but bounced off, landing on the grass.

Fangar watched him with a grin on his face. It made Sidry prickly, but he continued and threw the second dagger. This one hit the outer ring, while the third missed completely and flew wide of the tree. Sidry sighed.

"Do you mind if *I* have a go?" Fangar asked.

The boys turned to each other. Sidry thought it must have been obvious from their expressions that none of them appreciated the intrusion.

Rivan nodded grudgingly.

Fangar strode over to the tree and collected the daggers. He then made his way back to the spot Aylen had marked upon the ground, turned around and, with three practised movements of his arm, the blades whirled through the air. They all struck the centre of the target. Sidry raised his eyebrow in surprise. Only Aylen usually managed to get all three on mark.

"I see you've done this before…" Rivan commented dryly.

Fangar nodded. "I've delved," he admitted. "But you do realise that *this* means nothing?"

He pointed to the target on the tree.

"What do you mean?" Dareth said.

"How many encounters have you been in where you were able to stand still?" Fangar asked. "You need to practise accuracy while on the *move*!"

"He's right," Aylen admitted reluctantly. "But where is this going?" he asked, turning to Fangar. "We can't simulate a battle and run around throwing daggers at each other!"

Fangar turned around and took three large – impossibly far – leaps and, when he landed, stubbed the toe of his boot into the earth, carving a cross in the dirt. Then, he strolled a little bit closer to the tree and marked another spot in the same fashion.

He marched back, making one last mark on the ground when he returned.

"There…" he announced, pointing to the first mark he made. "You make your first throw from there, and then you sprint to *that* spot to take your second, and then your final one from *here*. Between each of them, you have to keep running…"

The four young men looked at each other. None of them liked the way this stranger had taken charge of their game, but refusing his challenge would seem like conceding defeat.

"Shall I try?" Aylen whispered.

Rivan nodded.

*   *   *

Aylen made his way to the first marker.

He was nervous. None of the others took dagger throwing seriously – a part of him suspected they only agreed to practise its art this evening to humour him – but, for Aylen, it was his forte. It was a skill the others recognised him for, and

Fangar just demonstrated marksmanship which rivalled his own.

If Aylen did poorly in this new challenge, he could lose some of his credibility.

He looked at the target. It was further away now, but it was for the benefit of the others rather than himself that he had set the mark closer before. For him, this first shot was no ordeal.

With a flick of his wrist, the blade was soaring towards the target.

Aylen leapt into a sprint towards the next marker. Upon reaching it, he threw the second dagger and, shortly after, heard the others cheer for him as he ran towards the last spot. He smiled – it seemed that they were impressed, but he would not know how well he had truly done until it was over.

He landed on the last marker and, in one single, fluid motion, twisted his body around as he flung the final blade. He watched it spin towards the tree. It struck the outer ring.

Aylen winced. To his standards, the outer ring counted as a miss.

But his first two daggers found their home in the centre of the target and his friends seemed to think he'd done well. They applauded him.

"What's going on here?" Kyra asked as she joined them.

The applause came to an abrupt end.

"Want to have a go, lass?" Fangar asked.

"Sure," she said.

Aylen was pleasantly surprised when Kyra greeted him with a warm smile. She even winked at him just before she ran over to the tree to collect his daggers. She'd been icy with him ever since he failed to cover for her lark into the village, but it seemed her mood had thawed now and he was back in her good books.

She threw the blades, running between each one she cast. She even added a bit of her own flair at the end by somersaulting to the last marker – which was a bit theatrical, in Aylen's opinion, but he would never tell her that.

Two of her blades struck the target which, for her, was enough to justify raising her arms in celebration.

"Who's next?" Aylen asked when she returned the daggers to him.

"Me!" Dareth said, snatching them.

*   *   *

Dareth smiled as he made his way to the first marker. He knew he had little chance of beating Aylen's score, but he had no great wish to best his friend. The only important thing to him was that he did better than Kyra. He wanted to wipe that smug look off her face.

He didn't take much time to aim for his first throw; he made a point out of doing it quickly, as he thought it would look more impressive that way. Dareth sprinted as fast as he could towards the next marker and threw the second. Barely had it left his hand before he leapt again and sprinted towards the final marker to cast his last.

He then looked at the tree and frowned in disbelief.

Only one of the daggers had hit the target, the other two had flown well past the tree.

Dareth could feel everyone staring at him. Even Baird and Jaedin had paused from their sparring to watch and had seen it.

"Better luck next time," Kyra teased.

Dareth caught sight of Jaedin placing a hand over his mouth to cover up the fact that he was laughing. Dareth clenched his fists. Not only had he been beaten by a *girl*, but Jaedin – *Jaedin* – was laughing at him.

"Baird!" Dareth said, strolling up to their leader. He kept his face composed, hoping nobody would see how embarrassed he was. "Can I duel someone?"

"Of course you can," Baird smiled.

"Maybe Jaedin?" Dareth suggested, and Jaedin's grin swiftly vanished. "Ain't it time he practised those moves you've been teaching him?"

Chapter 18

Loyalties

Jaedin glanced at his opponent: Dareth stood opposite him with a sword in his hand and pure malice in his eyes.

"Are you ready?" Baird asked.

Everyone had formed a circle around them. They would all be watching.

Why did you agree to this, Baird? Jaedin thought, turning to their leader pleadingly. *Can't you see he's only doing this because he hates me?*

Jaedin's palm was sweaty. He couldn't get a proper grip on the hilt of his sword. He wiped his clammy hand on his tunic and reminded himself that, even though they were wielding real weapons, this was just a spar. And there were witnesses. Dareth would never dare to actually hurt him.

Would he?

He probably just wanted to humiliate him.

"Jaedin!"

He jumped at the sound of Baird's voice and gave their impatient leader the signal that he was ready.

Baird began the countdown. Dareth's mouth curved into a cruel smile. Jaedin tightened his grip on his sword.

Jaedin could not even remember the count being over. Before he even knew what was happening, Dareth was charging at him.

Jaedin raised his blade and braced himself. The clashing of their swords sent Jaedin reeling back.

He steadied. Dareth skirted around him. He began to assail Jaedin with a series of lunges. Jaedin blocked each one as it came. The fight was in a deadlock, neither of them gaining ground. Dareth was merely swinging his sword around belligerently, and it took all of Jaedin's focus to defend himself. Most novices would have been unnerved, and it would have worn them down, but Jaedin's newfound reflexes meant that he could keep up.

Dareth had underestimated him. He continued with his relentless barrage, but his moves became more erratic, and

Jaedin could see from the expression on his face he was getting angry.

Time to surprise him, Jaedin decided. He sidestepped and flashed his sword in a full circle, but Dareth blocked.

Jaedin jumped back and prepared himself for the next onslaught. Dareth rushed in, his sword raised high. Jaedin prepared to shield his upper region, but Dareth made a sudden duck and swiped at his legs. Jaedin jumped, arching his sword in a counter as he landed.

Their swords locked and they looked at each other. Jaedin applied some force, and Dareth's heels began to skid across the dirt. Jaedin got a strange pleasure out of demonstrating that he was now stronger than the boy who used to bully him. Dareth, on the other hand, was furious.

Dareth twisted his sword out of the lock and skirted away. He narrowed his eyes.

It was clear, from his expression, he had expected this to be over sooner – that he only suggested this duel because he wanted to humiliate Jaedin and make himself feel better – but instead, he was struggling to defeat a novice. And everyone was watching.

Dareth rushed in again, and Jaedin, fuelled by a sudden determination to prove Dareth and the others wrong, charged to meet him. Their swords clashed. They circled each other and went into a frenzy of strikes and counters, both of them trying to find an opening.

Jaedin pulled all his concentration into the flashing movements of Dareth's sword and held his ground. He gritted his teeth. Now, he wasn't only determined to get through this duel unscathed, he wanted to do the impossible. He wanted to *win*.

Their swords locked again. Dareth twisted Jaedin's blade so that it almost slipped out of his grip. Jaedin gasped and took a step back but tripped over his own foot and almost fell. He swung his arms out to catch his balance.

As Jaedin was righting himself, Dareth raised his foot and drove it into his stomach.

Jaedin fell back, crying out as he landed on the ground a few feet away. He looked up. Dareth was striding towards him. He knew that, unless he did something soon, it would be over.

Jaedin remembered a manoeuvre Kyra had taught him a few

days ago. He rolled onto his upper back and pushed his hands against the ground to bounce himself back onto his feet.

It was too late. As Jaedin landed, Dareth grabbed hold of his wrist and forced the sword out of his hand.

Jaedin had been defeated.

At least it is all over, Jaedin thought to himself with relief, as his weapon fell with a thud.

But it wasn't. Out of nowhere, Dareth's sword flashed towards him. Dareth grinned manically; there was something baleful in his eyes that moment. Jaedin's heart skipped a beat. The blade was on a course for his neck.

He closed his eyes.

But then heard a clash. It sounded like two blades meeting.

When Jaedin opened his eyes again, Fangar was standing between him and Dareth. He had a dagger in his hand, and it was pressed against the edge of Dareth's sword. Everyone around them gasped.

"Got a bit carried away there, kid?" Fangar muttered.

Dareth opened his mouth to reply but was interrupted by Fangar's foot smashing into his chest. He fell to the ground violently, limbs flailing.

Fangar then strode up to Dareth while he was still down, leant forward, and grabbed him by the scruff of his collar. Pulled his face close to his own.

"If you *ever* hurt Jaedin, I'll kill you!"

*　　*　　*

Rivan's hand went to the hilt of his sword as he considered whether he should intervene.

Fangar was holding Dareth by the collar of his tunic, shaking with cold anger. It was impossible to predict what the man was going to do.

"Let go of him!" Baird yelled as he stepped in. "These kids are my responsibility! *I'll* decide what to do with them!"

Fangar regarded their leader with a sneer, but he did as Baird requested and dropped Dareth. The young man landed clumsily, and there was none of the usual hubris in his face; Fangar had truly scared him.

Baird grabbed Dareth by his shoulders and yanked him to his feet. Rivan had never seen his mentor so angry. Not even when Miles confessed to being a spy.

"You're coming with me!" Baird said through gritted teeth.

Rivan watched as Baird dragged Dareth away. He knew Dareth and Jaedin had always loathed each other, but he found it hard to believe that Dareth would actually try to *kill* him. Dareth liked to show off. Rivan thought it likely Dareth had been just about to pull his blow when Fangar intervened. That Dareth merely wanted to scare Jaedin, not cause him any actual harm.

But it was still dangerous, Rivan thought. At the speed that Dareth's blade had been veering towards Jaedin's neck, the slightest miscalculation of when to halt the blow could have proved fatal.

Rivan had never seen someone move so fast as the moment Fangar leapt in to defend Jaedin. No human could have got between them so quickly. It had been almost too quick for the eye to see. It troubled Rivan that a distrusted stranger in their midst had such dexterity.

Kyra spat. "That cavecrawling cunt should've just died in Jalard with the others!"

"That is not something to joke about, Kyra…" Rivan said.

"Who said I was joking?" she snorted.

Rivan suppressed a strong compulsion to hit her. It offended him that, after everything they had been through, she would use the massacre of their village as a means to make such thoughtless remarks. Dareth made a stupid mistake, but it didn't excuse such vile things coming out of her mouth.

"You need to watch your words…" Rivan advised.

"Dareth just tried to *kill* Jaedin, and you're worried about something I *said*?" Kyra retorted. "Sort your priorities out, Rivan!"

"Dareth wouldn't kill–" he began to say.

"Dareth is a killer," Fangar interrupted their quarrelling. "I could see it in his eyes."

"No," Aylen shook his head. "Dareth has a temper… but he wouldn't kill anyone…"

"Believe what you will," Fangar shrugged. "But I mean what I said. I *will* kill *anyone* who tries to hurt Jaedin."

Rivan was about to say something back but was rendered speechless by what he saw next.

Fangar put his arms around Jaedin. There was something

about it – a tenderness Rivan had never witnessed between two men before – as Fangar placed his fingers beneath Jaedin's chin and tilted his face up so that they were looking into each other's eyes, which forced Rivan into a double-take.

"Are you okay, Jaedin?" he asked.

*　　*　　*

Jaedin could feel everyone's eyes on him and Fangar and, for a few moments, he just wanted to disappear.

But that wish was short-lived. With Fangar standing next to him, Jaedin felt like nothing could hurt him.

He spent most of his life being called names and being derided. Their words used to hurt but something about Jaedin's disposition changed during that moment.

He realised their opinions no longer concerned him. They didn't hold any power over him. They were just *words*.

He didn't care what any of them thought of him anymore.

What started as one of the most uncomfortable moments of Jaedin's life became a leap of liberation. He felt like he was now seeing the world from a new perspective. Like a huge weight had been lifted from his shoulders.

And the feeling of Fangar's arms around him was pleasant.

Fangar looked him in the eyes. They were brown with flecks of gold and green, but Jaedin did not just see their colours. When he looked into them, Jaedin's heart raced, and a warm feeling blossomed in his chest. He felt excitement. Danger. Beguiling darkness.

Jaedin knew if he looked into them much longer, they would kiss. And then there would be no turning back.

He wanted to.

But he remembered what Baird said to him, and looked away. He had to resist. If Jaedin gave in, then Baird might do something to Fangar. Jaedin didn't want that to happen.

"I am fine…" Jaedin replied, stepping away. "Thank you. I just need to rest…"

"Come with me, Jaedin…" he whispered.

Those words sent butterflies fluttering around Jaedin's insides. He looked at Fangar again. Those wild brown eyes. The way he grinned. He wondered what his body would feel like pressed against him.

"I can't," Jaedin mumbled. "I'm… sorry."

Jaedin turned and, as he walked away, Kyra appeared beside him and put an arm around his shoulder. They walked back to the camp together.

"You should have gone for it," she laughed once they were out of earshot. "I know I would've!"

Jaedin blushed.

*   *   *

By the time Baird and Dareth returned to the camp later, the sun was setting, and the sky had turned to an indigo haze.

Aylen was sitting by the fire alone. It was his and Dareth's turn to keep the first watch that night and, with only one horned moon in the sky, it looked like it was going to be a dark one.

Aylen didn't like nights like this. The absence of moonlight meant more stars would appear, which was a rare sight – and it used to be one that conjured a sense of awe within him – but the thought that there might be Zakaras out there made him very aware of the darkness. The fire he sat by only illuminated their immediate surroundings. In Jalard, Aylen had always had the comfort of seeing the faint lights glowing from all the nearby homes, but here they were very much alone.

Baird made for his tent while Dareth joined Aylen by the fire. His head was hanging so low that Aylen could tell whatever Baird had said to him must have been severe.

Dareth kicked one of the logs and sparks flew. Aylen flinched.

Dareth then slumped by the fire and folded his arms over his chest. For a time neither of them said anything.

"You shouldn't have done that, Dareth," Aylen whispered.

"What's everyone's problem?" Dareth hissed. "I wasn't going to kill him! I just wanted to shit him up a bit…"

"What if you made a mistake?" Aylen asked. "You could have hurt him."

"I don't make mistakes!"

Aylen didn't believe that Dareth had intended to kill Jaedin either, but the incident still concerned him. Ever since they were children Aylen had made it his task to cool Dareth's temper and reason with him – it was within the foundations of their friendship – so, in a way, Dareth's misbehaviour felt like Aylen's own failure.

"When are we going ditch these idiots?" Dareth whispered.

Aylen turned to his friend in surprise. Dareth had made a lot of comments recently about how they should leave the others, but Aylen had not taken any of them literally. Dareth often said things he didn't mean.

But this time Aylen knew he was serious.

"We can't," Aylen whispered.

That was his initial reaction but, when Aylen paused to think about it, he realised it was tempting. Fraknar was looming ever closer, and he was scared. Sidry, Baird, Jaedin, and even Bryna had superhuman powers which would help protect them, but Aylen and the weaker ones were vulnerable. Aylen often wondered if he was even needed in what was to come, or just an accessory. A stray that Baird had flung onto the back of the wagon because he felt obliged.

Aylen and Dareth *could* leave. They could go somewhere safe.

But then Aylen thought of Kyra. He thought about the way she smiled at him earlier that day. How happy he was that they were talking again. He couldn't leave her. She was reckless. Someone needed to stop her from getting herself hurt.

He also thought about Rivan. Aylen looked up to him, and they'd bonded recently. And Sidry. These people around him were all that remained of Jalard.

"We have to stay," Aylen said.

"You have always been the wiser of us," Dareth admitted. "So I'll stick with your choice." He stared into the flames. "I'll stay with you for now, but when we get there, there will be more decisions for me and you, Aylen. The others will blindly carry on, but we're different. We have options."

Why does he keep speaking this way? Aylen wondered as he stared at him.

"Did you hear that?" Dareth asked, looking around them.

Aylen pricked his ears. Footsteps.

His heart raced. Aylen couldn't remember seeing any of the others leave their tents. The noise was coming from outside the camp.

Which could only mean they had an intruder.

He drew two of his daggers and got up from the fire. Dareth signalled Aylen to cover him and crept into the darkness to hide out of sight.

Aylen watched as Dareth drew his sword. The intruder stepped into the range of the firelight's glow. He was travel-worn and dirty, his eyes were hollow, and the vestiges of his clothes – threadbare and torn – hung loosely from his emaciated body.

A cold, chilling smile stretched his craggy face. It did not reach his eyes. Aylen recognised that icy expression. The man was a Zakara.

"What do you want?" Dareth asked.

"I used to be a citizen of Sharma," the man said in a raspy voice. "But now, I serve Lord Shayam."

Aylen crept up from behind him and pressed the point of his blade to the man's throat.

"Any last words?" Aylen asked.

The intruder raised his hands to show that he was unarmed, but that did not mean much to Aylen. All Zakaras had weapons they could summon when needed. Claws, talons, fangs, tentacles.

"I have not come here to fight," it said. "I bring a message from Lord Shayam."

I should just kill it now, Aylen realised. *Being this close is dangerous.*

"No!" Dareth exclaimed as Aylen sank his blade into the creature's neck. "Let him speak!"

Aylen paused. He had already buried his dagger into the man's throat, and a river of blood was trickling down his shoulder. The man didn't even flinch.

"Shayam wants you to know that if the three of you who stole the Stones turn themselves in, this will all stop. He will leave the rest of you in peace," the Zakara said.

"That is all he wants?" Dareth asked.

"Yes. Shayam remembers you, Dareth and he is looking forward to meeting you again. He says if you help him, you will find it rewarding."

"We are not stupid!" Aylen exclaimed. "We will not help you!"

"One last thing, Dareth," the creature rasped. "We know that the Descendant of Vai-ris is among you."

"Descendant of what?" Dareth blurted. "What do you mean?"

"That is all. Shayam no longer has any use for me so I will be rescinded."

He began to convulse. Aylen leapt away. Blood ran from the man's eyes, ears and mouth.

* * *

As soon as Jaedin awoke, he sat up. He could feel a Zakara – it was nearby!

He opened his mouth to call a warning and alert the others, but a terrible wave of energy passed through him. He gasped.

He felt Shayam kill the Zakara with his mind – Jaedin was partially attuned to the Zakara at the time, so he felt some of its pain as it was destroyed from the inside and its organs turned on themselves. Jaedin withdrew to save himself from feeling anymore and hurriedly began to dress.

"What's going on?" Kyra mumbled beside him as she stirred in her blankets.

"A Zakara was here!" Jaedin exclaimed. He pulled back the opening of their tent and scrambled outside. Kyra was soon behind him.

Jaedin found the others crowded around a spot near the fire. He ran to them, arriving just as Baird was leaning over to inspect the body. Or what was left of it, at least. Bones and withered flesh, tangled within sodden clothes, and a pool of blood. Jaedin held his nose.

"Shayam killed it with his Stone of Zakar," Jaedin said, turning away from the morbid sight. "I felt him do it."

"Are there any more?" Baird asked him.

"No," Jaedin shook his head. "He was alone."

"Why would Shayam just send one?" Rivan asked. "Only to kill it?"

"I don't know…" Jaedin whispered.

"What happened, Aylen?" Baird asked, turning to the young man.

Aylen paused from cleaning his knife on the grass and looked up at their leader. "He said he wants the Stones back," he said. "That he'll stop and leave the rest of us alone if you hand yourselves in."

"That's it?" Baird asked. "Nothing more?"

Aylen opened his mouth to respond but was cut off by Dareth.

"No," he answered, shaking his head. "Nothing."

"He didn't attack you?" Baird pressed.

They both shook their heads.

Baird cursed and turned his eyes back to the body.

"He's probably too busy taking over Fraknar to send a proper assault," Miles guessed. "So he just sent one here to scare and divide us."

"We still need to be careful, in any case," Baird said.

Jaedin suppressed a shudder. Somehow, Shayam had managed to track them down.

"Let me keep watch tonight," Jaedin volunteered.

When Baird opened his mouth to reply, Jaedin could already tell from his expression he was going to refuse.

"I can *sense* them!" Jaedin argued. "No one can detect them quicker than I can!"

"And I can smell them," a voice uttered from the shadows.

They all turned around as Fangar emerged from the darkness. How long he had been watching the interaction was a mystery, but now he was choosing to step into the light and make himself visible. Baird eyed them both sceptically, while Jaedin held his breath.

Jaedin was sick of being treated like he was useless. Why was he always left out of the watch duties when he could carry out the task better than any of them?

"Fine," Baird decided. "Jaedin, your duties begin as of now. Tonight."

*   *   *

It took Jaedin a few days to adjust to his new duties and, after the intrusion, Baird was even more cautious than usual. He often gave Jaedin extended watches, meaning he had even less time to sleep than the others.

Each morning, Baird woke them just before sunrise and Fangar continued leading them towards Fraknar. Despite all their vigilance, Shayam never sent any more of his creatures to them and each night was free from disturbance.

One evening, Jaedin found himself placed in the same shift

as Aylen, and the two of them sat at opposite sides of the fire, huddled beneath blankets. Autumn was on the way, and the nights were getting colder.

There wasn't much in the way of conversation. Jaedin always felt awkward in Aylen's company. The two of them had been friends when they were children – and they shared many fond years playing in Aylen's garden – but that felt like a distant memory now.

When they got older, Dareth came into their lives, and from the very first moment they met, Jaedin and Dareth took a dislike to each other. Dareth hounded Jaedin ruthlessly and, after a few rough tumbles which ended in Jaedin walking home with tears in his eyes, Dareth won the battle for Aylen's friendship. Jaedin spent the rest of his childhood indoors. He became a recluse.

Jaedin always felt betrayed by the boy who let Dareth bully him.

As Jaedin stared into the fire, Miles crept into his thoughts. Like he often did. Jaedin's former mentor had become even more distant recently. He and Jaedin had barely spoken a word to each other since Fangar came into their lives. Jaedin missed his company.

Jaedin had grown aware enough of his own desires by then to realise he was infatuated with his former mentor. Once, he had even fooled himself into thinking Miles harboured feelings which echoed his, but now he knew he had deluded himself. The time they kissed was now just a hazy memory, and Jaedin could not even remember how it happened; the only moment from it he could recall with arresting clarity was that Miles had been the one to pull away.

Jaedin made a complete fool of himself. He needed to accept the truth so he could move on. Miles was avoiding him, and it was probably because Jaedin was a sodd and it made him uncomfortable.

"Jaedin?" he was pulled out of his thoughts by Aylen's voice.

"What?" Jaedin droned.

"I was just wondering about something…" Aylen said. "You know stuff, right?

Jaedin raised an eyebrow.

"I mean, you're clever, and you read books, and–"

"Just spit it out, Aylen," Jaedin said.

Aylen cleared his throat. "I just remembered something from that night... you know... when that man visited us. He said something strange just before he died. I think it must've slipped my mind because I couldn't make sense of it, but–"

"What was it?" Jaedin asked.

"He said something about a... a descendant, among us," Aylen recalled, as he scratched his head. "I think he said Vai-ris? A Descendant of Vai-ris. Or something like that. Do you know what that means?"

The name did ring bells somewhere in the back of Jaedin's mind, but he couldn't remember where.

"I know it was probably nonsense..." Aylen said. "But I just thought... if any of us knew it'd be you."

"I'll look into it," Jaedin promised.

He turned back to the fire and tried to remember where he had heard that name before. Much of Jaedin's vocabulary consisted of words he absorbed from the pages of books, rather than the mouths of others, so he did not know to pronounce all of them. There was no exact and consistent formula when it came to translating the phonetics of the Ancient lexicon either.

"Does Kyra ever mention me?" Aylen asked.

"I don't know," Jaedin mumbled. "I guess so. Sometimes. Why?"

"I had sex with her."

Smoke from the fire got caught in Jaedin's chest, and he coughed. He covered his mouth and let it ride its course before turning back to Aylen.

"*What?*" he asked.

"We had sex," Aylen whispered.

Could it be true? Jaedin wondered. Kyra had not said anything to him. He knew Kyra and Aylen were friendly but never got the impression she'd taken a shine to him.

"When?" Jaedin asked.

"A while back," Aylen replied. "After we escaped from Shayam's camp."

Jaedin did not quite know how to take this news. He thought Kyra told him everything, but this was something she had kept to herself.

"Why are you telling me this?" Jaedin asked.

"Because I can't tell anyone else..." Aylen shrugged. "Don't tell her I told you... I don't think she'd like it."

Jaedin sighed. He did not know why, but this bothered him. He knew it wasn't because he was jealous, so he concluded it must be a form of brotherly protectiveness he felt for Kyra.

*   *   *

The next day Fangar announced Fraknar was close, so they stopped early. Baird wanted them all to rest and prepare for what lay ahead.

"Want to go hunting, Jaedin?" Kyra asked after they pitched the tents. Despite the impending danger, she seemed to be in high spirits.

Jaedin laughed, despite how nervous he felt. "I can barely hold a sword yet, let alone a bow. I think I'll pass..."

"Aww come on," Kyra said. "It's easier than you think."

Jaedin shook his head. He did not mention that the thought of killing an animal made him feel queasy.

"But Baird said I can only go if someone comes with me..." Kyra pleaded.

"Why don't you ask Aylen?" Jaedin suggested.

Kyra's eyes lit up. "Good idea," she turned her gaze to the other side of the camp where Aylen was pitching his tent with Dareth. "If I can tear him away from that creep..."

"Kyra, are you okay?" Jaedin asked.

"What do you mean?" Kyra raised an eyebrow.

"Well... just. I don't know... is there something you haven't told me?"

"Not that I can think of," Kyra shrugged. She got out her bow and began to string it. "Why do you ask?"

"It's nothing," Jaedin said. "Good luck."

Once Kyra's bow was ready, she walked over to Aylen. Jaedin watched her. She smiled at him as she approached and, perhaps it was just Jaedin projecting, but there was something a little flirtatious about it.

Who would have believed it? Jaedin thought when Aylen smiled back at her. *Kyra and Aylen...*

Jaedin worried about his friend though. Kyra was still going to great lengths to present a cheery persona, but Jaedin knew her better than the others and could see through it. Her behaviour was becoming more erratic. He wondered what lengths she would go to, as a distraction from her pain.

Jaedin was snapped out of his thoughts when his sister's face appeared before him.

"Danger is coming, Jaedin..." she whispered.

"What?" Jaedin mumbled.

"The clouds," Bryna pointed up to the sky. It was overcast. Gloomy. "They warn me. Danger is coming. These... *things*," she waved her arms around. "I can feel them. They are getting stronger. Jaedin... they scare me."

She continued mumbling incoherently and waving her arms around for a while. Jaedin felt his temper flaring. He tried to bite his tongue but there was only so much of this he could take.

"We are all scared!" he yelled, already regretting the harsh words the moment they left his lips but unable to stop himself. "We have lost our homes! Our families are dead! People want to kill us! But you!" he declared, pointing at her. "Are afraid, because of fucking clouds!"

Jaedin began to clap sarcastically. "Well done, Bryna! Your powers of perception have, once again, amazed me! We are about to enter a city full of Zakaras, but I never guessed we were in danger until you mentioned fucking *clouds*!"

Bryna turned away, her eyes rheumy with tears.

But a part of Jaedin was relieved to see her cry. It was the first emotional response he had witnessed from her for aeights. It reassured him there was still *something* human beneath that foggy consciousness of hers.

"I just wanted to warn you," she whispered. "I'm... sorry..."

"Well I already know that shit is coming, Bryna," Jaedin said. The sight of his twin upset almost made him falter on his words, but he was so angry he couldn't stop. "What is your problem?" he exclaimed. "Does the thought of speaking a lucid sentence pain you? All you do is wander around with your little basket picking flowers, occasionally turning your eyes to the sky and opening your mouth to bless us from your fountain of wisdom. It's getting really boring! No one understands you!"

She was sobbing now. It made Jaedin's own eyes well up with tears.

"No one understands you, Bryna!" he repeated. "Not even me! I want my sister back!"

He walked away.

That was their first ever argument. Jaedin had never even dreamed of shouting at his twin before. He made his way into the trees. He wanted some privacy. He had never felt so alone. His mother was dead, his sister was acting like a stranger, and Kyra was keeping secrets from him.

When he was far enough away from the camp, Jaedin stopped and wiped the tears from his eyes.

"Jaedin?"

He looked over and saw Miles sitting by the trunk of a tree.

"Are you okay?" Miles asked.

"I'm fine!" Jaedin exclaimed, turning away.

Of all people to catch me like this! he thought.

He began to walk away, but a hand grabbed his shoulder.

"Leave me alone!" Jaedin exclaimed.

"Tell me, Jaedin!" Miles spun Jaedin around, so they were face to face. "Is it Fangar? Has he hurt you?"

"No! It's not Fangar!" Jaedin yelled. Why were Miles and the others so fixated on catching Fangar out? It was almost as if they *wanted* him to be their enemy.

"What is it then?" Miles implored.

"I fell out with Bryna," Jaedin replied. "And I *don't* want to talk about it…"

Jaedin became aware of how close he and Miles were standing to each other. He stepped away.

"Miles, have you ever heard of the name Vai-ris?" Jaedin asked, in an attempt to shift the subject of his thoughts.

"Of course I have," Miles replied. "Don't *you* remember the tale of Vai-ris?"

"No," Jaedin shook his head. "I remember the name, but I can't place it…"

"Do you want me to remind you?" Miles asked.

Jaedin nodded.

"Okay, I will. But why don't you sit down? You look worn out…" Miles said motioning to a nearby tree.

"Fine," Jaedin said as he seated himself and rested his back against the trunk. He was reluctant to admit it, but he *was* tired. Baird had kept him up half of the night with watching duties, and his outburst at Bryna had drained the last of his energy.

"As you already know," Miles said as he sat beside him. "In the beginning, there were just four gods – The Ancients: Lania, Ignis, Ta'al, and Vaishra – and all the other Ancient gods were born from them. Then later came the Other Gods, and their leader was Gazareth."

Jaedin smiled and closed his eyes. This was beginning to feel like old times, back in Miles' study in Jalard, where they used to spend hours reading history and discussing lore. Jaedin missed those days. They were uncomplicated.

But they were a lie, he reminded himself. Even then, Miles had been an agent sent by Grav'aen. A spy.

"The Ancients distrusted these new gods, who brought chaos with them. But love works in mysterious ways, and Lania fell for Gazareth."

Jaedin nodded. The forbidden affair which led to the creation of mankind. He always found that part problematic.

"Lania and Gazareth gave birth to triplets; Flora, Fauna, and Verdana. Flora and Fauna brought abundance to the land, so the Ancients approved of them. But they didn't trust Verdana, for she was too much like her father. She became the womb of mankind."

This was the part that Jaedin found puzzling. He'd always found it peculiar humans would worship gods who opposed their very existence. Miles had said there were other versions. Versions Jaedin would gain access to if he ever made it to the Academy. He had been looking forward to reading them.

"Verdana's existence – and even the humans she created – were eventually tolerated by the gods but, when she had a daughter… that was a different story."

"Verdana had a *daughter*?" Jaedin asked. Already bells were ringing in his mind. He was beginning to remember.

"Verdana had an affair with her own father, Gazareth, and bore a daughter from that union. That is who Vai-ris was. Vai-ris was a dark child. They said she could talk to the dead and walk between worlds. The Ancients never trusted her, so they banished her to the mortal world to live as a human."

"What happened to her?" Jaedin asked.

Miles shook his head. "There are many tales about Vai-ris but I never cared to memorise all of them. Why do you ask?"

"Apparently the Zakara Shayam sent to us last aeight said something about a Descendant of Vai-ris among us," Jaedin replied. "It's obviously a load of crap, but I was just curious."

"Don't always dismiss things just because they seem unlikely," Miles advised. "You never know what is coming around the bend of the valley."

"A Descendant of Vai-ris, though?" Jaedin repeated. "Who among us could be descended from a mythical god?"

Miles shook his head. "I am not saying it is true. I am just telling you to keep an open mind. It could just be metaphorical. And remember, remarkable things are happening across the world. Prophecies indicate the powers of the gods are stirring once again."

A pox on you and your bloody prophecies! Jaedin thought, remembering that it was the direction of some goddess Miles dreamed up which drove him to make Jaedin the subject of one of Shayam's experiments.

"Be careful when we reach Fraknar, Jaedin," Miles whispered. "I don't know what I would do if something happened to you."

"I'm going now," Jaedin shuffled away and rose to his feet. "Thanks for the advice."

*   *   *

When Jaedin walked back into the camp, Kyra and Aylen had just returned from hunting and were skinning a deer they caught. Jaedin knew it wouldn't be ready to eat for a while yet so he decided to retire to his tent and catch up with his sleep.

As Jaedin made his way there, he saw Fangar in the corner of his eye. The rogue waved.

"Come here, Jaedin," he said from the opening of the shelter he had built for himself.

Jaedin wanted to. More than anything.

But he knew Baird would not approve. Jaedin didn't want to be the cause of any problems.

Jaedin also thought about Miles. The two of them were finally speaking again.

No, Jaedin thought, as he shook his head. *Sorry Fangar, but I can't. It isn't right.*

He retreated to his tent.

Chapter 19

Fraknar

They reached the town at dawn, when the sun was looming upon the horizon and the streets were streaked with long shadows.

The moment they entered the first neighbourhood, they knew that Fangar had not been lying. The first thing that struck Sidry was how disturbingly silent it was. The houses were dishevelled and empty.

It was the largest town he had ever seen. Its most distinctive feature was a fortress in the centre with four towers; it dominated the entire landscape and dwarfed everything else. Sidry kept staring at it because he had never seen such a sight before.

He pulled his hood tighter over his head. They were all wearing things to cover their faces; an attempt to stop Shayam recognising any of them through the eyes of any Zakaras he might be controlling.

They were still on the outskirts, but signs of devastation were already apparent. Splintered wood and shattered stone lay scattered across the road. One of the nearby houses was in a particularly sorry state; its roof had caved in and most of the windows were smashed. Its door dangled from its frame by a single hinge. Even though this town was built mostly from slate and stone rather than mud and timber, and vastly more modern than Jalard, the signs of destruction were similar, and it reminded Sidry of what happened to his own home.

"How many?" Baird asked.

His question was directed at Jaedin, who had wrapped one of Bryna's scarfs around the lower half of his face.

"Many…" he whispered.

Baird's mouth straightened into a grim expression. He continued leading them into the town.

"Don't use your power," Baird reminded Jaedin. "Not until I say. Don't let Shayam sense you."

Sidry reminded himself of his own instructions. Baird had

311

forbidden him from summoning his Avatar of Gezra unless it was truly necessary, as he wanted them to keep a low profile and stay undetected for as long as possible.

They marched. Sidry assembled beside their leader at the front of the group, and he scanned their surroundings, watching for any sudden movements. They were in a tight formation: Kyra and Aylen had their bows out and were covering their sides; Rivan and Dareth were at the rear, guarding their backs; and Jaedin, Miles and Bryna were huddled in the centre.

Sidry caught movement in the corner of his vision and saw two children watching them from behind a pile of debris. At the realisation they'd been noticed they scarpered. Sidry resisted the urge to run after them. He wanted to help them but knew he had much more immediate things to take care of.

He began to hear noises in the distance. A fusion of screaming, monstrous roars and clanging grated his ears. It was all one sound. The sound of Zakaras wreaking havoc upon the city.

They turned a corner, and a creature came hurtling towards them.

"Brace yourselves!" Baird yelled.

Kyra loosed an arrow and struck true, sending the Zakara skidding. It yelped and squirmed on its back for a few moments as it tried to right itself. Kyra nocked her bow, preparing to loose again, but Rivan beat her to it and ran in, swinging his sword down upon its neck.

Their first kill.

Baird gave Rivan a nod of approval and silently motioned for them to continue walking. They had only covered a few more paces when three more creatures appeared. Baird halted, and they all readied their weapons.

A succession of Kyra and Aylen's arrows flew past Sidry's ears. The monsters darted from side to side to evade them as they charged. Sidry gripped his sword and prepared himself. The creatures were getting closer. One of them was on a path straight for him.

An arrow caught the creature's leg, and it staggered. It opened its jaws and let out an angry roar, exposing its jagged, yellow fangs, but another arrow tore through its neck, bursting it in a cloud of red.

Sidry ran in and drove the point of his sword into its skull. The creature howled, and Sidry twisted the blade, tearing up the flesh inside the creature's head. Its body jerked one more time and went still.

Sidry took a moment to gather his breath and pull his hood back over his head; in the heat of combat it had slid down a little. He looked around and discovered that, while he had been busy, the other two Zakaras had already been dealt with by others. Aylen stood over the corpse of one of them with two bloodied knives in his hands and Baird was just in the process of pulling his sword out of the third.

"Everyone okay?" Baird asked.

After everyone had nodded, he once again led the way.

Men were shouting to each other in the distance, and the other noises of disturbance were getting louder. It was clear that there was a skirmish going on nearby. They quickened their pace. The clanging and shouting grew in Sidry's ears. Eventually, he saw movement up ahead.

"We should help them," Fangar said, sidling up beside Baird.

As they got closer, Sidry saw a group of men and women had formed a ring around a Zakara and were jabbing it with their spears. The creature shrieked and writhed.

It was a good sign. It meant the city had not been completely overwhelmed yet. The people were fighting back.

"Yes," Baird agreed with Fangar. "Come!" he ordered, motioning for them to all follow as his legs built up speed.

They raced to join the group of warriors, who had by then killed the Zakara and were pulling their spears out of its corpse.

"He's one of them!" Kyra yelled, pointing to one of the men who stood away from the others. His body began to tremble, but none of his comrades noticed because they all had their backs turned. "Watch out!"

But her warning came too late. Between his convulsions, the man thrust his spear into the back of one of the men in front of him. The wounded man screamed, alerting the others, who all turned around in dismay as their comrade fell face down to the ground with the offending weapon sticking from his body.

The betrayer's body began to expand as he shifted into a

Zakara. Some of the braver ones tried to take him out while he was still in the process of transforming, but he clawed them away with his hands which now more resembled paws. His flesh turned green, and his body continued to shift and stretch until he was almost as high as the rooftops.

Everyone drew to a halt and stared up at the gigantic creature now before them.

It was the biggest Zakara Sidry had ever seen. Bear shaped, but with leathery skin and huge black eyes.

It roared and came after the group of warriors, raking its claws and sending them scattering in all directions.

Sidry was at odds with what to do. He turned to Baird for direction. Their leader was staring up at the creature, weighing it up with his eyes.

The Zakara was getting the better of the warriors; two of them managed to get close enough to stab it, but their spears got stuck inside its rubbery flesh and the creature was still standing. It pawed one of the men to the ground and drew its claws across his body, ripping his guts open.

"Sidry, Rivan, and Fangar," Baird called, turning to each of them. "You three help me take it down. The rest of you stay back and protect Jaedin!"

The four of them drew their weapons and charged.

Fangar unleashed his claws and raced into the affray with astonishing speed. When the warriors saw him coming they scattered – as if they thought he was another monster – but Fangar ran straight past them.

Rivan was next in. The monster was too busy chasing after Fangar to notice his approach. He sprang into the air and sank his sword into the monster's abdomen. The monster twisted and howled, sending Rivan swaying back and forth with his legs flapping wildly as he kept a tight grip on his sword. He eventually used his own weight to pull it free. When he landed, blood oozed from the monster's belly, forming a dark puddle at its feet.

Rivan retreated, and Sidry ran to meet him.

"He's still standing!" Rivan exclaimed in disbelief.

The monster charged at them, causing the ground to shudder with each step.

"Cover me! I'll distract it!" Baird said as he ran past them.

Baird charged in fearlessly, and the Zakara veered from its

course towards Sidry to swing its claws at Baird. Baird proved himself surprisingly quick on his feet. He dodged and skirted around the creature as it tried to strike him a second time. And third.

"Sidry!" Rivan nudged him. "We need to take its legs out! Pin it to the ground. You take one, I'll take the other!"

Sidry nodded.

They charged in. The monster was too busy attempting a series of lunges at Baird to notice them at first.

"Peg him down!" Rivan roared, as they neared.

Sidry split apart from Rivan and veered towards the creature's right leg. He launched his body into the air and, as he came back down, drove his sword into the monster's foot, putting all of his strength and weight behind it. He felt his sword twitch in his palms – threatening to veer off course as it bore through the rubbery layers of skin and scraped through the bones and cartilage – but Sidry resisted and held on tight, keeping it on course until it passed through the other side of his foot and sank into the ground.

The creature roared, and Sidry made a hasty retreat, glancing over his shoulder and noting, with some satisfaction, that both of the monster's feet were pinned.

Once Sidry was safely out of reach, he halted and watched as the monster howled and squirmed. It eventually managed to free itself and limped towards Sidry, its feet bleeding, mangled, and dragging.

A shadow appeared from one of the buildings. It was Fangar. He leapt from a rooftop, landing on the Zakaras shoulders, and wrapped his legs around its neck. The monster tried to shrug him off, but Fangar clung on tight and drove his claws into the creature's eyes. The monster let out an abominable wail and swung its talons in a blind rage, but Fangar was long gone, and its raking claws met thin air.

"It's time to end this!" Baird spat, shoving Sidry aside as charged past him, towards the beast.

The creature was in a frenzy. Baird had to duck to avoid a blind swing from one of its arms but, once he was close, he drove his shoulder into the Zakara's hip and sent it toppling over. The creature let out one last final roar, but Baird brought his blade down on its neck, beheading it in one fell swoop.

Sidry breathed a sigh of relief; that was the biggest Zakara he had ever seen, and he felt a sense of pride that they managed to take it down with conventional weapons. He walked over to the corpse and pulled his sword free from its garbled foot.

Sidry checked on the others and discovered that, while he'd been busy, they had faced attacks from smaller Zakaras. Kyra was just in the process of finishing one of them off, and she pulled her bloodied sword out of its corpse. Further down the street, Dareth stood over the body of another, and Aylen was in the process of collecting his daggers. Miles, Bryna and Jaedin were huddled together, protected by a faintly glowing shield Miles had cast.

The warriors with spears stared at Sidry and his companions with wide eyes. Sidry knew it was not just the fact that Fangar had claws which caused them such bewilderment; it must have been clear from the proficient way they dealt with that Zakara that they had a history with them and had killed them before.

One of them lowered his spear and walked over to greet them. He was a burly man with a black beard and a scar above his eye.

"Who are you?" he asked.

"We have no time for explanations," Baird responded, raising his voice so they all could hear him. "We know what it is you face and are here to help. You can fight with us as long as you don't get in the way!"

The bearded man turned back to the rest of his comrades, and they conferred for a few moments. Many of them seemed wary.

"I suggest you hurry," Baird called out to them impatiently.

The bearded man came back. "Okay, we'll join you... for now," he agreed. "But we have some questions to ask you later. *If* we survive this..."

"That's fine," Baird agreed. "But be warned. Some of us can... do things. Things you may find surprising. But we *are* on your side, and you *have* to trust us."

"I can see that," the man said, eying Fangar. Fangar barely looked human now. His teeth had grown long and pointed, and his muscles bulged from beneath his dark, leathery skin. It seemed he was maintaining his transformation at some stage mid-way to his full Zakara form.

They marched further into the town with their new band of spear-wielding allies in tow. Sidry reclaimed his place next to Baird in their formation.

When they turned the corner, Sidry caught a glimpse of what was waiting for them in the next street and froze.

A horde of Zakaras stood in the middle of the road. Dozens upon dozens of them.

For a moment, there was silence. They stared at the Zakaras, and the Zakaras stared back. It was obvious that they had been waiting for them.

They were being hunted.

"I think Shayam knows we're here now..." Kyra muttered dryly.

"Almost certainly," Miles agreed from behind his glowing shield.

Baird nodded grimly.

The Zakaras began to rush towards them. Sidry turned to Baird pleadingly.

"Yes, Sidry," Baird confirmed. "You can."

Sidry called out to the crystal. The street vanished. There was only white light. The Stone of Gezra awakened, pulsating, sending waves of energy through him as it moulded his body into a new shape. Ethereal armour manifested around his limbs, and Sidry once again experienced that feeling of immense power.

He opened his eyes and saw the street with newly enhanced vision. Baird was beside him, also now an Avatar of Gezra, and together they charged to meet the monsters. Sidry was on top of one of them in moments, tearing the creature open with his bladed-arm. The rest of the Zakaras scattered. Another leapt at him, but Sidry sensed him coming and met it with his blade, skewering it like a rabbit ready for the spit. He flicked the body aside.

The creatures backed away in fear, realising that Sidry was a foe to approach with caution but, eventually, their anger flared again and they bounded towards him.

Shayam is controlling them, Sidry realised, as he summoned his second blade.

* * *

Jaedin watched from behind Miles' shield as Sidry and Baird charged to meet the stampede of monsters, swinging their blades and leaving a bloody trail of corpses behind them.

Some of the Zakaras were slipping through the cracks, and it was down to the rest of them to deal with those.

Fangar was now fully transformed. He leapt into the fray and whirled his talons. Kyra and Aylen were loosing a swift succession of arrows, but Jaedin could see their quivers were beginning to run low and they would soon be forced to unleash their blades.

Behind the safety of Miles' shield, Jaedin pulled Bryna's scarf from his face and felt a tingling in his forehead as he activated the crystal. His eyes glowed. He directed the focus of the crystal's power exclusively on the Zakaras nearby and reached into their minds to still them. The scene around him disappeared, and all he could see was their glowing forms under the red canvas of his crystal-sight. He tried to gain control of their minds, but Shayam was already inside. The struggle was such that Jaedin's head began to ache, and his knees shook beneath him.

The Zakaras became confused, their bodies trembling as two opposing forces fought over their psyches.

When Jaedin finally pierced through and assumed control, he felt a series of painful sensations – spears impaling flesh, Rivan's sword, arrows – as the Zakaras shared their experiences with him. They fought against his will, wanting to fight back, but Jaedin subdued them. Many of them perished. Jaedin maintained the assimilation for as long as he could, but it was taxing and Shayam fought back.

Eventually, Jaedin was pushed out. He fell to his knees and caught his breath.

"Jaedin you need to help them!" Miles said beside him. More Zakaras were coming.

Jaedin turned to his mentor. "Shayam..." he breathed. "He's too strong! I can't!"

Jaedin heard a clash, and the grey bubble around them flickered. A Zakara was assailing Miles' shield. Each time it struck Miles shuddered from the strain of sustaining it. Jaedin could tell that he was beginning to falter. He was running through his *viga*, fast.

Another horde of Zakaras rushed at them, and two of the

spear-wielding warriors – their newfound allies – were caught in the stampede. They screamed. Jaedin looked around; everyone was scattered. This no longer resembled a coordinated battle.

It was the beginning of a massacre.

Rivan staggered back, a hand on his chest. He was bleeding.

"Jaedin!" Miles shouted. "Do something!"

"I can't!" Jaedin cried, tears pouring from his eyes. There were too many, and Shayam's hold over them was impenetrable. He couldn't break it.

"I will help you, Jaedin," a voice whispered beside him.

It was Bryna. Her eyes were blackened opals. She reached into a fold of her dress and drew a tiny dagger.

"No," Jaedin said when realised what she was doing.

She ignored him, pulled back her sleeve. He tried to stop her, but it was too late; she had already drawn the blade across her wrist. Her blood clouded the air. He felt it seep into him.

"Do it, Jaedin," she whispered. "Our friends are dying. We must help them."

The adrenaline now coursing through Jaedin's veins quelled his objections. He closed his eyes, touched the mind of every monster around them; pushed Shayam out, stilled their forms.

Jaedin's power over the Stone of Zakar, when fuelled by Bryna's blood, knew no bounds.

He reached into the mind of every Zakara in the city.

*　　*　　*

The Zakaras had stopped moving.

"Tear them down!" Kyra roared as she leapt and drove her blade into one of them.

The warriors around her roared in triumph and charged at the beasts with their spears. They didn't even know why the Zakaras were standing still, but they were taking advantage of the moment anyway.

Dareth watched in silence.

This is stupid, he thought.

He was injured. One of the Zakaras had just raked his arm

with its claws, missing his neck by mere inches. He had almost been killed.

Dareth hadn't opted himself for this. He didn't want to die following Baird on a blind crusade.

Do I want to be with them when they're defeated by Shayam? he wondered.

He was pulled from his thoughts by Aylen. His friend's face was contorted with worry.

"Are you okay?" Aylen asked, examining Dareth's shoulder.

"I'll live," Dareth uttered.

Aylen nodded. "You should dress it. It's bleeding. They got Rivan."

He pointed behind them, and Dareth looked to see his comrade sitting by a pile of debris with a hand held to his chest. His tunic was red with blood.

"How bad is it?" Dareth asked.

"Bad…" Aylen said. "I… I don't know what to do…"

They were interrupted by Bryna passing between them. Her eyes were blackened, and her wrist was marked with freshly-made cuts.

Baird is fighting the Zakaras because they're monsters, but ignores the monsters among us… Dareth thought as his eyes lingered upon the acts of her self-mutilation. Dark magic beset an eerie haze around her.

"Let me look at him," she whispered as she breezed past them like a dark cloud.

Throughout the battle so far, it had been clear to Dareth that Shayam's monsters could have killed them many times over. The only reason they were still alive was because Shayam was holding back. He wasn't trying to *kill* them. He was trying to *capture* them. He wanted them alive. He wanted the crystals that were taken from him.

If they prolonged the battle much longer, Rivan would bleed to death.

This has gone too far… Dareth decided.

He looked at Jaedin. Now that the young man had gained control over the Zakaras, Miles had dropped his shield. Jaedin was the key. *He* was the one who was prolonging this fight.

Everyone was busy. Either by killing the monsters or

tending to Rivan. No one was watching Jaedin, aside from Miles.

Dareth looked at the debris scattered on the ground, searched through the piles of scattered stone and glass until he found what he was looking for.

A plank of wood. It was large and heavy. It would easily knock someone out but, as long as Dareth was careful, it wouldn't cause injury. He hefted it and ran at Miles.

As Dareth neared him, Miles must have heard his footsteps. He turned, and his eyes widened. He opened his mouth to say something, but Dareth's blow to the head silenced him. He toppled to the ground.

Dareth smiled to himself. Now it was Jaedin's turn.

Jaedin was so busy controlling the Zakaras he didn't notice his mentor fall beside him. He just stood still. His eyes glowing.

Dareth almost laughed out loud at how easy this was turning out to be. He raised the plank above Jaedin's head.

*　　*　　*

Rivan was losing blood fast. Aylen watched as Bryna wound a bandage around his chest. Her pale white hands streaked with the dark scarlet of his blood.

"Is he going to make it?" he asked.

Bryna didn't answer.

Rivan opened his lips to speak but struggled. Blood oozed from the side of his mouth.

"What is it?" Aylen asked, leaning closer.

Rivan raised his finger and pointed at something behind Aylen's shoulder.

Aylen turned around and witnessed the moment Dareth struck Jaedin across the head. He was unable to process it in time to shout a warning.

With a thud, Jaedin fell to the ground. Aylen stared, trying to comprehend why Dareth would do such a thing. Nothing about it made sense.

For a moment, time seemed to pause. The air went silent, and everyone turned to each other, as if they all sensed something was not quite right.

The Zakaras stirred back into motion.

There was no warning. None of them were prepared for it. Most of the warriors had scattered from their defensive formations and were vulnerable. Some of them tried to flee but it was too late. Aylen watched, in horror, as a Zakara fastened its jaws around one of the men and lifted him from the ground.

Aylen ran to Dareth. He was standing over Jaedin's body with a grimly satisfied expression on his face.

"What are you doing?" Aylen asked, thinking this must be a mistake. He knew that Dareth could be brash sometimes but never imagined he would turn against them. Aylen tried to think up an excuse for his friend's betrayal but he couldn't.

"You chose to bring us here, Aylen," he said. Aylen was expecting his eyes to be struck with madness, but they were clear and calculated. Dareth knew what he was doing and was prepared for the implications. "Now, it is my turn to choose our destiny."

Tentacles snaked around Aylen's arms. He tried to wriggle free, but they tightened and lifted him from the ground.

"I'm sorry," Dareth said, as he crossed his arms over his chest. "But this is for your own good."

*　　*　　*

Kyra ran at Dareth as fast as her legs could carry her, screaming in fury.

When she saw Dareth standing over Jaedin's body, she knew it could only mean they had been betrayed.

A swerving claw knocked her over. She cursed and pulled herself back to her feet. She dodged the next one and looked up, saw a Zakara slithering up behind Aylen, and yelled a warning he didn't hear.

The Zakara flexed its tentacles, coiling them around Aylen's limbs and pulling him from the ground, kicking and screaming. The Zakara carried him to the rooftop of one of the houses and leapt away.

Kyra ran. She knew it was too late to save Aylen, but she ran anyway. Her legs were charged with all her fury, yet somehow they still weren't fast enough.

A gargantuan, fuzzy creature galloped past her, beating her to reach Dareth. She screamed. The beast scooped up Miles and Jaedin in its giant paws and then bowed its head to the ground. Dareth climbed onto its back. It was his chariot.

"Give them back!" she screamed once Dareth was within earshot. She readied her sword. There were no excuses for him this time. She was going to kill him.

Dareth grinned spitefully as he placed his legs on either side of the monster's back.

"It's over, Kyra!" he replied. "Run while you still can."

"Fight! You coward!" she screamed in helpless rage as the Zakara turned and carried Dareth away. She chased after it, but it was too fast. It galloped down the street and turned a corner, gone within seconds.

"Kyra!" a voice yelled behind her.

It was Baird. He was back in his human form. Kyra looked around and saw that most of the Zakaras were now dead, and Sidry was picking off the remaining two.

"Where have they gone?" Baird asked.

"Dareth betrayed us!" she cried. "A Zakara took them! They went that way."

When she pointed, she realised it was towards the fortress.

"Shayam must be in there," Baird concluded.

"We have to go after them!" she said.

"No," Baird shook his head. "Rivan needs to be treated."

Kyra looked at Rivan. He sat against a wall, and his face was pale; he looked like he was at death's door. It was only then Kyra became aware of the devastation around them. Most of the local warriors were dead but, by some miracle, Sidry, Baird, Fangar and Bryna appeared to be unharmed.

"We must go!" one of the surviving warriors yelled to them. "Follow me! I know somewhere safe!"

Chapter 20

The Resistance

Shayam peered out from the embrasure in the wall of the tower and smiled to himself as he looked upon the desolated city.

A small rebellion still lingered within its shadows, but it was only a matter of time before it was crushed, and then the entire city would be his. The streets were rife with his creatures.

And Shayam couldn't help but marvel how easy it had been.

He had entered the town just a little over two aeights ago, and taking control of it had been a swift process. Within a couple of days, he had talked his way into the castle walls and, within a few minutes of entering the gate, Shayam had killed all the Elders and their advisors. He then killed all the servants and guards too, turning them into Zakaras and, finally, Shayam sealed himself up in the fortress and sent his henchmen out into the streets to conquer the city while he sat safely behind the walls built for its protection.

It had been that simple.

Baird and his followers had fallen right into the trap, just as Shayam knew they would. At this very moment, Jaedin was being carried to a room which would remain his prison until Carmaestre found a way to remove the Stone of Zakar from his head. Baird and Sidry were still out there, somewhere, but Shayam's Zakaras had the run of the streets so Shayam knew they could not escape. It was just a matter of finding them.

He sensed a presence drawing near and closed his eyes. It was his servants. They were dragging Miles up the stairs.

Shayam smiled. He was looking forward to chatting with his old friend.

He turned around just as the door swung open and grinned smugly as his guards guided the traitor to the table and dropped him onto a chair.

Shayam sent a telepathic command to his men. *Leave!*

The two of them were alone. Miles lifted his head from the

table, and Shayam saw a weary sun-scorched face covered with a shadow of stubble. His clothes were torn and weathered. He had clearly been out in the wilderness for quite some time. It was a strange state for Shayam to see the scholar in. This was a man he associated with dusty libraries and books and faded scrolls. A man who'd spent most of his adult life being the urban socialite, mingling with nobles and the academic circles of Mordeem. This was the man who had been one of Grav'aen's most trusted agents, and Shayam's friend.

This was the man who had somehow managed to deceive them all. Even Grav'aen, who was the most adept Psymancer in known existence.

"I hope your journey here was not too troublesome," Shayam greeted his guest with icy courtesy as he made his way to the table. He eyed Miles' haggard state with amusement. "I will arrange for my servants to make you a hot bath and bring you some clean clothes later. This is not a suitable state for Sir Miles, the great scholar, to be in, is it?"

Miles glowered as Shayam seated himself at the other side of the table.

"A whole city..." Miles whispered. "So many people, Shayam. How could you do such a thing?"

Shayam momentarily felt a twinge of guilt, but it was a feeling he swiftly suppressed.

Your betrayal caused the plan to change, he thought as he stared at Miles.

When Baird and the others all escaped from his grasp, Shayam knew that, unless he tracked them down, Grav'aen's punishment for his failure would be severe. Creating a stronghold in this town was the only way Shayam could think of to protect his future. He could lure them in, recover the Stones and, at the same time, provide Grav'aen with an added bonus which would make amends for his mistakes.

"I did not want it to come to this," Shayam told him. "You knew what the plan was – you were supposed to be a part of it! – come to Sharma, conduct some small experiments, and leave. *This* was never part of the plan. Thanks to *someone,* the original plan went wrong, so I had to improvise."

"I did what I thought was for the best," Miles said, looking at Shayam with contempt. "It was getting out of control.

Can't you see what you have created? Look around you!"

"*We* have created," Shayam corrected him. "Don't pretend you had no part in this."

Miles expression became one of guilt.

"Don't tell me you convinced your new friends that you've been working in their interests *all* this time?" Shayam guessed, reading Miles' reaction and feeling a wave of satisfaction that he had caught him out. "That this has all been for them?"

Shayam laughed out loud. "Of course!" he continued as Miles looked down at the table. "If they knew the complete truth, they would have killed you on the spot. You may have betrayed us later down the line, but never forget that *you* were the one who made all of this possible!"

"I realised it was wrong when I found out people were being killed," Miles' voice croaked. "The research was originally to save people from disease... not create a new one!"

"There were always mortalities," Shayam reminded him. "From the very beginning, there were failed experiments. Things that went wrong."

"I told myself it was a small sacrifice for all the lives that would be saved!" Miles cried out. "But Grav'aen isn't just interested in saving lives. He's creating living weapons!"

"Oh, give it a rest!" Shayam muttered. "You must have had some idea what those rituals and runes you uncovered were capable of!"

They were interrupted by the door opening. A group of Shayam's servants walked in carrying steaming platters of food. They placed onto the table a roast pigeon, meats stuffed with grains, freshly cooked vegetables with herby aromas, boiled potatoes, warm bread, and a number of extras. It was an exquisite feast. Shayam had requested it so.

For Miles was a very special guest.

As the servants filed out of the room, Shayam began to spoon food onto his plate.

Zakaras can even be great cooks, Shayam thought as he took his first bite.

Throughout the last few aeights, he had perfected his handling of Zakaras. He'd discovered that, if he used his Stone of Zakar to activate specific parts of their minds, it gave them enough intelligence to execute skills and tasks they used to perform back when they were human. Zakaras still had the memories of their human hosts stored within them, it was just a case of granting them the ability to access them.

But Shayam had also learnt that, if he gave them too much intelligence, it also increased their free will and they became harder to control. Dion had been evidence of this; he had been one of Shayam's initial experiments. Shayam had spent hours enhancing Dion, focusing the power of his crystal into awakening parts of Dion's mind and, in doing so, Shayam had moulded him in a Zakara with almost human intelligence.

But, as a consequence, Shayam had often found it difficult to control him. If Aylen had not killed Dion, Shayam would have been forced to eventually.

Shayam had perfected his use of his Stone of Zakar now. In the case of the cooks, guards, and other cogs of this fortress, he'd merely activated the parts of their minds which contained those skills, and now, all it took was a short telepathic command for Shayam to get them to perform their previous roles.

With the right amount of application, it had been that simple.

Shayam looked up. Miles was staring at him with a wary expression. The plate in front of him was still clean, but Shayam could tell that he was desperately hungry.

"Please, help yourself," Shayam urged. "The last thing I want is for my prisoner to starve."

"What is all this for, Shayam?" Miles asked. "If I eat, will you consider it my surrender? Is this one of your games?"

"This is no game, Miles," Shayam replied. "I want you to sit with me. We will eat this feast. You can even have a glass of wine, if you like. Just like old times."

Miles shifted uncomfortably.

It is nice to see him squirm, Shayam thought with amusement.

"I want you to enjoy this, Miles," Shayam continued. "I want you to eat this delicious meal prepared by my servants. The servants you helped to create. I want you to remember this moment because, you might find this hard to believe, I feel sorry for you. I don't know exactly what Grav'aen is going to do with you, once I hand you over to him, but I suspect you will discover a whole new world of pain."

*   *   *

The last hour had been a complete blur for Sidry, as he dashed through the streets with his wounded friend in his arms, following a stranger who claimed to be leading them to safety. They ran for their lives, while Baird and Fangar disposed of any Zakaras who crossed their path.

He had no time to dwell upon the betrayal they had just suffered. No time to be angry with Dareth. He didn't even have time to particularly worry about the friend who was possibly dying in his arms because, while he sprinted for life – through endless streets and alleyways, over walls, and around tight corners – with monsters chasing them from every angle, it was a desperate struggle for survival for *all* of them. Not just the wounded.

The bearded man who led them only had four of his comrades left. The rest of them had died in the skirmish and been left behind. They carried the loss so stoically, Sidry knew this must be far from their first brush with tragedy in recent times.

They were led through a series of rundown buildings which all seemed to be joined to one another by corridors, stairs, and passageways. It all passed by in a blur. Sidry began to feel so lost in the labyrinth of walls and tunnels that he no longer knew if he was above ground or below. The men leading him seemed to know where they were going though. At one point, they passed a pair of armoured warriors standing guard in a doorway. They raised their crossbows in alarm at the sight of Sidry in his Avatar of Gezra, but the bearded man intervened and somehow persuaded them to let them pass.

"Take the wounded in there," the bearded man said, motioning to a door. Sidry ducked through the arch and entered a dingy room with a few straw beds and blankets on the floor. He placed Rivan carefully upon the nearest one.

Sidry then closed his eyes and called out to the crystal, reverting his ethereal armour. White light flashed across the room, and Sidry experienced tingling sensations all over his body. When he opened his eyes, he was human again. He caught his breath for a few moments while he grounded himself. Whenever Sidry changed back from being an Avatar of Gezra, he always felt a little lightheaded.

He looked at the wound on Rivan's chest and winced. Sidry, like the other young men of Jalard, had been given basic training in first aid. He knew how to dress a wound, make a splint, and even a few plants which could slow bleeding, but he didn't have a clue where to even begin with an injury like this.

"Rivan needs help!" he called out.

"I will."

He jumped at the sound of Bryna's voice, realising that she was already beside him. She reached into her bag and drew out her medicine kit.

Even Kyra was there. She seemed anxious. Her rigid face, which usually made expressions of vexation in Rivan's presence, was contorted with worry.

"His lung is punctured. I need to drain it…" Bryna muttered to herself as she examined Rivan. "Kyra, get me hot water, and more light!" she ordered, her voice surprisingly firm.

* * *

While Bryna treated Rivan, the bearded man led Baird and Fangar deeper into his strange dwelling.

It was comprised of a vast network of tunnels. All the rooms and passageways were lit by glowstones or candlelight. Baird suspected they were underground for he had not come across a single window and the air was musky.

Baird could also see how this place managed to elude the Zakaras; not only was it hidden but, even if any Zakaras found a way in, they would still have to crawl through the tight corridors one at a time while fighting past the guards to reach the heart of this haven.

But it didn't take much stretching of Baird's imagination to guess what purpose this place had served to the city beforehand.

"So who are you and what is this place?" Baird asked as tactfully as he could.

"I am Jarndal," he replied. "And this place is safe from the monsters. Everything else will be explained to you soon. I am taking you to our leader."

*   *   *

Jarndal took them to a room which appeared to be their headquarters and asked them to stand by outside. He went in alone.

Baird waited patiently, while Fangar paced to and fro, occasionally tilting his nose up to sniff the air.

The door opened. "You can come in."

Baird scanned the room as he entered, his suspicions confirmed. He was in the presence of dastards and outlaws; he could tell from their dour expressions and the ill-matched motley of clothing most of them wore, which somehow managed to be simultaneously garish and shabby. Baird saw similar sights many years ago when he was a soldier and took part in a series of raids to break up a network of gangs in Shemet.

Keep your wits about you, Baird told himself. He eyed up their waists to calculate how many of them were armed and counted only a few crude swords and a dagger or two. Then he peeked at the openings some of them had in their sleeves and boots – to look for hidden pockets and straps – and realised that the number of concealed weapons was likely much higher.

A man came forward and greeted them.

"I am the leader here," he said. "My name is Kerdev."

Kerdev was surprisingly young for his station. Baird guessed him to be somewhere in his early twenties. His face was youthful, but he had wrinkles around his eyes, and part of his left ear was missing.

Baird's instincts were screaming at him to turn and run, but he couldn't; he knew what was waiting for them outside.

"So, what is this?" Fangar spoke out. "Some den for street rats and thugs?"

The energy changed. Everyone glared at him. Some even drew weapons.

He's causing trouble, Baird thought, regretting his choice to let the rogue accompany him.

Kerdev raised his hand; that was all it took, and his vassals stood down and sheathed their weapons. Their expressions, however, remained hostile.

Kerdev regarded Fangar with a firm expression. "Is there a problem?" he asked.

"Yes," Fangar replied. "In fact, there is!"

With a sudden flash of movement, Fangar leapt across the room. He moved too fast for Baird's eyes to follow at first. All Baird could distinguish was the flash of claws and a burst of red.

And then Fangar was standing before a headless body.

The head rolled onto the floor, and everyone gasped. A horrible stench filled the room.

There was no mistaking the putrid odour of a Zakara's blood.

"You have been infiltrated," Fangar finished. "He was one of them."

*   *   *

When Jaedin opened his eyes, he saw his mother looking down on him.

He stared at her in disbelief for a few moments, until her face twisted into a snarl, and then he knew it wasn't really her. This woman's hair was darker, her skin was chalky pale, and her eyes were cold.

"Where is the stone?" she rasped.

"What?" Jaedin blurted.

"The stone!" she repeated. "Your bastard sister has it! Where is she?"

"Bryna?" Jaedin breathed.

"Yes!" she screamed. She clenched her fist and struck the wall. "Bryna! Your sister! Are you simple or something? Is this what happens when people interbreed and spawn brats? Your sister wasn't much talk either!"

"What?" Jaedin blurted.

He had never been so confused in his life. The last thing he could remember was being in the streets of Fraknar, struggling to control the Zakaras while everyone around him was fighting. He didn't even know how that had ended, or how he had awoken in a room with this strange, aggressive woman who resembled his mother.

She laughed maniacally. "Oh, she never told you, did she? You don't even know about the incestuous sheets that seeded you! I suppose it's not the sort of thing you tell your children about!"

Jaedin gasped. His mother had never told him anything about his father, but he couldn't bring himself to believe what this woman was insinuating.

"Who are you?" he asked.

"She never mentioned me?" she asked. "Carmaestre? The sister she betrayed? Ring any bells?"

Jaedin shook his head, and Carmaestre's face snagged into a grim expression. The fact she had never been mentioned seemed to be her biggest grievance.

She screamed with rage, and the air around her glowed with purple light. Jaedin's body became consumed with pain. He convulsed, blinded by it. He tried to summon his own magic to defend himself but he was too weak.

Eventually, it ended, and he landed back on the bed with a thud.

Carmaestre glowered at him. Most of her rage seemed to have been spent.

A cruel smile broadened across her dark lips. "You're a disappointment," she said. "Most of our family inherit some form of talent, but it seems to have missed you. Trust Meredith to birth such a useless runt."

She brought her face close to his. "Your mother and sister are nothing but a pair of lowly thieves, and I *will* take back what is mine," she whispered. "I am the true Descendant of Vai-ris!"

She turned and left.

"Oh," she said, just before she shut the door. "By the way. Shayam sent me here to give you a warning. *Don't* try to meddle with any of his servants. Or any of the other Zakaras in this city for that matter. He has guards posted outside Miles' and Aylen's doors, and at the merest *hint* of you trying to use that Stone I put in your head, he will have them killed."

*   *   *

Fangar's discovery that there was an impostor within Kerdev's inner retinue caused much worriment within the lair. So much so that Kerdev sent Fangar and Baird on a quest to explore the rest of his underground kingdom and track down any other Zakaras who may have infiltrated but were yet to reveal their true forms.

It wasn't a pleasant task. Fangar managed to detect five more, and they were all people in sickbeds. Some of them even had families and loved ones huddled around them, praying for their survival, but the reality was that they were already dead and would soon become a threat. Each time, Baird knew what needed to be done but couldn't bring himself to do it. In the end, it had fallen upon Fangar to perform the acts of mercy.

After they'd finished their sweep of the entire territory, Baird was finally allowed to rest. Kerdev offered to escort him back to the room where Rivan and the others were.

"Your friend Fangar is an interesting creature..." Kerdev commented once they were alone. He stopped in the middle of the corridor and folded his arms over his chest. "And Jarndal gave me ear that yourself and one of the others you brought with you aren't exactly... *normal*, either..."

"What of it?" Baird asked, feeling impatient. He was anxious to find out if Rivan was still alive.

"Let me put it straight to you," Kerdev said. "I have seen some seriously weird shit of late, and many a man I thought a friend turn into one of those creatures... I want to know what the difference is between you and *them*."

Baird sighed, realising Kerdev's want for an explanation was justified.

He gave him a brief account of what happened to Jalard. How he and Sidry had escaped with the Stones of Gezra. Who Shayam was, and why he had attacked their city.

As they talked, Kerdev asked many questions. He seemed to show great concern for the people hiding out in his lair, and this didn't just merely include his pack of outlaws and cutpurses; Baird had just discovered – during his foray – that this place had become a refuge for hundreds of civilians who'd fled from their homes. Kerdev had not only taken them in during their time of need; he had taken them under his wing and made their survival his personal responsibility.

This confused Baird. He had met men of Kerdev's ilk before and knew that one didn't rise to his station by being benign. It was the end of a long and bloody road, most often filled with brutality and backstabbing. Such men were either ruthless from the very beginning or became jaded over time.

Why is he helping these people? Baird wondered. *Does he believe there is something in it for him?*

"Now I have some questions for you," Baird said after he finished relating his story. "What is your plan? Because let me tell you; if you stay down here you will either run out of food or they'll find a way in. What are you going to do?"

"Our plan is to stay alive," Kerdev said simply.

"So you plan to attempt an escape?" Baird clarified.

"If it comes to it..." Kerdev grimaced. "We've been taking each day as it comes... We haven't had time to think of a plan yet."

"You can't stay down here forever," Baird said. "Have you considered fighting Shayam?"

"We're outlaws, Baird..." Kerdev admitted. He said it flatly and unashamedly. "We're used to defending our territory and keeping our asses alive. That is all we know."

"Shayam is using this city to mass an army," Baird reminded him. "We *have* to stop him!"

"Shayam's in the fortress," Kerdev crossed his arms over his chest. "How do you expect us to fight our way past those monsters *and* get in there?"

"If you can help us get to the gates, that'll be enough," Baird suggested. "Me and Sidry could scale those walls no problem."

"I don't doubt that, from what Jarndal has told me," Kerdev admitted. "But how many men would I lose? I need them to protect the women and children I have down here!"

*Does he **really** care about all those people?* Baird thought. He still couldn't figure out what this man's angle was.

Kerdev narrowed his eyes. "I can tell what you are thinking. You think that just because we're outlaws we only care for ourselves..."

"I said no such thing," Baird shook his head.

"I could see it in the way you looked at me," Kerdev said. "I've a good eye for such things... don't long survive the life I live if you don't... I've orphans down here, Baird. Children."

"And you've been teaching them to pickpockets and crawl through windows, no doubt..." Baird muttered.

"Most of them are new..." Kerdev said wistfully. "Took 'em in when the monsters came."

"And what about the whores?" Baird asked, recalling the bawdy women he saw in one of the rooms he and Fangar came across during their search. "I saw those lasses. I know what they are."

"Aye..." Kerdev said. "First thing I did when I took charge was take 'em in... they were on the streets before that... being beaten... sometimes even killed. I didn't choose their way of getting by but I gave them a safe place to do it. What else could I do? Growing up... watching me mam come home each morning with bruises..." Kerdev's eyes misted briefly, but then he composed himself and slammed his hand on the wall. Cursed. "You know what? I don't need to justify myself to you. My men saved your ass, and you're in *my* den! If you don't like it here, you can scittin' leave! I'm sure those creatures out there would enjoy a nice little feast."

"I..." Baird hesitated. He looked at Kerdev and realised the man was serious. "Look, Kerdev, I'm sorry... I... can't pretend I agree with what you are and what you have going on here, but none of that matters right now. Not anymore. I'd pick you a hundred times over that Shayam bastard, and we have a much better chance of getting out of this alive together."

"First bit of sense you've spoken for a while," Kerdev muttered. His expression softened. "Fine," he said. "You can stay here, but this is *my* territory, Baird. *I* run this place."

"Agreed," Baird said, swallowing some of his pride. "I also want you to consider what I said about mounting an attack, because unless we stop Shayam *nowhere* in Sharma will be safe later down the line..."

"I will consider. I promise no more," Kerdev agreed.

*   *   *

Sidry had never been interested in healing techniques before but, as he watched his friend being treated, he found himself asking Kyra about every process Bryna carried out. From the draining of fluid from his lungs to the strong-smelling salves she applied to the wounds, the stitches, and even now, after bandaging him, Bryna still had work to do.

He watched as Bryna guided a steaming cup to Rivan's lips and gently coaxed him to drink her potion. It was a strange sight to see; the stalwart young man being fed like a baby, by the petite, dark and unearthly Bryna.

"What's that for?" Sidry asked.

"Probably some kind of booster to speed up healing... or fight infection," Kyra guessed.

The scene was painful to witness. Rivan had always been a pillar of strength. Sidry thought him invincible.

Even Kyra was anxious for him. Between fetching the things Bryna requested, she barely left his side.

Why is it we all seem to hate each other until moments like this? Sidry wondered. It reminded him of the time Kyra was taken away by Dion. How he had worried for her.

And right now it wasn't solely Rivan whom Sidry was fretting over. He kept thinking about Aylen too. And even Jaedin. He didn't know if they were alive or dead.

Thoughts of Dareth, however, made Sidry's fists tighten.

Could it really be true that he had betrayed them? Sidry had not witnessed it himself but Kyra had given him an account of it.

When Bryna finished coaxing Rivan to drink the potion, she placed the cup on the floor and rose to her feet.

"How is he?" Kyra asked as Bryna walked over to them.

"He needs to rest," Bryna whispered.

Kyra nodded. "But will he...?"

"Rivan is strong. He will fight," she said.

Sidry nodded solemnly. He wanted, more than anything, for Bryna to say he was going to be okay, but it appeared nothing was certain yet and she wasn't going to give false promises.

"I best go find Baird," Kyra decided. She stood up and took once last glance at Rivan before leaving the room.

Sidry was alone with Bryna. She sat next to him and ran a hand over her forehead. It seemed it was only when her work was done she permitted tiredness to show.

Sidry had never been so close to her before. Never found her so beautiful. He looked at her dark ebony hair, flowing down her pearly shoulders like threads of silk. He wanted to run his fingers through it.

She turned her head and their eyes met. Her irises were purple. The only other woman Sidry had ever seen with purple eyes before was Carmaestre, but hers had been bitter and cruel. Bryna's were intense and striking, arcane and unfathomable.

"Why is it that you always open your mouth, as if you want to speak to me, but say nothing?" she asked.

Because you are the most beautiful thing I have ever seen, but you scare me.

But he couldn't say that. He was flustered. He tried to think of words which would express what he wanted to say but differently. He couldn't find any.

"I think I know…" Bryna eventually said, turning away and ending their opia. "You are a nice man, Sidry, but I am not capable of returning such feelings. If you knew the truth about me, you would be scared. Don't fall in love with me. You will get hurt."

Sidry was rendered speechless. He didn't know how to reply.

They sat in silence for a while.

"Jaedin is still alive," Bryna announced. "I know he is. So Miles and Aylen should be too."

Sidry was glad to hear it. He somehow knew that, whatever Bryna was, and whatever it was she was hiding from them, he could trust her. She had said such things before and never been wrong.

"Thank you for helping Rivan," he finally said.

"I hope it is enough."

*   *   *

Shortly after his arrival, Dareth was escorted through the castle by an armed guard. They led him towards one of the towers and, after making his way up a spiralling staircase and through a door, Dareth found himself in a large chamber where Shayam sat behind a grand table made of oak.

"I would like to thank you for your assistance earlier," Shayam greeted. He waved his hand and the guards left the room. "Your friends were already fighting a losing battle, of course, but you did speed up the process."

"They are not my friends," Dareth replied. "I only care

about the one I brought with me."

Shayam sighed. "I'm afraid that *that* young man is proving himself quite troublesome. He's refusing to eat, using terrible language, and being aggressive to my guards... I'm considering having him altered so that he won't be so bothersome, but I thought to consult you first..."

Dareth tensed when he realised what Shayam meant by 'altered', but he tried to not let it show. He knew Shayam was being pleasant to him because he had earned his favour, but that could easily change.

But Dareth wasn't going to let Shayam turn Aylen into one of those monsters either.

"Let me see him," Dareth requested. "I can reason with him."

Shayam nodded. "Sure. You have earned my trust. You are no prisoner here, Dareth. You can wander this fortress as you like."

"Have you found the others, yet?" Dareth asked.

"No," Shayam shook his head. "The citizens of this town have been rebelling against me and it has proved a very tedious affair... I have managed to quash most of the rebellions now, but there is still a large faction of them left who are hiding out in an underground lair somewhere, and I believe your old friends are with them. I can't seem to find the entrance to this hideaway, but I am sure I will soon... One of my Zakaras will have it stored in their mind somewhere, I just haven't found the time to start the process of searching for it yet. I have been dealing with other matters..."

Dareth nodded.

"Are you not concerned for them?" Shayam asked.

"Not particularly," Dareth shrugged. "It's not that I want to see them hurt... it's just... well, they brought this all on themselves. And worse, they dragged me and Aylen into it. I had to put me and him first."

"That was a wise thing to do," Shayam agreed. "You are an interesting young man, Dareth... I think there could be a place for you among us."

Dareth wasn't sure working for Shayam was what he desired. He didn't know what he wanted.

Best to let him think I am interested for now though, Dareth realised. *Keep my options open... And at the moment he has Aylen...*

"You can leave now," Shayam dismissed him. "Give you some time to think... if you need anything – such as a warm bath, food, or even some new clothes – you need only ask my servants."

Dareth nodded. "Thanks."

*　　*　　*

Aylen was being held prisoner in a bare room and, with nothing but stone walls around him, he had only his thoughts to torment himself. He sat in the corner. Hours passed by. His mind replayed the moment Dareth clubbed Jaedin over the head, over and over again.

It's all my fault, Aylen realised.

He recalled all the peculiar things Dareth had said to him recently. All the times Dareth had tried to talk him into abandoning the others. Dareth had even said, once, that when they reached Fraknar they would have 'options'.

All of those things echoed in Aylen's mind with a new and terrible clarity.

Aylen remembered the message they received from the intruder.

Yes. Shayam remembers you, Dareth. He is looking forward to meeting you again. He says that if you help him, you will find it very rewarding.

Aylen received so many clues that Dareth was going to betray them, yet for some reason, he had not taken any of them seriously.

Why didn't I say anything? he wondered.

Because he had been scared of losing Dareth. Because he had always set himself the task of watching over him. Because he thought that, as long as he was around, he could keep Dareth's dark side at bay.

Because Aylen had been in denial. He convinced himself that, deep down, Dareth had some good in him. That he could change him.

Shayam had won, and it was all Aylen's fault.

He heard footsteps outside the door. Aylen cursed. Shayam kept sending servants to bring him messages and food, but each time they came Aylen spurned them. He didn't want to listen to Shayam's messages or eat food that was prepared by his monsters. He clenched his fists and prepared himself for the next wave of henchmen trying to coax him into obedience but, when the door opened, he was stunned to silence when he saw Dareth.

"Hi Aylen," he said, stepping into the room.

Dareth was wearing a brand new set of clothes. They were Gavendarian in style; made from red velvet, with black frills around the neck, waist and collar. Aylen was surprised how comfortably one of the poorest boys from Jalard carried himself in such attire.

His dark hair was no longer tangled, which made it seem longer. He swept a lock of it away from his face, and they looked at each other.

"You bastard!" Aylen gritted his teeth. "What have you done?"

"Oh, calm down," Dareth rolled back his eyes. "The others are still alive. If I didn't do *something* Rivan would've bled to death. Did you *want* him to die?"

Aylen frowned. "But the monsters... they were–"

"Shayam never wanted to kill us," Dareth explained. "He just wanted those damn stones back."

"So they're still alive?" Aylen asked. A glimmer of hope lifted his spirits.

"As far as I know..." Dareth shrugged. "They escaped, and they haven't been killed by Zakaras yet... I know that much. Whether they managed to save Rivan or not, that's a different story..."

"How long have you been working for Shayam?" Aylen asked.

"It's not like that," Dareth shook his head. "I don't work for *anyone*. Before you guys found me I got to know him a little, that's all... I did this for *us*, Aylen. You're like my brother. We're safe now."

Oh Dareth, how could you be so stupid? Aylen thought. He turned away. "Piss off, Dareth."

Dareth frowned. "Aylen..."

"Leave me!" Aylen shouted. "You fucked up everything!"

"I did this for you..." Dareth said solemnly. "You're the only one who ever cared for me. The only person I ever relied on. Can't you see that? When Jalard was destroyed, I didn't even care that much because I knew *you* were still alive."

Aylen was speechless. He couldn't imagine a world where he only had one person within it he cared about. Every time Aylen thought about Jalard – all the people, friends and family who perished there, that he would never see again – he experienced a pain so terrible he found it hard to breathe.

But Dareth was free from that burden. He never had many friends. And he hated his family.

Dareth did all of this for me... Aylen realised.

Aylen's knees gave way, and he dropped to the ground in despair, clawing at his face with his hands.

Dareth touched his shoulder.

"Aylen, if you don't start cooperating soon Shayam is going to kill you," he warned. "Please... Aylen, start eating and stop fighting. *Please*. I have talked him into giving you more time, but I don't know how much longer he will give you."

Tears of despair flooded from Aylen's eyes. He wiped them away. He cried for Jalard. For his family. For his neighbours. For his friends, who had just been betrayed, and his failure to stop it from happening.

When Aylen came around from his fit of anguish, he opened his eyes and realised Dareth had gone.

He had left a plate of food on the floor.

If I behave... maybe I can gain their trust, Aylen realised. *If they let me out of this room, maybe I could find a way to help the others...*

Dareth was lost in delusions. Aylen knew there was no hope in trying to talk his old friend around this time; his mind was set. Aylen had never seen Dareth more resolute in his life.

But if I find a way to help put things right... maybe then I can make it up to everyone else.

Aylen picked up the plate and began to eat. He was surprised by how hungry he was. Before, he had no stomach for it, but now he had a motive, a plan, and hope that his friends were still alive, he realised he needed his strength.

He ate it all and placed the empty plate neatly by the door.

Aylen then sat back down and began to rehearse in his mind how he was going to feign obedience.

*   *   *

When Baird returned to the others, Bryna was in the process of cleaning and redressing Rivan's wound. He watched as she wound a bandage over his chest.

She is more useful than I gave her credit, Baird realised. He had no doubt that without her help Rivan would have died.

He walked over and took a closer look at Rivan. He could tell from how pale he was that it was still unclear whether he would survive. Baird had seen men recover from worse, but he had also seen many more perish from far lesser injuries.

Baird was accustomed to the price of war, but he knew that, if Rivan died, it would be an onerous test to his fortitude. He'd nurtured the young man since he was a boy, and he was one of the most dedicated pupils Baird had ever had.

I led him into this, Baird reminded himself.

But he knew that, if he had the chance to go back, he would have done it again. They were fighting for something that was bigger than themselves, and such quests often required sacrifices.

"Thank you, Bryna," Baird said.

She tilted her head up and smiled faintly. It was the first time she had ever looked at him directly and it caught him by surprise. Something had changed about her since they entered this town. She seemed more coherent. It was like disaster made her more alive.

She continued winding the bandage around Rivan chest.

There is nothing you can do but wait, Baird told himself.

He sat down, rested his head against the wall, and dozed off for a while.

*   *   *

Baird was awoken some time later by a knock on the door. He got up and answered it.

It was Kerdev.

"I have news for you," Kerdev announced. "I have spoken to my advisors, and we are willing to discuss the matter you mentioned earlier."

"Good," Baird replied. "I hope I can talk you into seeing sense."

"There is one other matter though…" Kerdev said.

"I am listening."

"In the morning, I am going to send Fangar on another sweep to check on the sick and wounded… make sure they haven't… well, you know… *changed.*"

"That is a good idea," Baird agreed.

"I am sorry to tell you this, but the young man you have in there don't get no free pass…" Kerdev gestured into the room. "He'll be needing the all-clear too."

Baird paused. It had not occurred to him that Rivan could turn into a Zakara, but now Kerdev had said it he knew the man was right.

Rivan *could* change. And if he did, he was no exception and must be dealt with just like everyone else.

"You're right," Baird said. "But… please don't tell the others… they have been through a lot and I don't think they can handle it just now. *If* it comes down to it, don't let Fangar do it either… I'll do it… I owe him that much."

*　　*　　*

Jaedin knew they were coming for him before they even arrived outside his door. He sensed it when Shayam sent the telepathic command to his guards, telling them to collect him.

When the door opened, Jaedin was waiting for them. Obediently, he stood in the middle of the chamber and placed his hands by his sides. They grabbed him, pulled him out of the room, and Jaedin let himself be escorted without a word of protest.

I am such a coward, Jaedin thought, wretchedly, as he followed them through the corridors of the fortress.

He was powerless. Not only had guards been posted outside Miles' and Aylen's doors – ordered to kill them if Jaedin tried to meddle – but Jaedin also knew by now that Shayam's mastery over his Stone of Zakar was somehow much more advanced than his own.

They led him outside. Jaedin glanced behind himself, noting that he had just exited the tower on the eastern side of the castle. Knowing which part of the castle he was being detained within could be useful information somewhere later down the line.

He glimpsed several small buildings as they passed through the courtyard. He guessed them to be halls, kitchens, and living quarters for servants. To his right, he saw a set of steps leading up to a platform circling the outer wall. It was a parapet: a place for archers to access the crenulations in the event of a siege. Jaedin knew because he had read about castles in books but had never seen any of them in use before. Very few people from western Sharma had as most of the nation's fortresses fell into decline hundreds of years ago when the Synod rose to power, and the feudal age came to an end. Some of the fortifications near the Gavendarian border were still in operation, but everywhere else they either lay abandoned or had been repurposed into administrative centres.

They entered a tower on the other side of the bailey and Jaedin was led up a staircase. When they opened the door, Shayam was waiting for him.

"Hello Jaedin," he greeted.

Jaedin looked down at his feet. He couldn't bear the smug expression on Shayam's face.

"I'm glad that you've taken my advice and stopped trying to meddle with my creatures..." Shayam remarked. "That was wise of you. I am sure you don't want to see any more people needlessly killed for your stupidity."

A lump formed in Jaedin's throat and he swallowed it.

"Nothing to say for yourself?" Shayam asked. "I remember you having quite a lot to say last time I met you."

"And you are full of horseshit, just like the last time I met you," Jaedin said. He looked up at the Gavendarian. Met his gaze. "Just cut to the chase, Shayam."

Shayam smiled thinly and one side of his moustache curved upwards. "I just want to tell you that it will not be long till I apprehend the rest of your friends. Then your aunt – the woman you met earlier – will remove that stone from your head."

Jaedin's blood froze. Would he survive such a procedure?

And even if he did, what would they do to him afterwards?

"I believe your friends are hiding somewhere in the city... with the rest of the townspeople who have somehow eluded me," Shayam speculated. "I have not managed to find this mysterious location yet, but I will soon begin searching through the minds of my Zakaras for it. One of them will have a memory of it tucked away somewhere and, when I find it, my mission here will be almost complete."

Shayam lifted his hand, revealing a red gem fused into the flesh of his palm. His Stone of Zakar. Jaedin stared at it as it began to glow.

Why is he so much more powerful than me? Jaedin wondered.

"You will never be able to control the Zakaras like I can," Shayam said, almost as if he had just read Jaedin's mind. "Myself and the others have been given guidance on how to use our Stones. *Your* ability to control the Zakaras is undisciplined. That is why you are no match for me, Jaedin."

Jaedin turned his eyes to his feet again. Miles believed he was some prophesied saviour of the world, and even Baird wanted him to use his power if war came. Fangar had followed his scent, crossing a whole country to find him, because he believed Jaedin was their only hope.

And all this time, Jaedin thought them wrong. Because he wasn't strong or brave enough to be a hero.

Now, he knew, even *if* he learnt to be those things, he would still be useless.

"There is a festival tonight. Do you know which one it is?" Shayam asked.

"Why are you asking?" Jaedin muttered.

"Just humour me…" Shayam said.

Jaedin had noticed the seasons pass since he left Jalard – if anything, he had been even more aware of them than usual because he had been out in the wilderness and at the mercy of the elements – but he and the other survivors had always been too busy fighting for their lives to worry about marking the festivals.

There were eight festivals of the year, in all, and there were exactly six aeights between each one. The Festival of Ignis – which marked midsummer – passed three aeights before Jaedin and Bryna's birthday and, since then, another three aeights had passed. "Tonight is the Festival of Verdana," Jaedin answered.

"What does this mean in Sharma?" Shayam asked.

"Verdana is the Goddess who created *us*. Humans," Jaedin replied. "She is Goddess of birth and death and rebirth. Endings and beginnings. She is the harbinger of disaster and new opportunities. When Ignis discovered Verdana's existence, he knew that Lania had been unfaithful to him. It sparked the war between the gods."

"Tell me..." Shayam stroked his chin. "What is said to have happened *after* this war between the gods?"

Why is he asking me these questions? Jaedin wondered. With Shayam's monsters roaming the city there was no chance of anyone celebrating the Festival of Verdana this year. "After the war was over, Vaishra – the goddess of water – emerged and saw the desolation around her," Jaedin replied. "She refused to take part in the war, so only she was strong enough to take care of the world in the aftermath. That is why Vaishra is the Goddess of Autumn, the season where it rains and everything turns barren."

"And what about Verdana?" Shayam asked.

"Vaishra found Verdana amongst the wreckage and took pity on her. Verdana no longer had to hide from Ignis so she was finally free to live out her purpose. She created humanity."

Shayam nodded and smiled. "There are a few differences, but it is a similar story to what we tell in Gavendara. It is a strange fate that the Festival of Verdana – one of death, decay, rebirth, and new beginnings – falls tonight, don't you think?"

Jaedin grimaced.

"I have summoned you here because I am about to send a message to your friends. Undoubtedly, you would have heard it anyway, but I wanted you to be present... I wanted you to see what a *true* master of a Stone of Zakar is capable of!"

Shayam raised his palm, and his Stone of Zakar began to glimmer; red light dazzled the room. Jaedin covered his eyes and turned his head away.

He heard voices all around him. The Zakaras in the room. The ones in the corridor. Even the ones outside the window.

Jaedin could not only hear them, he could *feel* them. The Stone of Zakar in his forehead quivered. It felt Shayam's command.

Every Zakara, in the entire city, opened their mouths and

spoke as one. Their words echoed through the streets. The whole city seemed to tremble, as hundreds of Zakaras chanted in unison.

"Baird. Sidry. And Bryna. I know you are out there, and I will find you. Surrender yourselves. Return what is mine. You have until sundown. After that, we will hunt you. And no mercy will be spared for those who help you hide from me."

When it was over, it took Jaedin a few moments to ground himself. He had felt every Zakara in the city respond to Shayam's call. He had felt the power Shayam had over them.

And now, Jaedin knew there was no hope. That they would never be able to defeat Shayam.

"Take him away," Shayam dismissed him with a wave of his arm.

Cold hands pulled Jaedin to his feet and dragged him from the room.

Chapter 21

Bryna's Secret

There was not a soul in the city who did not hear Shayam's message. The chanting of hundreds of Zakaras in unison echoed through every wall and rooftop.

Bryna heard it rumble through the ceiling above her and chills ran down her spine when she heard her name.

Shayam wants me, she thought. *Not just Sidry and Baird. Me.*

Which could only mean one thing.

He knows¸ Bryna realised. *Carmaestre must have told him.*

She reached for the Stone of Vai-ris and tightened her fingers around the heirloom. Carmaestre wanted it, and she was using Shayam and his monsters to get it.

Bryna then became aware that the room had gone silent. Everyone was staring at her. Baird. Sidry. Even Kyra.

Baird isn't going to give up so easily this time... she sensed.

"Why does Shayam want you, Bryna?" Baird asked.

She opened her mouth to reply but couldn't bring herself to speak. There was so much to tell them. She didn't even know where to begin.

"Tell me, Bryna!" Baird yelled as he rose to his feet and strode up to her. "If Shayam – our *enemy* – knows something, it's about time we knew something too!"

She turned away. How was she supposed to explain it to them when she had not yet even come to terms with it herself?

Ever since Bryna escaped from Jalard, she had tried to suppress her new identity but entering a city full of restless spirits had been like a splash of cold water to her face. Her power was awakening, and she couldn't hold it back anymore.

The spirit world was close. The city was teeming with energy. Like places always did when there was death in the air.

Bryna understood this now. She knew that, when souls

departed from the mortal realm, it was not just their spirits which left their corporeal bodies behind, but their residual *viga* too. This energy lingered and, ever since Bryna had been reborn, she found she could draw upon it.

She was charged now. There was so much magic within her that it was hard to contain.

And the spirits were calling.

She closed her eyes and, once again, reinforced the barrier. Blocked out the voices trying to reach her from the *aythirrealm*.

When Bryna opened her eyes, Baird was still staring at her. He was determined to get answers.

They will know what I am soon enough, Bryna thought darkly. *But it is not the time yet.*

"Sundown," she said to him. "You will know by sundown."

She could tell from his impatient expression that sundown wasn't going to be soon enough, but luckily they were interrupted by the door opening. A face stuck its head into the room.

"Baird!" the man said with a tone of urgency. "We need to talk. *Now!*"

*   *   *

It was Kerdev. Baird suppressed a groan and reluctantly turned away from Bryna.

I will get it out of her as soon as this is over! he promised himself as he joined the outlaw in the corridor.

"I'm afraid you and your friends will have to leave before sundown," Kerdev said, once Baird shut the door and they were alone. "I'm sorry, but I can't risk the lives of everyone here."

Baird wasn't surprised. He'd half expected Kerdev to turf them out then and there.

I need to think up a plan, Baird realised.

"Me and Sidry will go," Baird agreed. "But the others must stay."

Kerdev shook his head.

"Rivan's wounded!" Baird argued. "He's not even conscious! How do you expect him to–"

"Rivan can stay," Kerdev agreed. "But Shayam named three people, not two. I want Bryna gone as well."

"But she's just a girl..." Baird muttered.

"You heard the message!" Kerdev said. "'No mercy will be given to those who hide you'. Do you know how many people we have down here?"

"Do you honestly think Shayam is going to let you live once he has dealt with us?" Baird asked. "He is massing an army, and he is going to use it to attack Shemet. Just by *knowing* this, you are a threat to him!"

Kerdev's face dropped, and Baird caught a flicker of the pressure he was under. The strain it was having on him. "I don't know what to think anymore, Baird..." he admitted.

"If you try to hide down here, Shayam will kill you," Baird said. "He will kill *everyone*. He has done it before, and he will do it again. Tossing us out will distract him for a while and buy you some time, but he will get you eventually."

*   *   *

When Baird left the room, Sidry and Kyra both stared at Bryna.

"Whatever happens, Bryna," Kyra got up from her chair and walked over to her. "I am here for you. You know that, right?"

She put a hand on Bryna's shoulder.

She doesn't know what she's touching, Bryna thought. She felt an impulse to squirm away but a deeper longing within her needed the comfort her friend was offering. Shayam's message had chilled her to the bone. With every moment, sundown was drawing closer.

At sundown, they were going to have to leave this place and confront Shayam. By tomorrow everyone would know her secret.

"I need to rest," Bryna said, stroking Kyra's hand. She got up and claimed one of the pallets, tucking herself under the blanket and nestling into the pile of hay.

She knew she was going to need her energy later.

*   *   *

Kyra watched Bryna as she drifted to sleep. She seemed peaceful.

Kyra was deeply curious over what her friend was hiding from them but, more importantly, she was concerned. That was why Kyra refrained from harassing Bryna like the others did; she knew it caused her distress.

Whenever Kyra looked into Bryna's eyes these days, she sensed deep grief. And heartache. Kyra did not understand what was going on with her, but she knew her friend must be carrying a heavy burden. Bryna needed their support, not persecution.

The door swung open, and Baird and Fangar entered the room. Their attention was immediately drawn to Rivan, and they strode to his bedside.

They've come to make sure he hasn't turned into a Zakara, Kyra realised, and she shuddered.

She closed her eyes, made a quick prayer, and waited for the verdict.

"He's fine," Fangar announced.

Kyra let out a breath she didn't even know she had been holding in.

"What do you mean?" Sidry asked. "What's going on?"

"Fangar has been checking the wounded to see which ones have turned," Baird explained.

"Shayam's little rant made this morning's run easier," Fangar commented dryly. "That little prick does have a taste for the dramatic, doesn't he?! I have to commend you guys. You've *really* pissed him off!"

"You mean he could have..." Sidry mumbled, looking at his unconscious friend.

"Of course he could have," Kyra said. "He may be a stubborn old ox, but he's no different to anyone else in that regard."

"The most important thing, for now, is that he *hasn't*," Baird said and then looked across the room. "I see Bryna has fallen asleep... how convenient..."

"Let her rest, Baird," Kyra pleaded. "I think we're in for a long night."

*   *   *

Aylen was surprised how easy it had been to earn Shayam's trust. All it took was a day of keeping his head low and being obedient, and his good behaviour was rewarded by a summons to Shayam's quarters.

When that happened, Aylen sat down at a table with him and recited a speech he had spent hours rehearsing in his head.

He mostly blamed Baird. He told Shayam that he had simply been following orders, and he was deeply sorry for all the terrible things that his mentor had made him do. Aylen assured Shayam that he was seeing things differently now. That he had learnt his lesson and wanted to make amends for his mistakes.

He thought it was obvious he was lying, but he must have put on a fairly convincing performance because, afterwards, Shayam granted him permission to leave his room and freedom to roam the fortress.

In the hours which followed, Aylen explored every part of the castle where he was allowed access, but he didn't discover anything he could do to sabotage Shayam or help his friends. He wasn't permitted entry to all of the rooms though. Many of them had guards stationed outside who blocked his path if he tried to get inside. Aylen realised that, in many ways, he was still a prisoner and yet to earn Shayam's complete confidence.

Eventually, there was only one room left for Aylen to visit. He had delayed this last one for a while because he was nervous, but he knew it needed to be done.

It was time to talk to Jaedin.

He knocked upon the door but there was no response. He looked questioningly at the guards outside as he unbolted the lock, but they made no move to stop him, so Aylen swung the door open.

When he peered into the room, he became the subject of a surprised stare which quickly turned icy.

"Jaedin..." Aylen greeted nervously as he closed the door behind him. "Are you okay?"

Jaedin nodded, but Aylen knew this not to be true. Jaedin sat on the floor with a forlorn expression on his face, and his emerald eyes, which usually shone bright with keen intelligence, were dim and despondent. Something inside him was broken.

"I..." Aylen began, stumbling to find a way to explain what it was he was doing. "I am sorry about Dareth. About everything. He's... confused right now. But I am trying to–"

"Dareth?" Jaedin hissed. "Confused? Aylen, give me a fucking break. Dareth knows exactly what he is doing! He always has!"

Aylen hesitated. There was nothing he could say to vindicate Dareth or himself for what happened. Dareth committed a grave betrayal, and Aylen failed to notice the signs of his swaying loyalties in time to warn the others. There was no excuse.

"Why are you here, Aylen?" Jaedin asked tiredly.

Aylen leant closer and lowered his voice. "I am pretending to be on Shayam's side. Just so I can get around. See if I can do something to–"

He was cut off by Jaedin laughing.

"Oh, Aylen!" Jaedin exclaimed, putting a hand to his chest. "I should have guessed. You'll never change! Always trying to please people. Always going along with what's easiest!"

"No," Aylen shook his head. "Jaedin, I am trying to–"

"Give it a rest!" Jaedin retorted. There was a bitterness to his voice which Aylen had never heard before and made him realise just how much Jaedin had changed. What happened to the shy and acquiescent boy who hid behind books and his mother's skirt? Did he die in Jalard, or somewhere along their journey since then?

"Why can't you ever think for *yourself?*" Jaedin asked. "All your life, you have been clinging to Dareth, putting up with his shit. Or tagging along with Rivan and Sidry, agreeing with everything they say. When we were younger, I thought that we stopped being friends because I was too soft and I wasn't enough of a boy for you – and maybe that is partly true – but do you know what I think the *real* reason is?"

Aylen turned away. This was the first time in many years that either of them mentioned the friendship they once shared. It was something that had often played on Aylen's conscience. Those days of playing in Aylen's garden when they were children had been simple and uncomplicated but, when Dareth came along and started picking on Jaedin, Aylen never had the guts to stand up for him. Back then, with childhood naivety, Aylen convinced himself his two friends would learn to like each other, but instead he lost one of them. Jaedin stopped visiting him. They didn't speak for years.

Aylen had never had the guts to say he was sorry. Or make amends.

"You're weak, Aylen," Jaedin said. "I know everyone calls me a soddy. I know I'm feeble. But you are weak in a different way. You need people to guide you and tell you what to be. The real reason we stopped being friends is that I never told you to be anything!"

Aylen felt tears welling up in his eyes, but he forced them back. Men were not supposed to cry. Dareth had taught him that.

Aylen stared at the wall because he could no longer look Jaedin in the face. There was so much he wanted to say, but he knew Jaedin wouldn't listen or believe him.

*But I **will** find a way to correct this!* Aylen was determined. *I have to…*

"Can I just ask one question?" Aylen said. "Whether you believe me or not, I *am* trying to help, and I came here to ask you something."

"As long as you're quick and promise to never bother me again," Jaedin said irritably.

Jaedin's harsh and dismissive reply hurt Aylen more than he would ever admit. He swallowed a lump which had grown in his throat. "Why aren't you using your power anymore?" he asked. "Why don't you turn the Zakaras against Shayam, or at least make things difficult for him?"

Jaedin turned his eyes to the floor. Aylen sensed from his forlorn expression that the fact Jaedin was *not* doing these things was killing him inside.

"I am no match for Shayam," Jaedin replied. "I was just an experiment… I don't have the discipline."

"Discipline?" Aylen repeated. "What? Like when Baird–"

"No!" Jaedin snapped. "Not *that* kind of discipline! Gods… how do I describe this to someone as *stupid* as you?!" He paused and shook his head. "Okay… think of it this way: remember when Baird taught you how to fight? He gave you a sword and showed you the stances and moves… and then you sparred against other people who were also learning and that helped you improve? Well, that's like what Shayam and those other bastards who have the rest of the Stones of Zakar have been doing – they have been given guidance. But me," Jaedin shrugged. "I've just been whacking a stick at a tree. Nobody taught me to fight so when I'm up against someone like Shayam I don't stand a chance. He has complete control, and even if I try to thwart him, the impact I would make would be minimal at best. Do you understand now?"

"I think so…" Aylen said. His heart sank. Their situation was even more dire than he previously believed. He had not thought up a plan yet, but he knew that Jaedin would have played a key role in it.

"And Shayam said he will kill Miles if I attempt anything," Jaedin added. "Can you go talk to him for me?" Jaedin asked. "Tell him what I just told you? That my power is useless? He needs to know. He thinks I am some prophesied saviour or some goosecrap."

Aylen nodded. "Is there anything else I can do?"

"Tell him that I…" Jaedin hesitated and then shook his head. "No… Nothing else. That's all."

"Okay," Aylen agreed. "I know you don't believe me, Jaedin, but I *do* want to help and I am going to do everything I can. And I am sorry about Dareth… I think you were right about him all along."

Aylen opened the door and took one last look at the young man who used to be his friend. How much they had changed since then.

"Bye Jaedin," he said and closed the door behind him.

It is a shame you feel that way, because I never stopped caring about you.

*   *   *

Jaedin…

He heard it. Faintly. Like a whisper.

Jaedin looked around the room, but there was no one there.

Jaedin…

It sounded like Bryna. Her voice was in his mind. Jaedin shook his head in disbelief. He hadn't heard Bryna's voice like this since they were children.

But it wasn't just her voice he could hear. He could feel her presence too.

Jaedin...

The voice called out to him again, and this time it was more apparent.

Is she psyseering? Jaedin wondered.

There was only one way to find out. He closed his eyes and stilled his mind. After a few minutes of slowing his breathing, he tuned into his *psysona* and felt a presence nearby.

Bryna? he called out.

Yes, Jaedin. It's me, her voice filled his mind.

I thought we'd stopped doing this? he asked. They had spent much of their childhood being able to speak mind to mind without needing to *psycalesse*, but as they grew older it ebbed away.

I have always been able to find you this way, Jaedin.

So it was only me who lost it... Jaedin realised.

He remembered what Carmaestre said to him the previous day. *Most of our family inherit some form of talent, but it seems to have skipped you. Trust Meredith to birth such a useless runt!*

I see you've met her... Bryna commented.

Jaedin felt a flush of embarrassment, as he was reminded that, if you weren't careful, thoughts could slip through when two *psysonas* were linked this way.

How are the others? he asked, changing the subject. *Are they still alive?*

Yes, Bryna replied. *Rivan is healing. The others are well.*

Jaedin was relieved, but they were still in grave danger. Their situation was dire. It would take a miracle to turn it around.

It is time for me to tell you about what happened to me, Bryna announced. *About why I am this way... Are you ready?*

Jaedin paused. He had known for a long time now that there was something not right with his sister and he had been desperate to get to the bottom of it. Now she was finally going to tell him, he was apprehensive.

Yes.

Bryna touched his spirit, and he let her in. She delved into his consciousness. Images streamed into his mind, and he began to see memories of her past as if they were through his own eyes.

* * *

Bryna was back in their home in Jalard. She was sitting in the kitchen, drumming her fingers upon the table.

Something terrible was coming. She could feel it in her bones. It felt like a black cloud was descending upon their village. But not a cloud one could see or hear or smell. It was not the sort of cloud which brought rain or thunder. It was the kind which brought gloom and change. You couldn't stop it any more than you could the flow of a river. It was coming for them.

Bryna had woken that morning shaking from a nightmare she couldn't even remember.

The door opened, and Meredith stepped into the house. Bryna could tell immediately that her mother was in a state of distress. It was early in the morning, but Meredith's face seemed worn and tired.

"What's happened?" Bryna asked.

Meredith sighed deeply and shook her head. "You know Tarvek? That drunk who lives with that Dareth boy and his mother?"

"I think so…" Bryna replied.

"He was murdered this morning."

Bryna gasped. Such a thing had never happened in their village before.

"Are you sure?" she asked.

Meredith nodded grimly. "Yes. He was stabbed. It was done with a kitchen knife."

* * *

Dareth! Jaedin realised, and his reaction pulled them out of the memory.

Yes, Jaedin, Bryna confirmed. *It was Dareth.*

*You **knew** about this?* Jaedin asked. *Why didn't you tell us?*

It's complicated, Jaedin… I didn't tell you because I knew Dareth had his reasons for doing what he did… I wanted to believe that there was still some good within him.

You should have thought differently! Jaedin exclaimed. *I have always known he was a nasty piece of work! This could have changed everything!*

Jaedin, I haven't finished yet. There is more.

* * *

It was a few hours later, and Bryna idly sat at the table while her mother tried to distract herself with some sewing. They had been instructed by the town Elders to stay indoors and tell no one the disturbing news. Dareth was missing, and they were trying to find him so they could find out what happened before they announced anything to the rest of the village.

The quiet was suddenly disturbed by the sound of a woman screaming. Meredith dropped the garment she was mending, and she and Bryna looked at each other from across the table. Other noises followed. A window breaking. Something large fell. Men shouting at each other. Meredith's eyes widened, and then there was another scream, but this one didn't even sound human.

Meredith and Bryna both ran to the window and opened the shutters. Men were fleeing down the street.

"Bandits!" Meredith gasped.

"I don't think its bandits, mother..." Bryna whispered.

The black cloud Bryna had foreseen was finally upon them. She didn't know whether to feel terrified or relieved.

And then they caught a glimpse of what the men were running away from. It was moving so fast Bryna only saw it briefly as it charged after the men on all fours, its paws tearing up the ground and leaving a trail of deep gashes upon the dirt. Meredith placed her hand over her mouth.

"Did you see that?" Meredith breathed. "What was it?!"

"I don't know," Bryna shook her head.

Meredith's healer instinct seemed to take over, and she rushed over to her cupboard to retrieve her medicine bag. "Stay here, Bryna!" she ordered. "I'm going out!"

But just as she was running to the door, it burst open, and a man stumbled inside. It was one of the farmers from the village. His face was red, and he put a hand to his chest as he caught his breath.

"Meredith!" he called out. "You're okay?"

"What's going on?" she asked.

"I don't know!" he gasped. "We're being attacked! By these *things*! You wouldn't believe me if I told you!"

Meredith reached for the door, but he blocked her path.

"No!" he said. "I came to tell you to stay in here! It's too dangerous!"

"I need to help the wounded!" she said. She squared up to him, but he stood his ground. "Get out of my way!" she ordered. "I am the Devotee of Carnea here, and I will–"

"Trust me, Meredith, stay here! Someone will come and get you when it's safe. A lot of people will need you, and you won't be able to help them dead!"

Meredith's lower lip trembled. The severity of the situation finally seemed to dawn upon her.

"What do you want me to do?" she asked.

"Bar the door, block the windows, and hide!" he said. "Don't come out until someone tells you!"

*　　*　　*

Meredith barricaded the door, while Bryna drew upon her magic to manifest fields of energy over the windows which she hoped were strong enough to stop whatever was outside getting into the house. She wasn't used to calling upon her Blessing for such things, so her efforts left her feeling faint and drowsy. She staggered over to the nearest chair and held her head to stop it from swaying.

A few moments later, a blaring sound tore across the entire street, and the ground beneath her feet trembled. Meredith ran to the window and peered through a crack. Whatever she saw made her gasp.

"What is it?" Bryna asked, fear rising.

Meredith turned around and composed her face into a calm expression. "Bryna, go upstairs to your room, please."

She said it coolly, but Bryna knew she was faking it.

"No!" Bryna refused. "I'm staying with you!"

"Bryna! Go to your room!" Meredith screamed, pointing to the stairs.

And then Bryna realised that, whatever Meredith had seen outside, it was so terrifying she didn't believe Bryna's shields and all the barricades would be enough to keep it out.

Bryna tried to argue, but her mother grabbed her and pulled her across the room. Bryna was still drowsy from all the magic she'd just used. She fought against her mother, but she was weak and dizzy, and Meredith was surprisingly strong. Her eyes rolled into the back of her head, and she fought to stay conscious. When she opened them again, her mother had dragged her halfway up the stairs. Everything went dark once more, and the next thing Bryna knew, she was being pushed through a doorway.

She cried out a final protest, but her mother ignored her. Meredith's eyes went to the chain dangling from Bryna's neck. She touched the stone she had given to her daughter only a few nights ago and smiled faintly. "Keep it safe," Meredith said. "There is someone out there who will stop at nothing to take it from you!"

She slammed the door shut, and Bryna heard the bolts, that were once used to keep her and Jaedin inside when they were disobedient as children, click into place.

*   *   *

Jaedin felt a wave of overwhelming guilt consume his conscience as realisation struck him.

Oh my Gods… Bryna, I am so sorry…

What for? she asked.

He remembered what he saw the last time he walked into the house. He had nightmares about it regularly.

Seeing what the Zakaras did to their mother had been enough for Jaedin. He ran. He never went upstairs to check if his sister was up there. He'd thought her already dead and been too much of a coward to venture any further.

You were locked up there all that time! Jaedin realised. *I left you there! I swear, if I had any idea that you were still alive I would have-*

I haven't finished yet, Jaedin, Bryna interrupted him. *My story doesn't end here.*

*   *   *

There was a loud crack which shook the entire house, and Meredith screamed. Bryna hammered her palms on the door, trying to break it open so she could run down to help her but it wouldn't budge. She heard glass breaking, followed by a strange growl. Her mother's screaming got louder, and then she let out a final, agonising wail, which tore into Bryna's soul.

And then the house went quiet. Bryna rattled the door a few more times and then her legs gave way. She collapsed. She didn't even have the will to cry. She opened her mouth, but all that came out was a choked moan. Her mother was dead. She not only knew it was likely; she could *feel* it.

She heard more sounds. Furniture being turned over. It was the creature. It had finished with her mother, and now it was seeking new prey.

The stairs began to creak, and Bryna trembled at the realisation. It was coming for her. Meredith died trying to protect her and Bryna had wasted that sacrifice. She made too much noise. That thought filled her with guilt, and Bryna was instilled with an overwhelming desire to survive so that it wasn't in vain.

She fled, scrambling to the other side of the room, but it was too late. The creature already knew she was there. The door shuddered, and then there was a crunch. A leathery, black arm broke through. Bryna pressed her knuckles to her mouth to stop herself screaming.

The door swung open. The first things Bryna saw were its eyes – which were just a pair of soulless black spheres without any whites – and then its twisted, slimy body slithered into the room. The creature was so tall that it had to arch its back just so it could stand.

Bryna stared at it, paralysed by fear. She had no idea what it was, or where it had come from.

She just knew she was about to die.

She used the last threads of her remaining *viga* to summon a small flame in the palm of her hand. She had heard some creatures were scared of fire.

But this was no normal creature. It continued advancing. Bryna had nowhere to go. She was trapped in the corner. The creature lifted one of its arms, but it wasn't really an arm, just a shiny, dark appendage which was sharp and pointed. Bryna stared at it, and then there was a flash of movement followed by blinding pain. Bryna screamed. Her abdomen had been torn open, but the agony it ignited spread to her every extremity. She opened her eyes again and watched as the monster ripped the tentacle out of her.

The monster then apathetically turned and slithered away.

Bryna's hands went to the hole it had created in her, and she felt her own blood flood over her hands.

She was dying. She knew it.

She fell, face down, and closed her eyes, hoping it would be quick.

*　　*　　*

The pain ended a few minutes later. Bryna stared at her hands, noticing that they had turned silver and that she could almost see through them. She realised she wasn't breathing either. For the briefest of moments, she panicked, but then she came to the understanding that it wasn't a bad thing that she wasn't inhaling or expelling air. It wasn't necessary anymore. She didn't feel the need.

She was surrounded by grey mist. Bryna recognised this place. She had visited this desolate dimension once before, when she had the vision which told her to let Jaedin leave Jalard, but this time it felt different. Before, Bryna had only dreamt of it. Now, she was truly there.

And *She* was there again. The woman sat on an ancient throne of twisted tree trunks. Her ageless face was sharp and full of grim wisdom, and her hair was a dark grey mane which floated around her head weightlessly.

This time, Bryna knew who she was.

Verdana.

Bryna was dead, and it was time for the goddess to claim her soul.

Bryna held her head up defiantly. She was angry. She felt cheated. She didn't want to die. She didn't want her mother to die.

"Many spirits have passed before me this day," Verdana spoke in a voice which was somehow both seraphic and caliginous, which Bryna could not just hear, but feel all around her. "And the things I have seen through their eyes disturb me."

The goddess smiled grimly, and her eyes ventured from

Bryna's face to her neck. Bryna looked down and realised the necklace her mother had given to her had somehow travelled with her in death. The stone was glowing.

"Dark powers have been unleashed upon the world, and I fear that many more will pass my way in the future to come. But you... it's not your time yet. Come closer."

Bryna was scared, but she found herself unable to refuse the goddess before her. She climbed up onto the roots of Verdana's throne.

Verdana reached down and caressed the glowing stone with her fingers.

"It has been many aeons since I have seen the stone of Vai-ris, but I see that it has finally passed into the hands of someone who has the true bloodline of my daughter."

She looked Bryna in the eyes. The grey irises of the goddess up close were overwhelming. Bryna turned away, fearing that they would consume her soul.

"Understand, my child, that your path is one of great sorrow and responsibility. You will be both feared by humans and hated by gods. Death will be the curse of your existence and your greatest boon."

She pressed her palm into Bryna's forehead, and Bryna fell back into the grey mist.

"Go back, Bryna. Descendant of Vai-ris."

*   *   *

Bryna felt solid ground beneath her again, followed by a wave of nausea. She choked a breath of dusty air and opened her eyes to see the walls of her wrecked room around her.

She was back in Jalard.

She shifted, and looked down to see her gown was caked with blood, but the gaping wound in her abdomen was no longer a cause of pain. Bryna gasped. She knew it was impossible for her to have survived such an injury.

But she was no longer human. Bryna felt that fact within the core of her being. Her body felt as if she didn't belong inside it. Her skin was as cold as her faintly beating heart.

And then she began to hear the voices.

Help us, Bryna.

Bryna had always been sensitive to energies around her but

had never sensed *this* before, nor anything else so tangible. The dead souls of the village were calling out to her. She could *feel* them. Feel their anger.

She clawed at her face and let out a scream.

*   *   *

Bryna lay there for hours, still and silent, while the restless spirits spoke to her. She ignored them. She didn't like this new reality. She wanted to die again. To go back to the grey abyss.

But she wasn't free to leave her body behind and float into the sky like the apparitions around her, no matter how much she willed herself to.

The voices could not be ignored forever, and sometimes Bryna couldn't help but listen to them. Mostly, they were people from the village who felt angry and cheated over the way their mortal existence ended so abruptly. Bryna envied them. Unlike her, they were free. They could go to the afterlife in peace, but instead they were clinging to the *aythirrealm*. Bryna had experienced the blissful liberation death offered. Being confined to a human body again felt oppressive. Simple processes she used to take for granted, such as hunger, thirst, and the need to breathe air to stay alive, felt vexing and cumbersome.

One of the spirits that spoke to her was Tarvek. He came and sobbed a self-pitying story about how he drank his life away and never knew how to express the love he buried for his son. Memories from crucial moments in his life leaked out of his spirit and Bryna was able to assemble an accurate picture of the abuse Dareth suffered at his hands.

Go away! she commanded, and banished him. *You got what you deserved!*

For a while, Bryna became vaguely aware of feeling her brother's presence nearby. At one point she even heard him enter the house, but she didn't have the will to call out to him. It felt so far away and, after everything she had been through, reality seemed like a mere dream. How could she face him or anyone else in her current state?

It was only when Bryna became aware of her mother's spirit beside her that she began to come to terms with the reality of her situation. She felt a cold sensation on the back of her head. It was her mother running a hand through her hair.

Bryna, she whispered. *You need to get up*.

"I can't," Bryna mumbled from the floor. "I don't want this. I just want to die."

For years, our family have waited for someone to awaken the Stone of Vai-ris, Meredith whispered to her. *And you have finally done it. This is not a coincidence, Bryna. And you know it.*

"I don't want it!" Bryna choked "I'm a freak!"

You are not. You are special. And beautiful.

Her mother's ghostly hand continued to stroke Bryna's hair. It was soothing. Bryna finally let herself cry, and was forced to rub her eyes when the tears blurred her vision. It was the first time she had moved a single muscle for hours.

Bryna remembered that Jaedin was still alive. She could feel his distress through the link she had with him. He needed her.

She sat up. It was night now, and Bryna saw Teanar glowing through the window. Its light shone upon her stomach, which made her look at it. The wound had healed and closed itself; she didn't even have a scar. The only evidence which remained from her fatal injury was her gown, which was torn and sticky with blood.

Bryna pulled herself to her feet and became possessed by a newly found equanimity. She calmly walked over to her wardrobe and changed into one of her black dresses. And then she filled a bag with some of her possessions.

When Bryna walked down the stairs, she averted her eyes from the bloody remains of her mother. That no longer mattered. Bryna knew her mother still existed. She could feel her essence floating beside her. Bryna collected her medicine bag and made her way to the door.

She stepped outside, into the moonlight.

The monsters must have caught her scent or heard her, because some of them were already stalking towards the house. Bryna narrowed her eyes at them. They had done this. They had killed everyone. They had done this to her.

Bryna wasn't scared of them. Not anymore. The massacre had not only left Jalard swarming with angry, restless spirits who were not quite ready to depart yet, but the village was also teeming with residual *viga* these people left behind when their souls were separated from their mortal bodies. Both of these things were a source of power to Bryna.

Use us, Bryna.

We will help you.

Avenge us.

Bryna smiled. Now, she found their voices oddly comforting.

She knew what she needed to do.

Come spirits of Jalard, she called, raising her arms to the air. *You will have your vengeance tonight.*

The spirits swirled, spiralling around her. They gifted her with their energy, and in return, she gave them substance, turning them into glowing phantoms of light. Bryna saw her mother's face in one of them, but only for a brief moment. She soared away, like the others, and swooped down upon the monsters.

*   *   *

What happened after that, Bryna could not fully remember. The next memory she had was of sitting upon a hill just outside the village and watching it burn. A tear glistened down her cheek but she felt strangely numb. This place had been her home, once, but it was no longer a part of her. It was her past, and she was no longer the girl she used to be.

She walked into the night. It was time to find her brother.

*   *   *

We are the Descendants of Vai-ris, Jaedin. The Stone has chosen me, and it came at a heavy price. I made the sacrifice that came with it. I am neither alive nor dead. I never wanted this, but I can't hold it back anymore.

Carmaestre said we were born from incest. Is it true? Jaedin asked.

I don't know, Jaedin, Bryna replied. *But I sense it is not just the Stone that Carmaestre feels our mother stole from her; I think she loved our father too. Even if it is true, does it matter? Incest is forbidden among humans, but the bloodline of Vai-ris had to be preserved somehow.*

Jaedin said nothing. This was all a lot for him to digest. The thought that he and Bryna were somehow descended from gods was hard for him to take in.

Tonight is the Festival of Verdana, Bryna reminded him. *It is the night of destruction and rebirth. The night that the spirit world is closest to our own. This is the night of the year I am most powerful, and I am going to help you.*

Bryna! Don't! Jaedin called out. *You'll get yourself-*

Killed? Bryna finished for him, with a hint of dryness. *I am already dead, Jaedin. It is almost sundown. It is time.*

* * *

Bryna opened her eyes and looked about the room. Everyone had left apart from Rivan, who was still sleeping.

She went over to him and checked his pulse. It was steady. He was going to make it.

Bryna placed a hand on his face and stroked his cheek. *He is handsome*, she thought. If she was human, she might have even let herself be attracted to him.

But she wasn't human, and Bryna knew, in her heart, no man would ever want to lie with her.

"Stay here. Where it is safe, Rivan," she whispered. "I am going to help us."

She knew she had to leave now. Before any of the others tried to stop her. She made her way to the door and awakened her senses. Angry spirits were all around her, screaming for vengeance.

She was going to give it to them.

Chapter 22

The Festival of Verdana

It was the Festival of Verdana, but no citizens were celebrating in the streets of Fraknar that night. The only remaining survivors – those who were still human – were either hiding underground or within pockets of the devastation.

As the sun set, a strange tension filled the air – it was as if the city's very walls were aware of Shayam's ultimatum – and it swept into the streets like a baleful wind. A prelude for events to come.

But all was silent.

When night descended, the sky turned black, leaving only two crescent moons casting a dim luminescence upon the outline of the rooftops.

From the towering fortress, something stirred. The gate lifted, and hordes of monsters marched across the bridge and swarmed onto the streets. They had one purpose; it was time to hunt their prey. Their keen noses only dimly sensed the presence of humans, but they began searching the alleys and houses for an entrance to their underground lair. That night, they were determined to find a way inside.

A lone figure emerged from the darkness. A young woman, wrapped in a hazy purple aura. Glowing orbs of light swirled around her. She walked purposefully, without fear, almost serene.

The creatures nearby stared at first, wary that she did not seem afraid of them.

But the thunderous call of their master filled their minds, urging them to continue with their objective.

Hunt them down. Bring me the Stones. Hunt them all if you must! She is just a girl!

They barrelled towards her, but her gentle steps towards the walls of the castle didn't falter. When the first Zakara drew close, the purple stone hanging from her neck blazed with light, and the spheres spinning around her shimmered. They materialised, growing pearly white arms and legs. They assumed faces, taking on the appearance of men and women. They were translucent, ghostly, and glowed in the darkness.

The dead citizens of Fraknar were being summoned back.

A pair of the phantoms swooped down upon the Zakara – the one who got too close – and the creature shrieked as their pale forms collided into him. The creature's body dissolved in a cloud of smog.

Once there was nothing left of the Zakara but rendered flesh, the phantoms withdrew, returning to the woman. There were dozens of apparitions now, forming a circle around her. Their arms linked.

The monsters continued rushing. Some even let out a battle cry as they neared. The phantoms readied themselves.

As the first wave of Zakaras leapt at her, claws swinging, they were met by a wall of the glowing beings. Their claws ran through their transparent forms with little consequence.

The phantoms smote them. Monsters howled, flesh seared by their touch. They fought back with defiant rage. Each time a Zakara struck a phantom, the glowing beings lost some of their substance, but they did not injure nor tire. They simply ebbed away. Occasionally, a finishing blow would cause one of them to dissipate into a cloud of ethereal fog but, just as quickly as they faded away, more appeared. The woman summoned them in a tide which rippled and swelled.

The monsters received a new order from their master.

Attack the girl! She is the key!

Zakaras continued bounding towards her, newly determined. They came from every direction, but the glowing apparitions held their ground; a phantasmal shield between her and the horde. She was their master, and they would protect her with everything which bound them to this world.

She raised her hands to the sky, and her outline shone with amaranthine brilliance. The spirits swirled around her, stirring up a cyclone of wind which swept up her hair and the tassels of her dress.

She opened her mouth. No sound came from her lips, but the city felt the effects of her silent call. The land stirred, more phantoms appeared. They floated out of the ground, emerged from the houses. They lit up the streets and filled the sky.

Her arms fell back down to her sides and, as chaos

consumed the city around her she, once again, continued marching towards the fortress.

*   *   *

"These are the men and women who will fight for you," Kerdev said as he guided Baird into the room.

Baird scanned the group. He counted about eighty, in all. Some were wearing leather armour and had swords hanging from their waists; Baird guessed them to be Kerdev's mobsters and a few mercenaries. Jarndal stood at the front, and the warrior smiled when their eyes met.

The rest were a ragtag bunch. Fathers with axes more suited for cutting wood, farmers with bows, and Baird was sure that he recognised one of the women – who was holding a makeshift spear – as one of Kerdev's whores.

He found the youngsters at the back the most morally challenging. Baird could tell some had been just boys and girls not long ago. He wondered if they knew what they were in for.

Baird had led many into battle before, knowing some would not make it back but, on this occasion, he knew there was little chance of any of them returning.

Unless we stop Shayam, they are all dead anyway, Baird reminded himself. In circumstances like this, everyone had a right to choose between fighting or waiting to die.

"Thank you," Baird said to the outlaw beside him. "I promise I will do all I can to bring this to an end."

Kerdev nodded grimly. "I will wait down here with the others. If you don't come back by sunrise, we'll attempt an escape."

"Good luck," Baird said, repressing a sigh. He didn't want to tell Kerdev that running would be hopeless.

Baird turned his attention back to the mob before him and began to think of a speech. What could he say to motivate them and heighten their morale which wouldn't just be lies?

"You have one missing," Kerdev said, looking behind Baird and noting Bryna was not there. Just Kyra, Sidry, and Fangar. "The lass. The one Shayam named. You must take her too."

"No," Baird said. "Bryna needs to take of Rivan–"

Kerdev shook his head. "I'm sorry, Baird, but she has to go. I have given you these people, and in return, you've got to do this for me. I hate to make this about numbers, but I have dozens of children down here, and she is just one lass. I have healers who will take care of Rivan."

Baird didn't want to take Bryna with them. She was slow, and they needed to be swift if they were to stand any chance of fighting their way to the castle.

Three men burst into the room.

"Kerdev!" one of them exclaimed, panting for air.

"What's going on?" Kerdev narrowed his eyes at them angrily. "You're supposed to be keeping watch! Who's looking after your post?"

"You wouldn't believe what we just saw!" one of them gasped. "There was this girl! She–"

"A girl?" Kerdev repeated. "Can't you see I'm busy? Get back to your post, *now*!"

"But Kerdev, you've got to see!" he argued. "She walked right past us, and there was these lights–"

"You let her *out*?" Kerdev gasped.

The guard raised his hands helplessly. "We tried to stop her, but couldn't... you wouldn't believe it. There were these *things* flying around her. Kerdev, I saw my wife! She's dead but she spoke to me!"

If the man had been alone in his wild claims, Baird would have disregarded this story as the ravings of a madman, but there were two others with him, and all three had the bright eyes of people who had just witnessed something miraculous and profound.

And, when he mentioned a girl, Baird had a creeping suspicion who they were talking about.

"Where did she go?" Baird asked.

"She went outside!" one of them said. "We tried to stop her but–"

He paused as a chilling breeze swept through the room. Baird shivered. There was something unnatural about it.

And Baird was not the only person who sensed it. Everyone cast their eyes about them.

"Look!" one of the guards exclaimed, pointing upwards.

A small boy was floating across the ceiling. He was pale and translucent.

"Like that!" the man said, grinning. "There were more of them! They were following her!"

Everyone stared at the diaphanous boy in disbelief as he soared above them.

"Let's go..." Baird said. He didn't like being in the presence of magic and sorcery, but he pushed his discomfort aside. He signalled everyone to follow him.

"Wait!" Kerdev called. "Bryna—"

"Check our room if you want," Baird said over his shoulder as he walked away. "I think Bryna has already left."

*   *   *

From behind the walls of the fortress, high up in one of the towers, Miles watched as the Zakaras crossed the bridge and entered the city.

He had not seen Shayam since the meal they shared when he was first captured. Since then, he had been kept in confinement.

His prison was surprisingly luxurious. Miles had a personal garderobe, a dining area, a four-poster bed, and a large mirror in the corner. It had confused Miles at first – why would Shayam treat him to, what appeared to be, one of the finest rooms in the fortress? – but that mystery was solved when Miles discovered a door which allowed him access to the open roof on the top of the tower. It had a tremendous view of the city.

His old friend had a spiteful sense of humour, and he had given Miles a front row seat to watch the destruction of Fraknar.

When Miles looked down at the courtyard below, he saw an easy way to end his misery. He thought about what Grav'aen would do to him when Shayam handed him over. The long drop was a tempting way out.

But Miles didn't jump. He was to blame for all of this, and he owed it to the world to witness the outcome of his mistakes.

You helped create this, he told himself, as he watched the monsters swarm onto the streets.

*   *   *

Miles thought back to when he first met Grav'aen, eighteen years ago.

Back then, Miles had been young and idealistic. He had just left his father's estate for the first time to go to live in Gavendara's capital, Mordeem.

He wasn't sad to leave his home, for Miles had never been close to his family. His mother died from The Ruena when he was very young, which turned his father into a cold, bitter, and distant man. Miles' childhood was a lonely one, with only a hired nanny to show him any care and the books of his father's library to offer him distraction. It was in Mordeem that Miles finally found a place where he felt he *belonged*.

He enrolled himself at the University, and his undertakings there began in the School of Arcane Studies where he focussed on developing his long neglected aptitude for magic. This endeavour did not take him very long, for Miles soon learnt that he was Blessed by Diammna. As far as Blessings go, it was a powerful one, but limited in its scope.

It was in the School of Arcane Studies that Miles met Grav'aen.

A friendship between the two of them seemed unlikely at first, considering that Grav'aen was a powerful Psymancer and Miles' own abilities meant that his mind was one of the few in the world that Grav'aen could never probe. Or perhaps that was *why* they became friends. They certainly had much in common. Like Miles, Grav'aen was an idealist. They were both from broken homes and had lost loved ones to The Ruena. They both wanted to make a difference. Change the world for the better.

Within a few months, Miles' lessons in the School of Arcane Studies reached a dead end, so he went on to nurture his long interest in history. He and Grav'aen remained friends though and, a few years later, Grav'aen asked him if he would like to help him investigate some ancient ruins which had been recently rediscovered in the mountains to the north. Miles was more than happy to join his friend, seeing it as a chance to broaden his knowledge and maybe even – if he discovered something of value – gain some recognition. He soon found himself spending days at a time shining candlelight upon walls, translating runes and inscriptions written in Ancient. Much of the information Miles found in the beginning was boring, but he didn't mind because, for the first time, he felt like he was in his element.

He eventually came across a set of caverns, in which engravings detailed procedures that were claimed to make people stronger. Miles noted them down and showed them to Grav'aen that very evening. His friend was excited by the discovery. He believed it could even lead to a cure for The Ruena.

Miles had misgivings – countless examples from history, legends and myths came with a clear message that there were often consequences when one interfered with nature – but these feelings were outbalanced by his curiosity. He justified it by telling himself it was all for the greater good.

The studies began on a small scale. People at death's door were asked if they wanted to attempt a possible cure, and many willingly gave what life they had left to the cause. Grav'aen's project soon caught the attention of others, including academics from the University, skilled healers, and even young men like Shayam; men who came from rich, powerful families and brought more money and proficiency to the venture. In Gavendara, almost everyone knew someone who had died from The Ruena, so it wasn't hard to find people willing to dedicate themselves to finding a solution.

But some were prepared to achieve it at costs which were far too high.

Some of the experiments began to produce results that Miles found disturbing, but Grav'aen carried on regardless. Miles also began to suspect Grav'aen was using his telepathic abilities to influence people's minds and stop them objecting to the continuation of his research. There were only so many people Miles could see die, only so many times he could watch convicted criminals experimented on against their will, or peasants offering their healthy children because they desired the money, before Miles admitted to himself that it had all gone too far. But, by that time, he was in too deep. He had provided Grav'aen with crucial information which made everything they achieved possible.

Grav'aen had always spoken loathingly of their Sharmarian neighbours who were blessed with more fertile lands and free from The Ruena, and the subjects of his experiments were turning into docile creatures which Grav'aen could impose his will upon – with both of these facts in mind, Miles realised that it was inevitable that the things they were creating would one day be used to wage war.

But he was too afraid to defy Grav'aen, so he had no other option but to feign his support and carry on with the research.

One night, his dreams were disturbed by a vision. He found himself weightless, in a cloudy dimension of fog.

Before him sat the Goddess Verdana on a grand throne and, as she spoke to him, he didn't just hear her; he felt her voice in his mind. Everything about it was too vivid to be merely a dream. He knew her to be real. When Miles looked into her penetrating eyes, they crept into his soul and communicated a message beyond words. He realised the gravity of his actions. He became aware that, when his lifetime was over, he would pass through her hands.

And that thought terrified him.

She told him she had a task for him. He must find a way to pass on one of the Stones of Zakar into the hands of a Sharmarian. He would be a frail boy, with eyes of jade. Miles would know who it was when he met him.

The next day, Grav'aen asked Miles if he would like to become a spy and infiltrate the people of Sharma. His ability to shield his mind from Psymancers was an asset which made him the perfect candidate for such a mission.

Little did Grav'aen know how true that was.

* * *

Miles clasped hold of the merlon before him in despair as he watched the Zakaras swarm into the city. Creatures he'd helped to create.

He had done what the goddess told him, but it had all been in vain.

A few hours ago, Aylen had come to his room with a message from Jaedin. He told Miles that Shayam had learnt the secrets to harnessing the full potential of his Stone of Zakar – secrets that Jaedin didn't know – and therefore Jaedin was powerless against him.

A goddess made Miles risk his life and betray his own people for the sake of granting powers to a boy; powers which were not strong enough to save them.

And now, there was nothing Miles could do to stop Shayam.

*   *   *

When Miles ventured to Jalard, all those years ago, most of the villagers treated him with suspicion. He found them a cold and backward people. Stubborn and set in their ways.

With one exception. Meredith. She welcomed him into her family with open arms.

Miles was inexplicably drawn to the ageless witch. And her unusual children with their dark hair and fey eyes. The first time Miles saw Jaedin and noted the colour of his irises, he remembered Verdana's message. Miles wasn't surprised it was Meredith's family, out of all of the others in the village, whose son had a special destiny. Meredith and her children had an otherworldly aura which set them apart from most people. Bryna was a sweet girl, but she was mysterious and often hard to understand. Jaedin, on the other hand, was shy and timid, but Miles soon came to the realisation he was sharp of mind.

Very few of Jalard's children held an interest for scholastic pursuits; most of the youngsters left his study to never return after mastering the basics of reading and writing. Jaedin, however, became a frequent visitor so Miles gave him guidance. He taught him history, critical thinking, and the language of the Ancients.

Miles settled down in the lifestyle of the village, and Meredith's house became his second home. He knew he was letting himself get too close to the people he was destined to betray, but he couldn't stop himself. He grew to love the people of Jalard, for all of their simplicity. The thought that the only way he could save them was to one day betray them was always in the back of his mind.

When the twins grew into adolescence, Miles noticed a change in the way Jaedin acted around him. He often caught the boy staring at him from over the pages of a book while they were in his study. Jaedin started to act flustered and nervous when he was around him. It didn't take long for Miles to realise why the boy was behaving this way. He did his best to ignore it and hoped it would pass when Jaedin got older.

But it didn't. And, as Jaedin transformed from a timid boy into a handsome young man, Miles unwittingly found himself noticing him in a way he wished he didn't.

This shamed Miles. Not because Jaedin was a man, for Gavendarians did not have the same taboos as Sharmarians concerning relations between people of the same sex. Nor even because of the difference in their years, for Jaedin was an adult now and it wasn't uncommon – in both Sharma and Gavendara – for someone of his age to court or even start a family with someone of Miles' maturity.

It was because Miles had known Jaedin since he was a boy and had once been his mentor. To desire him in that way felt like a betrayal of trust.

When Meredith died, Miles only became even more determined to suppress his feelings for Jaedin out of respect for her memory. Meredith had been his friend, but Miles deceived her for all those years and betrayed her beyond forgiveness. Giving in to his desires for her son was a line he could not cross.

*　　*　　*

As Miles looked upon the city, he thought about all the people who died in Jalard and what he would have done differently if he could go back in time. He tortured his mind with the outcomes of his mistakes.

Most of all, Miles thought about the young man that he loved but deceived. Nurtured. Betrayed. Who believed himself a coward when the real coward was the man who ruined his life.

*　　*　　*

When Baird emerged from Kerdev's lair, the first thing he saw was a flash of light streak across the horizon. He ran out onto the street and found himself amidst a scene of chaos. Shimmering beings of white light were descending from the sky, swooping down upon Zakaras. The monsters fought back, screaming as they burned in ethereal fire.

He stared, wide-eyed, at the glowing beings. They seemed to be able to shift form at will. One moment they were just an orb of light streaking through the air, the next they assumed ghostly figures of men and women.

"Oh my gods..." Kyra uttered from beside him. She pointed to a group of the luminous phantoms. "That one looks like Dion! How can *he* be here?"

Baird shook his head. He didn't know.

"Well fuck knows what's going on here, but it seems to be working in our favour so let's not complain..." Fangar commented with a chuckle as he sidled up to them. "The castle is that way!"

He pointed up to the black sky ahead and, when Baird squinted his eyes, he could just make out the outline of four towers in the distance.

"And I'm sorry, but I have business to attend to," Fangar finished. "So I will see you there when you catch up!"

Baird opened his mouth to object but the words fell from his lips as Fangar shifted into his Zakara form, leaving just a pile of torn clothes where he had been standing. A monster galloped away on four legs.

"Wait!" Baird called. *We're supposed to stick together!* he thought as the renegade disappeared into the night.

"Watch out!" someone yelled.

Baird turned and caught sight of a Zakara leaping towards them from one of the alleyways. His hand went to his sword but a group of the warriors behind him beat him to it. They charged right past him, roaring a battle cry as they raised their weapons. The beast whipped its tail around in a full circle as they closed in but one of the men met the swinging appendage with his axe. The monster let out a shriek as it drowned in a sea of flashing steel.

A few moments later they all stepped away, leaving just a sanguine mess of body parts on the road.

Not bad for a mob, Baird thought, noting that they had dealt with the first attack without any direction and none of them appeared to have been injured, either. The encounter jolted them out of bewilderment, and now they were alert, waiting for Baird's command.

He looked to the direction of the castle and saw a long trail of ghosts and Zakaras fighting each other in the path towards it.

"Follow me, and keep your eyes open. Kill anything that

comes near!" he called as he raised his sword into the air and led the way.

Just a few feet ahead of them, Baird caught a glimpse of Dion's face on the body of one of the phantoms. The apparition smiled and then continued soaring down the street.

"It *is* Dion!" Kyra exclaimed as she ran after him. "He's leading us!"

* * *

Miles watched in amazement when the dots of light appeared in the distance. He leant over the wall, trying to figure out what they were as they floated down the streets and across the rooftops.

A cluster of them soared towards the castle, to a street not far from its outer walls. They flew in a tight formation, giving them the appearance of a glowing, nebulous sphere of light. A Zakara bounded towards the strange phenomenon and, when the monster reached it, the shining orbs dispersed, shifting into guises of human shape. They surrounded the monster, and ethereal fire poured from their hands.

Miles watched it all in disbelief. He had seen many a strange thing in his time, but none of them came close to matching this.

He became aware of a presence beside him. Turning his head, Miles gasped when he recognised the face hovering beside him.

It was Meredith. But she looked somehow both younger and older than he remembered her. Her flowing hair was like white fire, her face was free of all its wrinkles, and her eyes were gleaming with the wisdom one could only possibly obtain when they have passed beyond.

She smiled at him.

"She did it," she whispered.

"Meredith?" Miles gasped. "Is that really you?"

"Yes," she said, holding her pale white hand up to the black sky. "Bryna summoned us. She is the Descendant of Vai-ris, and she has awakened."

Miles turned his eyes back to the chaos rife in the city. Could it really be that Bryna was responsible for all this?

He remembered the legend of Vai-ris. The message they

had been given. The peculiar way Bryna had been acting. The strange glamour which all of her family seemed to have.

And it all made sense.

"I know what you have done, Miles. I know about you. Your past. And I have seen the way you... are, with my son," Meredith said. "And if I was alive right now, I would kill you."

Miles turned away in shame. Had she been watching from a window of the otherworld when he had held back the full truth from them all, or when he had let his desires get the better of him and kissed Jaedin?

"But I am dead... and being dead makes you see things differently..." Meredith continued. "We will discuss such matters later... if we have the chance. For now, come with me, Miles. He needs our help."

* * *

Kyra ran down the streets as fast as her legs could carry her, ducking and diving as debris from rooftops and burning houses crumbled into her path. Most of the Zakaras were too busy fighting off the phantoms to pay any attention to her.

Dion was always ahead of her, no matter how fast she ran. He was glowing in the night, gliding down the street with other spirits around him, and they moved as a collective entity, like a swarm of bees. They led the way to the castle, sporadically separating to deal with Zakaras who crossed their path.

"Kyra!" Baird called out to her. "Slow down!"

She turned around, realising that Baird and the other warriors were now twenty paces behind her, and cursed. She'd got so absorbed with chasing after Dion she'd got ahead. She ran back to join them but, just as she was nearing, she caught sight of a Zakara crawling across one of the rooftops above.

"Watch out!" she yelled, pointing.

Her warning came too late. The monster dropped, landing in the midst of a crowd of people. Everyone scattered, but a few were too slow and were flattened by the beast. The Zakara – large and green, with a reptilian head – lifted its neck to the sky and tentacles grew from its body.

One of the tentacles struck a man through his chest. He dropped his axe and kicked out frantically as the appendage came out of the other side of his back and lifted him from the ground. Some of the people around him tried to help by grabbing onto his legs, but they only made his plight worse. He screamed in agony as the monster and his comrades both tugged upon his body.

He was only dropped when one of the other warriors beheaded the creature, but by then it was too late.

"Come!" Baird called, urging them to carry on moving. Some of them gathered around their fallen comrade but it was clear they could do nothing for him. "We must move on!"

"Come, Kyra…" a voice whispered into her ear.

She turned, and Dion was standing beside her with that familiar grin on his face. His eyes and skin shimmered with the moonlight, and she knew that, this time, it was the *real* him. Not the imposter who stole his body but failed to impersonate his soul.

But then a stampede of warriors charged past her and Kyra leapt out of their path.

When she turned back again, Dion was gone.

Kyra sighed. She had fallen behind and was now at the tail of the group. She ran to make her way to the front of the horde again, but everyone suddenly skidded to a halt. Another wave of Zakaras had appeared.

Kyra scanned her surroundings to make sure they weren't surrounded and noticed a movement in the corner of her eye. A Zakara emerged from one of the buildings.

"Over there!" Kyra called to the woman in front of her as the creature pounced.

The woman jumped out of its path, and the monster missed her by inches. The woman had dropped her spear whilst dodging, so she drew out her second weapon – a rapier – and assumed a defensive stance.

Two pincers snapped down at her from above, she ducked and rolled.

Kyra rushed in to the woman's aid, closing in behind the creature as it prepared to pounce upon the woman again. She struck one of its legs with her sword, and the blade cracked through the creature's brittle bones. A coarse shriek rang from its mouth.

The Zakara scurried away with one of its hind legs dragging across the ground at a morbid angle, leaving a trail of ichor. The woman gave Kyra a brief nod of gratitude before she turned her attention back to the monster. It growled, and Kyra could see by the flexing of its muscles it was preparing to pounce again.

Kyra reached for one of her emergency knives and threw it. The blade stuck its carapace but bounced off. It caused the creature's attention to shift though, and it turned its black, soulless eyes upon her. Kyra braced herself for its onslaught but, while it was distracted, the other woman raced in to assist her and drew her rapier across the creature's throat. Its body went limp.

"You okay?" Kyra asked.

She nodded. "Thanks for that."

Kyra smiled grimly.

The woman opened her mouth to speak again but something dropped onto her from above and she fell. It was another Zakara; a small, simian one with a coat of black fur. It wrapped its body around the woman's shoulders and dug its claws into her neck, ripping her throat open. For a moment, the woman turned to Kyra in desperation, but her face abruptly went still and lifeless.

Kyra bit her lip to hold back a scream. The initial shock of what just happened was swiftly overwhelmed by fury. She charged, swinging her sword feverishly, catching the monster by surprise and knocking it off the woman's body.

The maimed creature shrieked as it fell, but bounced back onto its small legs. Kyra brought her sword down on it again. It dodged, and the edge of her sword scraped against the ground.

The creature jumped at her one last time but Kyra raised her sword to meet it. Her blade met its outstretched arms and Kyra drove forward, using the force of the creature's fall against it.

The monster and its dismembered arms fell to the ground, separately. The monster screamed, and its bleeding stumps wriggled. Kyra hacked off its head.

She caught her breath for a moment and then cast her eyes around to check for more signs of danger. It appeared the worst of the onslaught was over. The last few Zakaras were being picked off by the other warriors.

Kyra looked at the corpse of the woman and saw a glowing figure standing above her.

Kyra gasped. This new phantom had the same appearance as the woman who'd just been killed. She stood over her own corpse; an exact copy, only translucent and glowing. A glowing rapier in one hand. A spear of light in the other.

She wasn't the only one who had been summoned back. Kyra looked around her and saw that there were now several phantoms dotted throughout their numbers. They marched, once again, among their mortal comrades.

"Come," the phantom said to Kyra, ushering her to follow. "We move on now."

*   *   *

Jaedin scrunched his eyes shut and covered his ears but there was no way to escape the onslaught of painful sensations. He felt Zakaras from the city dwindling out like faint lights in his mind as they were burned away by the spirits of the dead. He caught glimpses of random events through their eyes but had no control over these visions. Occasionally, he caught a flash of a familiar face, and he would try to sustain that vision for long enough to gain an idea of their situation, but it was no use; just as quickly, the vision would end, and a new Zakara shared its pain with him.

But Jaedin did know one thing. His sister was raising the dead, and they were fighting back.

Shayam now had an obstacle in his way. But was it enough? From the visions Jaedin witnessed, Bryna was wielding onerous magic. He wondered how long she could keep it up, and at what cost to herself.

The Stone of Zakar in his forehead tingled again, but this time the artefact had been triggered by something closeby. A Zakara near to Jaedin was in pain. Jaedin tried to zone in on its mind and find out what was happening but was too late. The creature was already dead.

Something had killed it. He wondered if Bryna had sent some of her spirits to come and rescue him.

The door to Jaedin's cell burst open, but it was not a glowing spectre on the other side; it was a dishevelled, naked man, covered in blood.

Fangar.

"I found you," he said, grinning as his claws shrank back into fingers,

"Where are the others?" Jaedin asked. He ran to him and peered down the corridor. No one else was there.

"They're probably still fightin' their way through the town," Fangar replied. "I went on ahead."

He placed a hand on Jaedin's shoulder and looked at him with wild, feral eyes.

"Come," he said and handed Jaedin a sword. "Let's end this."

*　　*　　*

As they drew close to the castle, the fighting escalated. Scores of Zakaras stormed in from the shadows, but they were outnumbered by the phantoms which circled the sky and swooped down at them from above.

Sidry did not let this lull him into a false sense of security though. He kept his wits about him because they were still far from being out of danger.

"We're almost there!" Kyra exclaimed, sprinting past him.

"Kyra! Wait!" Baird called, but she continued running.

They turned a corner and saw the outer walls of the fortress. Something was going on outside the drawbridge. Globes of lights were swirling around in an elaborate dance. The peculiar display made Sidry forget his sensibilities. He ran.

As he drew closer, Sidry noticed a dark figure in the centre of the marvel. A woman. And he recognised the black dress she was wearing.

"Bryna!" Sidry realised, calling out to her as his legs gathered more speed.

She was holding her arms up to the sky, hair flailing, phantoms whirling around her.

"Bryna!" he called again, racing to reach her. He caught up with Kyra, and the two of them ran side by side.

She turned, but the face they saw was not Bryna's. Not as they had ever seen her before. Her skin was as white as the moon, and her eyes were blackened opals, dark as obsidian. The powers she was wielding seemed to have transfigured her almost beyond recognition.

Bryna... Sidry thought in dismay. *What has happened to you...* Her beautiful face had transformed into something lurid and ghoulish. He wanted to grab her and stop whatever it was she was doing to herself but was afraid to go near her.

The phantoms were dancing around her, waving their arms and swirling up to the sky. Their mouths were open. They sang a faint, ethereal song so sombre it almost brought tears to Sidry's eyes.

"I have opened the gates," Bryna uttered, in a voice which was dry and seemed to echo all around him. "You must go inside. I can't hold this up much longer."

"You did all of *this*?" Baird asked.

There was a burst of light, and Dion appeared before them. Sidry's eyes widened at the sight of his deceased friend.

"Bryna is the Descendant of Vai-ris," Dion said, standing beside Bryna. He crossed his arms over his chest. "She has sung us back into this world."

"But how, Bryna?" Kyra asked.

"There is no time!" Bryna shook her head. "You must go!"

Dion floated to Kyra and touched her face. At first, Kyra flinched, but she stilled herself.

"Go live a good life, Kyra," he said.

Dion then turned to Sidry and smiled. "You too, Sidry. I would ask you to look after her for me, but it seems someone else has already taken on that duty."

Sidry didn't understand but had no chance to ask. They were interrupted by Bryna's strange voice. "No time! You must finish it! Go to the castle! I will hold them off from here!"

"Bryna! Stop it!" Sidry pleaded. He could see the strain the magic was having on her. She looked almost inhuman.

"Go!" she screamed. With her blackened eyes it was hard for him to tell if she was looking at him or not. "I can't keep this up forever!"

"Come on, Sidry!" Baird roared into his ear as he dragged him towards the gates. "You heard her!

Chapter 23

Aylen's Redemption

Dareth and Aylen stood at the window and watched as the glowing phantoms of light swarmed the city. The beings were closing in on the castle.

"What are they?" Aylen breathed.

Dareth shook his head. He was worried. He didn't know what they were, but in his gut he knew that weird sister of Jaedin's was somehow behind it. It would also explain why Shayam and Carmaestre were after her.

He turned to Shayam for answers, but the Gavendarian was occupied. He was sitting in a chair. His eyes were closed, and the crystal he used to control the Zakaras was glowing.

"Shayam!" Dareth exclaimed.

No response. The Gavendarian was either ignoring him or too busy to hear.

Dareth walked over and snapped his fingers in front of Shayam's face. He had no patience for being kept in the dark anymore. He'd put his life in danger to help this man and was promised safety in exchange.

"What the fuck is going on!" Dareth yelled.

Shayam's eyes shot open. At first, they were glowing red from the power of the crystal, but eventually they cleared. Dareth saw fear in them.

"They've reached the castle..." he murmured in disbelief.

"Yes! They certainly have!" Carmaestre's voice tore across the room as she entered. "That damn bitch let them in! What's your plan now, *Lord* Shayam?"

He turned to her, at first indignant, but his expression became forlorn. "Is there nothing we can do to stop her?" he asked.

Carmaestre shook her head violently. "No! Don't you see it?" she said, motioning to the window. "She feeds off the dead, and you've certainly handed over to her an abundance of those things, haven't you! You *fool*! May I add that your choice of attacking on the night of the year the spirit world is closest to our own was impeccable! Grav'aen is going to have your guts for chicken feed! *If* you're lucky enough to survive this!"

"You never told me!" Shayam retorted, his face turning red with anger. "She's your fucking niece!"

"I didn't know how her power worked until now!" Carmaestre shouted back. She pointed at him with one of her long, black fingernails. "You're the one who's in charge of this operation – as you so often liked to remind me – and every step of the way you have ignored my advice! We wouldn't even–"

She was interrupted by a rumbling below. Dareth felt the wood beneath his feet shudder. Everyone turned their eyes to the floor.

"Carmaestre," Shayam said, composing his face into a calmer expression. "Get the waystone."

She frowned. "But Grav'aen said–"

"Just get it!" Shayam struck the arm of his chair. Dareth could tell that, whoever this Grav'aen person was, Shayam was almost more afraid of answering to him if he escaped than being hunted down by Baird and the others. "I'll deal with that when it comes. Just get us out of here!"

"As you wish," Carmaestre muttered and made her way back to the adjoining room. As she breezed past Dareth, their eyes met, but he turned away. He still found her attractive, but the revelation she was related to Jaedin came as a somewhat repulsive surprise.

"What's a waystone?" Dareth said, turning back to Shayam.

"It's Enchanted," Shayam replied. "It will vanish us from this wretched place, and we'll reappear in Gavendara."

"What?" Dareth blurted. That seemed a little farfetched to him.

Shayam narrowed his eyes. "Do you want me to repeat it a little slower for you?"

"Why didn't she want you to use it?" Dareth asked.

"They're rare. Very expensive. Grav'aen gave it to me but told me to only use it when I had captured your friends. It seems we have no choice now, though," Shayam explained. He then shooed Dareth away with a motion of his hand. "Now leave me. It will take her a while to activate it, and I need to buy us some time."

He closed his eyes, and the crystal in his palm glowed again.

Dareth sighed. He thought that once he handed Jaedin over to Shayam things would be simple – that he and Aylen could be free – but things had become even more complicated.

Dareth had always known that there was something not quite right about Bryna.

"What are we going to do?" Aylen whispered into his ear.

Dareth turned to his friend. He felt a wave of guilt for getting him into this situation but quickly suppressed it. If Dareth could go back, he would have done it all again.

Before, Dareth was a nobody, obliged to follow Baird's orders out of fear, but now he was a man. One who had earned his place among others.

He took a deep breath and reminded himself he was one of the only survivors from a devastated village. He'd even got away with murder. After all that, he would find a way to get through this. Somehow.

"It's not too late," Aylen whispered into Dareth's ear. "We could still stop him." He nodded his head in Shayam's direction. "When Baird gets here we can say–"

"No," Dareth said. "Baird would never forgive us. We picked our side. There's no going back now."

Dareth could tell his friend was not fully convinced. He saw uncertainty in his eyes. Conflict.

"Don't worry," Dareth reassured, placing a hand on Aylen's shoulder. "We'll get through this. You'll see."

*　　*　　*

The warriors charged across the bridge. They had fought their way to the dark walls of the castle, and now the arched entrance loomed over them. This was the final step of their journey. Many were nervous, but their sense of triumph fuelled them with courage.

Baird held his sword to the sky, and the sea of warriors followed, their weapons glinting in the moonlight.

Seven dark, disfigured shapes emerged from the opening.

Kyra braced herself as the monsters charged at them. The warriors around her all panicked and they scattered but had little room to move. Many of them collided into each other, and some fell and were trampled in a stampede.

Kyra retreated and squared herself up against a wall. A group of men ran past her with a rampaging Zakara at their heels. She saw a Zakara only a few feet away grab a man with its jaws and shake him around before throwing him up into the air.

The monster fixed its eyes on Kyra; it had chosen its next target.

It leapt at her, but Kyra ducked and rolled. A man came to her aid, charging in with his spear. The Zakara shoved his weapon aside and raked its claws across his stomach.

Just as Kyra was about to intercede, a flash of light blinded her.

When it ended, she opened her eyes. Sidry had changed into his Avatar of Gezra. He dived at the Zakara and, with a blur of his bladed arms, dismembered it. The monster made an ear-piercing cry of fury as its limbs fell to the ground and Sidry raised his blade to make a finishing blow.

Suddenly, another Zakara jumped upon Sidry's back. Sidry tried to shake it off but it clung on, sinking its claws into his shoulders.

Kyra spotted yet another Zakara preparing to attack Sidry while he was distracted, and rushed to his aid. Her sword met the hard surface of its black body and cracked its shell.

The Zakara jerked and turned to her with its dark, dead eyes. It raised its rawbone arms, and barbed fingers swooped down at her. She dodged and skirted. She tried to block with her sword, but another claw came down and grazed her shoulder. She cursed, raised her sword to block another strike, this time using her blade to twist its arms away. She rolled to the side and leapt back to her feet before it had time to turn. She charged in and thrust her sword at the exposed shell of its abdomen, this time breaking through.

It wrangled and screamed. Kyra held on to her sword, tearing through the flesh inside as the monster jittered around.

Eventually, it became still, and Kyra landed back onto her feet. She pulled out her sword. The Zakara collapsed to the ground with a shudder.

She caught her breath and wiped the blood from her hands. Her eyes quickly scanned the others; Sidry was landing the final blow to the only Zakara which remained, and the rest of the warriors were either examining the fallen or heading deeper into the castle. Kyra followed them to the end of the runway where Baird was waiting for them.

"What do we do now?" she asked him.

They were now in the courtyard. Kyra looked at the walls around her and suddenly felt very small. She had never been in a place so expansive before. She didn't even know where to begin searching for Shayam and the others.

"Split up into groups," Baird decided, raising his voice so the others could hear. "Search the place! If you find Shayam, kill him."

*   *   *

Aylen watched Carmaestre through a crack in the door. She was standing in the centre of the adjoining chamber with a grey stone in her hand, muttering words from an obscure language as she stroked it. Aylen didn't understand any of it but every now and then the stone glimmered.

The sounds of conflict in the castle were getting louder, and Aylen knew it was only a matter of time until someone found them. He prayed it would be before she finished the incantation.

"How long is she going to take?" Dareth muttered.

"She needs to tell it where we want to go," Shayam explained. "The world is a big place!"

Most of Shayam's men were in the courtyard now, fighting off the intruders. Only three remained in this chamber. They stood by his side. They were his bodyguards. Although they were still in human guise, Aylen could tell from the vacant expressions on their faces they were Zakaras. They would be Shayam's final defence if anyone found them.

If that happens, Shayam will be distracted. He will not bother watching his back, Aylen thought darkly.

His hand wandered to the dagger tucked into the waist of his leggings. He felt a temptation to do it there and then, but the bodyguards were watching, and Aylen knew he would only get one chance. He needed to wait for the right moment.

I'm going to make it up to you guys, Aylen promised, as he thought about his friends who were out there, fighting. *I'm going to make a difference.*

*　　*　　*

The castle was in mayhem. Its very foundations were rumbling, and Kyra could hear the sounds of swords hacking, walls crumbling, and cries of men in the final throes of death. Zakaras shrieked all around her.

She scampered through the corridors, swift and silent. She avoided any sign of conflict. She wasn't interested in killing Zakaras anymore. She was on the hunt for bigger prey.

She was going to kill Shayam.

She hugged a wall and peered into the corridor ahead. She had taken so many turns now she wasn't quite sure which part of the castle she was in anymore. It had not taken her long to get lost in this place.

She heard a sound ahead and hid behind the corner, pressing her back against the wall and quieting her breathing. She pricked her ears and focused on the footsteps she could hear. Human steps – too soft to be the heavy trundling of a Zakara – but she knew that didn't necessarily mean she was safe. Shayam's men tended to disguise themselves as humans most of the time. Until they wanted to kill you.

The footsteps were getting closer. She reached for her dirk. She didn't want to draw any unwanted attention to herself, so she decided it would be best to catch whoever this was out by surprise. Kill them swiftly.

When they drew near, she leapt out from behind the corner and brought the blade to their neck. She was just about to draw it across their throat when she recognised the face.

"Oh… it's *you*," Kyra muttered, as she remembered the last time she had held a knife to this man's throat. The day her family were murdered.

Miles.

"Kyra!" he exclaimed, his eyes lit up. "You're alive!"

Kyra cursed under her breath. Technically, he was an ally, but she'd never been able to trust him since that day. She was just about to begin interrogating him – ask him what he was doing wandering the corridors of Shayam's fortress freely – when she noticed a glowing figure.

"*Meredith*?" Kyra gasped.

She was just as Kyra remembered her, only her face had a perfect agelessness about it.

Kyra had always admired Bryna's mother. She was one of the few women from the village the men feared and, despite the countless tantrums Kyra threw because she didn't want to learn to stitch and weave with the other girls, the Devotee of Carnea had always been a kind and caring source of guidance and support. Kyra's esteem for Meredith was ingrained into her childhood. Just being in her presence made her feel safe.

Kyra lowered the dirk from Miles' neck. If Meredith trusted the traitor, then she would too.

"It's good to see you, Kyra," Meredith's lips parted, and a soft yet sovereign voice swept through the corridor.

"Where are the others?" Miles asked.

"They're here," Kyra replied, turning back to Miles. She realised this was no time for chatting and hearty reunions. She wasn't in the mood for swapping stories, she was in the mood for slitting Shayam's throat. "Where are you going?"

"We went to find Jaedin," Miles said, motioning to the corridor behind them. "But someone's already broken him out! He's not there!"

Kyra frowned. "Fangar went ahead. It must've been him. Do you know where Shayam is?"

Miles shrugged. "I don't know. They dragged me to his chambers once, but I was barely conscious."

"I know where he is," Meredith said. "I will guide you."

*   *   *

Jaedin followed Fangar up the last few circuits of the spiralling staircase. They reached a large wooden door at the top and stopped.

"This is it," Fangar whispered.

Jaedin nodded. He knew. It was the same tower he'd been escorted to when Shayam summoned him a day ago.

"There are three Zakaras in there," Jaedin warned, sensing them.

"I know," Fangar said, sniffing. "Are you ready?"

Jaedin nodded. He felt a tingle of fear, but it was distant. He possessed a new equanimity. Only a few minutes ago, he'd thought himself a dead man. He'd accepted it as inevitable. Now, he felt like he was living on borrowed time. That numbed his fear.

His fury was much stronger.

How much I have changed... he realised.

The Stone of Zakar in his forehead tingled. It was trying to warn him of something.

"They know we're here!" Jaedin realised. "They're coming!"

Fangar rammed his shoulder into the door. It swung open, and he charged into the room. Jaedin followed closely at his heels.

Jaedin spotted Shayam. The Gavendarian Lord stood on the far side of the chamber.

Jaedin hefted the sword Fangar gave him. He wanted to end Shayam then and there, but three figures were blocking his way. It seemed Jaedin would have to fight his way through them first.

The three men were clad in green robes, and Jaedin knew monsters lived beneath their human faces. He braced himself, expecting them to shift form, but they just stood there. No one made a move.

"What are you waiting for?!" Fangar growled at the three men blocking their path. He clenched his fists, and his body trembled. His legs twisted and grew, his hands turned into claws, his back arched, and his neck craned forward. Only his face remained human, apart from his teeth which became long and tapered.

Shayam stared at the display with his mouth gaping open. When Fangar's mutation was over, the Gavendarian Lord crossed his arms over his chest and regarded him. "Who are you? Why does my Stone have no effect on you?"

"Stop stalling and fight!" Fangar growled.

"Fangs..." Shayam muttered out loud as his eyes travelled down Fangar's body. "Claws... You look like a Zakara, yet..." He put a hand on his chin and one side of his moustache curved upwards. "You're that failed experiment I've heard about. 'Fangar'? Is that what you call yourself?"

"This is the last face you'll ever see!" Fangar spat.

"I see a problem with that," Shayam replied. The Stone of Zakar in his palm pulsed with red light and the three men in the middle of the room shifted form. One of them bulged outwards and grew a layer of thick green fur. The one in the middle: his body became covered in a crustaceous shell, and his arms turned into pincers. The third became tall and black, with several long, elasticised arms.

"There are three of them and one of you..." Shayam finished.

"*Two* of us!" Jaedin said as he brandished his sword.

"That soddy can barely hold a sword!" a voice jeered in the background.

Jaedin looked for the speaker and only then noticed that Dareth and Aylen were in the room. A cruel smile touched Dareth's lips, and Jaedin's hand tightened around the hilt of his sword. During that moment, he wanted nothing more but to run his blade through that face.

But between him and Dareth were Shayam and three Zakaras.

"So, *Fangar*," Shayam called out mockingly. "Let's see how you fare against the real thing!"

Fangar's legs flexed, and he sprang, circling his claws. The Zakaras scattered from his flashing talons. Two of them fought back, while the third broke away and closed in on Jaedin.

Jaedin held his sword between himself and the incoming Zakara. Memorisations of Baird's duelling lessons flashed through his mind, and he positioned himself into a protective stance.

The Zakara crossed the room on its thin, spidery limbs. It had a black, elongated body and an oval head with barbed yellow teeth. It lashed out, and Jaedin lifted his sword to meet the black tentacle. The edge of his blade met the creature's rubbery flesh and drew blood, but it barely seemed to notice.

Jaedin swung his blade, aiming for its head. The Zakara ducked, but one of its arms came out and pounded Jaedin in the abdomen. Jaedin put a hand to his stomach and backed away.

The monster came for him, swinging its arms. Jaedin dodged and ducked. He tried to surprise it with a twisting blade attack that Kyra taught him but, as he was in the motions, the monster struck him again.

Jaedin staggered. Tried to regain his balance. A tentacle coiled around his shoulder and pulled him in. The creature opened its jaws, and Jaedin's whole body went cold at the sight of its teeth.

"Jaedin!" Fangar yelled, leaping to his aid. The man-beast crossed the gap between them and, in one blurred movement, drove his claws into the monster's abdomen. A piercing scream rang from the creature's mouth and brown blood leaked from four parallel gashes in its belly.

Jaedin was dropped. He steadied himself. He was dizzy.

When his vision cleared, Jaedin caught sight of one of the Zakaras leaping at Fangar.

"Watch out!" Jaedin tried to warn him.

But he was too late. The monster drove its claw through Fangar's spine. Fangar's face contorted and, for a moment, time seemed to slow. Fangar and Jaedin looked at each other. Jaedin watched, in horror, as the end of the Zakara's pincer burst out from Fangar's stomach.

Jaedin rushed in to help him but, as he was doing so, caught movement in the corner of his eye. The other Zakara – the one Fangar wounded – had drawn itself back to its feet. Jaedin clenched his teeth together and faced it.

Before the creature knew what was coming, Jaedin buried his sword into its chest. Brown ichor sprayed all over Jaedin's hands but he didn't care. He screamed in fury, yanked the sword out, struck again.

The Zakara's wail came to an abrupt end.

Jaedin didn't even have time to register that he'd just made his first ever kill because, while he'd been busy, the green Zakara had dragged Fangar across the room, leaving a sticky trail of blood. Jaedin ran to him, but another Zakara stepped into his path and snapped its forceps at him. Jaedin backed away.

The Zakara dumped Fangar at Shayam's feet.

"I have to admit..." Shayam said, leering over Fangar. "I expected better."

Fangar was still alive, but his chest heaved from the effort it took him to breathe. He put a hand to the gaping hole in his abdomen and looked up at Shayam. He tried to say something, but it provoked a fit of coughing and he choked up blood onto his chest.

"I've heard the stories," Shayam continued. "You hit and run. Do as much damage as you can and leave before we can catch you. You, Fangar, have even killed the innocent if they stood in your way. What's changed? How did a ruthless killer like you end up giving his life for someone else?"

Jaedin felt his blood drain from his face. What Shayam said was true. Fangar just saved him.

"Could it be you now have a weakness?" Shayam asked.

"Stop it!" Jaedin screamed. He raised his sword. It was still dripping with blood.

"Don't move!" Shayam warned. He drew a dagger and pointed it to Fangar's throat. "Take *one* step closer, and I will end the very short moments this *thing* has left!"

Jaedin's lips trembled with latent emotion. His eyes met Fangar's. The man tried to say something, but he choked again, and more blood streamed from his mouth.

"Very quaint..." Shayam said, and a smile lit up his face. "It seems my enemies have bonded. You two are more than comrades, aren't you?" Shayam turned away from Jaedin and brought his face up close to Fangar's. "You put up a good fight before you turned away," he taunted him. "For a while, I was even a little worried. It was your feelings which stopped you defeating me, Fangar. I want you to die knowing that."

* * *

Meredith led them through the castle.

At one point, they passed a window, and Kyra caught sight of Zakaras and men brawling in the courtyard. She didn't spot Baird, but she heard his voice as he barked out orders. She heard a man scream so loud she was almost certain he'd been mortally wounded. Kyra resisted the urge to run out and join them. Help them. She wanted to, but she wanted to kill Shayam more.

The sooner Shayam dies, the better for us all, she told herself as she continued down the corridor. Shayam was the one controlling these monsters, and she knew the swiftest way to end this was to take out the source.

"How much longer?" she asked.

"Not far," Meredith called back. "We're almost there."

Kyra heard something behind them. "Wait!" she hissed, halting. She nocked her bow and pointing it down the corridor. "We're being followed."

"How many?" Meredith whispered, floating beside her.

Kyra strained her ears. It was hard to judge because of all the echoing, but she could make out several pairs of footsteps, all of them too heavy to be human.

"Four," she guessed. "They're Zakaras."

They were coming in fast. Kyra tautened the string of her bow and readied the arrow. A shadow appeared in the doorway. She released. The arrow flew down the passage, and the monster screeched.

It lifted its head, fixed its hollowed eyes on Kyra, and charged. Kyra reached into her quiver for another arrow. She was just nocking it to her bow when Meredith floated past her.

"Go!" she said

"But Meredith–" Miles said.

"*Go!*" the phantom exclaimed. "There are too many of them! Head down the corridor and up the staircase! I will take care of these things!"

Miles tried to object again but Meredith ignored him. She soared, manifesting a sphere of light in her hand as she descended upon the monsters. She threw it at one of them, engulfing the creature in flames.

While it burned, the other Zakaras leapt at her. Meredith's silhouette flickered.

"She's right!" Kyra realised. "There's too many of them. We need to go! Now!"

The Zakaras had Meredith surrounded. They ravaged her, tearing at her translucent form with teeth and claws. Ethereal fire poured from her hands, burned them, but they didn't relent. Every time they struck her, her glowing figure dimmed like a waning candle.

"But she–" Miles muttered.

"She's already dead!" Kyra reminded him. "And unless you want to join her, *move!*"

She grabbed Miles' arm and dragged him away. As they fled, she turned and took one last look at Meredith. Their eyes met, and Kyra hoped she knew how grateful she was.

*　　*　　*

"Carmaestre!" Shayam yelled. "Is the waystone ready yet?"

"I need more time!" her cacophonous voice shrieked back.

Jaedin was startled when he heard Carmaestre's voice. It was coming from a door on the other side of the chamber.

Could it really be that she was preparing a waystone?

Jaedin knew what waystones were. Many people considered them merely a myth, but Jaedin had read about them and knew that they existed. They were just extremely expensive and hard to come by.

He's trying to get away! Jaedin realised.

On the other side of the room, Dareth bared his teeth in a smug smile. Jaedin glowered at the boy who'd made his childhood a misery. Dareth betrayed them all, and now he was trying to escape. He was going to get away with it!

"Fight me, you coward!" Jaedin screamed at him.

Dareth's eyes lit up at the challenge. "I thought you'd never ask!"

"No!" Shayam yelled.

But Dareth ignored the Gavendarian. He drew his sword and marched towards Jaedin.

"Stop Dareth!" Shayam shouted. He extended his hand and a stream of red magic flowed from his palm. A wall of light manifested in the middle of the room, blocking Dareth's path.

"Let me kill him!" Dareth screamed. He tried to push his way past the barrier but it flashed and propelled him backwards.

Shayam shook his head. "We must take him *alive*."

"I'm not going anywhere!" Jaedin yelled at them.

The Zakara in front of Jaedin stirred into motion again, as if it had just roused from sleep. Its cadaverous eyes looked at Jaedin.

"You didn't think I was going to go without you, did you?" Shayam asked Jaedin as the Zakara closed in on him. "Your damned sister has ruined everything, but if I bring *you* back, at least I won't return completely empty-handed."

Jaedin backed away from the monster but came up against a wall. He felt the cold stone against his back. His heart raced. He had nowhere to run.

The Zakara reached for him with its pincers. Its forceps flexed.

Suddenly, Jaedin heard the sound of piercing wind. An arrow burst into the Zakara's side. It shrieked.

Jaedin looked towards the doorway and Kyra marched into

the room. She reached into her quiver for another arrow and nocked it to her bow.

"They're here!" Dareth exclaimed. He rammed his fists at the wall of energy, but the field remained. "Let me through, Shayam!"

Shayam ignored him. His eyes were drawn to the second figure that had just entered the chamber.

It was Miles.

"Jaedin," Miles called, as he and Shayam stared at each other. "Are you okay?"

Jaedin nodded. *I am still alive... but I can't say the same for Fangar...* he thought sadly.

Jaedin looked at the body beneath Shayam's feet. Fangar had stopped moving.

Don't let his sacrifice be in vain, Jaedin told himself.

Kyra loosed an arrow at Shayam, but the field of red light in the middle of the room flashed and it bounced away. Shayam watched as it clattered to the floor and narrowed his eyes.

"Kill them!" Shayam yelled at the Zakara who'd cornered Jaedin.

The Zakara turned away from Jaedin, pulling the arrow out of its flesh as it marched towards Kyra. Kyra readied herself, discarding her bow and drawing her sword.

When it reached her its arm came swooping down, but she raised her weapon and its forceps met the sharp steel of her blade. They remained locked for a moment, but the monster was stronger and pushed Kyra back.

Jaedin ran to her aid, leaping at the creature from behind and hacking one of its legs. The monster shrieked and spun to face him, its arms flying wildly. One of its pincers swerved dangerously close to Jaedin's neck but he ducked.

The creature righted itself and came for Jaedin, screaming in rage. Its damaged leg trailing across the floor, it limped. Jaedin skirted around it, taking advantage of the creature's lack of mobility while he considered his tactics. He carefully watched the movements of the creature's most dangerous weapons; its chelae, which were both dark and shiny, with red tips. The right one swung towards him, but Jaedin blocked, and the two forceps snapped together in front of his eyes. The left one then came next, and Jaedin dived.

Jaedin rolled back to his feet and took a moment to gather his wits while the creature stumbled towards him again.

Kyra appeared behind it, her sword a silver blur as she swung down on its arm. The bony, elongated limb cracked off and rolled to the floor, leaking blood.

The Zakara hollered, thrashing its remaining pincer at her. Kyra dodged and, while the creature was distracted, Jaedin found an opening. He tried to thrust his sword into its body but the blade bounced off the hard shell of its exoskeleton. The monster roared again and turned its attention back to him.

Jaedin retreated, but the monster went berserk, charging as fast as its crippled leg could carry it. Kyra came to Jaedin's aid again, rushing in from behind and severing the remaining leg.

The monster fell onto its back, wailing. Kyra smiled and brought her bloodied sword down again. This time on its neck.

The body jerked one last time as the blade tore through its throat, and then went limp.

Kyra caught her breath and wiped some of the sweat from her brow.

"*Aylen?*" she said when she noticed him. "What the fuck are you doing *there?*"

Aylen turned his eyes to his feet in shame. He couldn't even look at her.

"You know this doesn't change anything," Shayam said. "You have saved a mere corpse of this town, but this is far from over."

"Yes, you're right!" Kyra said, raising her sword. "This isn't over yet!"

She drove her sword into the barrier. The wall of energy flashed and sent her reeling back, but she clenched her teeth and struck again.

The expression on Shayam's face became concerned. He turned back to the doorway behind him. "Carmaestre! Hurry up!"

"I'm doing it!" she screeched back.

"He's using a waystone!" Jaedin yelled at Miles. "He's trying to get away!"

Kyra's face twisted into an expression of grim

determination. She hefted her sword and continued to assault the wall of energy. Each time she struck, it flickered, and Shayam flinched from the effort of keeping it alive. Jaedin realised that, even though it was merely an irrational act of rage on Kyra's part, she was draining Shayam's *viga*. He could see no other way for them to get to him before the waystone was ready, so he ran in and helped her.

The first flash of light as his blade met the shield almost knocked him over. He clenched his teeth together and charged again, this time steadying his weight on the back of his heels.

"Kyra," Miles appeared behind them. "Once you get through, you can't kill Shayam. Not yet."

"Screw that!" Kyra yelled back as she thrashed her sword, continuing her barrage. "He's *mine!*"

Miles opened his mouth to argue but something on the other side of the room grabbed his attention. Jaedin followed his gaze and noticed that Aylen had a dagger in his hand. He was staring at Shayam intently as he lined up the blade with his eye-line. He rocked it back and forth.

And then, with a flick of his arm, Aylen sent the blade spiralling towards Shayam.

"*No!*" Miles yelled as the blade closed upon the back of Shayam's head.

Just before the dagger struck, a sphere manifested around Shayam and there was a flash of light. Shayam flinched. He looked at the dagger as it skidded along the floor and his eyes widened.

The room went completely silent. Aylen stared in dismay at the blade which failed to meet its target. His guilty expression made it clear to Shayam who the culprit was.

Shayam's eyebrows drew together. "Kill him," he said, pointing at Aylen.

The Zakara beside Shayam stirred into motion again. It lumbered towards Aylen, its footsteps heavy on the floor.

"No!" Kyra screamed, resuming her affray upon the barrier.

At first, Jaedin could only stare in horror as the fuzzy being closed in on Aylen. The Zakara's protuberant muscles bulged as it marched.

Then the gravity of what was happening hit him. He

snapped out of his stupor.

I need to stop him! he realised.

Jaedin briefly attempted to activate his own Stone of Zakar, but was met by a wall and realised it was futile. Shayam had pulled all his focus into controlling that one Zakara alone – abandoning the rest of the creatures in the city to their own devices – and Jaedin's command over his own Stone of Zakar was still weaker than Shayam's. He couldn't pierce through.

So Jaedin instead continued his barrage on the wall of energy, praying he and Kyra could exhaust Shayam's *viga* and breakthrough before the monster killed Aylen. He found himself possessed of a speed and strength he never knew he had.

But it wasn't enough. Jaedin watched, helplessly, as the Zakara reached Aylen. It had its back turned so Jaedin didn't even see what it did to him. He just saw the movements of its arms and heard Aylen's muffled screams.

Dareth tried to intervene and help Aylen, but the monster just shoved him aside.

Shayam smiled, and the stone in his hand continued to glow. He pointed it towards Aylen, commanding the creature to carry on clawing him.

They were killing Aylen. And there was nothing Jaedin could do about it.

Jaedin then noticed something move beneath Shayam's feet.

It was Fangar's corpse. Stirring.

Is he still alive? Jaedin wondered.

The man-beast opened his eyes and his face twisted into an expression of pained anger. The shape of Fangar's head began to shift. His jaw stretched out, and his teeth grew longer and sharper. Fangar's body was shifting form again, becoming darker and leathery. He looked more monstrous now than Jaedin had ever seen him before.

Once Fangar finished shifting, he rolled over. A trail of blood still oozed from his body, and he was moving so jerkily Jaedin could tell he was in an extraordinary amount of pain.

But Fangar was, somehow, alive.

Before Shayam even became aware of what was

happening, Fangar's jaws snapped around his wrist.

Shayam screamed. It was one of the highest screams Jaedin had heard that entire night.

The shield flickered. Jaedin rammed his shoulder into the waning barrier once more and tore through. He ran, brandishing his sword. The next thing he knew, he was on the other side of the room, driving his blade into the monster's back. The creature jerked, and Jaedin made a hasty retreat, pulling his sword out. Blood ruptured from the wound, and the creature turned and faced Jaedin, baring its teeth.

It charged. Jaedin sidestepped from its path and Kyra ran in, meeting the creature head-on. The monster shoved aside her sword with a heavy bash of its arm, and Kyra rolled to stem her fall. Jaedin saw an opening and drove his sword at the monster's side, but the Zakara was aware of him this time. It raised its foot and kicked him away.

Jaedin felt the impact on his chest and flew backwards. He landed on the floor.

To Jaedin's surprise, Dareth rushed in to aid them. He was red-faced and yelling in fury as he charged at the beast. He pulled out a dagger and stabbed the monster in the back. The creature twisted around to face him.

Jaedin leapt back to his feet and ran in to help. The monster was swiping at Dareth with its paws, and Kyra rushed back into the fray too, launching herself onto its back. The creature wriggled and writhed to shake her off, and her legs swayed around the room wildly. She wrapped her arms around its neck and clung on. The Zakara caught Dareth with one of its wild swings and knocked him away. Jaedin rushed in while it was distracted, pointing his sword at the monster's midsection. The Zakara was too busy trying to shake Kyra off to notice him coming. He drew close and drove his sword into its belly.

Claws came down and raked his shoulder. Jaedin gasped. Lines of pain enflamed his flesh. He felt his blood trickle warmly down his arm. He fell back and placed his hand on the torn flesh at his collar.

When Jaedin looked up again, the Zakara fell, making one last final roar as it collapsed with the handle of Jaedin's sword protruding from its belly.

Kyra and Dareth ran to Aylen's side.

Jaedin winced, trying to ignore the pain as he forced himself back to his feet. He limped over to join them.

"I'm sorry," Aylen wheezed between laboured breaths of air. "I let you down… but I hope I–"

"Don't worry, Aylen," Kyra said, touching his shoulder. She tried to smile reassuringly, but Jaedin could see that she was holding back tears.

Jaedin looked closer and saw why.

Aylen's chest and stomach were ripped open and mangled, and his organs were dangling from his body. Jaedin knew that there was nothing they could do for him. It was a miracle he had even lasted this long. He had lost a lot of blood, and his olive skin had almost turned white.

A smile touched Aylen's face. "I'm just glad I helped."

Tears poured from Jaedin's eyes. He remembered his last encounter with Aylen. He doubted him. Scorned him. He wanted to say he was sorry but, when he opened his mouth, the words wouldn't come. Their eyes met, and Jaedin saw a decade's worth of apologies in Aylen's gaze. The two of them had been close once. Aylen never stopped caring. Jaedin just didn't see it.

"Aylen, why did you do it?" Dareth croaked.

Kyra glared at Dareth. She had murder in her eyes, and Jaedin didn't blame her. If he still had his sword, he'd have been tempted to run Dareth through himself. Could he not see this was his fault?

But now wasn't the time. This was Aylen's final moment, and he deserved better than to see his friends slay each other.

Aylen didn't respond to Dareth. He looked at Kyra. The pain on his face just from the effort it took him to breathe was clear.

"I did it for you," Aylen said to her. "I wanted you safe. I wanted you to love me."

"I do love you!" Kyra said, her voice cracking.

Aylen shook his head weakly. "You don't. Not like…"

He looked up at her one last time, and Jaedin witnessed the moment when the light left his eyes.

"I…"

Aylen's head dipped.

He was gone.

Kyra wailed, finally letting her tears flow. She reached

forward, wrapped her arms around Aylen's lifeless body, and cried into his shoulder.

* * *

Dareth stared as Kyra held Aylen's corpse in her arms.

At first, his mind was blank. All he could do was watch. It was all so sudden. All too much for him to comprehend.

But then his blood began to boil.

Aylen had not even looked at him. His final moments were for her.

He died for *her*.

It was all *her* fault. Aylen sacrificed himself for *her*, the reckless, emotional fool.

Aylen had always been *Dareth's* friend. For years, it had been just the two of them. What gave her the right to wrap her arms around him? To be the one he said his final words to? She barely even knew him.

* * *

"Kyra!" an urgent cry pulled her out of her anguish.

When Kyra heard Jaedin's warning call, something inside her knew what was coming and she dived out of the way. When she looked up, she saw the flash of Dareth's blade stabbing down upon the spot she had been only a moment ago.

Shit! she thought. She should have guessed the truce between them would be over after Aylen drew his last breath.

Dareth glowered at her with madness in his eyes. She rose to her feet and stared back at him. Her whole body quivered with anger. She clenched her jaw as her rage sent waves of tension through her entire body. The last time Kyra felt like this, the only way she could deal with it was to take a blade to her own flesh.

This time, she was going to take her blade to Dareth.

She had always despised him. Now she had an excuse to kill him.

"Jaedin," she murmured when she caught him retrieving his sword in the corner of her eye. "Stay back."

"But–" he began to object.

"*Go!*" she yelled. "This is *my* fight. Check on the others!"

She reached into her belt for one of her daggers – a large one – and brought it out of its sheath. Dareth held his own blade out before him and smiled callously.

There was no signal. They didn't need one. They both charged.

Kyra jabbed her knife from every possible opening she could see to his body, but he kept dodging and deflecting. Their blades met in the middle with a clash and, for a moment, they were face to face. Dareth tried to push her back, but Kyra sidestepped and twisted away.

Their weapons flashed between them in a flurry of thrusts and parries. They grappled around each other. She wasn't even fully aware of what moves she was using. She let her anger guide her.

The end of his blade cut into her thigh, and she bit her lip. She jumped away and took a quick glance at the blood running down her leg to make sure it wasn't fatal. She ignored the pain. Charged in again to give him payback. She aimed for his neck but his blade met hers and they locked once more. She raised her foot and kicked him in the chest.

He flew back and collided into the wall.

Kyra smiled grimly. She had him now.

She was just about to finish him off when a woman appeared out of the doorway beside him. Kyra opened her mouth in shock at the sight of her face. She looked like Meredith but Kyra knew it wasn't her. Her hair was too dark. Her eyes were cold, and her face was cruel.

The woman leant down and placed her hand on Dareth's shoulder.

"Who the fuck are you?" Kyra asked.

The woman just smiled back and opened her hand to reveal a stone glowing.

With a flash of blue light, they were gone.

*   *   *

Jaedin ran to Fangar's side just as his body was shifting back to its human guise. The rogue rested his back against the wall. He seemed weary but no longer in pain.

"I thought you were dead," Jaedin whispered.

Fangar smiled faintly.

Jaedin looked at Shayam. The Gavendarian was staring at the bleeding stump where his arm once was. "Animal!" he wailed. "He bit my fucking arm off!"

Jaedin kicked Shayam in the chest. The Gavendarian whimpered and curled up into a ball. Jaedin got a peculiar pleasure out of seeing the man responsible for ruining his and so many other lives now so pathetic. He drew his foot back and kicked him again. This time harder.

Miles interceded, grabbing Jaedin by his shoulders in an attempt to restrain him. "Stop it!" he said.

"Piss off!" Jaedin shoved Miles away, driving his elbow into his chest. "This isn't about you!"

"Jalard was my home too…"

"Not it wasn't!" Jaedin turned and squared up to him. "You were faking it the whole time!"

"Jaedin, please, *listen*!" Miles said, looking into Jaedin's eyes.

Jaedin clenched his fists by his sides. He wanted to hit Miles across the face but couldn't do it. No matter how many times Miles' loyalties came into question, Jaedin's heart would never fully let go.

He wished that Miles didn't have such power over him.

"I've figured it out," Miles said. "Shayam says your Stone of Zakar is useless because you don't know *how* to use it. Well… Shayam has all of that. In his *mind*. We can get it from him."

If I psycalesse with him, Jaedin realised.

But did he *want* to?

Jaedin knew if he did this, he would open a door and his life would never be his own anymore. He wouldn't be able to study at the Academy and live a peaceful existence surrounded by books. He would be expected to fight until all of this was over.

All that this struggle had caused him so far was pain, and as long as he had the power to help, people like Baird would always be dragging him from one situation to another.

Jaedin was brought out of his thoughts by the sound of footsteps. He turned around. It was Kyra. She had a murderous look in her eyes and a dagger clenched in her fist. She was marching towards Shayam.

"Stop!" Jaedin yelled.

He blocked her path and grabbed her by her wrist.

"What are you *doing*?!" she screeched. The knife quivered in her hand as she tried to free herself. The look in her eyes was one of cold anger. "Don't listen to Miles' crap! Let me *kill* him!"

"Soon…" Jaedin whispered into her ear. "Soon… But not yet."

"Kyra," Miles implored. He held up his hands as he approached her. "Shayam is just one man. He is but a pawn on Grav'aen's chessboard. There are others out there. And they are far more capable and cunning than he is. You want revenge, don't you?"

She nodded her head stiffly.

"You want to kill *everyone* responsible? Not just this man?"

Kyra looked at Shayam, and the sight of him made her jaw quiver and her hand tighten around the dagger.

But, eventually, Kyra turned back to Miles and nodded.

"If you want to do that, I can help make it happen," Miles said. "And, when this is all over, and I have done all I can to help you get your revenge, you can even kill *me* as well if it makes you feel better… I just need you to let me do this one thing to make it all possible. Will you let me?"

At this point, Jaedin knew that Miles was lying. If there was one thing Jaedin had learnt about Miles recently, it was that he had a remarkable drive for self-preservation. Miles would never sacrifice himself needlessly. When this was all over, he would never give his life away.

He was even better at deceit and manipulation than Jaedin originally believed.

Nevertheless, he won Kyra over this time. She nodded.

* * *

"You're going to reveal everything to me," Jaedin said coolly as he placed his hand on the cowering man's forehead. "All the secrets to using the Stone of Zakar."

"And if you don't," Miles said, pressing a blade to Shayam's groin. "Then I promise you, the pain you are feeling right now will be a mere tickle compared to what I will do to you."

Shayam was pale from loss of blood. Even without Miles' threats, he would have been too weak to object. He closed his eyes in solemn acceptance.

Jaedin slowed his breathing and awakened his inner self. The room around him disappeared. All that existed was his *psysona*. He reached into Shayam's mind and spiralled into a streaming vortex of his consciousness. Thoughts. Memories. Disjointed information. The thoughts rippled frantically from waves of fear. For a brief moment, Jaedin felt all of Shayam's pain, but he blocked out the sensory feelings by forming a barrier. He calmed his mind. He calmed Shayam's mind, then delved into his thoughts. The Gavendarian opened up to him without a fight. His mind became still.

Jaedin began to search through his memories for what he needed.

Hello Shayam, Jaedin said. *Tell me...*

*Tell me **everything**...*

*   *   *

When Jaedin finished, Miles held him by his shoulders and led him away, knowing the young man might not have the stomach to witness what was about to come next. Miles didn't care to see it either.

"Kyra!" Miles called over his shoulder. "He's all yours."

Kyra's face brightened, and she walked over to Shayam.

"I have been dreaming about this moment for a long time," she whispered, leaning over him so that their faces were close. She playfully stroked the point of her dagger across his cheek, making a faint red line. "A. Very. Long. Time."

"No!" Shayam begged. "Please! No! Miles! Help me! She's–"

Chapter 24

Farewell to a Friend

The end of the Festival of Verdana was marked by Ignis breaking the sky and streaking beams of light upon the devastation. The phantoms faded away. The city became silent.

Sidry looked at the corpses around him. The grass was red and sticky, and the combined dirt and ichor oozed in puddles beneath his feet. A while ago, such a sight would have sent Sidry into a fit of retching, but now he had become all too used to it.

The handful of warriors who had survived the night were now wandering around beheading the corpses so they wouldn't rise again.

Sidry decided to help them. He readied his sword and walked to the nearest body. He was just about to swing his blade down upon its neck when its eyes snapped open. Sidry hesitated, wondering whether this man was a survivor who needed attention. The man's lips parted.

"If I am speaking right now, it is because I am no longer human," he said, but Sidry heard those words not just from his lips alone. They echoed all around him. Many of the other corpses spoke them too. "I am a monster. I am being controlled," the voices uttered in unison. "I may have the face of someone you cared about, but I am dead. I am no longer that person. If I am left this way, I will try to kill you, eventually.

"This is why I must be destroyed. The fight is over. You can all come outside again. If you can hear this, you are a survivor. Goodbye."

The corpses then began to jitter and shake. Blood ran from their noses and ears.

Sidry smiled. It was a morbid sight, but it brought good tidings.

It meant Shayam was dead and Jaedin was in control of the Zakaras now.

* * *

When Jaedin came round, his body was shaking.

He'd only just acquired the secrets to using his Stone of Zakar, but already he'd performed something very advanced.

He knew implementing his new abilities on such a large scale so soon was risky, especially as tired as he was, but Jaedin wanted to end it all before anyone else was killed.

With Shayam gone, Jaedin had exclusive control over the creatures. If Jaedin wanted to, he could have kept them alive and put every one of them to his bidding.

But he knew in his gut that utilising Zakaras – even if it was for the purpose of good – would be morally reprehensible. Some things were just wrong no matter what the circumstances or intentions were. Jaedin was not going to cross that line.

So he destroyed them. Each and every one.

It was only when Jaedin opened his eyes again that he realised just how exhausted he was.

"Are you okay?" Miles asked him, putting a hand on his shoulder.

As Jaedin's vision cleared, he looked into Miles' eyes and this time he *knew* his former mentor desired him. There was no mistaking it.

"I can't…" Jaedin said and turned away. He looked at the wall. The ceiling. Anywhere but Miles. "I'm not going to let you manipulate me."

Miles expelled a long breath of air and removed his hand from Jaedin's shoulder. "I don't want to–"

"You *do*!" Jaedin exclaimed. "You manipulate people! It's what you do. I have seen it. And I am not going to let you do it anymore."

"Jaedin," Miles implored him. He reached for one of Jaedin's hands but Jaedin pulled it away.

"When I was in Shayam's mind, I saw things," Jaedin said. "Shayam trusted you too, and you betrayed him. You are a liar, Miles. It is what you do… I can't trust you anymore."

Jaedin had made the most of the opportunity when he had access to Shayam's thoughts and found out all he could about Miles. Some of the things he saw troubled him. Shayam had known Miles for a long time. He had witnessed him slither his way up the social ladder of Mordeem, bedding women to gain their husband's secrets and deceiving those below his status to curry favour. He was cunning. Calculating.

"Whatever you saw was from Shayam's perspective," Miles tried to explain. "It was a long time ago... I was... different. I know I have been deceitful in the past, but I have changed. The lies were to help you."

Jaedin shook his head. "I saw *everything*, Miles. I have seen the horrible things you have done. The help you gave to them. The Zakaras wouldn't even exist if it wasn't for you!"

Miles hesitated and then chose to say nothing.

"And do you know what else I find interesting," Jaedin said. "I've seen Shayam use magic before and his *viga* was always red. But when Aylen threw that dagger at him the shield which saved him wasn't the same. It was grey. That is the colour of *your* magic, Miles."

Miles didn't even try to lie his way out of that one. His jaw dropped and he turned away. Unable to hide his guilt.

"I know why you did it," Jaedin continued. "If Shayam died, I would have never obtained the secrets of controlling the Zakaras from him. You were just doing what you always seem to think you are doing – making sacrifices for the greater good of all – but that will never change the fact that, if it wasn't for you, Aylen might still be alive. For that, I will never forgive you."

Miles looked like he was on the verge of tears, but Jaedin didn't know whether or not it was genuine. He didn't know what to think of the man sitting next to him anymore.

"Are you going to tell Baird and the others?" Miles asked.

"About what?" Jaedin asked. "About how you helped create the Zakaras? Or how Aylen is dead because of you?"

"Both..." he whispered.

"No," Jaedin shook his head. He considered it. And he knew that he should, but he couldn't. Kyra would kill Miles, and Jaedin had seen too much bloodshed that day. Too many people that he cared for die.

"Why?" Miles asked.

Jaedin paused. He didn't know why. He guessed that it was because there was still a part of him which wanted to believe Miles had some goodness in him.

They were interrupted by the door opening. They both

jumped when Baird walked into the room, and Jaedin shuffled away from Miles, abruptly conscious of how close they were sitting. Baird seemed too distracted by his own grief to notice the tension in the room. Very rarely had Jaedin witnessed their stoic leader let emotion show but, now the battle was over, Baird's composure had slipped. The expression on his face made it clear he'd just seen what had happened to Aylen.

"Aylen died bravely," Jaedin found himself saying. "If it wasn't for him, we probably wouldn't be here."

Baird nodded grimly. "Kyra... she is down there with him, but I couldn't get much sense out of her... Can you try, Jaedin? I think she needs you. Go to her. Please. Miles can fill me in on what happened."

Jaedin didn't want to go back to that room but was too weary to argue. He rose.

"Jaedin?" Baird said as he was making his way to the door.

"Yes?" Jaedin replied, turning around.

"You did well," Baird said.

Jaedin was startled by those words. It was the first time Baird had ever complimented him.

"I know I am often harsh," Baird continued. "I push you all... but it is only because I want you to live. Today you made me proud. You proved yourself. You are someone I can rely on. Someone I can trust."

When Jaedin' heard the word 'trust' he looked at Miles and guilt crawled within his chest.

He looked at the floor and nodded humbly.

He knew if Baird ever found out the secrets he was hiding, he would never forgive him.

Jaedin made his way down the stairs. When he entered the bloody chamber, the first thing he saw was Fangar. He still sat with his back against the wall. He gave Jaedin a grim smile.

"Think there's a lass over there who needs you," Fangar said.

Jaedin looked at the spot where Aylen died. His body was still there. Blood was running from his ears, which made Jaedin realise that, after Aylen died, he'd become infected; he was one of the many Zakaras Jaedin had just killed with his Stone of Zakar. The words Jaedin got them to chant out loud had come from Aylen's lips, just as they had from all the other Zakaras in the city before Jaedin destroyed the monsters which lived within them.

Kyra had her arms draped around Aylen's neck and was crying. Jaedin had never seen her as weak and vulnerable as he did at that moment. Aylen's blood had pooled around her knees but she didn't seem to have noticed.

Jaedin put a hand on her shoulder and gave her a gentle nudge to try and pull her out of her well of torment.

"Kyra," Jaedin leant in and whispered into her ear, softly. "Come... Let's go."

"He did it for me..." Kyra whined. "Why?"

Jaedin opened his mouth and tried to think of an answer. Tried to think of something to say which would make her feel better.

"You stupid idiot!" Kyra breathed, thudding her fist upon Aylen's shoulder. "*Why!?*"

* * *

When they left the castle, they found Bryna by the drawbridge. At first, they thought she was dead because her body was so cold, but Jaedin examined her and discovered she was breathing. Nothing they did could wake her, so they carried her back to Kerdev's base.

Bryna slept for an entire day and, when she woke up, there was something different about her. Her manner was more coherent, and her eyes were clearer. She was more lucid.

They buried Aylen the following morning, and Bryna performed a small rite to bid his spirit a peaceful rest.

Sidry watched her as she sang. They all knew what she was now. They knew how such a frail young woman survived the attack on Jalard. The wary suspicion with which they had once regarded her had been replaced by awe.

Without any precursor or warning, two men loosened the ropes and Aylen was lowered into the pit. Sidry had no time to emotionally prepare himself for that moment – watching it happen made it seem so final – and the grim reality struck him. Aylen was gone.

Baird and Fangar each grabbed a spade and began to fill Aylen's grave.

Kyra tiptoed up to the edge and dropped one of her most treasured daggers for Aylen to take with him. And a bundle of white flowers. Her face scrunched up and angry tears streamed from her eyes. She walked away, and Jaedin followed, putting an arm around her.

Rivan picked up a third spade, limped over to the pile of earth, and helped. His injuries still pained him but he was trying to hide it. Sidry saw it in the way every movement made him wince.

There was no fourth spade, so Sidry sat upon the grass and watched.

"I felt him die," Bryna said, and Sidry became aware that she was sitting beside him. "And I gave him the chance to come back. To fight again. But he didn't. He wanted to see his family. He is at peace."

Sidry looked at her. He knew what Bryna was now. He knew an ominous power lurked within her.

But she was still Bryna.

And, as Sidry watched his young friend – one whose time had been cut short and still had so many things to do with his life – being laid to rest, he realised he didn't want to live with any regrets.

Sidry summoned some of his courage.

"I know what you are now, Bryna," he said. She looked at him with her purple eyes. "And I admit it scares me. But I still…"

He fell silent, not knowing what to say. She smiled faintly and, in that moment, Sidry knew that somewhere, deep within her, she had feelings for him too. But there were so many other things in her eyes it was hard for him to know if that was enough. She had so many things buried inside her. Burdens she carried every day.

She placed one of her hands upon his. Her fingers rested between his knuckles.

"You are a sweet man, Sidry, but I don't think I can give you what you want. Being the Descendant of Vai-ris is… complicated. I am not human. I would break your heart."

"But you have a right to a life as well, Bryna," Sidry said. "I can help you. You don't have to bear it all alone."

She shook her head. "I couldn't do that to you. I care about you too much."

"I don't care!" Sidry blurted, trying to hide the desperation in his voice. "You're worth it. If I get hurt, that is *my* choice. Don't you see that?"

"What about Kyra?" Bryna asked.

The sudden jump in conversation made him frown. "What about her?"

"Dion died. And now Aylen too," Bryna said. "She needs me right now, and I can't be distracted. I don't think seeing one of her friends… happy with someone, would help."

Sidry paused to consider this. He'd had an inkling something was going on between Kyra and Aylen. Now Bryna had confirmed it.

But the fact that, once again, Bryna was willing to sacrifice her own happiness for someone else made Sidry feel even more endeared to her. She was so selfless. Most people never even noticed. Or appreciated it.

"So you're admitting that I would make you happy?" he realised.

"Maybe…" she admitted. "But not yet, Sidry. This isn't the time or the place."

*   *   *

Jaedin watched as Baird scooped up the last pile of dirt and tossed it upon the mound.

Everyone stared at Aylen's grave.

Shayam's Stone of Zakar had been buried with Aylen's body. It only seemed fitting. It was partially thanks to Aylen they managed to defeat him. Baird initially suggested they should keep it but, after making some attempts to harness its power, Jaedin discovered the artefact was now defunct. It seemed that its function had died with Shayam.

Some of them made speeches. Baird spoke of how brave Aylen was. Kyra regarded his kindness. Fangar complimented the way his daggers always struck true. Rivan retold a couple of humorous stories about him which made everyone laugh softly between their tears.

Jaedin didn't say anything. How could he, in good conscience, speak a hearty eulogy when he felt that he was responsible for Aylen's fate? How could he say anything when the truth was that Aylen was dead because of him?

Aylen was dead, because Miles betrayed them.

Miles had betrayed them again, and Jaedin was keeping it secret.

After a few minutes of peaceful, reflective quiet, Baird spoke.

"We leave in the morning," he announced. There were a few reluctant groans. "I know you are tired. I know you are grieving. But we must press on. We must reach Shemet. We must stop this happening anywhere else. We must do this out of respect for those who are not with us today."

*   *   *

They walked back to the ruins of Fraknar to collect their things and speak to Kerdev. Now that the ordeal was over the young rogue had become the city's de facto leader – above ground as well as below – and he had begun coordinating its restoration. The fact that most of the survivors had decided to stay and repair their homes surprised Jaedin. He'd assumed that after the terrible ordeal they'd been through they'd want to start anew, but it seemed the people of Fraknar possessed a stubborn determination.

As a parting gift, Kerdev gave them some horses. His only condition was that they used them to reach Shemet as quickly as possible so they could inform the Synod of what had happened to Fraknar. Baird agreed and humbly thanked him. The two of them shook hands. Kerdev then led them to an abandoned inn that they could sleep in for their last night in the city.

They went inside. It was eerie to see the common room of an inn empty. There were still cups of ale which had gone stale on one of the tables, and no sign of the owners. Jaedin assumed they were dead. They searched the rooms. The pantry was full of food and some of it was still edible, so Baird set Jaedin and Sidry to the task of sorting through it all.

Jaedin almost refused. It felt wrong to steal from the deceased and benefit from the misfortune of others, but pragmatic sense eventually won over.

Once he'd finished, Jaedin went up the stairs to look for Kyra and Bryna and found them in one of the rooms. They'd each claimed a bed and were resting.

"Isn't there one for me?" Jaedin asked, looking around the room.

"No," Kyra said apologetically. "None of the rooms had three beds…"

Jaedin sighed. Throughout the entirety of their journey, he had always shared a tent with the girls. It had become habit. Something he was used to. He didn't want to sleep alone that night. He kept having nightmares.

"There's loads of other rooms, Jaedin!" Baird yelled from somewhere down the corridor.

Jaedin sighed as he stepped into the hallway.

As he walked down, one of the doors opened. It was Fangar.

He was naked. He smiled at Jaedin, and Jaedin felt his blood rushing into his face. He tried to resist the urge to stare at Fangar's body but couldn't.

"There's one down here," Baird called. "You can have it all to yourself…"

"It's okay," Jaedin found himself saying. "I've found one."

He stepped into Fangar's room. Baird must have seen him because Jaedin heard him march down the corridor to try and stop him. Baird's voice became enraged. He streamed a list of objections, but Jaedin didn't even listen to what he was saying. He didn't care. He had never been so sure of anything in his life.

Fangar closed the door behind them and bolted the lock. They were face to face, their bodies pressed close. Their lips met.

"Jaedin! What are you doing in there?!" Baird hollered as he banged his fist on the door. "Come right back here!"

Fangar lifted Jaedin's tunic over his head and pushed him down onto the bed. Jaedin laughed.

"Jaedin!" Baird yelled. "I order you to come out here *now*! This is not right!"

"Fuck off, Baird."

Epilogue

The Third Avatar of Gezra

Grav'aen stared at a map of the world, as he considered his plan.

The Valantian Mountains had always been an unforgiving and relentless terrain – it had divided the two nations for thousands of years – but it would not be difficult for Grav'aen to get an army of Zakaras across. He just needed to build one.

Grav'aen's gaze went to the contours of Sharma's landscape, and he narrowed his eyes. Grav'aen had never set foot in Sharma. He had never even known anyone *from* there, but just the thought of the nation stirred ireful feelings within him.

Sharma was full of rich farmlands. It even had forests. It was a glorious bounty of abundance. Sharmarian people hoarded fertile lands, free from The Ruena, while the people of Gavendara dwindled in their barren mountains.

They could not continue like this.

Despite all of the reasons Grav'aen had to hate Sharma, he did not mean for the situation to escalate the way it had. Shayam had failed him catastrophically. Even if he'd managed to escape from Fraknar, Grav'aen would have disposed of him. It was only justice after all the trouble he had caused.

It had been a simple plan, in the beginning. Miles, Shayam, and Carmaestre were to experiment with some procedures somewhere off the beaten track. Grav'aen had never meant for the Zakaras to spread. He had never meant for all those people – Sharmarians they may be – to die.

But now Grav'aen had no choice but to act. Those people had escaped Shayam's grasp, and soon the whole of Sharma would know what he was up to. There was a war coming.

Grav'aen slammed his fist upon the table. He had also lost two of the Stones of Zakar.

He placed his hand on his forehead, where there was a new scar. Last night, Carmaestre performed the procedure on him.

Grav'aen was attuned to his Stone of Zakar more potently than ever now. The experiment had been a success. They knew how to harness the full potential of their powers now. This, at least, they had gained.

But Grav'aen had also lost two Stones of Gezra.

Those relics had been found years ago, and none of his magicians or scholars could ever discover any use for them. Thinking them useless artefacts, Grav'aen gave them away to Carmaestre's curiosity.

But Grav'aen knew their true potential now. The people Carmaestre attuned those relics to could now transform into the avatars of a god. For that, Grav'aen could only blame himself. He should not have underestimated the potential of those stones so easily.

The ruins where they had been found had been excavated again recently. Grav'aen had been hoping to find many more, but they found just one.

"Bring him in," he said to his servants.

A young man was escorted into the room. Most people who were brought before Grav'aen's presence these days cowered in fear, many of them even performed a little bow, but this boy merely shrugged his guides off indignantly and stared up at Grav'aen with a scowl on his face.

"What do you want from me?" he asked, crossing his arms over his chest.

Grav'aen would usually have a person punished for such insolence, but instead, he smiled to himself. There was something about this man he liked.

Grav'aen closed his eyes and awakened his telepathy. Reaching into the boy's mind, he studied his thoughts and feelings.

"You are from Jalard?" Grav'aen asked, looking at him.

The young man nodded. "And you must be that Grav'aen guy everyone talks about," Dareth replied, meeting his gaze. "If you're expecting me to beg for my life, you'll be disappointed."

Grav'aen studied him. His posture. His thoughts. His feelings. This youth had a lot of anger. A yearning to prove himself and be recognised in some way. He was impulsive. Bull-headed but not very bright. Bold in action but weak of mind. Most of the men who were under Grav'aen's command were intellectuals – they performed the tasks he set them mostly out of greed and want of personal gain – Shayam was one of them, and those were the flaws which made him fail.

Grav'aen needed someone special for the new task he had at hand. He needed someone who would perform it out of personal yearning. Someone who could be easily manipulated.

To get what you want out of someone, exploit their weaknesses, Grav'aen reminded himself. He searched Dareth's mind and found it.

The boy was riddled with guilt over the death of his friend.

Deep down, Dareth knew he'd played a part in Aylen's death, but he was in denial. To escape this guilt, Dareth had shifted the blame onto others.

"You hate Jaedin, don't you? And Kyra. Baird too..." Grav'aen said.

The boy's face hardened. "What of it?" he asked.

"You have not answered my question," Grav'aen said. "Do you hate them?"

He nodded.

"Aylen sacrificed his life for them," Grav'aen said. "How far would you go to avenge his death?"

"I will *kill* them," Dareth vowed between gritted teeth.

Grav'aen smiled to himself. He was satisfied with his choice.

"Come in, Carmaestre!" he called.

She emerged from the shadows, and her white teeth flashed in a ghoulish smile. She appeared behind Dareth, placed her pale arms over his shoulders, and draped her hands across his chest. Dareth turned. Faced her. And Grav'aen – still within Dareth's mind – felt him try to deny the sexual arousal she stirred within him. It was amusing to watch. Dareth was a young man, and she would have no difficulty seducing him.

But not tonight. There was something which needed to be done first.

"Carmaestre, begin the preparations," Grav'aen said. "Congratulations Dareth of Jalard, the third Stone of Gezra is yours."

End of Book 1

Acknowledgements

Foremost, Roy Gilham and Jamie Slack, who were my first ever beta-readers.

Simon Llewelyn, Andreas Wiesner-Zacarias, Alex Brown, Tom Jennings, Liam Leeson, Simon Woodsell, Tom Livingstone, Tristan Treagust, Ian Graham, Chris Brookes, Paul Wright, James Eldridge & Ros Jackson, whom have all given me feedback at some point throughout this novel's extensive drafts over the years. Also Russell Flinn, for his early guidance, and whose passing instilled in me a determination to make every year count.

All the friends I have made in the SFF community. Most notably Anna Smith Spark, Allen Stroud, Karen Fishwick, Chris Nuttall, Danie Ware, Joanne Hall, Douglas Thompson, James Bennett, Alan Gowing, Adrian Chamberlin, Cheryl Morgan & Rebecca Hall.

The team at Elsewhen Press. Especially Pete, Alison and Sofia.

Chuck Ashmore for all his support, and much patience.

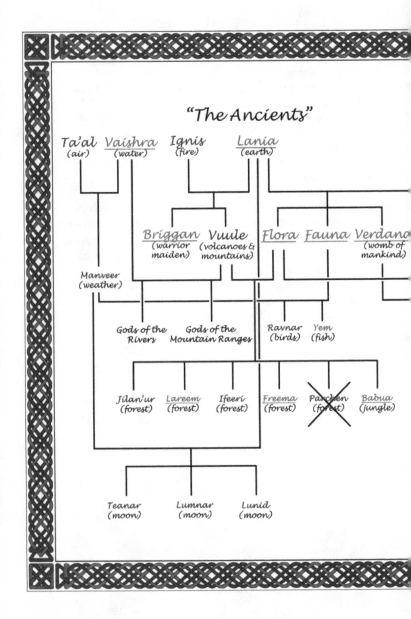

"The Ancients"

Ta'al (air) Vaishra (water) Ignis (fire) Lania (earth)

Briggan (warrior maiden) Vuule (volcanoes & mountains) Flora Fauna Verdana (womb of mankind)

Manveer (weather)

Gods of the Rivers Gods of the Mountain Ranges Ravnar (birds) Yem (fish)

Jilan'ur (forest) Lareem (forest) Ifeeri (forest) Freema (forest) Parchen (forest) Babua (jungle)

Teanar (moon) Lumnar (moon) Lunid (moon)

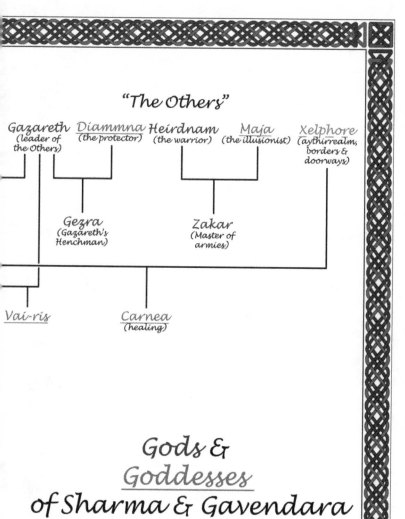

"The Others"

Gazareth (leader of the Others)   **Diammna** (the protector)   **Heirdnam** (the warrior)   **Maja** (the illusionist)   **Xelphore** (aythirrealm, borders & doorways)

Gezra (Gazareth's Henchman)   **Zakar** (Master of armies)

Vai-ris   **Carnea** (healing)

Gods & Goddesses
of Sharma & Gavendara

Elsewhen Press

delivering outstanding new talents in speculative fiction

Visit the Elsewhen Press website at elsewhen.press for the latest information on all of our titles, authors and events; to read our blog; find out where to buy our books and ebooks; or to place an order.

Sign up for the Elsewhen Press InFlight Newsletter at
elsewhen.press/newsletter

Existence is
Elsewhen
Twenty stories from twenty great authors
including
Tej Turner
John Gribbin
Rhys Hughes
Christopher Nuttall
Douglas Thompson

The title *Existence is Elsewhen* paraphrases the last sentence of André Breton's 1924 *Manifesto of Surrealism*, perfectly summing up the intent behind this anthology of stories from a wonderful collection of authors. Different worlds... different times. It's what Elsewhen Press has been about since we launched our first title in 2011.

Here, we present twenty science fiction stories for you to enjoy. We are delighted that headlining this collection is the fantastic **John Gribbin**, with a worrying vision of medical research in the near future. Future global healthcare is the theme of **J A Christy's** story; while the ultimate in spare part surgery is where **Dave Weaver** takes us. **Edwin Hayward's** search for a renewable protein source turns out to be digital; and **Tanya Reimer's** story with characters we think we know gives us pause for thought about another food we take for granted. Evolution is examined too, with **Andy McKell's** chilling tale of what states could become if genetics are used to drive policy. Similarly, **Robin Moran's** story explores the societal impact of an undesirable evolutionary trend; while **Douglas Thompson** provides a truly surreal warning of an impending disaster that will reverse evolution, with dire consequences.

On a lighter note, we have satire from **Steve Harrison** discovering who really owns the Earth (and why); and **Ira Nayman**, who uses the surreal alternative realities of his *Transdimensional Authority* series as the setting for a detective story mash-up of Agatha Christie and Dashiel Hammett. Pursuing the crime-solving theme, **Peter Wolfe** explores life, and death, on a space station; while **Stefan Jackson** follows a police investigation into some bizarre cold-blooded murders in a cyberpunk future. Going into the past, albeit an 1831 set in the alternate Britain of his *Royal Sorceress* series, **Christopher Nuttall** reports on an investigation into a girl with strange powers.

Strange powers in the present-day is the theme for **Tej Turner**, who tells a poignant tale of how extra-sensory perception makes it easier for a husband to bear his dying wife's last few days. Difficult decisions are the theme of **Chloe Skye's** heart-rending story exploring personal sacrifice. Relationships aren't always so close, as **Susan Oke's** tale demonstrates, when sibling rivalry is taken to the limit. Relationships are the backdrop to **Peter R. Ellis's** story where a spectacular mid-winter event on a newly-colonised distant planet involves a Madonna and Child. Coming right back to Earth and in what feels like an almost imminent future, **Siobhan McVeigh** tells a cautionary tale for anyone thinking of using technology to deflect the blame for their actions. Building on the remarkable setting of Pera from her *LiGa* series, and developing Pera's legendary *Book of Shadow*, **Sanem Ozdural** spins the creation myth of the first light tree in a lyrical and poetic song. Also exploring language, the master of fantastika and absurdism, **Rhys Hughes,** extrapolates the way in which language changes over time, with an entertaining result.

ISBN: 9781908168955 (epub, kindle) / ISBN: 9781908168856 (320pp paperback)
Visit bit.ly/ExistenceIsElsewhen

About Tej Turner

Tej Turner has spent much of his life on the move and does not have any particular place he calls 'home'. For a large period of his childhood, he dwelt within the Westcountry of England, and he then moved to rural Wales to study Creative Writing and Film at Trinity College in Carmarthen, followed by a master's degree at The University of Wales Lampeter.

After completing his studies, he moved to Cardiff, where he works as a chef by day and writes by moonlight. He is also an intermittent traveller who every now and then straps on a backpack and flies off to another part of the world to go on an adventure. So far, he has clocked two years in Asia and a year in South America. He hopes to go on more and has his sights set on Central America next. When he travels, he takes a particular interest in historic sites, jungles, wildlife, native cultures, and mountains. He also spent some time volunteering at the Merazonia Wildlife Rehabilitation Centre in Ecuador, a place he hopes to return to someday.

Bloodsworn is his third published novel. His debut novel *The Janus Cycle* was published by Elsewhen Press in 2015, followed by his sequel *Dinnusos Rises* in 2017. Both of them were described as 'gritty and surreal urban fantasy'. He has also had short stories published in various anthologies.

He keeps a travelblog on his website (http://tejturner.wordpress.com/) where he also posts author-related news.